Wanjiru's Sons

By Rod McCormick

~

Word's Brook Publisher

Word's Brook Publisher
6 Bashaw Drive
Essex Vermont 05452
USA

Paperback Edition 2010

ISBN   0-615-33943-3
EAN-13 978-0-615-33943-6

Chapter 1, 1975 Njoro Kenya

Wanjiru's eyes flickered open to see her mother leaving through the front opening of their hut. Her mother was rushing off to make breakfast for her Englishman, who lived in one of the teachers' houses a few doors down. Her sister Muthoni was still snoring away on her blanket, and her sister Warimu was stoking the charcoal cooker trying to get it going again. Light was seeping through the smoke hole in the thatched roof of their hut so that she could find her way across the dirt floor to the opening. Pushing open the cloth, she was out in the bright early morning - the dazzling rising sun blinding her. She found her way to the latrine trench, and spread her legs and urinated.

Dogs were barking. She was finding her way back to her hut, as her mother's friend Wambui came rushing by with her baby Ruthy attached to her back, saying good morning in Kikuyu, and hurried on. Wambui suddenly turned around and said, "Njiru! I have to go to my *shamba* for two weeks, does Muthoni want to do my work for my *mzungu* again?" Wambui was a tall, brown woman with short hair and bucked teeth, who was always joking and laughing around.

"Muthoni is still asleep." She stated. "Is that the same *mzungu* she worked for?" Wanjiru knew that Wambui had worked for several *mzungu* teachers. She had heard her sister's stories of working for the young *mzungu* teacher at the high school.

"Yes, for my Lodi. He said he would pay a hundred shillings for two weeks, and pay me too for vacation to go to my *shamba*." Wambui laughed.

"Maybe I could work for him this time," she said thinking of the tall, white man, or boy really, who often walked by the hut on his way to the bus stop. He often looked at her with his sky blue eyes through wire glasses and smiled with straight, white teeth that made her tingle. He was not much older than her own eighteen years - or so he appeared to Wanjiru. Wanjiru's own father was English, her mother was Kikuyu, and being half-caste made her feel a bit akin to the white boy. He must feel like an outsider as much as she had been made to feel.

1

"He will want the…" and she motioned with a finger poking into the other hand. Wanjiru felt the tingling in her groin that always happened with thoughts of sex. "Come to his place with me now, and I will make tea and bread for you. I will ask if you will do." Wambui giggled, and started walking off, as if to say, if you are coming, come now. They rushed up to driveway, which was lined on both sides by evergreen hedges. They turned to walk around the stone house to enter the backdoor near the small garden. As they entered, the coffee pot was perking, and she heard *gitaa* music playing in the next room. "*Jambo*, Lodi!" Wambui shouted and peeked around a corner into the living room.

"*Habari*." Came the voice in the next room, and the music stopped, and in Americanized Swahili he asked, "I want fried eggs and toast." Wambui took Wanjiru's hand and pulled her into the living room. There was a huge, pale boy wearing wire glasses and was sitting in a chair strumming a very small *gitaa*. "Who is this is beautiful girl?" he asked standing up to greet Wanjiru. He was very tall, with long, light brown hair streaked with yellow.

"This is Wanjiru. She is Esther's daughter. Esther works for Keogh." Wambui stated, and the tall boy reached out to shake her hand. "Perhaps she can do my work when I am at *shamba*. She can do everything I do for you. Her mama works for Keogh." She repeated. Wambui looked at her as if she should say something, and Lodi looked her up and down. Wanjiru knew that she was attractive to Europeans since so many of the white tourists in Nakuru would eye her and say *Jambo*. She was *nusu nusu*, meaning half European and half Kikuyu, having many features that attract Europeans but ugly to Kikuyu.

"I will give her a try." Lodi said in his Swahili. She looked into his sky blue eyes as he said in English, "You are beautiful. It will be nice having you around." With that Wanjiru laughed, since she knew English fairly well. Seeing that she understood, he continued to say, "Have Wambui teach you what she does for me, and what she does not do for me also. Like, only I make coffee, so do not bother with that." Wambui was not following, and pulled Wanjiru back into the kitchen.

"Njiru! What did he say?" Wambui asked in Kikuyu.

"He said you should teach me what you do for him." With that Wambui just laughed and began preparing breakfast, putting the coffee pot off the stove, the frying pan on the electric burner

2

and slices of bread in the oven. As music of the little *gitaa* came from the other room, Wambui poured some milk into a pan, which she had boiling in a matter of minutes. She poured some milk in with coffee into a cup, added some sugar and disappeared into the living room. Coming back, she threw some tealeaves into the milk, added water from the filter tank and sugar and set it to boil again. She took the toast out of the oven, flipped them and put them back for the second side. She put some margarine in the skillet and cracked two eggs into it to fry. She took four slices of toast out of the oven.

"Spread margarine on these. Put two on the plate. One each for us..." She slid the fried eggs onto the plate next to the toast. She sliced up an orange, put it on the plate, and disappeared into the dining area. "Food ready..." Wambui announced in Swahili, and returned to the kitchen.

"May I ask?" Wanjiru asked nervously in Kikuyu. "Does he sex you?"

Wambui laughed. "An African woman working for a man will have sex." She giggled. "He does not want as much as my other *mzungu*, but he will find someone else if I do not make him happy."

"And pregnancy?"

"I got the wire thing in my womb that stops pregnancy. It hurt for a month until it settled in." Wambui rubbed her pubic area and winced. "No more children for me. Three are plenty. Dead husband and no one want a widow to marry." Then as if to calm her concern, "Tell Lodi to use *Durexi* because you do not need a baby."

"Is Lodi a boy or a man... how old is he?"

"Twenty-seven... The students say he is very smart and very educated. He shaves his beard, too, every morning, so he looks like a boy."

There was the sound of a chair moving in the dining area, and Lodi came in. "I go now," he said, and added in choppy Swahili, "I will be back for lunch. No teaching in afternoon... *Kwa heri*." He turned and left, with the sound of the front door closing and being locked.

Wambui laughed and said, "If he says no work for him in the afternoon that means he wants sex. Did your sister Muthoni tell you he did her?" Again, Wanjiru felt the tingling in her groin. Her

3

imagination started working. "Lodi told me how he tried to do sex with her. Lodi said she too young. He worried she too young and could not do her. He said he was too embarrassed to try again, even after he learned she was of age. You know he did sex with your older sister Warimu, too?"

"No, she never told me. She wants a baby very badly but cannot get a pregnancy."

Wambui laughed, "He used *Durexi* and was as fast as a rooster. He said Warimu was too shy to take off all her clothes. Lodi say he just want to get it done."

"You take off all your clothes for Lodi?" Again, the tingling began. Wambui giggled and nodded covering her mouth to cover her big teeth. Wambui took the dirty dishes and began washing them in the sink, and began describing her daily routine. The baby began whimpering on Wambui's back. Wambui pulled Ruthy around to her front, sat on a chair and began nursing the baby. Wanjiru had no child yet, and watching Wambui's pleasure, looked forward to a baby on her tit. The baby was soon fed and back on Wambui's back.

After doing dusting and a bit of waxing of the floor, she showed Wanjiru how she made the bed and washed laundry. Wambui put the sleeping baby on a spare bed, so she could do the laundry. There was only two shirts, some underwear and socks which she hand-washed in the bathtub when the water was clear. Sometimes the water was filthy, and she would have to wait for it to clear up. As they were washing the clothes in the tub, the voice of a small boy was shouting for her in the kitchen.

"Come in here, almost done." After a minute, a five-year-old boy came in wearing tattered rags. "You know my baby brother. I wash him in the laundry water. The boy came in and Wambui squeezed the laundry into a basket for hanging. Then grabbed the boy, stripped off his so-called clothes and stuck him in the tub. "Njiru, wash him. I need to hang these clothes in the sun." The boy was stretched out in the water playing with his penis. Wanjiru soaped up a cloth and started rubbing the boy all over. As the cloth rubbed over the penis it stiffened up and the boy giggled. She pulled back his foreskin and rubbed it with soap, splashing water on him until the soap was gone. The boy giggled and played with himself again.

4

"I wish I had a fine boy like you." Wanjiru said trying to flatter the boy. Wambui returned with one of her own towels and stood the boy up in the tub, drying him off.

"Get your clothes on and go home." Wambui ordered her brother. "Our turn to get clean." Wambui turned the water on in the tub and removed her clothes, standing in the tub. She began washing herself all over. "Take your clothes off, and get clean with me." Wanjiru felt the tingling in her groin again as she soon stepped naked into the tub to use a washcloth as Wambui had done. Wambui heard Ruthy crying, left and returned with the baby nursing. Wanjiru wondered if Lodi suddenly returned to see two naked women, one washing and one nursing a baby. Would he be angry or aroused? She chuckled to herself.

Wanjiru felt especially clean when Wambui showed her how to use the *mzungu* toilet and paper. She showed how to flush the toilet and how to keep it clean. Wanjiru used the toilet and the paper once before in Mombasa and thought it was a bit complicated compared to using the latrine in the field, or the Arab toilets at her school. She chuckled to herself at the thought of *mzungu* squatting in the field.

~~~~

Wanjiru nervously walked up the cinder road into the school compound. Some students were standing by the dormitories in the sunrise. She felt very self-conscious as she walked into the driveway to the *mzungu* teacher's house. She walked along the back to the kitchen door and unlocked the door using the key Wambui had given her. As she opened the door, she was shocked to see Lodi standing next to the electric stove putting the coffee peculator on the burner. "*Jambo!*" he smiled at her. He was wearing black slacks and light blue dress shirt without the tie that other teachers wore. He was so tall and his skin so pale, she thought, probably like her own father. His hair now looked reddish-brown with streaks of yellow in it, likely due to the strong sun. "You are right on-time," he said in English, and she took it as a compliment. Then he said in his poor Swahili, "Two fried eggs, two toasts and sliced orange, please." Then as if remembering she knew English, repeated it in English. She stood for a minute transfixed. His eyes scanned her up and down, and stopped at her open-top blouse she was wearing, and he was enjoying the bit of light brown breast she decided would be a treat for her *mzungu*

5

employer. He stroked her back as he walked by into the living room; his touch sent excitement throughout her body. She was alone with a man in his house and the thought fired another spark. She tried to remember the last time she was with a man. She was so unattractive to the Kikuyu men, who generally ignored her. She started the toast, making three slices, including one for herself. She quickly tried to emulate what she had been taught, but the toast was half-black, the eggs runny and she forgot sugar in the coffee. The white boy said nothing as he ate and drank his coffee. She came back into the dining room as he was finishing, and he said in Swahili. "Kenyatta is coming this afternoon to his Njoro farm." He looked Wanjiru up and down, and sipped the last of his coffee. Then back to English, he said. "The students will all be going to the dancing. Are you going, or will you be here?"

Wanjiru knew she could have the afternoon off, but since the white boy was American, he did not have to go to Kenyatta's dance. She had gone many times to see the *Mzee* sit looking bored with his fly tail swishing the air as he watched the traditional dancing and singing. She did not know what to say. Then he said in English, "I will take a hot bath this afternoon and take a nap." That helped her to decide.

"I will make you lunch and help you with your needs." She said in English, wondering if that was correct. He smiled, stood up and walked over to a pile of books and papers and picked them up. She followed close behind. He seemed very tall for a boy, and he looked so delicate. He turned off the radio.

"If you want music," he said in Swahili that was so obviously book-learned. "Press this and it will play a cassette of African music." She was stunned that he gave her permission to listen to music when she worked. He handed her some money, "Go buy a half pound of beef and a quart of milk." Again, she was surprised at being trusted… or was it a test to see if she could be trusted? He patted her back again and waved bye. He left locking the front door and headed off across the lawn to the archway in the hedge. She was alone in the *mzungu's* house. The first thing was to press the button and out came music so beautiful that she was motivated to get working and clean the house. She had to explore the house to see what he had. On the wall near the dining table were dozens of photographs of what must be his parents, brothers and sisters, nieces and nephews. He had many books and

6

magazines on the living room shelves. At school in Mombasa, she often checked out English novels from the library. They were mostly romance stories about living in England.

On Lodi's shelf, she tried reading the titles. There were many math and science books. One caught her attention had "sex" in the title, which was one English word that, invariably, caught her attention. She pulled it off the shelf and looked at the title, "Everything You Wanted to Know about Sex: Picture Edition." She opened it up and there were photos of people having sex in every imaginable way: Men with women, women with women, men with men! She thought, how did he get this book into Kenya? She read a few pages, and realized this job might be an education as well.

~~~~~

Wanjiru locked the back door and adjusted her woven bag on her shoulder. She felt good about how clean the house was and now worried about walking through the school compound and the foul-mouthed boys. She walked through the thick grass in the back yard to the break in the twelve-foot tall hedges. Walking down the driveway, she saw some older boys basking in the sun near their dormitories. She looked down, making herself small. She walked by them as one of them shouted in Kikuyu. "Did the *mzungu* do you this morning?" This made her shake a bit and she shook her head and looked down shyly. Two tall boys stood up and soon she heard them following her as she left the school compound. She walked a bit faster and headed into her mother's hut. Her older sister Warimu was still there sipping tea. She opened her mouth to say something just as a voice outside, "Girl, we have a few shillings. We want to do you." Wanjiru looked nervously at her sister.

Her sister, smiled, "Come in boys." The two students who had followed her came into the dark hut. "You can do me. She is working for your teacher." This made the boys shuffle nervously as if something horrible would happen if they had Wanjiru.

"Anyway, we do not do *nusu nusu*." The taller one said.

"I would rather go without." The other one said. Wanjiru heard such insults so often it meant nothing to her.

"Show me the shillings." One boy handed Warimu a five-shilling note. "Take off your clothes." Warimu said as she began taking off her clothes. "Wanjiru, buy us some meat and bread…

go!" Wanjiru took the money but waited until one very black boy had taken off his grey shorts and white shirt, then his briefs, and was naked and ready for sex. The boy was very proud of his manhood and was eager for Warimu to get ready on her cot. Wanjiru left the hut and waited outside in the sun for a moment. She was not a virgin, but she did not think she would like such students because they were too quick to be satisfying, and so few Kikuyu men find *nusu nusu* women attractive. Her first and only boyfriend was with a student who was Luhya-English mix. Kikuyu students later beat him so badly, that he returned to Nairobi. He wrote her letters for a while, but stopped.

She headed toward Bondeni, that part of Njoro where there were shops and a small market of folks selling their farm goods. The air was nippy as she crossed the railroad tracks and the highway onto the field where buses and taxis stopped. She had taken the bus many times to Nakuru, on to Nairobi and down to Mombasa to visit an uncle who had a good job there. Mombasa was dreadfully warm and too many people. Although she did years of school in Mombasa, she did not miss the heat.

She crossed the field and headed to the butcher to buy two slices of beef, and after that to find a shop with some fresh bread and cartons of BHT milk. There would be more to eat than just *ugali* and tea tonight.

Heading back towards the school she could see from afar two boys coming out of her mother's hut. By the time she reached it the sun was beginning to warm her shoulders. It was about time for the students to head off to Kenyatta's farm for the dancing. She went into the hut and gave some food to her sister, who was still naked on her bed dozing off. She tried to wake her, and Warimu rolled over. "How many times they do you?" Wanjiru asked looking her sister.

"I don't know... I fell asleep." Several more came. I have some more money to give mama." Warimu said proudly. "I hope one of them gives me a pregnancy." Wanjiru shrugged thinking that it was not likely since she never had bleeding. Her sister began washing herself from soapy water in a bowl as Wanjiru decided it was time to get back to Lodi to make his lunch. As she headed towards the school, students in clean uniforms were streaming out headed towards Kenyatta's farm several miles away. They all

8

looked very serious as if headed for an execution, which it might be if there was an assassination attempt.

Back at the house, she heard water running in the bathtub as she entered the kitchen. There was bread, peanut spread, marmalade sitting on the counter. Wanjiru put away the food that she had purchased in the village, and set the change on the counter. Then she remembered what she was to make. She went out looking for Lodi. Just as she came into the living room, she saw him walking the hallway holding a towel in front of him going into the bathroom. She followed him into the bath just as he was settling into water. He was so white! He looked up and saw her, "*Jambo*, Wanjiru!" he said. "Could you make me a sandwich for lunch and some tea with sugar no milk?" I will eat it in here. Make yourself tea and something too." She returned his smile and thought how trusting he was. She turned to head back, when someone tapped at the front door. It was the headmaster, a very black Luhya, who everyone loved. She went to the door and said, "Lodi is taking a bath." He looked bewildered then shrugged, and pushed his way into the living room, disappearing into the bath.

She heard him saying something about driving to Kenyatta, but Lodi said, "Kenyatta hates white people. I would not be welcome there."

As they continued to talk, she went into the kitchen to prepare lunch, setting a pan of water from the filter tank on the stove. She heard the Headmaster say something and she went out as he was leaving.

"*Kwa heri, asante sana.*" He said as he pulled the door shut. She went over and locked the front door, and headed back to the kitchen to slice bread. The water began boiling. In a few minutes, she had a plate and a cup of black tea, heading back to the bath. Lodi was stretched out in the large tub making himself very comfortable. A wash cloth covered his privates and his eyes were closed, but his eyes popped open as she came in with the plate. He set the tea on the side of the tub and took the plate.

"Sit here and talk to me." He said, and she was stunned. Why did the white teacher want to talk to me? "You married, you have children, where do you live, why do you know English?" he asked just as a teacher would in English. She sat down on the edge of the tub and watched him eat the sandwich.

In her school English she said, "I am not married, and have no children yet. I live with my mother and two sisters. I think you know them. My mother Esther works for Keogh. My sisters Muthoni and Warimu -" And immediately she saw a bulge under the wash cloth in the water. "I went through form two in Mombasa and came here with my mother. I live here for maybe two years." The bulge under the cloth decreased. He finished the bread, handed the plate to her and began sipping the tea.

"Why did you not finish high school?"

"My father in England died in a car crash and no more money came for school fees."

"Oh, I am sorry about your father. Do you want to finish school? You could get a better job than this." He smiled, and she thought what an easy job this was.

"This is a good job. No, I do not like school anyway."

"Is that the same Muthoni who worked for me when Wambui was away?" he said in English, and again the bulge grew. Wanjiru nodded a yes, but had a hard time not watching the wash cloth rather than his face. He laughed and spoke in Swahili, "I tried to do her, but I got too worried if she were too young." The bulge got long. "She now likes a friend of Wambui's. Wambui says I need to try again."

"You did my other sister too. *Haraka*." She giggled. He looked baffled. "She says she not take off her clothes. She told me she saw you naked and you put on a *Durexi*." She giggled again.

"Oh," he said in English, "She wears a white dress? You are beautiful. She is cute. You are not as dark brown as your sisters. Your younger sister is nearly black. In fact, I think you have a beautiful face." He said and Wanjiru felt her face burn in embarrassment.

"She wants a pregnancy very badly and has sex with anyone now. My father was an Englishman my mother worked for. He left Kenya before I was born, I think." Wanjiru noticed that he had finished his tea, and was listening to her. "Wambui says she washed you sometimes."

He laughed, "Not really, she does my back and legs, not everything." He pulled the washcloth off and handed it to her. She stared at his white thing with the pink tip getting longer in the water. He chuckled at the way she stared at it, and sat up and turned on hot water to replace the water that had leaked out. She

10

leaned down and took the bar of soap and the washcloth, soaped it and began rubbing his back. The skin on his back was white but turned pink if you rubbed it. She became too shy as he leaned back obviously hoping she would touch him all over. His white shaft entranced her with the pink tip sticking now out of the water. Suddenly she was aware of his watching her stare at his manhood. Wanjiru felt embarrassed and turned away.

"Hand me the towel. If you wanna take a bath it's okay." He said in his American accent, standing up waiting for the towel. She turned around with the towel stunned by the very tall, white man dripping wet. She just stood and stared holding the towel. He stood like a statue for a moment then put out a hand, and she gave him the towel. He stepped out of the bath to dry himself off. She stood watching. He glanced at the water, which was still hot and clear, and she knew she wanted to take a bath. "Do you want to be alone?" he asked, but she felt the tingling in her groin, and shook her head no. His arousal had lessened and he put the damp towel across his shoulders.

She loosened the knot holding her skirt up and let it drop, pulled her blouse over her head. He obviously was enjoying the show as she pulled off her underwear, and unsnapped the button on the front of her bra. She let it fall and let him return the favor of staring. "Oh, holy mother of God! You are beautiful... perfect." His manhood looked as if it might burst. Wanjiru smiled and stepped into the tub and stretched out. Lodi bent down, took the bar of soap and began leathering bubbles onto her belly in wider and wider circles until he reached her breasts. With soap on his hands, he circled her breasts covering every inch, then up her neck, down her arms, back to her breasts until she felt the tingling in her groin and nipples of her breasts. He lathered more soap bubbles and lathered her legs down to the bottoms of her feet, massaging the bottom of the feet. His hand found its way up to her curly mound. He rubbed soap into the hair and lathered it white, he put the soap on her belly and ran a finger inside her then up to place he knew how to touch, and with his other hand, he pinched the nipples on her breasts. He did this until the tingling excitement spread from her groin and caused her whole body shudder in pure pleasure. Her entire body tensed in excitement as he strummed her womanhood. It was too much; she thrashed in the water and fainted.

11

She awoke to his holding her head above water, "Oh my, are you okay?" he was saying.

She laughed and said, "I never had that feeling before… it is too strong." She looked into his blue eyes, and knew she would forever think of him as special.

He chuckled, and stood up, left the room and came back with a towel. He took his towel off his shoulders and hung it over the sink. "When you are done, hang the towels in the sun to dry." He disappeared into his bedroom. She stood up weak in the legs, but dried herself off and got dressed again. She took the towels out to the line in back and pinned them to dry. She ate a bit of lunch as she cleaned the kitchen. She was washing dishes, when she wondered what Lodi was doing. She turned around and was startled to see him sitting on the kitchen counter. She looked directly at his ivory teeth through his parted lips. Whiskers were showing on his cheeks as if he had missed a few when he shaved today. A streak of his yellow hair had fallen down onto his forehead. He was so much larger than the Kikuyu men she knew. She stood and watched as he took off his glasses to look straight into her eyes, reaching out and stroking her neck. His blue eyes and ivory teeth made her want to do anything for him. He said in English, "Do you want to go to my bedroom with me?" This sent electricity through her.

"Yes, I want." She said simply.

~~~~~~~

Wanjiru woke with a start. It took her a few seconds to realize she was in Lodi's bedroom, under a sheet in his bed. It all came back to her, and she realized she was alone in the house. She sat up and saw all her clothes in a pile on the floor. She stood up and felt a trickle down her leg. She went into the bathroom to wash and returned to put on her clothes. On the dining table was a note. "I am at Keogh's house. See you tomorrow." That was the Englishman where her mother worked. She was free this evening, so she straightened up and headed back to her mother's hut.

Smoke was coming out the top of the hut as she approached. The school was strangely quiet, which meant that the students were still at Kenyatta's farm. The sun was low on the horizon which made it about 5:30 or so, and her mother would still be at her Englishman's house. She pulled back the cloth and entered the hut. She was surprised to see both her sisters and her

12

mother there roasting meat and maize on a fire. The flames painted the grass roof, cast dancing shadows on the wall. The smoke was drifting up towards the hole in the center of the roof. She found her way to her cot and sat down, while her mother handed her a plate with roasted meat and an ear of roasted maize. "You smell like *mzungu*," her mother said in Kikuyu and laughed, which startled Wanjiru. "Did he do you?" she asked more out of curiosity than piousness. She knew her mother liked stories about men, and probably wanted all the details.

Trying to change the subject, Wanjiru asked, "Why are you not working?"

"Beatrice, Keogh and Lodi went to the golf place to drink." Esther said. "Did you work all afternoon?"

Warimu laughed, "Did he show you everything?" She stoked at the fire with a stick, making it flame up. Wanjiru knew Warimu had seen everything also.

"Yes, everything." Wanjiru spoke quietly. "He bathed me and his finger danced with my privates and gave me pleasure like I never knew before. Later he did me for two or three hours in many ways."

"Did he use a Durexi," Warimu asked, probably recalling her experience.

"No he planted his seed in me."

"Maybe you will get the first pregnancy." Warimu said with a bit of jealousy in her voice. They looked at their mother who was very quiet. "Mama, what do you say?"

Esther was quiet for a while. "Children are wonderful to have but such a big responsibility. Each of you is my blood. Wanjiru your father was an Englishman. He had a wife but no children and I was their housekeeper. Whenever his wife was away in Nakuru, he would do me. He would push me on my back on the dining table." The girls giggled nervously. "He would pull off my underwear and pleasure us. He would talk to me as he did it, asking me if it felt good." The girls giggled a bit. "Then he would squirt into me and stay there inside me talking, asking me questions. He looked like your *mzungu*, Wanjiru, but not as tall, and crooked, brown teeth. He had blue eyes too, and brown, straight hair that always was in his eyes. Very thin. His thing was long and fat." The girls murmured what thing what thing, but Esther went on, "He did me like this often, and it went on for years

13

with no pregnancy. Then the Englishman had to go back home, and he did me even in the grass when he escorted me home at night after work. Then I got a pregnancy. When he was leaving, he could tell I was pregnant, and his wife knew also, I think. When they were ready to go, he gave me an envelope with his address in England. He sent me money for years for Wanjiru's schooling. I am told they separated back in England. His name was Tatton, but there are many by that name in England. I cannot say it the way he says his name."

Wanjiru wondered if her life would be as her mother's life to raise a *mzungu's* child and struggle to stay alive and find food for everyone. Wanjiru was about to say something when a student pulled back the curtain of the door. "I have five shillings." Was all he said, and Warimu jumped up and left the hut.

Wanjiru wanted to know about her father. What else was there to know since her mother repeated details of each of three men who fathered the three daughters? Two she knew and they worked at the school. One the night watchman and the other was a cook who already had two wives and ten children. "Do you know what my father taught at the school?"

"I don't know what it is called, but it is like how to mix things together for medicines."

"Like the chemist in Nakuru?" Muthoni asked and Esther nodded. "Must be very smart."

"He could fix anything, cars, radios, electric stoves, water heaters, motorcycles." Just then, Warimu returned and gave Esther some money, and went over to the water pail to wash herself. "*Anafanya haraka*!" Esther said suggesting the boy had done her quickly.

"He was just a boy with a little thing, a few sperms and five shillings."

"You think he has more money?" Muthoni asked, as if this is good business, especially since they all wanted a man anyway.

"Does your friend Kimani pay you?" Wanjiru asked. She knew him as a former student and friend of Wambui. Kimani had done Muthoni in Lodi's house whenever Lodi was gone. She had told her stories of Kimani doing her on lumpy beds in unused rooms in the house. She thought that Wambui would lose her job if Lodi found out.

14

Muthoni looked perplexed. "Kimani pay me? No, he always used *durexi* so no pregnancy. He just wanted pleasure. I hope Kimani wants to marry me." This caused her two sisters burst out in laughter.

Esther warned her daughters, "Stop that! Kimani has money to pay bride price. Wambui says he teaches in Molo. Her *mzungu* went to visit his family in Embu. His *baba* owns a big *shamba*. He would be a good husband and he likes Muthoni."

Warimu snickered, "How many goats would he pay for Muthoni? Two? She is not a virgin. If a boy is cute she goes out to the maize field with him and does not charge."

Wanjiru laughed, "None of us are holy holy virgins. We love men ... and boys. If we do not have sperm in our *kuma*, we think we are starving." They all nodded in agreement. Wanjiru smiled to herself, she was "starving" for many months, but now well fed. There was a long silence as they all watched the flame flickering off a log. Esther would bring home several split logs every evening from her Englishman as part of her pay. He was hardly ever around, since he spent a lot of his time at the Njoro country club drinking. The silence was broken by a boy's voice.

"Wanjiru, it is Wambui's stepson, Njuguna." The boy came in and stood dumb as if waiting for permission to speak. Esther waved her hand as if to say sit next to me. "My mother wants word how Wanjiru did with her *mzungu*." Strangely he had a pencil and a school writing booklet.

Esther laughed, "You will come every night to write down what happened?"

"This is my mother's want." The boy said very seriously. Wanjiru looked at the skinny ten year old, who was Wambui's stepson - her dead husband's son by his first wife. He had a long face and a shaved head... reminding her of his deceased police officer father...at least Wambui's photo of him. The boy was ready to write what Wanjiru spoke. She looked down and saw the list of questions, and could see they would get personal. He is only ten, so will he be embarrassed to ask those questions? "First question. Did you make the meals?"

~~~~

Waking up, it took Wanjiru a few seconds to realize where she was. The bed was soft and warm, the man next to her was asleep, and breathing lightly. The walls were a light blue color and the brightly decorated curtains were letting in the Friday afternoon light. She looked at Lodi and petted his chest hairs but not wanting to wake him. She liked working for him, since the work was easy and fun. The school was having a fund raising and Lodi snuck out to come home and spend it, as he says, "making love." She laughed and thought it was more like "making babies." She looked at his nakedness, and thought, he must be cold, and pulled the sheet and blanket up over them both. She studied his face. A long lock of yellow hair, as usual, fell across his forehead. His long white nose reminded her of his thing, and she giggled silently.

She heard some voices outside of a man and a woman, and walking up the gravel walkway. She carefully rolled out of bed and slipped her dress over her head, without her bra and underwear. She looked at her bra on the floor and laughed at the first time she did it with Lodi. She wore a lace bra and underwear that Lodi said was beautiful, but then maybe he said that about her breasts. She buttoned the top just as someone was knocking at the door.

Wanjiru headed through the living room to the front door. She saw what she thought was a Chinese woman and a short, skinny and very black Luo boy. Then she remembered, Wambui had told about the woman. She was that American who used to share this house with Lodi. She unlocked the door, and greeted the two, "Hello, Miss Lee."

"Hello, you remember me? I came to visit my old housemate. Is Mac around?" Miss Lee said, and Wanjiru assumed she was referring to her Lodi.

"Come in. Lodi is taking a nap. I am Wanjiru but call me Njiru." She looked from Miss Lee to the boy, who was as tall as Miss Lee was and shorter than Wanjiru, thin but at the same time quite muscular in the arms. They both wore khaki shorts, and his very black legs contrasted to her very white legs. Wanjiru wondered if he was her boyfriend.

"Lodi? Oh, yes, of course. This is Ivan a student of mine."

"Lodi has some sherry or gin for guests." Wanjiru pointed to the chairs, and the two relaxed. Wanjiru brought two glasses and two bottles, sitting them down on the coffee table.

"Njiru, we brought some Tusker too. Kinda warm, but relaxing. My school in Kisumu is funding raising, too. Looks like it is going on down there too." She observed, opening three bottles of Tusker. "Where is Wambui? She finally get fired?" She

16

wondered, handing Wanjiru the beer. Miss Lee poured some gin in a glass and swallowed it all at once. Wanjiru recalled the nasty things Wambui had said about Miss Lee.

Wanjiru sat down and took a sip, and as usual thought the first sip was too bitter. "No, she is at her garden until Monday. I work for two weeks here and keep Lodi happy." She heard a sound come out of Ivan, and looked over at the jet-black face. Luo hated the Kikuyu, so she did not think there was much hope for a friendship.

"Yes, you are beautiful. I am sure you keep him very happy."

"I recall you had a big *mzungu* boyfriend with a big *pikipiki*."

"*Mzungu*?" she thought a minute. "Oh, yes, well American, anyway. Big motorcycle, yes. He left his contract early and went back and married his fiancé. I was sort of shocked that he had a fiancé."

"Very sorry. I hope you are done with him." Wanjiru said hoping that was the right English phrase. Beyond form two, her English was from movies in Nakuru and on the village square.

"Yes, I am over him. Ivan's father works in Nakuru, so he is traveling with me. He wanted to see Njoro School. If I could stay here, Ivan will go on to Nakuru, if not I will go with him and see if Beth is around." Miss Lee said, and Wanjiru saw that Ivan was looking between her legs. She had forgotten that she had no underwear and her dress pulled up. He has no manners, looking at a woman that way, she thought, that stinking boy! She put her legs together and pulled her dress down over her knees, and Miss Lee gave Ivan the look of death. "Ivan, go take a walk around the school." The boy looked dejected, stood up and left.

"Oh, yes, Beth. He told me she is coming here on Sunday, or was it tomorrow night? I am sure you are welcome here, unless you two are still bad." Wanjiru forgot who told her, but the gossip was that Lodi and Miss Lee were mad at each other when they separated.

"Well, that is why I came. We separated very mad at each other. I thought we should kiss and make up." Miss Lee chuckled and finished her beer, took another shot of gin, and began working on the beer Ivan had yet to drink.

17

"Wambui told me about your fight." Wanjiru took another sip, thought it too bitter, and pushed it towards Miss Lee, hoping she would want it.

"Well, I did the screaming, and he sat there and took it. I am still ashamed the way I acted. He had some idea that I cared for him. Mac didn't know about my boyfriend until Steve showed up one weekend. It totally surprised him." She finished Ivan's beer, and took the beer Wanjiru offered. Wanjiru wondered if she could hold that much beer.

"Oh! You had another boyfriend and Lodi did not know?" Wanjiru felt a pang shoot through her. "Wambui told me that Lodi liked you." She looked into the woman's eyes, whose "Chinese" eyes were really not that different from many Africans, just that she was quite white instead of brown. Her black hair was course like African hair, but perfectly straight instead of tight curls. Wanjiru, being *nusu nusu,* had brown hair with wider curls.

"Yes, I know. I did not like him, though. I never did like white boys. We had to share the house until another house came free. We could not get along. Whenever Mac hit on me, and I always turned him down." She slowed a bit drinking the third beer, but Wanjiru assumed the woman needed company, so she sat with her until she was nearly done. "I really need to go pee. *Kwenda choo.*" She stood up, weaving a bit from the gin and beer, and headed towards the toilet. Wanjiru got up and went to the kitchen to clean up, thinking Miss Lee might be a while. She spent a few minutes cleaning, and took out the rubbish. She came back in and washed her hands. She returned to the living room but Miss Lee was gone. She went to see if there was a problem, but the toilet and bath were empty, but the door to Lodi's bedroom was open.

Miss Lee was standing by the sleeping man and began removing her own clothes, apparently too drunk to sense that Wanjiru was standing behind her. Pangs of jealousy were shooting through Wanjiru, realizing that Miss Lee was taking her place. But Lodi did her for maybe two hours, so he may be empty. She was sore from so much sex. Conflicted by jealousy and curiosity, she watched as the naked woman slowly got in next to her Lodi, and began petting him. Lodi stirred a bit as Miss Lee stroked his thing making it stiff. He turned around and petted her breasts, just like, Wanjiru thought, the way he does me. He was quite long and hard, and rolled over on top of her as she spread her very white thighs

18

apart for him. He spread them farther apart with his knees, and his white shaft began probing around looking for an entry point. He found something and Wanjiru smiled seeing his hips dance, and it reminded her of the way he got inside and the delightful sensation when he did. Miss Lee let out a sound when he plunged deep and withdrew. That is how he does that! She thought. Then it was like a machine going in and out and mysteriously hitting target every time. It went in deep, withdrew all the way, then plunged deep again all very rapidly. That is how he drives me insane with pleasure. Miss Lee was letting out little sounds very much like Wanjiru's. This went on with the bed vibrating and sweat began forming on his back. Suddenly he plunged in and stopped and his whole body quaked, and Wanjiru could see the muscles in his back and legs quivering. He paused for a while then rolled off her with a tremendous sigh.

"Wanjiru, that was hmmmm" he said, and Wanjiru thought he was going back to sleep. Miss Lee was about to go to sleep too, but Wanjiru thought better.

"I go *choo*, Lodi" Wanjiru said, hearing him grunt something. She pulled the naked woman out of the bed, standing her up. By now she was quite drunk, so Wanjiru led her to the toilet and sat her down, and returned to get her clothes. She came back with the clothes, Miss Lee had fallen backwards with her arms and legs spread out, and she was slipping off the toilet. Wanjiru was curious and fingered Miss Lee, taking a sniff, knowing then that Lodi had planted seed in her. Wanjiru wondered what to do. Should they know that Lodi did her? He may think he did me, and she was too drunk to remember – well, maybe. She looked at the unconscious, naked woman sprawled out on the toilet. She had nice breasts, and very black pubic hair.

"What is going on, who is that?" Lodi's voice came from behind. She turned and saw her naked boss standing there looking. "Is that Ann?" He asked. "Why is she naked on the toilet? Hmmm, great body." He chuckled. Wanjiru realized that this was the first time he had seen her without clothing.

"She came for visit with one of her students. A boy named Ivan. When she waited for you to wake up, she drank beer and gin and she lay next to you. She got you happy and you did her and went back to sleep."

"I did?" he looked guilty. "I thought it was you and you were doing – hmmmm. It was different. It never occurred to me that someone would take your place. Is this Ivan guy here now?"

"She wants to stay for the weekend. You did her already. She told Ivan to go away, then you did her." She repeated as if he was not understanding what he had done.

"But did she really want it?"

"She came to you and took off her clothes. She wanted it." Wanjiru laughed, and he laughed along.

"Help me take her back to bed. In the little room though." He said, as he lifted the naked woman off the toilet, and they both led her into the small bedroom and put her on the hard mattress. Suddenly Miss Lee woke up acting very bewildered.

"Wanjiru, please start the water for a bath for Ann." Lodi said, and Wanjiru felt a stab of jealousy, thinking of all the fun times she had with Lodi in that wonderfully warm water, and his gentle petting. Just the thought was arousing, but she turned and went to the bath, inserted the plastic plug and turned the knobs for hot and cold water, making a warm mixture. As she turned, Miss Lee was standing still attached to Lodi hiding her nakedness. Lodi let Wanjiru pass, and pushed the naked woman towards the bathtub. Wanjiru wondered why the woman is suddenly shy, covering her breasts and privates as she stepped into the tub. Did the beer and gin make her so bold? Lodi got a towel and washcloth and set them by the tub. He closed the door, and Wanjiru was relieved that he did not get in the tub with her. She would feel so jealous. Miss Lee had too much of Lodi already.

"Wanjiru, I guess. Is she staying for the weekend?" He asked and she worried her Lodi would do the China woman all weekend. She looked him in the eyes and nodded. "You should sleep with me this weekend so that I will not do her. You are my girlfriend, right?"

Wanjiru felt relieved. "I want to be, but I need to ask mama."

"She hate *mzungu*?"

"I am *nusu nusu mzungu*. She likes me." And they laughed together.

"Ask her if you can sleep with me every night and be my girlfriend." He said and she felt herself getting excited, but then it hit her that he might want to marry her and take her to America.

"Maybe I live in Kenya all my life and you can give me twelve kids like my grandfather had." He said, and now she knew he was crazy. Kenya is trying to get rid of white people. As they reached the kitchen, he started singing, "Sugar in the morning, sugar in the evening, sugar at suppertime, be my little sugar and love me all the time!"

He watched Wanjiru starting the oven to bake potatoes, and some oil a frying pan for the meat. She was getting better at cooking, but still nothing as good as Wambui did, or so she believed. She got plates and dinnerware and set it out on the table. "Wanjiru, go ask your mother if you can be my girlfriend and sleep with me every night."

"Really?" Wanjiru said. She left Lodi in the kitchen to watch the food, and ran out the back door, around the house. She knew her mother would still be at work, so she headed next door, running around to the back of Keogh's house. Her mother was putting trash in the can out back as she approached. Her mother looked surprised, but she started right off in Kikuyu, "Mama, Lodi wants me to be his girlfriend and sleep with him every night." She said and the older woman looked stunned. "He wants me to give him twelve babies so he can live in Kenya."

"Twelve? Twelve babies? Sleep with him every night?" her mama asked. "What if he is not allowed to stay in Kenya? Are you going to America? That place hates *nusu nusu* people like you. He take your babies to America and leave you here? Babies, yes, make all you want, but stay here in Kenya. No, do not spend a night with him. He will think you are his wife and own you. Do not spend all night with him."

"Mama!"

"You will do what you want, but you asked me, and I say no."

She returned to Lodi's kitchen sadly, and he knew right away. "Your mama thinks it is a bad idea? Am I right?"

"She would not give blessing. You do me, and I sleep at her house tonight. Do me until you too tired to do Miss Lee again." She said and he chuckled stirring the beef in the pan.

"I don't know. My body makes sperm like Tusker makes beer." He laughed, repeating a phrase she also heard from the students, and she laughed at the idea that his body was a like a big factory making truckloads of sperm. "Steam some *majani* and I

21

will check on Ann." He said suddenly and disappeared into the other room. The beef and sauce were simmering in the pan, and the potatoes still had maybe thirty minutes. It was too early to put on the *majani*. Lodi had opened a Tusker and it was sitting open on the counter. She took a sip, then another. She got up on the counter, sitting as Lodi often did to hear her stories as she cooked. Soon the beer was nearly gone, but Lodi was still gone. She put the *majani* in the steamer and turned on the stove. She went to the bathroom and heard a conversation, and turned back to the living room. She found two more beers in Miss Lee's bag and opened them, wondering what happened to the Luo boy. Returning to the bath, she found Lodi sitting on the edge of the tub, chatting with Miss Lee. She gave him a beer, and turned to give Miss Lee a beer. She was no longer shy, sitting in the clear water with one knee up, hiding nothing. She handed her a beer, and announced that food was ready, and left, but listened a bit more from around the corner.

"So, when Wanjiru told me I did you, I knew something was different..."

"You enjoy? I did." Came the female voice.

"Yes, good. Wanjiru's skin is warmer and has like the perfect body." He said, and Wanjiru thought that her Lodi was insulting the China woman, or make her try harder next time. She laughed to herself wondering if Miss Lee cared.

"Maybe that is why Steve went back to his fiancé. I am not that good in bed. Should I ask Wanjiru for some tips?" She heard the woman say, and Wanjiru wondered what she meant by tip. The woman continued, "She obviously makes you very happy."

"I would marry her and take her home if I could."

"I bet your dad would like that."

"I think the bigger problem would be Wanjiru's family. They hate whites more than my dad hates half-breeds."

"And Chinks?"

"I never heard a bad word from my family about Orientals. My dad's brother died in the Korean War. We should get supper. Your clothes are in the little bedroom. Nice body by the way."

"Thanks." She heard the woman say. Wanjiru tried to get back to the kitchen before Lodi found out she was listening, but he caught her just as she stepped into the living room. He pulled her back and pressed her against the wall, sticking his tongue into her mouth, a taste she loved. A hand pulled up her dress and found its way to her left breast, while another hand slipped into her underwear and found her special place and delicately began rubbing it. Tingling from that place to her breast grew until her whole body trembled in pleasure. She wrapped her arms around his neck and held on tight as her body convulsed with her legs losing strength. He stopped and held her tightly until she calmed down. "I'm afraid the *majani* might be ruined." She ran in and found the water had just started steaming. She jabbed the potatoes with a fork and they were ready.

Bringing out the food, she found that there were three plates on the table, and she was concerned that another guest was coming she had not planned for. Lodi was putting music in the cassette player, and turned to look her in the eyes. "I want my girlfriend to eat with us." He said, and she felt a quiver of nervousness shoot through her. She sat the bowls of food down, just as Miss Lee appeared.

Lodi pointed to a chair for Miss Lee and said, "Wanjiru sit next to me, please." She looked at Lodi and Miss Lee, and no one was surprised that she would be eating with them. "I'd serve wine, but I think Ann will get rowdy again."

"It is not as good as Wambui's cooking, but I hope you like it." She said.

"The stew looks great." Miss Lee said, and they all took a share of food. Wanjiru was concerned about her table manners, since it had been a long time since she sat at a table to eat rather than sit with food on her lap. She had etiquette lessons in form one in Mombasa. However, Lodi picked at food with his fingers, and probably did not take that etiquette lesson.

Her Lodi asked, "Wanjiru, you told me you read romance novels in school in Mombasa. What was your favorite?"

"The one I like best was not from the library. I got it from my uncle who got it at his hotel. Someone left it at the hotel and he thought I would like it. *Lady Chatterly's Lover*. It was very sexy book.

"You got to be kidding! I read that when I was in Swahili training in Likoni." Lodi laughed. "When I was done, I gave it to a waiter."

"Likoni? Sea Breeze Hotel? That is where my uncle works." She laughed, finding it unbelievable that she read a book her Lodi read. They had actually touched the same book long before they met, and her uncle perhaps prepared food for her Lodi to eat. "I still have that book in my box!" They laughed and he stroked her back.

"It's a small world." There was a silence as they continued eating.

Finally Miss Ann spoke. "Mac, the reason I came was to beg forgiveness for being such a bitch to you when we shared this place." Miss Lee said, and Wanjiru felt a sudden chill, thinking they would start fighting again.

"We were both very upset. I have always hated myself for showing anger." Her Lodi replied.

"Mac, I think any other guy would have strangled me, just to shut me up." She said, and Lodi just chuckled.

Wanjiru was very curious. "You know, your fight was the talk of Njoro. The students in the dormitories heard, and Wambui had to tell everyone. What was the problem?"

Miss Lee looked down at her food. "I really used you, Mac." She frowned. "I led you on in order to get things out of you. Steve said I did the same to him, and got tired of it. I manipulate men to get things I can't otherwise get." Miss Lee said. Wanjiru did not understand a word.

"What does *manipulate* mean?"

Her Lodi said, "It means to lie or misrepresent, make promises you do not intend to keep, in order to get things. I think I was easy to manipulate. I never had a girlfriend before I came to Kenya." He said, and Wanjiru was very surprised. "I was too serious a student. My brother got married at seventeen and was a father at eighteen, which made me scared of women."

"You were a virgin?" Miss Lee asked.

"I got the impression that American girls were not interested in me, so I gave up on them. I asked a lot of girls or women out, but was always turned down." He said. Wanjiru was wondering if this was the truth. Was all he knew about sex from that book?

"I sort of knew that, and took advantage of you. You were a perfect gentleman and I screwed you over." She said and seemed to be telling the truth. "What do you mean a virgin?"

"Well, not in the strict sense. There was a college girl who boarded in our house, she got me."

"How old were you?"

"Eight years old. She taught great technique."

"She was a pedophile - that doesn't count. Anything else?"

"Well, a student friend in college invited me over, got me drunk and took advantage of me."

"She good looking?"

"It was a *he*." Her Lodi said looking down at his plate and chuckling. "I woke up in *his* bed with a very sore bottom. That was the last time I got drunk in a long time. So, technically not a virgin."

Miss Lee seemed very interested now. "So, how did you lose your virginity with a girl?"

"About a week after I arrived in Njoro, another teacher and I went down to the Equator bar in Nakuru. He chatted up a couple of girls, and they agreed to come back to Njoro with us. I got the younger one, who turned out to be as much a virgin as I was. There was more blood than pleasure." He said, and Wanjiru remembered her first time was very painful, and bloody, as the boy tore her hymen. "It lasted a few minutes, but then we sat for a long time with her pressing a towel until the bleeding stopped. I walked her over to the taxi stand and gave her money for the ride back."

"Yeah, my first time hurt like hell." Miss Lee said. "But it was like smoking the first cigarette. Hurt like hell but I could not wait to have another." They all laughed.

It was later after an evening of music, sherry and conversation that Wanjiru hoped that Lodi would not ask her again to spend the night with him. She heard some voices in the kitchen, and went out to see that her sisters had come to escort her home. "Mama said you might have to work late, so we bring you back." Warimu stated, sounding confused about the change in schedule.

"I will explain when I get home." Wanjiru stated. She went back, announced that she was going home, and Lodi stood up giving her a hug and kiss.

"Well, think about being my girlfriend. Maybe your mama will change her mind."

"Maybe." Wanjiru said and headed out the back with her sisters towing her along. She knew Ann Lee would end up in bed with him again. How could he resist such a beautiful woman?

~~~~~

Beth Kropp walked up the gravel walkway to the front door of her American friend's house. She had been thinking. Why

25

does she keep throwing herself at him only to be turned down? She stepped up to the veranda and saw that the curtains were wide open and she could see the housekeeper. She tapped on the glass door and opened it up. "Hi, Wanjiru, is Mac around?" Beth asked, suddenly remembering only the Americans called him "Mac."

"*Hujambo*, Beth! Lodi told me you would come today."

"Yes, I went to the market early, and there was a bus for Njoro, and I said what the hell." She came in, sat her bag by the window and shook Wanjiru's hand. "You are looking great. What is your secret?" She said with a chuckle.

"You know all my secrets. Oh, Miss Lee arrived yesterday."

"Yes, she wrote and said she would either be here or my place. Where is Mac anyway?"

"He is in the *choo*."

"Tell me, did he sleep with Ann?" she asked, and Wanjiru knew from novels that *sleep with Ann* meant to have sex with Ann.

"Have sex last night? *Sijui*. I had to sleep at my mother's place."

"No, I meant actually sleep in the same bed."

"Oh, sorry. Miss Lee slept in the small bedroom in a sleeping bag. She's still there. Go wake her up. Lodi made coffee for everyone."

Beth headed for the hallway to run into a wall of a man coming out. He gave her a hug and a peck on the cheek. "Hey, Sis, you came early! Ann is still asleep I think. He looked at his watch. "Nine forty. Let's wake her up." Beth followed him, and Wanjiru followed her into the small room.

Ann said, "I heard you coming, I'm trying to get up. Too comfortable."

"Beth, you get her going, Wanjiru and I will get some toast for you."

The other two disappeared, and Beth sat down on the bed, as Ann kicked the sleeping bag back. Beth leaned down and the two kissed, with Beth stroking Ann's hair. "Hey, I read in your letter about Steve. That was a rotten thing to do." Beth said, and Ann nodded. "So, you here for some rebound sex?"

"Rebound sex? With him?"

"You never did like him, did you?"

"Well, I don't get all mushy over him like you do, no." Ann said. "At least he is helluva more gentleman than Steve, for sure. He doesn't lie to you just to get into your pants, he tells you straight up what he wants."

"Well, I recall a few lies dropping from your lips."

"Hey, I'm no saint. I came to apologize to Mac."

"So, did you get any of Mac or not?" Beth pressed, looking at Ann's long black hair hanging off the bed. She was wearing a large t-shirt that might be Steve's. She could see through the thin cloth that her friend was not wearing a bra or panties. Beth pulled up the t-shirt and petted Ann's breasts, which she always enjoyed.

"Well, I tricked him yesterday. He was asleep and I took Wanjiru's place in bed. He nailed me good before I passed out from too much gin. After Wanjiru went home last night, I cornered him coming out of the toilet. He nailed me to the wall. Being naked helped," she laughed. "He picked me up like I was light as a feather and pressed me against the wall and did me like I was on my back."

"And?" Beth knew there was more.

"I got into his bed early this morning to take advantage –"

"Of his morning –"

"You know. Anyway, he nearly turned me inside out before I cried uncle."

"You told him to stop before he was finished?" Beth said and absent-mindedly squeezed a nipple, then played with her thick, black pubic hair.

"Yes, and came back here for safety." Ann laughed. "Hmmm, that feels good." Beth leaned down and stuck her tongue into Ann's mouth and at the same time found her clitoris. Within a minute, Ann was convulsing in pleasure, and then slowly calmed down. "Wow that was nice. I owe you one." Ann added as they were still face-to-face.

"Sure, the things you do… Anyway, I bet you still don't like him." Beth snickered, sitting up and sniffed the finger that did Ann. Hmmm that is his smell, I would bet, Beth thought.

"If he were Chinese-American or half oriental like Steve. He knows? I don't like white boys. Just getting rocks off. Besides he does too many black girls." Ann stated cynically. Beth always thought Ann's racism was a bit rude, but she tried to look past it.

"Let's get some coffee and toast." Beth suggested. Ann stood up and the t-shirt came down halfway to her knees, and did not seem to intend to wear anything more for clothes. In the kitchen, they found buttered toast, boiled eggs and coffee all on the stove. There was hot milk and sugar on the counter. They wondered where their friends were, but helped themselves and sat in the living room, listening to the news on VOA that Gerald Ford had announced that he would run for his own term as President. Beth wondered where they had gone, but then thought… she got up and looked down the hall and saw that his bedroom door was closed, so she went back to sip her coffee. Ann seems angry about her life, Beth thought. I suppose Steve dumping her would hurt. At least the guy I like best is not leading me on. If a guy calls you "sis" you know your only chance with him is if he has an incest habit. "You over Steve yet? What are you going to do?"

"No, I am still mad as hell. My doc gave me some valium to calm me down. Makes me feel like my head is stuffed with cotton, so I would rather be angry." She paused and took the last bite of her toast. Beth heard the water running in the bathtub, thinking something will happen soon. "I came here to apologize to him. I think, let him nail me – you know someone I really hate – is my way of getting even with Steve. Anyway, Mac said some stuff last night that made me understand why it is so easy to mislead him. He thinks American girls just don't like him."

"I'm American! Hey, I have lost all self-respect asking for him to screw me, but he calls me sis and kisses me on the cheek."

"He must be getting even for all the rejection. I tricked him, so that broke the ice. Maybe you can break the ice, too."

"Probably too late. You see the way he is all puppy eyes for Wanjiru?"

"Yeah, pretty pathetic. What? Not even high school education, and lives in a grass shack. He told me last night after she left that he wants to marry her, take her back to Illinois and have a bunch of beautiful kids."

"Why doesn't he?" Beth said, already knowing.

"Wanjiru would never leave Kenya, and he knows he will be thrown out after five years. He is really love struck though. Poor thing."

"For someone you so detest, you sure take pity on him." Beth laughed. "I got to go pee." She got up, headed for the toilet, and passed the bath, which is a separate room. Wanjiru was in the tub with Mac, and he was soaping her with a washcloth. He smiled and waved as she passed. God! Let that be me someday! She said to herself, probably not in this lifetime. She got out of the toilet room and the bathroom door was closed, so she went back to drink her coffee and chat with Ann.

After a few minutes, Wanjiru came out, "Lodi say you do bath now." She went on into the kitchen.

Beth and Ann looked at each other, Beth said, "You think he wants me to share the bath with him?" They both stood up and headed for the bath, but it was empty.

A voice came from behind. "Hey girls. You two want a hot bath? I'd love to watch you two bathe each other. At least you, Ann, really need a bath." He said, and Beth knew that was a poke at her for what Beth imagined, was a lot of sweaty sex. As if from nowhere, he added. "We should take a hike out to Egerton Castle for exercise." Ann went into the bath and started the water bending over and showing her pudenda. "Nice view, Ann." Ann pulled the t-shirt over her head and gave them a nice show of her sliding into the warm water. "Ann, you need someone to wash you? Me, Beth or Njiru?" Ann answered by sticking out her tongue and reaching out a hand and pushing the door shut.

Beth leaned into the huge man copping a feel. God! Is he some kind of Satyr! Mac let her explore for a moment before he took her hands, gave her a hug, and led her to the living room. He let loose and went to tell Wanjiru something. Beth turned off the radio. Strummed the mandolin on the shelf and found a Newsweek International to read until everyone was ready.

Ninety minutes later, the three could just see Egerton Castle at the end of a long field. It was the abandoned home of former British settler. It was a large two story, stone house, supposedly over fifty rooms, which was a version of an English country home plunked down on the highlands of Kenya.

Ann complained, "What is it, a ten mile hike here? Your legs are so long it is hard to keep up with you." Beth thought that if she complained too much, Mac would leave her home next time – which would be good. Keep complaining Ann!

"I think about four miles or so. I usually make it in less than an hour, but you are kind of slow." Mac snickered. "If you want, you can ride on my shoulders. I used to give my nieces and nephews horsy rides around the house." Ann stuck her tongue out at him. "So, Beth, I was saying, that Wambui's friend Kimani is really cute, about your age, and I thought you might like to meet him. He used to be a student at Njoro and teaches in Molo now. He used to be a close friend of Wambui's other white teacher. I went up to Embu with him to visit his father's place. A little cross-cultural experience. I had a meal with his family in his mother's grass and stick house, slept in his cow-dung covered single-man's hut in a hammock, and went to a Kikuyu wedding."

"Interesting." Beth said, wondering why the suggestion for a cute Kikuyu guy. "He must be a gentleman like you or you wouldn't suggest it."

"Gentleman? Me? Surely you jest. Kimani is definitely not a hairy he-man. He is somewhat effeminate, non-threatening."

Ann barged into the conversation sarcastically, "You must have done him already."

"Ann!" Beth exclaimed, but Mac just rolled his eyes.

"I would bet he is still a virgin on that side. I asked Wambui why Kimani came around so often. You know I am not a really likable guy." He chuckled at his own self-deprecation, which Beth enjoyed hearing from Mac. "Speaking of which, I think I told you that guy's theory on sex?"

Ann was finally interested. "Which guy?"

"I wish I could remember, but I had to read it in college. I think it was Erich Fromm and the art of love or loving. I have it back at the house. Every person carries a male and female polarity, receiving and penetrating. Bisexual. I probably have my books mixed up, but because of cultural norms or pressures, the ..."

Ann interrupted, "Beth that would explain you and me, then."

"What's that?" Mac asked, and Beth felt her face blushing. "Oh, you and Beth. Everyone knows you two get it on. I'd love to watch sometimes and learn a few tricks on pleasing women." Mac smiled at Beth who could feel her face burning with embarrassment, knowing that Mac always knew that she had a side thing with Ann. "Anyway, since we are telling all, I have to be honest there are a few guys I would like to explore."

Beth felt relieved with this tell-all, and Mac's idea that people are not gay, straight or bi, but just sexual opportunists. Like a flower child, if it feels good it must be right. That probably explains Mac's semi-hippy ways. Alcohol and sex are his only apparent addictions, though.

Ann was still in her mood, "Well, an asshole like Steve might learn that honesty can do a lot less damage in the long run."

"I'd drink to that!" Beth agreed. "Mac, I hope there are some alcoholic beverages in that backpack of yours."

"I'd thought I'd surprise you. Get you two drunk and watch you get it on!" He laughed, and Beth's felt her face flush again. "So, I'll check out Kimani to make sure you'd like him. I'll bring him to Nakuru." Beth looked up at her giant friend, with his long, blonde strands of hair falling onto his face and wondered. He added tangentially, "If that is I can get over my obsession with Wanjiru!"

"Let's see what happens."

Ann changed the subject, "It sort of looks like a castle, not like the ones in Europe."

Mac began lecturing for Ann's benefit, "Lord Egerton apparently built the house to impress the love of his life, and convince her to remain with him in Kenya, but upon seeing it, she did not like it and returned to England. This turned Lord Egerton into a recluse who announced he would shoot on site any woman coming near his house." Jesus! Beth thought, and here we are. "That is what I was told," Mac laughed, "so, I can't attest to the veracity of that story. But if the Kenya government would let me, I'd buy the place and start a school here." Beth thought, where the hell would you get the money to buy this place?

In the past, they have checked out the "castle" hoping that the caretaker would give them another tour. Beth recalled the first time she came here was when she, Mac and one of his students was given a tour inside, and were impressed with its pristine condition.

Beth looked at the front stairway and the stonework on the front, as Ann said. "I read that these Kenya Brits were pretty promiscuous." Beth turned and studied Ann who was wearing a tank top, a skirt and sandals. She had thought jeans would be better, but it got so warm and the air dead still, she realized Ann had a more comfortable outfit. She could see her nipples through the fabric of the top, and knew she was trying to be tempting. She then looked at Mac, and briefly fantasized her perfect *ménage à trios.* Discussing sex with Mac was having a liberating effect on her, albeit temporary.

Beth laughed, "Yeah, as if that's changed."

Mac smiled what Beth always thought was a killer smile, but said, "Probably not here, since women were not allowed here after he was jilted."

Beth started to say, "Maybe we could..." but a voice came from behind.

"*Jambo sana.*" It was the caretaker, who was an older man wearing work jeans and blue shirt. Beth knew that Ann like herself never learned much Swahili. Mac reached out to shake the man's hand.

"*Habari. Unakumbuka mimi? Dadangu* Beth here is from Nakuru, and *Mwalimu* Ann is from Kisumu. You are *Bwana* Njuroge?"

"Yes, yes, my name Njuroge." He said. But Beth heard ju-LOW-gay. "You *Bwana* Lodi. I showed you and *Bibi* Beth the big house one time." He said and Beth knew enough Swahili to know that *bibi* is for married woman and *dadangu* is "my sister." Should she be insulted being called *bibi*? The caretaker is pretty handsome, though, so no. They all shook hands with the fellow, with the fellow taking a bit longer to shake hands with Beth, as if checking her out. Hey, I would not kick him out of bed, Beth thought. "I get *tabu* if you go inside. Solly. You can walk and look." The caretaker walked away.

"*Asante sana*, we are just out for a walk. Uh, *ngoja kidogo.*" Mac said and walked up to him and began talking in Swahili that was over Beth's head, although she heard *dadangu* everytime Mac motioned towards Beth.

As they talked, Ann asked, "Beth, what was that look you gave him, that old man?"

"Well, he is not that old, but he is attractive."

Ann said disapprovingly, "That old, black man? Beth!"

Beth thought, there we go again, "Ann, don't worry about it. Anyway, you are getting Mac to nail you, and you hate him. You could really disgrace yourself letting that old man nail you, right?" Beth said, and regretting what she said almost immediately. Strangely, Ann did not act offended, and merely shrugged. Beth watched the two men talking, and Mac handed something to the caretaker, then turned towards them.

"Girls, he agreed to give us a tour of the castle." He said following Njuroge up the front staircase, with Beth stopping a second to look at the goofy lions holding the front lanterns.

Beth hurried up and asked, "What did you tell him that made him change his mind?"

"I told him my sister and the China lady thinks he is very sexy, and Njuroge could probably seduce either one or both of you."

"Jesus!" Beth said acting insulted, but then checked out Njuroge. "Well, you are right. I would not refuse him. Did you give him money?"

"No, a couple of condoms." He laughed, and, oddly, Beth felt relieved. "I made him promise to use them if he were able to persuade either of you."

"God! You think of everything. Since Ann is into sick-o sex, she'll probably give it out."

"You think?" he asked as Njuroge opened the large wooden, front door. Beth went in first and was again impressed with the grand staircase and the large paneled rooms. Although it was called a castle, it was more like a well-built stone mansion. As they strolled through the house, Beth was walking close to Njuroge to hear what he had to say. Most of the time he was hitting on Ann and Beth, and Beth was flattered. After Ann had walked ahead, Njuroge asked Beth a weird question, "Why your Kung Fu lady friend not wear *chupi* – uh - underwear?" Beth was stunned, and looked at Njuroge, who apparently saw a Kung Fu movie. The man was Ann's height, brown and just a bit wrinkled. Had closely cut hair with some white hair mixed with black.

"She what? I didn't know." Beth said, and realized how unobservant she was.

He led them to a ballroom that was built for dances, but only used for political meetings. There was a small stage at one end and some benches along one wall.

Ann got up on the stage, and twirled her skirt, giving the guys an eyeful, making them laugh and applaud. Beth was embarrassed for her. She came back and sat down next to Njuroge on the front of the stage. Beth sat down on the other side of Ann.

"Lord Egerton was in love with some British woman. They say he was a shrimp, less than five feet tall." Mac laughed, taking his backpack off, digging through the contents. "Girls, Njuroge, I have water, High Life sherry, cookies, crackers, apples and oranges, too, for a snack."

Beth piped up, "Cookies and sherry for me."

"Me, too, if you have enough." Ann said, and she got the bottle of sherry, while Beth took the box of cookies to open.

"You do the sherry, I just want water. Someone has to stay sober to find the way back."

Ann screwed off the cap and took a long swig of sherry and handed it to Beth, who did the same, passing it over to Njuroge, who took a small drink and giving it back to Ann. She took a deep drink and passed it on to Beth.

"I bet you brought the hard stuff and are holding back." Ann laughed.

"You must be psychic." He said and took out a bottle of whiskey, and handed it to Ann, who read the label.

"McCormick Old Style Bourbon. How appropriate." She laughed, unscrewing it and took a deep swig. "Where did you get this?"

"I snuck a supply into the country. They never checked my sleeping bag." He said. Ann offered the whiskey to Beth.

"Too strong for me. The sherry will get me high enough."

Beth passed the whiskey to Njuroge who tried to match Ann with a long swig, but nearly choked. "*Chang'aa!*" he gasped and gave it back to Ann. Beth was betting that Njuroge was hoping to get the girls drunk so he could have his choice.

"The sherry and whiskey are getting me hot!" Ann declared and kicked off her sandals, and stood up on the stage, and began dancing again. She twirled her skirt, again showing off her stuff, with Njuroge and Mac clapping as if in a strip bar. Ann pulled her top off, threw it at Njuroge and shook her tits to some imaginary music. Beth was so embarrassed for her friend on one level but sexually aroused on a different level. As Ann danced she unbuttoned her skirt, gave a twirl and it slid off her. The two men applauded as she danced shaking her tits and lifting her leg to show off everything. Beth hoped that Ann would not remember later.

Ann jumped down next to Njuroge, "Old man, come with me. Show me what you got." Ann said brazenly, and pulled Njuroge's hand. He obediently followed her into the hallway. Beth looked at her tall friend, who merely shrugged, and sat down on a bench, crossing his legs. Beth began nibbling a cookie watching him sip water, hoping the occasion would get him aroused enough to make love with her. Right here on this stage would be so cool, she thought.

He stood up and walked over to look where Ann and Njuroge had gone. "They are in the hall. Ann is having a tough time getting his clothes off. If the voyeur in you wants to peek..." He walked over to her and stood between her parted knees, looking into her face for an answer.

"No, I couldn't do that. When she gets over Steve, she will regret everything anyway."

"Even me?"

"Especially you." Beth said, looking up at his eyes peering through his wire spectacles. Then she looked down at the blue striped t-shirt, then his khaki shorts. Damn, right between my thighs, and no reaction.

"Yeah, I know. She's turned from a hopeless romantic into a hopeless slut. And she is not even that sweet."

"You mean compared to Wanjiru?" Beth said looking at his eyes behind the glass of his spectacles.

"No one could be sweeter than Wanjiru." He smiled.

"Wanjiru's going to break your heart, you know." Beth said, leaning forward and gave him a hug, wrapping her arms around his chest, and her legs around his thighs. Damn! She thought, wearing jeans makes this too complicated!

He massaged her back. "Wanjiru? Yes, for sure. She's not going to Illinois, and I'm not allowed to stay here." He said, and Beth listened to his heart pounding in his chest.

"Mac, make love to me here - please." She said and realizing that she was pleading. He pushed her back and smiled at her.

"Sis, wouldn't that would be incest? Besides Wanjiru wore me out." Beth dropped the grip of her legs on his thighs. He shrugeed, and added. "How about this?" he said, sticking his tongue out and gave it a flutter, sending a bolt of electricity to her womanhood. She leaned back on the edge of the stage, with her feet dangling down and unsnapped her jeans. "I can't promise that I am the best." He took off his glasses and handed them to her helping her with the jeans. He looked her directly in her eyes as he lifted her bottom and pulled both her jeans and panties down to her

35

ankles. He pushed her legs up and parted her knees. He bent down, sliding his head between her thighs. That's it! She thought. His tongue played with her clitoris as if he was well acquainted with every nerve ending. It felt fantastic. She sent her fingers through his head of hair as it bobbed back and forth between her thighs. She rested her feet on his back as his hands found their way under her blouse up under her bra to squeeze her nipples. He drove her insane with pleasure. His tongue knew exactly what to do. Beth began convulsing, crushing his head between her thighs. The orgasms came one right after another like major sysmic events. It was too intense. She pushed his head from between her thighs and rolled over on her side shaking. Through a cloud she heard. "Sorry, sis, did I hurt you?"

"Okay. Okay, incest is best." She sighed, and he belted out a laugh. "Was that the college girl when you were eight who taught you that?" Beth asked, remembering his story he told her a while back.

"That's not really sex, is it? Yes, I got fat on chocolate syrup and candy that she gave me for rewards." He began helping her with her jeans. She put herself back together as he watched. "Great body, by the way. Too bad you're my sister. We could make love."

"I'm *not* your sister!" Beth shouted, thinking it was funny while at the same time frustrating. "Hey, I'll always remember this."

"Me too. You taste like beer." He joked. She had heard that before, and glad that he did not say fish.

"I should return the favor."

"Buy me chocolates. Just something I provide to friends to make them happy."

Beth heard footsteps, and saw Njuroge coming back, zipping his jeans and saying something in Swahili that Beth thought meant animal. "Njuroge, *bwana*, she is not a Kikuyu girl is she?"

"Kung Fu girl is animal. She scares me!" Njuroge muttered. "I must to go to church and confess for the priest." He said, and Beth chuckled to herself, not knowing whether he did the deed or not.

"Njuroge, *ulifanya yeye au la?*" Mac asked him.

"*Hapana. Siwezi.*" He replied, with Beth barely understanding that he was not able. "You leave now." He demanded, and Beth knew that Njuroge had determined it was not worth the risk now that sex was not in the picture.

"*Ndiyo*, we leave. Ann is probably asleep." He said, heading for the hallway, with Beth and Njuroge following. Ann was naked, rolling on the floor, trying to get up. She seemed very drunk and disoriented. Beth hoped that Ann would pull herself out of this soon and stop degrading herself this way. Mac scooped her up as if she were a three year old who fell asleep in front of the TV. "Get her clothes and my backpack would you, Beth?"

"She heavy?" Beth asked, but they all headed out of the building, and ended up on the far side of the building. Njuroge soon disappeared, as Mac set her down in the grass. "I'll try to get her clothes back on." After struggling with the drunken woman, Beth was able to get the skirt and top back on, and he carried her to the southwest of the building under the shade of a tree, hoping she would sober up.

He asked aloud, "I don't know why it occurs to me now, but do you think she is taking birth control?"

"Now you are worried about knocking her up?"

"Hey, she did me first. I think I'd like to know if there is going to be a little half-Chinese, little Mac."

"Or maybe a little Annie? I get your point. She told me what happened yesterday. Hey, Mac, you having a half-African kid with Wanjiru?

"Uhhh. That would be a miracle. Wanjiru is half white."

"Oh, that's right. Well screw me and have an all-white." She laughed. "I am taking the pill, but to have your kids I'd stop." Beth said and her friend rolled his eyes. What is it? A sex addict like Mac puts her on a pedestal.

"You are the first American woman who ever expressed any interest in me. Don't stop taking the pill though. I think you will like Kimani." He laughed, and Beth wondered what he meant by her being the first.

"Taking the pill. I was for Steve, Steve. I stopped." Ann began talking, slurred her speech. Her face puckered up and tears streamed down her face. Beth wondered if it was her brand of pill, which was not very effective. "He said he wanted kids and was going back to his fee- Fiancé." Ann said. Beth wondered where this was coming from. Ann sat up, and Mac handed her the water bottle, which she sipped.

"Well, it is a long walk back. We should get ourselves together."

Beth looked around expecting to see the caretaker come and shoo them away, but the only living things around were the various birds, plants and trees. Perhaps the spirit of Lord Egerton was around, but not making himself known. Recalling the story of the Egerton's unrequited love, she looked at Mac helping Ann up. He flashed his baby blue eyes at her and winked, then gave her his pearly white smile.

~~~~

Wanjiru was setting out four plates and dinnerware when she saw her Lodi coming through the gap in the hedge, with Miss Lee on his back. Beth came through the hedge carrying two bags, saying something. These *wazungu* do such silly things. They all burst into the house, and Beth ran into the other room, apparently for the toilet, while Lodi turned and eased the China lady into a chair. She acted drunk. Lodi approached, "Wanjiru, I missed you." He said giving her a hug.

"Is Miss Lee sick?"

"She is drunk. Too much whiskey." He said, but she did not know to what he referred. She looked at Miss Lee who had fallen asleep on the chair, and was exposing herself. Wanjiru walked over and pulled Miss Lee's skirt down over her knees. "Maybe I should just put her to bed." He said, and a pang of jealousy shot through her, thinking he meant he would do her.

"You do her?" Wanjiru asked in Swahili.

"Me? No, she wanted Njuroge at the castle to do her, though."

"Njuroge at Egerton house? He is a holy, holy man."

"Yes, he said he needed to see a priest." Lodi picked up Miss Lee and carried her into the small bedroom, just as Beth was coming out of the toilet.

"He see priest? He is a guilty, holy man now."

Beth asked, "Oh, Mr. Njuroge? I think Ann corrupted him." Wanjiru turned and looked at Beth, who was tall and hardy looking, built for making babies, Wanjiru thought. Miss Beth touched her Lodi too much. She must want him badly.

"She should sleep it off." Lodi said, fitting Ann into her sleeping bag. "Wanjiru, you really need to sleep with me tonight so that Beth and Ann do not fight over me." Wanjiru looked at Beth, who was smiling and nodding her head in agreement. Wanjiru looked down at the drunken woman.

"They will fight to sleep with you?" Wanjiru was amazed. Wanjiru pulled the sleeping bag to cover her. "Just do them both and sleep alone." Everyone laughed.

"Sounds like a good plan." Beth said.

"Wanjiru is my love now," Lodi said, "I will have to build a castle to convince her to share her life with mine." Wanjiru felt such conflicting emotions, knowing that it would never happen, but not wanting to hurt him.

~~~~

It was a sunny Saturday morning and Kimani and Muthoni were headed to Lodi's house to see if Wambui would let them use her mzungu's bedroom again. They had walked up the cinder drive excitedly, and rounded the hedge through the backyard. But as they passed the bathroom window, Kimani thought he heard the water in the bathtub running. Hoping it was just Wambui doing the laundry, they walked in through the kitchen door.

"Wambui?" Muthoni asked. She was wearing only a blouse and *kitambaa*. When he picked her up, she was washing herself. He was in such a rush that she quickly put on the blouse and wrapped a cloth around herself. Kimani pulled his t-shirt out of his jeans, as if to speed up the process.

"*Natya*, Muthoni. Kimani, *nike*? You are early. Wait until he goes to Nakuru." Wambui said, and Kimani was disappointed. He looked at his watch and realized they were early, and he needed to reduce his expectations.

"Is Miss Lee still here?" Muthoni asked, and Kimani thought of Wanjiru's stories about her.

"No, she left early this morning for Kisumu."

Muthoni looked at him and said in Kikuyu, "We could go back to my mama's place."

Kimani replied, "No, I don't like your sisters watching. We can wait a while. We are early."

"Wambui!" came a call from the dining room, and Lodi entered wearing nothing but a towel around his waste. "Oh, Muthoni, *jambo*. Kimani." He said shaking hands with them both.

"Good to see you. He added in Swahili, "Wambui, if it be Wanjiru comes, I want her, and," he patted Muthoni's back, "where is my soap?" With that, Wambui disappeared, leaving the three at the back door. "Kimani, how is your mother? I hope she is well." He asked reminding him how well he got along with his mother when they visited Embu together. "Muthoni, it is good to see you. You look thinner than when you worked for me." He stood between the two and put his arms around each of them in a very friendly way. Kimani enjoyed the way his white boy was stroking his back.

"And a year older. More experience now." Muthoni said.

"Really? So it should feel very sweet?" he asked, and Kimani laughed, and the white boy patted Kimani's *matako* as if in approval. Muthoni did not understand, so Kimani repeated it in Kikuyu, and Muthoni laughed. Kimani returned the favor and stroked his white boy's bare skin on his back, then patted his *matako*.

"Yes, that is right. You can take your time too. No hurry." She said in English and chuckled as did he. Kimani thought that referred to Lodi's first hurried attempt. "Maybe try again sometime, if Wambui lets me." She said and moved in close and petted the hair on the white boy's belly. Kimani noticed Lodi getting aroused under the towel. He felt a bit of jealousy that Muthoni was making suggestions to the white boy, who pulled them both more closely to his side. Maybe his white boy will do us together? Kimani asked himself while stroking the white boy's back. There was a tap at the back door and it opened.

"Jambo, Lodi!" Wanjiru's head popped in, and Lodi walked over and pulled her in, giving her a hug and kiss. "I cannot stay. Muthoni, mama wants us to help her now." Just as Wanjiru came in she was followed in by Wambui's friend Virginia.

"Virginia, *karibu*!" Lodi said, shaking her hand. "Wanjiru, you cannot stay? You break my heart!"

"No, Keogh went to Nairobi and mama says it is a good day for us to care for the garden. We will work all day. I will miss you. Muthoni, come!" Lodi gave her another kiss as the two sisters left. Kimani felt frustrated. He had his morning of fun on the lumpy bed all set and now just as quickly it was snatched away.

Wambui returned and said, handing him a wrapped bar of soap. "Solly. *Natya*, Virginia, you want tea?"

40

Virginia nodded and Kimani was surprised when Virginia asked Wambui in Kikuyu. "Did Lodi do you this morning? Anything left?"

"He not do me. Miss Lee here last night." Wambui said as she went to pour tea. Virginia moved closer to Lodi and petted the hair on his belly.

"Lodi say he make sperm like Tusker make beer." Wambui chuckled. Kimani looked one by one at the two women, wondering if he could seduce either one. He looked at the older woman, who was maybe a few years older than he was, thinking maybe she would let him do her. He looked at the young Virginia who sat down on a kitchen chair sipping her tea, knowing she was interested in Lodi and would not be interested in him. Kimani thought that he would explode if he did not get sex.

"Wambui, you think Muthoni will want me later?" He asked in Kikuyu and realized he sounded pathetic.

"Maybe, but she will be tired from working with mama." Wambui said, but asked in Swahili for Lodi to hear. "You want me to say honestly?"

"Yes."

"Lodi is a boy who satisfies women like a man, but you are a man who satisfies women like a boy." She said, and a humiliating pain shot through his gut.

"Why is that you think?" He hoped for ideas to make women want him.

"Lodi reads books about satisfying people." Wambui said.

"You two crazy for Lodi, I think." Virginia smiled.

"He is good to me and Ruthy." Wambui spoke in Kikuyu, but added in Swahili. "Lodi is my *bwana*."

Lodi laughed and said, "Wambui thinks I married her."

Virginia put her cup on the ironing table and asked, "Kimani, you come around a lot. You take him to your father's. Travel with Lodi. Maybe you crazy in love with him also." She suggested, and Kimani laughed at the idea.

"Maybe like a brother."

"No, I see how you look at him. Not like brother."

"Really? You see that?" Kimani was getting uncomfortable with this line and tried to deflect. "Is Lodi going to do you?"

"No." Virginia said. "I have my month. You his friend?"

"You don't think I am a friend?" Kimani asked.

"Kimani, you want to be my friend?" Lodi asked him, but Kimani was not sure how he meant that.

"I do. Very much. I want to be your flend – frrriend." Kimani said, having a hard time with r's, realizing he was getting nervous.

"Even though everyone thinks I am not normal? Strange? Weird? I'm told everyone thinks I do everyone who comes here." Lodi chuckled.

"Yes, that is true. You are interesting, and my mother liked you, so I knew you were good." Kimani wanted to take that back, since it sounded like having introduced a girlfriend to his mother. "I'm curious. Did you do Miss Ann, too, this morning?" he asked trying to change the subject.

"Ann? Well, I woke up with her doing me. But she was finished before I finished." He said, and Kimani noticed a bit of swelling under the towel.

"You had Wambui this morning, too, I guess."

"No, she is an afternoon sort." He smiled, and Kimani could see he was aroused under the towel, thinking about the women.

"What is Wanjiru like? I guess you did her, too?"

"*Hapana*, no," he said in English, "but I would be happy doing her all day. Something about her makes her like the perfect woman for me. I love her so much! Yes, I could make love with her day in and day out." Kimani saw that he was quite happy under the towel.

"Well, I need to take a bath and head to Nakuru. Kimani come talk." He said, as if he expected Kimani to follow him. "You want to go to Nakuru with me and meet my sister?"

"You have a sister in Nakuru?" He asked as the white boy dropped the towel and stepped into the bath.

"Not really. Beth is a good friend who is in love with me, but she reminds me too much of a sister. You might like her for a girlfriend." The white boy soaped himself all over, then slid down into the water to rinse himself. He stood up as if reaching for a towel on the rack, but it had fallen to the floor. Kimani studied the naked white boy, being the first naked one he had seen.

"I would like to go with you." He said watching him dry off.

42

Later, as the two walked towards the bus stop, having just crossed the highway, Kimani had to know. "You ever do this girl Beth?"

"No, no sexual intercourse." Lodi laughed. This made Kimani think there was something else.

"But you did something else, and you did not like it?"

"No, I liked it. I'm a cunning linguist." He laughed.

"What?"

"I licked her, uh, you know."

"Oh, you do that? I never did."

"Some women like it, many don't. Beth does. She tastes like beer, so enjoy!"

"I was hoping for Muthoni this morning."

"For you, the day is not done. It is not eleven o'clock yet. Beth has a young housekeeper named Hanna who is very good to do. Many times, I show up at Beth's and Beth is out shopping. Hanna loves it on the dining table." The white boy bragged. "She says she wants a baby."

"She wants a *nusu nusu* baby?"

"*Nusu nusu*? Any baby, big and strong is what she wants. But Beth says she lets the students do her if they show up when Beth is out. The last time, I think she had the swelling for a baby. Maybe." He said as he pointed at a bus that some kid was shouting Nakuru.

"You like African girls a lot."

"Yes, I want to get them all pregnant then return to America, and have dozens of *my* kids running around Kenya. My IQ is 162, so I should share my genes for human improvement."

"You are joking!" Kimani was astonished.

He laughed, "Yes, joking. If people come around wanting it, should I turn them away? Did you get what you were after?"

Kimani felt a bit guilty, looking at his white boy. "I was okay."

"Be honest." His white boy laughed.

"Honestly, when I missed Muthoni, I thought Wambui or Virginia. I even thought you would relieve me."

"Of course, if you love me. Whatsoever ye shall ask in prayer, believing, ye shall receive."

Kimani thought that was a weird idea, but indeed felt love for his white boy.

They got on the stuffy bus and found seats across the aisle from each other at the back of the bus. A young mother with a baby was on his left. Lodi set his backpack between his legs. Kimani noticed he kept looking at the young mother, and he turned to see a woman nursing a baby. The brown baby would stop and look at the white boy with the wire glasses, and long brown and yellow hair. Kimani looked and saw Lodi staring back. Lodi said to the young mother in Swahili, "Your baby is beautiful. Good health. Sweet eyes." Lodi took a five shilling note and gave it to the mother. "This money is from God. Buy the baby something it needs." The mother smiled and nodded. "Kimani, when we get to Beth's place, Beth will want you to do her right away. Wait a week. Be a gentleman."

"Oh, okay, sure." Kimani said, as the bus pulled out of the field and onto the highway. The bus speeded up and they would soon be shopping in Nakuru and meeting new people.

Chapter 2, Improbable Love

It was a beautiful morning, with the dew thick in the grass as Wanjiru returned to her mother's hut from the latrine. Just as she was about to enter, her mother appeared beside her. She thought her mother was at work, but the thin woman looked her in the face, "You sleep good?"

"Yes, mama. Good."

"You still have a stomach?" she asked, referring to the nausea and vomiting the last couple of mornings.

"Yes, a bit." Wanjiru answered. Her mother took a letter out of her woven bag and handed it to her. She must have used pencil, paper and envelope from the Keogh's place.

"This is to my brother in Mombasa. He has a good job at a hotel there. I ask him to take you in and find you a job until you have your baby."

"Mama! Baby?"

"We all know the *mzungu* did you everyday, what all day long? You have the stomach in morning. You must have a pregnancy."

"If I do, I can stay here, yes?"

Her mother's eyes narrowed, "No, the *mzungu* will take the baby away like the Luhya men do."

"Mama, he is not Luhya. He wants me to be his girlfriend and he wants to marry me." Wanjiru said.

"No, all men lie. When he has to leave, he will take your baby to America, and you never see baby."

Wanjiru knew there was no arguing with her mother once she was determined. For such a small, thin woman, she carried a lot of determination. "Yes, mama, I will go to the post office."

"Here is money for a stamp." She said giving her a few coins, then turned to head back to work. Wanjiru stood looking at the coins with Kenyatta on them, then the envelope with her mother's childlike writing, and the postal box in Mombasa. She went inside the hut and saw Muthoni pouring tea into tin cups.

"Here, drink tea, *bibi*." Her sister suggesting that she was a married woman already. She just giggled and took the tea. "So, mama is going to send you to Mombasa to have the baby so the *mzungu* won't steal it?" Muthoni asked, and Wanjiru nodded and sipped the tea. "I will miss you very much. I want to help with the baby."

"Thank you. I will miss you." They both sat in silence sipping their warm tea that their mother had made for them. Half milk and the other half sugar, she thought, boiled for thirty minutes until it is thick and brown. "I will miss mama. She always knows what to do."

"You are not stupid. You will do well in Mombasa. There are lots of jobs there and money."

"Well, I am going to the post office. You want to go with me?"

"No, I have a date. Is it open on Saturday?"

"A date? This early? This is Saturday?"

"A cook at the school wants a quick one. Yes, it is Saturday." And repeated in Swahili, "*Jumamosi!*"

"Maybe I could see Lodi before he goes to Nakuru."

"Too late. I heard his motorcycle."

"He takes the bus to Nakuru, since his motorcycle is not strong enough to come back up the hill." She laughed, thinking about the huge boy on the little *pikipiki* trying to get up the hill to Njoro. "I should go talk with Wambui."

"No, leave her. She thinks you want her job, and take her *bwana* from her."

"No!"

"Lodi told her he wants you to be his girlfriend." Muthoni said. Wanjiru remembered her Lodi insisting, but she turned him down. Mama refused.

"I will not see Wambui until she calms down." Wanjiru suggested. "So, is the cook free or paying?" She asked as she stood up and pulled back the curtain. She saw that her other sister, Warimu, was still asleep under her blanket.

"Yes three shillings."

"I'll be back." Wanjiru stood outside the hut holding the letter. She wondered if she should take a shortcut through the school compound or around to avoid the students. If it is Saturday, then they all will be cleaning their dormitories. She headed up through the school. On her left the long white dormitories and her right were the tall hedges hiding the teacher houses. She walked the narrow road without a single insult from the students, although they stared at her. Some actually nodded respectfully. She wondered if that was because they knew their teacher... No! Not everyone knows everyone's secrets here." She reached the crossroads and was about to take a left towards the post office when she saw him on his motorcycle coming towards her. The wind was blowing his hair flat. She wanted to run into the maize field and hide. If Wambui saw her with him, she might kill.

"Wanjiru!" he came roaring to a stop right next to her, kicking up gravel and dust. "Where are you going?"

"Post office. I need to buy a stamp and mail a letter to my uncle."

"I was just there. Here, I have extra stamps." He said taking off his backpack and pulling out several, and tore off one for her. She took the stamp, licked it and pressed it on the letter. "Get on, I will ride you over to post it." He said. She had always wanted to ride a *piki*, but her *kitambaa* skirt would be a problem. "Ride side saddle." He said in English, but she had no clue. "Oh, put both legs on one side. Pull your skirt up so it does not get caught in the wheels." She understood that, and got on, tucking her *kitambaa* skirt between her legs, and resting her feet on a metal peg. He put his backpack on the front of the bike. She wrapped her arms around him and he pulled away slowly. The engine whined, then he shifted gears and it whined some more, but quickly she was in front of the post office dropping the envelope into the mail slot. She turned and saw him sitting on the *piki*, with the sun glancing off the long yellow streaks in his hair. He smiled at her. "I was going to go explore Egerton Castle area, then maybe up to Menengai."

"Not Nakuru today?"

"No, Beth is going to Nairobi, so no friend there."

"Beth likes you. Why the sleeping bag?" She wondered, looking at the sleeping bag tied to the front of the *piki*.

"I just want to go, and if I am far from home, maybe find a hotel."

"Oh, now I will worry about you." Wanjiru said, thinking she should not say that, since she was not allowed to be his girlfriend.

"Well, if you will worry, I will stay close to home. You ever been to Egerton Castle?"

"No. You took Miss Lee there? Miss Beth, too, right?"

"Yes, and Miss Lee made a fool of herself, taking off her clothes and seducing the caretaker."

"Yes, yes. She's not right in the head. Can we go now on your *piki* to Egerton house?" She said, hoping for another *piki* ride.

"I would love it. You will have to ride like I do, so pull your skirt up. I will go slowly." He kick started the piki and it began whining again. She did as instructed, straddling the *piki*, and wrapping her arms around him, pressing the side of her head into his back. Having him between her thighs once again made life a joy. The piki headed up towards some houses took a left and whined past a row of houses, took a right onto a dirt road. Soon they were beyond the town and whining past fields of maize and beans, and cow pastures. People were weeding their gardens, and women carrying loads of firewood on their backs. The *piki* was whining past small farmhouses and a few trees. They came to a tree-lined intersection and he stopped as if he was trying to decide which way to go. He bolted off once again. She peeked over his shoulder and saw outline of Menengai Crater on the horizon, and vast stretches of farmland in all directions. The piki whined to a stop again, as if he was not sure, then took a right and a quick left and headed off again. The day was beautiful, and she felt wonderful holding her Lodi so tightly to her breasts, with the *piki* bumping and vibrating him between her thighs. She saw the large stone structure off to her right, before the piki made two right turns and came up to the building, stopping at the large staircase. The engine shut off and she stood up to look. She had seen larger structures in Mombasa and Nairobi, but out here miles from cities, with rolling land and nothing but farms, it seemed out of place to her, but she recalled Lodi's story of Egerton building this to impress a girlfriend.

"Maybe we can get Njuroge to give you and me a tour." Lodi said as he set the *piki* on its stand, looking around. "Odd place isn't it?"

"Jambo, Lodi!" came a voice from behind, and she turned and saw the old man standing. "Oh, I know you. You are one of Esther's daughters."

"Wanjiru."

"Oh, yes, the *nusu nusu*." He said matter of factly in Swahili with Wanjiru feeling a bit insulted. "Lodi, what happen your China lady?"

Lodi laughed and said in Swahili, "You gave her a pregnancy, and she went back to America."

"Oh, too bad. I want to try again. *Lakini*, not my pregnancy. She scare me, I could not do her." He laughed, and Wanjiru was a bit embarrassed for Miss Lee, that a man could not do her because she made him afraid. "Lodi, is this your girlfriend? She pretty for *nusu nusu*."

Lodi said, "To me no woman in the whole world exceeds her beauty." He smiled and stroked her back, "*Dunia yote!*"

"If you have bottle sherry, I let you use the big house."

"For sherry?" Lodi said and looked at her, "He said we could use the castle for a while. You like?" He stroked her back again. She was tingling in excitement, and nodding a yes. Lodi grabbed the sleeping bag and backpack and climbed the stairs with Njuroge following. "*Kuja!*" He shouted and she climbed the concrete steps to the front door. Njuroge unlocked the front door, and Lodi handed him a full bottle of sherry. She knew they would get drunk on each other today, and would not need alcohol to get happy. She looked up over the door to the date 19 and 38. Trying to remember but she thought her father was born long before that.

"I lock you in. It opens from inside, close door when done." Njuroge smiled and raised the bottle to Lodi and disappeared. Wanjiru thought, for a holy holy, he loves his wine. She thought how they looked down at her at Njuroge's church for being *nusu nusu*, making her feel like she did not belong there. She walked into the house, and saw the huge stairway up and the large paneled walls.

"My Lady Egerton, welcome home." He said and pulled her up the stairs and began exploring the empty rooms. Each one seemed large enough to hold her mother's grass hut.

"I don't know which room is Lord Egerton's bedroom, but this is large enough to work. Nice view of the farms. Is that Menengai over there?" He asked but she was not sure. She was hoping he would do her right away, since she needed him so badly, but he seemed all excited about the big house. He searched through his backpack and pulled out his camera. "Stand by the window." He said, doing something with the camera, he set it on a side shelf, clicked it. The camera made a mechanical sound as he ran over and stood next to her, holding her close and the camera clicked. "I think it got us." He said, turning her around and giving her a kiss, slipping his tongue in to play with hers. She could feel him removing her clothes as they kissed, and she returned the favor, removing his. They could not wait to be coupled. He picked her up and pressed her against the cold wall, and slid deep inside her. She felt herself merging together with him, becoming one person with pleasure so intense she nearly passed out. His strong arms held her up with her head pressed against his chest, her hands were holding tightly to his shoulders as he thrust again and again. Then it hit as a thunderbolt of intense pleasure radiating to every point in her body, every muscle in her body contracted and she let out a scream. He stopped and merely held her tightly as she convulsed in his arms. As sanity returned, she wondered if such could expel the baby that her mother was sure in her womb, or would it merely make it stronger? He slowly let her down, and backed off a bit. He was still very aroused, but went back to the camera and repeated the settings, running back with his stiff thing bouncing up and down. He stood behind her and put his hands on her belly just as the camera clicked automatically. She thought, why did he put his hands on her belly? Did he know? He went over to the huge sleeping bag and unrolled it onto the hard floor, and stretched out on it. "*Kuja!*" he said and she was glad to see he was still aroused and lying on his back, she knew what he wanted was what she wanted. She got on top of him and taking hold and directed him inside her. She balanced her hands on his chest, and her legs folded back with her knees on the floor and her feet on his thighs. He had the look of a happy drunk as he played with her breasts. "That is wonderful. Thank you, thank you. Your breasts are larger; you're putting on some weight." He said as she went up and down on him in slight motions that he seemed to love, and she definitely loved. One hand went down and he stroked her pubic hair, then her belly. She felt the tingling coming back, starting where he was inside, and it began to flow out to her whole body. She began convulsing just as his muscles went tight all over, he moaned loudly, and she felt the hot fluid flowing inside her. She went weak and fell on top of him with her head on his shoulder. He pulled the cover over her chilly back just before she fell asleep.

"I have some cookies and orange juice." Came a voice through her dreams. Her eyes popped open to see blue eyes and a yellow strand of hair against his pink, sunburned face. She felt so cozy and safe in the sleeping bag pressed against his body, but she was feeling a bit hungry. "I have some whiskey, but I hear that is not good for babies." He said. Babies? Babies? What does he mean? "I may be wrong, either you are pregnant or you are eating better."

She had to think fast. What is her excuse for her the weight? "I work for you. Make good money. Buy good food. Eat your food." She said, and realizing she was sounding defensive.

"Okay, I guess. Remember. You need anything. Come to me. Let me know. Okay?"

"I need cookies and juice." She said and he laughed. "Then I need you again. Please, do me a favor. Do not tell Wambui."

"Yes, my love, my Lady Egerton." He said rolling over to get the food out of his backpack. He came back with a box of vanilla cookies and gave it to her. As she pulled out cookies, he said, "I would bet we are the only one who ever made love in this room. Maybe the whole castle."

"Not Njuroge?" She asked munching on the delicious cookies.

"I think there is a curse. Because Lord Egerton forbade women in this house, only people truly in love can make love in Egerton Castle." As she munched on the cookie, he stroked her breast and belly, feeling him becoming aroused against her. She put the cookie box down and pulled him over on top.

~~~~

The sun was coming up through the grandstand at the running track. Wambui circled around and through the playground so that she did not have to deal with the rude students at the dormitories. School always started slowly with students trickling in over several weeks. She cut through the gap in the arborvitae hedge, and headed through the knee-high grass to the kitchen door.

She could already smell the coffee as she inserted a key in the back door. It creaked open and she heard the radio in the living room, probably Voice of America. Wambui's *mzungu* will be going back to America in December for a one-month visit, and everyone assumes he would not return, so she dreaded his leaving. She peered around the kitchen door to see if her Lodi was in there, but he was not. She padded her way down the hall and saw him shaving in the bathroom. She went back to the kitchen, poured some milk in a metal pan, and turned on the electric stove. She set out two cups and a bag of light brown sugar. The coffee was looking very dark, so she set the glass perculator onto a pot holder. The milk began to bubble, and she poured some in a cup. She added some water and tealeaves to the remainder and put it back on the burner. She poured coffee into the large cup - Lodi called a mug, and added a bunch of sugar.

"*Jambo, habari gani?*" Came the voice behind her. Lodi came in and took his coffee. "I just want bread and marmalade this morning and a vitamin." He said in Swahili. He turned around and left. She took out a loaf of bread, and sliced off three pieces, put margarine on one slice and orange marmalade on two other slices. She put the two on a plate, took a vitamin out of a bottle, and went into the living room. Lodi was reading a book and making notes with his coffee mug balanced on the arm of the chair. "*Asante,*" he thanked her and went back to his reading, and nibbled on the bread. She headed back to the kitchen, but turned to watch him from around the corner. He put the vitamin in his mouth and sipped the coffee. Lodi was very skinny when she first started working for him, but got fatter over the years. Lodi will be going to America for a visit at Christmas and he said that he would get even fatter with his mother's cooking. Wambui stared at the young man. She really had doubted that Lodi would want to come back to Kenya after a month in America.

He suddenly looked up and caught her eye. "What is it?" he asked.

"When are you going to Nakuru?"

He laughed, "Soon. Why?"

"I want that thing," she said and covered her mouth.

"I will get back afternoon… you be around?"

"*Sijui*, maybe this evening," she said and returned to the kitchen where her tea was simmering. She poured it through a strainer into a tin cup, and took a bite of bread. She sipped for a while and finished her bread. Suddenly Lodi came in with the cup and plate.

"I am going now. *Kwa heri.*" He said, then in English, "I will eat in Nakuru at my friend Beth's house." She stared at him standing there. He patted her on the shoulder and turned to leave. "Is there anything special I should buy?" He asked, but she shook her head no and he disappeared and the last she heard him locking the front door. She turned to begin cleaning up, when she heard tapping at the door. She turned and unlocked the door and Wanjiru came in.

"Do you have some tea?" she asked.

"Come in." Wambui said and looked her over. "Your mother said you are getting fat." Wambui has been telling Lodi that Wanjiru did not like him, when the opposite was true. Wambui grew tired of Wanjiru constantly asking about Lodi, what he was doing. She kept asking to have him do her again, but Wambui worried that Lodi would want Wanjiru and Wambui would lose her job. "But I think you are pregnant. Is it Lodi's?"

"What? No, Yes, it could be. No, it is." She said, and Wambui handed her a cup of hot tea. Wambui thought, if Lodi finds out he would want to marry her or something crazy.

"If Lodi knows he maybe want to take the baby back to America with him." Wambui said.

"What? No, he would not do that... would he?" She paused and looked down. "Mama agrees with you, though."

"Lodi is crazy. He has a fierce temper. He thinks he knows what is right and what is best for people and becomes very angry when people refuse." Wambui knew she was lying, hoping to change Wanjiru's opinion of her Lodi.

"He is so sweet and gentle with me." Wanjiru said.

"Did I tell you about the *bangi* crooks?" Wambui asked, and Wanjiru shook her head no. "You know the *bangi* crooks come around the school compound after dark and sell *bangi* to the students?" She asked and Wanjiri nodded a yes as if everyone knew that. "When Lodi escorts me home at night, the *bangi* crooks are sometimes out there. One time we were crossing the pasture behind the school and the *bangi* crooks came in their little truck. They drove very near us like they wanted to run us down. Lodi got angry and hit the truck with his ax handle weapon he has."

"That is crazy. Does he want to die?"

"He is crazy. He knew they were the *bangi* crooks and I think he wanted to start a fight. The truck stopped and three Kyuks jumped out. They were short little men. Lodi could step on them like bugs, but they screamed at Lodi, and Lodi screamed back, saying he knew they were selling *bangi* to the students and it was going to stop now or something like that. He said it in English and the three Kyuks were using English. The screaming went on... did you not hear all that screaming? Maybe Esther told you."

"When we go to sleep, the hut could burn down around us and we would not wake." She laughed. "What happened?"

"Lodi had a flashlight and saw one Kyuk pick up a rock and came at Lodi. Lodi jabbed the Kyuk in the throat with the ax handle. Now Lodi had put nails in one end, so if he hit a dog it would leave teeth marks. The Kyuk dropped the rock, grabbed his throat, and could not breathe. Lodi hit the other two Kyuks in their knees and they fell to the ground. The first one fell out on the ground, then Lodi hit the other two on the back of their heads and they fell out."

"Oh dear Jesus!"

"He ripped off some cloth off one Kyuk's shirt and took it to the back of the truck, and started a fire. He ran and got me and told me to run to my home with him. When we reached my house, we heard an explosion and I saw that it was the *bangi* crook's truck. It was burning very brightly and I could see the three Kyuks crawling away from the flames. After a while the smoke came across the pasture and I could smell the *bangi* burning. The police had come but they let the truck burn. A group of school workers brought the *bangi* crooks out for the police. Lodi was there with me and he just laughed. He said the police will maybe pay him a visit. But it has been a year and the police never asked him anything."

"Lodi is crazy, but not a fool, since it all worked out well."

"Yes, with God's help." Wambui laughed covering her mouth. "There are other times too."

"Other what?" Wanjiru wondered.

"A few months after he first started he was very angry because the older boys treated the new students so bad."

"Do they beat the new students? What do they do?"

Suddenly, the story was interupted by a tapping at the door, and the door opened, and first Muthoni came in followed by Kimani. They stood in the side room as if waiting for permission.

Kimani piped up, "You telling about the older student doing the younger one?" Wambui looked at the short, skinny Embu Kikuyu. She nodded, having told him the story before.

Wambui continued. "Yes. Lodi will want to take his child to America. He does not want his child treated like this... like an African."

"It will be *kidogo* African..."

"*Nusu nusu.* As much American as African."

"*Hapana. Nusu* American and *nusu* English African. I will go to my uncle in Mombasa until Lodi goes back to America. My uncle wants me to work for an Arab that he works with."

Both Kimani and Muthoni looked at Wanjiru. Kimani, who already knew from Muthoni the news about Wanjiru's pregnancy, said, "We all have to deny your child is Lodi's or he will want the child. He is foolish enough to claim the child."

Suddenly Wambui realized why Kimani and Muthoni were here on a Saturday morning. "You are here early... did you see Lodi leaving for Nakuru?" As if it were their own house, Kimani and Muthoni disappeared to the other end of the house and the unused bedroom with the horsehair mattress. Wambui looked at Wanjiru. "Who is doing you now that you are pregnant?"

"No one. Lodi only man for many many months." She sipped her tea, "I dream of Lodi only."

"Oh, yes, I remember that when Mwangi made Ruthy, I think of Mwangi all the time." She said, and for a few minutes they sipped their tea in silence. "You know I let them use the room if they leave the door open and let me watch." Wambui giggled. "Let's go watch."

"No, I see too much at my mother's place." They both burst into laughing. Wanjiru hopped up on the kitchen counter to finish her tea. After a few minutes of chatting, they heard the front door unlocking and opening.

~~~~~

Wanjiru was suddenly very uneasy as Wambui turned to head into the living room but met Lodi who came into the kitchen. "*Jambo*, the police have a road block up and no buses are headed to Nakuru." He said and looked straight at Wanjiru, "Oh, *habari gani*, Wanjiru," he said, then switching to English, "You are looking even more beautiful than ever. Where have you been? I missed you." She felt a tingle in her groin up to her nipples. He walked up to her, "What a pretty dress you have... you look like you have gained some more weight." He got very close to her and she tried to press her knees together and cover her legs with her dress.

Wambui was saying something to them, which she did not hear. Lodi took off his glasses, set them on a shelf, and moved in close to her resting his hands on her thighs. She suddenly recalled

55

Muthoni and Kimani in the other room. If Lodi found out, Wambui would surely lose her job. She said to Wambui in Kikuyu that she would distract him, while Wambui got the couple out the front door. She reached forward and stroked the front of his trousers.

Everyday for the two weeks that Wanjiru worked for Lodi, they copulated in nearly every room of the house at one time or another. This counter was used several times before, so she knew what she wanted to do. She reached out and undid his belt, top snap on the trousers and the zipper, letting his trousers drop to the floor, while he was unbuttoning her dress down to her waist. His hands found her bra and the front button, releasing her breasts. "Perfect... they seem to have grown." He said as he stroked them. She tugged at his briefs trying to free his manhood, but could not, so he did it himself, and out popped his white shaft with the pink tip. His hands flew under her dress and expertly slid her *chupi* off, taking her sandals to the floor at the same time. He slid his hands under the dress, picked her up by the buttocks, and slid himself inside her, making both gasp in pleasure.

~~~~~

Wambui quickly ran into the bedroom to find the two asleep naked on the mattress. "Wake up, Lodi returned, wake up." She said urgently in a muffled voice. They started waking, not sure what was happening, so Wambui grabbed their clothes as a bundle and gave them all to Kimani. He got up holding all the clothes. Muthoni was still bewildered, but rolled out of the bed, and the two naked figures quickly and quietly hurried down the hall and through the living room to the front door. They hurried out the unlocked door to the far corner of the yard where the grass was several feet high. Wambui quietly closed the door and went back to the vacant bedroom. There were several wet spots on the mattress, so she turned the mattress over and left the room as it was earlier in the day. She went into Lodi's bedroom and peered through the curtains to see Kimani and Muthoni in the tall grass at the corner of the hedges. The sun was reflecting off his sweaty back. "Animals!" she said, but then laughed.

She returned to the kitchen only to see Lodi doing Wanjiru on the counter. His white buttocks were going back and forth with her light brown legs wrapped around him. Wanjiru's eyes popped open to see Wambui watching. Wambui could see Wanjiru was enjoying herself, so Wambui turned and decided to do the laundry,

56

which she did by hand in the bathtub. Wambui was seething with jealousy.

Wambui had finished washing the clothes and was carrying the basket of clothes through the kitchen out to the line. She saw that they were still going at it, but that his shirt was now on the floor with her dress and bra.

After she hung the clothes, rather than go back in, she decided to weed the garden, although the vegetables were not doing well for want of rain. She walked around to the front of the house and to the corner of the hedges. The two were gone but the grass was beaten down. She returned to the garden. After clearing out all the weeds, she headed to the back door only to meet Wanjiru coming out buttoning her dress. "What is it?" Wambui asked.

"I told Lodi that I have to go to my uncle in Mombasa. Lodi was very sad and began to cry real tears. He said that he would miss me very much." He gave me this money, and Wambui saw the hundred shilling note, and told me to come see him if I return. I will never see him again, I think."

Annoyed with the sex and money, Wambui said sarcastically, "He cries as much as he laughs... everything is either funny or sad." She then asked seriously, "Did you take all his sperms?" She was thinking more of her own wants than Lodi's sentimentalities.

"Wambui! I am telling you he is sad that I have to go away." Wambui was actually annoyed that Lodi was doing Wanjiru and not herself, and showed it on her face. "He did not fill me, he was very hard but dry." Wanjiru said and Wambui giggled in relief. "*Kwa heri*... oh, Lodi said he is changing his clothes."

"See you later," she said in Kikuyu, and hurried back into the house, locking the doors as she went. Lodi was about to put on khaki shorts. "It has been a long time since you did Wanjiru. Is she still sweet?" She said and he turned looking at her holding the shorts.

Lodi looked up and smiled, as if he knew where she was headed. "Sweet? Yes, very, very sweet." He said, which made her want him even more.

"She is more beautiful than me, though?" she said fishing for more compliments. "My breasts are old and limp."

"Old and limp?" he repeated the Swahili, apparently not knowing what it meant. "Show me and I will tell you." He laughed as if he was joking. She took off her blouse and bra as a matter of feminine ego. She could see the bulging in his briefs. These white boys always get aroused seeing milk bottles. Her other *mzungu* boy acted the same way.

"I should feel to see if they are old and soft." He said not using the word for limp. They should be soft, but she leaned forward and let him massage them... it did arouse her and him quite obviously.

"Wanjiru has very firm, young buttocks, too. Mine are old and limp, too." She said, but he was still massaging her breasts.

"For twenty-nine, your breasts are perfect. Show me your buttocks." He said in Swahili, *matako* was one of his favorite words. She took off the cloth that served as a skirt and hung it on a rack, removed her *chupi* or "panties" as Lodi called them. She offered her buttocks for massage, and he leaned forward to check the firmness. "Very good," he announced.

"My *kuma* is loose and big, and cannot satisfy you like Wanjiru's young and tight thing. I had two babies, so it is worn out." She said, knowing that she was not at all old, and was still flexible.

"I forget how you do." He smiled. With that, she lay back on his bed and spread her legs with him following into position, and feeling his shaft slide deep into her. She looked into his blue eyes and he smiled in delight whispering, "*Kuma mzuri kabisa.*" He began thrusting and she knew this could go on for hours and she would be exhausted after ten minutes. After a while, she was satisfied and rubbed the small of his back, which was their signal to finish it. He began thrusting more vigorously, making her whole body grip in intense pleasure, then suddenly she felt his hot fluids flowing into her. He relaxed on top of her with her ear to his chest, listening to his heart pounding, gradually slowing down as his manhood shrank and finally fell out of her. He rolled off, and she felt secure with her Lodi satisfied and resting next to her.

~~~~

Wanjiru was supposed to help her mother at Keogh in the garden, but as she saw the entrance to her Lodi's place, she paused. On Sunday afternoons, the students scatter, Wambui is at her home. She is still savoring yesterday morning in Lodi's kitchen. He was so sweet and gentle, she thought, and perhaps he is home. She could not resist and headed up the driveway and around to the front veranda. She heard music playing as she came around the corner. Someone was playing a guitar and Lodi playing the little *gitaa* he called a mandu- something. She stopped and listened to the music, and Lodi singing something about a girl left behind. She stopped before the veranda to listen awhile, but worked up the courage to go to the front door. She could see the back of the guitar player was Keogh, and Lodi saw her and jerked his head as he sang. She took that to mean come in. She listened while they finished the song. Lodi patted the chair next to him for her to sit. Lodi kissed her on the cheek and rubbed her back, sending ripples of pleasure through her.

Keogh said, "Hey, Njiru, your mama said you would be helping her in my garden. Thank you." She looked at the Englishman, who was almost a twin of her Lodi except all his hair was all yellow and he was not as tall. She looked closer into his eyes and noticed they were green. He was the only person she knew with green eyes.

"Yes, I was on my way there. I heard the beautiful music and had to stop by and give my greetings, and hear more music."

"If I may suggest, Mac, sing your version of the House of the Rising Sun." Keogh began fingering a tune that made Wanjiru admire the rich tones of the large *gitaa*. Her Lodi strummed the little *gitaa* and began singing.

"There is a house in Njoro Town. They call Ma Ko Ma Ki. And it's been the ruin of many a poor boy. God one of them is me! My mother was a teacher. She taught me how to grow. My daddy was an en jin ear. Up in Chi ca go. Oh mother, tell your children. Not to live your life like me. Spend your lives in sin and misery. In the House of Ma Ko Ma Ki. There is a house in Njoro Town. They call Ma Ko Ma Ki. And it's been the ruin of many a poor boy. God one of them is me!"

Wanjiru laughed. "Lodi, I hope you are joking!"

"Yes, yes. I made that up after Wambui got pregnant. Keogh here thought I was living in sin. He thought I was doing everyone that came to this house." Lodi said, and then Wanjiru thought how Keogh would believe that since he was a holy holy Catholic, and a good friend of the priest.

"It was very nice. And the *gitaa* are very nice."

Lodi said, "Well, I could have sung more in key, and keeping up with Keogh is hard."

"You're too hard on yourself. You play the *man-do-lin* quite fine." He said, and Wanjiru memorized the name of the little *gitaa*, since it was something her Lodi did.

"Well, for a Brit I like the way you do bluegrass."

"Blue grass?" Wanjiru asked.

"Oh," Lodi laughed. "It is American music. Long ago, the Scots, English and Africans brought their music together. It became what they call blue grass. The grass there is not really blue."

Wanjiru laughed, "So, that music is part English and African? Like me?"

"Well, yes, actually. Africans provided the banjo and the rhythm."

"Play a blue grass song for me." Wanjiru begged.

He looked at Keogh and asked, "Shady grove?" Keogh began strumming and her Lodi made the little mandolin sing. "It's shady on the mountain top, shady in the hollow. Anywhere my true love goes, I am bound to follow. Shady grove, my little love, shady grove I say, shady grove, my little love, I'm bound to go away." Her Lodi's voice cracked, but continued. "Cheeks as sweet as a blooming rose. And eyes are the prettiest brown. She's the darling of my heart. Sweetest girl in town." Her Lodi looked up from picking and winked at her. "Peaches in the summer, apples in the fall, If I can't have the girl I love, I'll have none at all." Lodi sang but strummed a chord finishing as someone opened the door.

"Love it, Mac, that is sweet." The black haired, *mzungu* woman walked in and sat in a chair next to her husband.

"Thanks Beatrice. How are you doing?"

"Well, I think I felt a kick this morning." She said rubbing the little bulge in her belly, giving Wanjiru the urge to rub her own belly, but she held back. "Miss Wanjiru, your mama said you would be here. She needs your help. I know it is really hard to pull yourself away from Mac, but she could use your help. It won't take an hour and you can come back."

"Well, Mrs. Keogh, Lodi sang me such a nice song I can go help mama and come right back." Wanjiru said.

"You promise?" Her Lodi asked, "It was great having you around." He stood up and walked her to the door. Gave her a kiss, and added in a whisper, "When you get back, I'll give you a hot bath and wash every bit of that beautiful skin." Wanjiru's whole body tingled in excitement, looking forward to returning to his gentle touch. She headed out the front door, turned down the drive and ran right into Wambui.

"Why are you here?" Wambui shouted at her. "You doing my *bwana* Lodi?" Wambui was standing in the middle of the drive between the tall hedges, waving her arms in anger.

"No, no." Wanjiru felt Wambui's rage, and did not want to exchange blows. "Just listen to music. Mr Keogh is here."

"You do him every morning everyday?" She screamed at her as if she wanted to kill. "Go away, never come back here. Lodi is my *bwana*. You want to take my *bwana* and my job?"

Wanjiru was horrified at the rage, and circled around her and ran over to Keogh's house and the safey of her mama.

Chapter 3, Mombasa

The little train was packed tightly with people as it pulled into Mombasa's railway station early in the morning of a hot, cloudy day. Wanjiru was sitting with her feet on top of the box of her belongings, so that she could sleep and not be bothered. The train silently came to a halt at the landing. People poured out and Wanjiru followed the crowd out carrying her ugly rope-wrapped box, hoping a cousin would be waiting. Several tall, brown-haired, white boys were getting off the train, and each one reminded her of her Lodi. As the people cleared away, there was still no sign of family. She found a bench to sit and wait.

She hated the heat of Mombasa. She intended to stay here until she learned that Lodi was back in America for good, and her baby was safe.

Finally, she saw two of her cousins, who were two young folk several years younger than she was. One young man Murangi and a girl also named Wanjiru, but everyone called Jeri. She gave Jeri a hug and offered Murangi a hand shake, but he gave her a big hug pressing himself against her, which made her feel awkward. Jeri was her blood cousin, but Murangi was the son of his uncle's second wife. Murangi's father was dead. He was short and very black - reminding her a bit of Kimani - and a cobbler by trade, spending the day repairing shoes to look like new. In previous visits, Murangi was always touching her and making suggestions – obviously very infatuated with Wanjiru. Jeri was about thirteen, skinny with breasts just beginning to pop out. She always admired her older cousin. However, what would she think once she hears about the pregnancy?

"Baba wants to go over over to Hussein's house today and see if he wants to hire you to watch his children." Murangi said as he picked up her box. They walked down to a bus stop and waited.

"I met Hussein before… very nice man… very fat." Wanjiru giggled.

"He lives just off the island in Likoni." Jeri said. "He works at a hotel there. He said he could get my sister Wajiko a job in the hotel, and she would not have to watch Hussein's children." Jeri handed her a scarf, and they both covered their heads for the bus ride. The cars were zipping by on the road, and many white tourists were walking along the road, smiling and saying hello as they passed by. The bus finally came, and they saw it was nearly empty except for a woman with her children. Wanjiru did not know the way to her uncle's, but it would be good to see him again since he treated her like a daughter.

~~~~~~~

The big white Likoni ferry was loaded and ready to pull away. Wanjiru and Wajiko were sitting on benches on the deck above the cars. Wajiko was nearly a twin to Wanjiru, except she was darker, tighter curl in her hair and not pregnant. She had seen her aunts and shown the bed she would share with Wajiko if she stayed there at her uncle's. Wanjiru told her aunts and cousins that she was pregnant, and they were all very happy for her.

Wajiko was to take her over to Hussein's house in Likoni to talk about working for him. This was her first trip on a ferry and it was exciting with all the different people... Blacks, Arabs, Whites. It was a quick trip, just a broad river really with no bridge. She could see the buildings on the other side, which looked like grain storage. Two white, young men came up and one sat next to Wajiko. "Jambo!" the younger one said. He had long, curly, yellow hair. He said in halting but nearly perfect Swahili. "I am in Mombasa to learn Swahili. I am a teacher from Meru." His friend was standing with a big smile on his face... he reminded her of Lodi but maybe younger, and had the same coloring. Wajiko said their names, and the young men said theirs, which sounded like Bob and Dug, who was sitting next to Wajiko. "We are staying at the Sea Breeze Hotel and we have Swahili class every morning. We go talk to people in town to learn." Dug said in very proper Swahili.

Wajiko giggled, "Your Swahili is very nice, very proper."

Bob said, "I teach in Embu. I come from America." He said in simple Swahili. The ferry had reached the other side already.

"My father works at Sea Breeze as a cook. You must eat what he prepares." Wajiko said, and Bob looked perplexed, but Dug told him in American what was said. Dug had strange green eyes that reminded her of Mr. Keogh, and the more she looked at Bob, the more she longed for Lodi. Bob was thinner and darker hair. His eyes were brown as was his hair, instead of blue. His skin was so white it was almost pink. He was quite hairy, since it was showing through the top of his blue shirt. The ferry had landed at Likoni, and the people were pressing together to get off the ferry, but Wanjiru was still sitting and chatting with the boys.

Dug offered, "We have some *pambe* at our hotel room. Would you like to have some?" And without asking Wanjiru first, Wajiko said that she would. Wanjiru looked at her cousin.

"We have to go to Hussein's house."

"We will get there. Just one beer and we go. Yes?" Wajiko promised. They pressed their way through the crowd and up the hill into Likoni. They saw the small sign to the hotel, and turned up the dirt road that separated the hotel from the Indian Ocean. Wanjiru could hear the ocean surf crashing in the distance. The palm trees were waving in the wind and the air smelled of the sea. Bob was walking next to her following Wajiko and Dug. He was saying something in Swahili but she did not understand him. She tried to use English, but he said that because of the Swahili school he was required to use only Swahili.

They entered the hotel room, which had adobe walls and had wired windows with curtains and no glass. The two beds had mosquito nets hanging over them. The wind was blowing through the outside bushes that provided privacy, and the sea smell was strong. The two beds were next to each other, and Dug pulled the mosquito nets up to the headboard so that the women could sit down. At first Wanjiru sat down beside Wajiko on one bed, but after Dug and Bob came back with bottles of Tusker beer, Wajiko got up and sat on one bed with Dug, leaving Bob to sit next to her.

They chatted for a while, Wajiko had downed the beer quickly, and Dug offered her another. Bob downed his as quickly, while Wanjiru only sipped her beer, thinking it was too bitter. Dug returned with another Tusker and Wajiko took a gulp. As they chatted Dug sat very closely to Wajiko, and started talking about sex. Wanjiru knew where this was going, but she did not know whether she wanted out or not. Dug said, "I will take off my shirt if you do." Bob and Wajiko giggled, and Dug pulled his shirt out of his jeans and pulled it over his head. His skin was very white and he had a small patch of yellow hair on his chest. Wajiko slowly removed her blouse, sipping her beer in her bra. Dug looked it over, found the catch in the back and unsnapped it. Bob put his beer down and took off his shirt, which made Wanjiru feel compelled to follow suit, but she was not drunk, so she just watched. Dug admired Wajiko's brown breasts with her large nipples, and began petting them. He stood up and pulled off his jeans and briefs with his huge white shaft bobbing around. He handed Bob something from the table and then Dug opened a condom packet and quickly put on a condom in front of the two women. Wanjiru was stunned and could not move, and looked at Bob who was also naked and putting on a condom and his short white shaft. Dug pushed Wajiko back onto the bed and pulled off her sandals and pulled down her panties, leaving her skirt on. Wajiko just giggled as Dug positioned her and mounted her.

Bob stood up in front of Wanjiru with his one-eyed, condom covered shaft, with an upside down beard, staring her in the face. She was too stunned to do anything. He took her beer and set it on the table, and pushed her back onto the bed. Quick as a flash, he pulled her panties and sandals off, and got on his knees on the bed, pulled her around and positioned her in an instant and penetrated her before she was aware what was going on. Dug was thrusting frantically in and out of Wajiku who had turned her head to watch her cousin being done by the skinny white boy. Bob was not at all as vigorous as Dug, and seemed to enjoy short even strokes, which sent electricity through her body and made her scratch his back and pull at his brown hair. He stared into her eyes as he thrusted away. Suddenly she heard Dug going into spasms making Wajiko scream. Bob went all goofy in the face and stiff all over, which indicated that he was finished and collapsed beside her on the small bed. Dug was still pumping away and Wajiko screamed again, when suddenly Dug stopped and went limp on top of her.

A few minutes passed and Wanjiru crawled out of the bed and found her panties and sandals. Wajiko pushed Dug off and started looking for her clothes. The two white boys were happily asleep, so the women got dressed and used the toilet waiting for the boys to wake up. After a while, Wajiko said, "We should get to Hussein's." As they were leaving, Wajiko noticed Bob's wallet part way out of his trousers on the floor, picked it up and took four one-hundred shilling notes out and gave two to Wanjiru. "For your baby." They left quietly, but quickly leaving the boys sleeping with their used condoms.

Hussein lived five minutes from the hotel with his three wives and seven children. He was also a cook at the hotel with Wajiko's father. They arrived at the small adobe covered house with a tile roof. They reached the door and one of Hussein's wives answered the door and was very happy to see Wajiko, giving her a hug. "Are you back to help us with the children?" she asked.

"I bring a cousin to help you. My father may get me a job at the hotel." Wajiko said as they were shown into the deceptively large living room. Two other wives were there with five of the children. "Wareesha, is the eldest wife." Wajiko smiled at the older woman holding a child on the floor. "Middle wife is Nasra, and the youngest wife is Nathifa." The two women stood up and gave Wanjiru a hug for welcome. Although they were Arabs, they had darker complexions than did Wanjiru, almost the same as Wajiko. Nasra hugged her, then stroked her belly.

"You are two or three months along?" she asked. Wanjiru was too stunned to say anything. "Our two older boys are at the hotel with their father... they all should be back soon." Wanjiru was nervous. Perhaps they saw them leaving the white boys' room.

They sat on the floor for the children to get used to Wanjiru. The children knew Wajiko and were playing with her and sitting on her lap and offering toys. One of the wives brought out a tray with some thick milky tea, which they drank waiting for Hussein to show up. When he showed up Wanjiru was surprised to see a dark, hairy Arab who was almost as wide as he was tall. He was wearing food stained white uniform and flour dust covered his two young sons. The sons were eager to get back to their toys. He like, Wajiko's father, went to the same Catholic church, she was told, but he also went to mosque.

Wajiko introduced Wanjiru who shook the large meaty hand, which was soft as a baby's bottom, and he smelled of curry and *pilipili*. She glanced down at his bulge in his white, food stained trousers, and wondered if he was excited ... or was it just massive? On the walk to the ferry, Wajiko had told her that he had several times come into her room after bedtime and tried to do her, but he would run out of strength before he could finish. His thing was so huge. Wajiko said she thought she was giving birth. Nothing like the tiny Kikuyu things, she said.

Hussein asked, "Please stand up. Are you pregnant?" Wanjiru was stunned. How do they all know? He laughed. "Your uncle told me to make sure I would not object." He said in Swahili, then switched to English, "I understand up country Africans and how everyone does everyone else several times a day. That is why the population up country is exploding." He continued in English, "I suppose Wajiko told you that I paid her visits at night?" He waited for her response.

Wanjiru looked at her cousin who said in English, "Yes, I told her, but I did not tell your wives." He smiled. Was it their secret? Wanjiru knew why he disclosed it. He would pay her visits as well.

"They know... it was their idea since they are tired of me. So, Wanjiru, your job is to live here and help with the children. My wives will help you with your pregnancy and you can visit your uncle's family any time. I can pay you twenty shillings each month." He waited a while.

"Please, I want to accept. I will go back to my uncle's house and get my things and return tomorrow to work."

"Fine." I will show you your room... it is the same that Wajiko had." He took them down a long hall and showed her the small room with a mattress on the floor, made up with sheets and blanket. There were shelves over the bed and just enough space to get dressed in. He pointed out the small Arab style toilet, which was much better than the pit latrine she used in Njoro. They shook hands and the two young women left Hussein's house. It was dusk with the sun setting over the city. Wanjiru had no idea which way Wajiko was taking her, but she soon recognized the hotel.

They were back at the room of the two young men. "Wajiko, why are we back here? We should go back to your father's."

"Maybe we can get more beer and money." She laughed. "They will want to do us again." She tapped at the door and Dug opened and let them in with a laugh.

"Bob, our sweeties have returned... pop open the beers."

Chapter 4, Where's Wanjiru?

It made Wambui self-conscious whenever Lodi would want to talk as she made supper. She would tell stories in up country Swahili and he would comment about it. As she diced vegetables, she would tell stories. He would sit on the counter listening and watching. Lodi had told her that Miss Lee had gone back to America early because of pregnancy. Lodi said it was probably her boyfriend's baby, but Wambui thought it was Lodi's. After her boyfriend left her, Miss Lee stayed her for over a week. Then Lodi asked, "Whatever happened to our friend Wanjiru Tatton?"

"Wanjiru Tatton? She is in Mombasa. Her uncle promised her a job with an Arab."

"With an Arab… they can have four wives… is she going to be his wife?"

"I don't know. Maybe. But men like African girls to do when they get tired of their wives."

"Hmmm, well Wanjiru is definitely sweet. If my family would like brown women I would take her to America and marry her. You know I asked her to marry me." He said and Wambui's heart fell to the floor… marry her? He continued, "Even being half English, some in my family only like white people and would make it hard on me."

"Same here. If I marry Luo, I would not be welcomed at my father's again. I married a Luhya because I had to. But a Luo or an Englishman? My father was Maumau, so he would kill me to marry an Englishman. American almost as bad." She said and he laughed.

"If I could stay in Kenya I would marry her. But your government is trying to get rid of whites… too many whites in Kenya." There was a long silence since Wambui agreed with the government… too many Luos also. Stinking Luos. He added. "You know I go to the country club with Keogh. There was an old Englishman who told me about Wanjiru's father. He helped set up this school. It was first for British children. Lord Egerton started it with the farm college. The old man told me that Wanjiru's father was the bastard son of Lord Egerton."

"Bastard? What is that?"

"*Haramu mtoto*." He tried. "Bastard means the mama and baba not married. Lord Egerton did one of his house keepers at his house in England." Lodi said in Swahili, and Wambui was having difficulty understanding. She had heard of Lord Egerton as a crazy man who hated women.

"Oh, people call my Ruthy bastard."

"Yes, so Wanjiru is the bastard daughter of the bastard son of Lord Egerton. Wanjiru might be the sole heir of the Egerton estate." He said in very difficult Swahili.

"That means what? Wanjiru owns Egerton house?"

"Maybe, but the English did not like bastards." He laughed so loudly it hurt her ears. She wanted to change the subject, since she was having such a hard time with what the English thought was so important about bastards.

"When I came, the students were laying in the grass by their house," she said in Swahili, then added in English, "dormitories" and back to Swahili. "One of your students asked me a question. He wanted to know if you do me." She laughed. "And if not is Makomeki holy holy?"

"What did you say?"

"Makomeki is holy holy." She laughed very loudly.

"You know students come here for tutoring after I take you home? They wait out in front until I return, then bring their books and ask questions. They ask me questions about my girlfriends too, but I do not answer. Several said they want to be my boyfriend."

"Yes, one told me he was waiting for you and he could see through the curtains of your bedroom. Shut off the light because students outside the window can see through the curtains what you do. You never wear clothes." She laughed and added, "I told you that. I think the boy loves you."

"Really? Only Virginia likes to have the lights on when she comes. So, my students already know who my girlfriend is." Wambui thought that he did not seem to care if he had students watched him.

"Maybe, but they also know what you do." Wambui said. "Everyone knows now maybe." There was a long silence as she cooked and he sat quietly watching.

"Remember, I am teacher on duty this week, so I have to check the dormitories at lights out. Is your brother coming again to escort you home?" He asked and she nodded as she cooked. "Last night I was walking through a dormitory and saw a boy leave his bed and go over to sleep with another boy. Today I told the deputy headmaster and he just said that the boy must have been on a mission."

"Mission?" she asked, not knowing the word.

"Like a soldier in the army out to penetrate enemy defenses." He laughed, but she was quiet for a while then giggled.

"Animals." She said, emphasizing her negative opinion of the students. "Food is ready, go sit down."

While her *mzungu* was eating, Wambui cleaned the kitchen. She could hear Voice of America on the radio. She took a look into the dining room and he was reading a textbook and making notes as he ate and listened to the radio. These *mzungus* have to do three things at a time. There was a tapping at the back door and she unlocked it and in came her brother Kimani and her friend Virginia. Her brother hardly ever spoke but she poured some tea for him, and asked her friend an obvious question, "Virginia, you want my *mzungu* to do you?" and before Virginia could answer, Lodi came in with dishes and handed them to Wambui.

"Virginia, Kimani, *habari gani*?" he shook their hands. "What is it?" Virginia took his hand and led him out of the room. Wambui looked at her brother, who seemed curious about what was going on.

"Come with me," she said to her brother, and they went out the back door and circled around to the side of the house where several younger students were looking into Lodi's bedroom window. The students saw her coming and bolted away. One tripped and fell to the ground. Kimani helped the boy up and held on to him by the ear. Wambui saw through the thin curtain Lodi and Virginia taking their clothes off. Wambui led her brother and the student back to the kitchen.

"You are Muwera, I know you. You are always coming around." Wambui said to the student. "You like to see your teacher without clothes?" The student looked very nervous. He was a form two, very black skin and thick curly hair, maybe sixteen and a typically short Kikuyu male. He had his green school sweater on, grey shorts and long white socks and tennis shoes. "You sit on the floor. Your teacher will know what you do." She said harshly to the boy who sat on the floor with his arms around his knees

70

waiting for his punishment. Kimani went back to finish his tea and chatted with his sister waiting for Virginia to return.

It was a while when Virginia returned to the kitchen. Wambui went to Lodi who was still on his bed pulling on his socks. "Kimani and I caught a student looking in your window watching you and Virginia. He could see everything." She said and Lodi laughed.

"Did you see everything also? I should shut the lights." He laughed out loud. "Let's talk to him," and they went to the kitchen. The student was sitting on the floor, Virginia and Kimani were sipping tea. "So, Waweri, you saw me without clothes. Why do you want to see your teacher without clothes?"

Muwera looked nervous, but finally said, "I am curious." Wambui was disgusted with him.

Lodi just laughed, "So, Muwera, what is the punishment for a student who wants to see his teacher without clothes?" Lodi towered over the puny student. He motioned the student to stand up and he studied the nervous student. Wambui did not know what a good punishment should be other than caning. "Muwera, I have to go do my master on duty duties. I will take you back, and we will talk with the headmaster in the morning."

The student looked extremely nervous, shifting from foot to foot, " He will expel me ...I cannot be expelled... I will do anything you ask, but not the headmaster, please." He begged in English. Wambui looked at the young man and realized there must be more than curiosity that made him come around so often.

"So, you will do anything I ask?" he asked the student, then looked up, "Wambui, go home." Lodi leaned forward and placed his hands on the young man's shoulders. Kimani pushed the two women out the back door. As they left, Lodi was telling Muwera something that she could not hear.

Chapter 5, Muturi Arrives

Wanjiru removed the second safety pin and pulled back the wet stinky diaper off the baby Yaqub. It was full and the little boy was happy to have it off himself. He kicked his feet and tried to turn to the side. Wanjiru pushed him back, wiped the poop off the boy's butt and rolled the diaper up and gave it a toss into the diaper pail. She took a wash cloth and wiped the butt clean and let him air out for a minute. It always made him calm down. She put a clean diaper on him and covered it with plastic pants. She let him down and he went crawling to his mother wanting to nurse. His mother took out a tit and the little boy attacked it ravenously. It was late and Wanjiru said, "I go to bed now, call me if you need help." She left the living room and walked down the hall passing Hussein's room where he was listening to the radio. "I go to bed now. Good night." He waved back and she went on to the toilet.

She collapsed exhausted on her bed, feeling the weight of her pregnancy, which she felt was due very soon. She often felt the baby kicking, and she felt as big as a house and a bit of cramping. Her head sank into her pillow and her memories of the last few months came back vividly.

The months went by very fast. She helped take care of the children and helped with shopping at the market. The family was wonderful, and Hussein was very gentle and caring. Wajiko was working at the hotel, making a lot of money doing the guests, and somehow not getting pregnant. Her uncle and Hussein were well-paid cooks at the hotel, which was very popular among young tourists since it was right on the ocean.

She went down to the beach with Wajiko during their off hours to watch the tourists, which were mostly German, English and some Kuwaiti. Wajiko called them brats, because they all had money and expected everyone to give them what they want. Wajiko made sure it was worth it. The sand was almost white and the waves would break about a quarter mile out. One day in particular came back vividly. The palm trees were waving in the wind. Young men would approach to chat them up, but seeing the pregnant girl, they smiled and went on. Wajiko would whine about missing the cute boys because of this pregnant girl with her, but

laugh aloud at her own joke. Wajiko wore a large hat to ward off
the sun, and a light yellow sundress for the beach. They never went
swimming or basking. Though she was dark brown she was badly
burned once and hated the blisters. For someone who cleaned the
rooms, she dressed very nicely since she was making so much
money from the men. When she spent the night with them, she
would tell her father she is staying with Wanjiru, and would give a
few shillings to keep her quiet. If her father found out she were
prostituting, she would be thrown out of his house. It was one
thing to get pregnant from a lusty boyfriend, but very different to
service strangers for money. Wajiko pointed to a tall, young man
basking in the sun on a large towel nearby. They walked over and
sat in the sand nearby. "Hello." Wajiko said to the young man.
Wanjiru looked him over, and he was so white that she thought the
sun would burn him like frying *ugali*. He wore a bikini swimsuit
and did not have much in them that she could guess. He was a bit
chubby with no hair on his chest. He turned towards Wajiko, then
looked at Wanjiru. "My name is Wajiko, and this pregnant girl is
Wanjiru. You are cute. Where are you from?"

"I am Hans, I from Germany," he said in broken English.
"I holiday here. It ist very kalt in Germany now." He laughed.
"You are very pretty. Pregnant girls very sexy." He laughed and
the girls laughed along. "Say, do me ein favor and lotion on my
back? I vill burn mit out it." Wajiko got up and went over to Hans
who had turned over onto his belly. She squirted cream on his back
and began rubbing it in. Wanjiru watched what she did. She spread
it evenly over his back and the back of his legs, and pulled down
his swimsuit and rubbed some onto his remarkably white buttocks.

"Turn on your back, I will do your front." He turned over
and was obviously aroused by the touching, since his thing was
peeking out of his swimsuit. Wajiko could not resist and straddled
him with her sundress hiding the connection. She reached for
something in her bag, then was doing something with her hands
under her dress, that Hans was enjoying. Wanjiru apparently had
made the connection and was servicing Hans. Wanjiru saw a
condom wrapper rolling in the breeze towards the ocean, and knew
she was protected. Wajiko squirted the lotion on his chest and
began rubbing it into the skin while going up and down on his
thing. Wanjiru looked around and there was no one within a
quarter mile. There was a line of people out where the surf was

breaking. She looked back at Wajiko and watched as she was pleasuring the young man. The wind caught her skirt and she saw how she was doing it, having pulled the swimsuit down and her underwear to the side to fit herself together with Hans. Suddenly, Hans went stiff all over and bent forward. Wajiko stopped to enjoy the moment. Wanjiru wondered how many men she serviced everyday, since she seems to know so well how to get them to finish.

"Das var vun da bar," Hans said but Wanjiru was not knowing what it meant. Wajiko got up and moved off to the side leaving Hans with his wet thing still out of his swimsuit. She pulled the condom out and buried it in the sand. He rolled over towards the women, unaware that it was hanging out. "Would you like to come to my room for a beer?" He said, and Wanjiru knew his cousin could not refuse that. Since he only had a towel and a room key, his money must be in his room.

Wanjiru's recollection continued vividly. In the room, he had cold beer from the little frig and gave them some pretzels. Wanjiru watched the two sipping beer and chatting on the bed, this was when Wanjiru learned about new ways to pleasure a man with the mouth, and apparently, Wajiko knew how to do it well. She watched her cousin from the corner of the room servicing the German man. After an hour, she left with Wajiko and five hundred shillings better off. Wanjiru thought that she would have to work for several years with Hussein to get that much. Wajiko laughed, "Here is a hundred for you for standing guard."

But the memory faded and as she heard the door open. The room was dark except the light from the open door. It was Hussein. He pulled the covers off her and began removing her panties. He turned her around on her knees and bent her down for rear entry. She was philosophical about it, since his thing was so big it would widen her birth canal and his sperms would help the baby slide out easier. Or so she hoped. It took a while for her to adapt to his huge thing. The first few times was painful with tearing and bleeding but as she got wider she looked forward to his occasional visits. He grabbed with one hand her hipbone and guided his thing into her, sinking it as far as it would go. The sensation was different this time since it set off birth contractions, and gratefully he quickly squirted into her a large amount of lubricant for the coming birth. He left her to fall onto her side in a major contraction. After he was gone for a while, she called out to Wareesha the eldest wife that the baby might be coming. The woman came in, timed the contractions, and pronounced an hour or two... enough time to get her to the health center.

~~~~~~~~~

Wanjiru sat on the edge of the hospital bed admiring the husky newborn sucking at her brown breast. The huge baby learned sucking quickly and seemed to have an endless appetite. He was nearly five kilo at birth, ripping his way out of her, with a pain she never knew could exist for any reason. But the pain was replaced with a mixture of joy, depression and anxiety for the future. Things always worked out, but now she had to worry for the boy. She had five relaxing days in the hospital, healing and learning from nurses how to take care of the baby. Wajiko had given some of her money to extend the stay in the hospital.

A nurse popped in with some paperwork for her to read and sign. It was the birth certificate form, which is something her mother did not have for her daughters. They were all born in a hut before the health service. The nurse also had a bag of baby supplies and papers with instructions. The nurse was a young, very black woman, chubby with a nearly shaved head, whose name on the badge was "Rebecca Sang." She smiled, "What a handsome young man you have there... you should be very proud. I need you to check this form to see all the information is correct." Wanjiru looked at the woman, thinking she looked very familiar.

"You look very familiar to me. Have you ever been to Njoro?"

"Yes, I was a nurse at the health center there for a while late 1974 until early last year."

"Oh, yes, when my friend Wambui had her daughter you were there. I remember you now." Wanjiru took the form and read the typewritten information. Mother's name, mailing address – her mother's address in Njoro – and some other information about her education. Then the father... she had hesitated about this, but looking at the blue eyes that smiled back at her, she had decided to tell all. Father's name: Lodi Makomeki, tribe/nationality: American. Education: college. Occupation: Teacher. As she read through it, and looked at the baby blue eyes, all the memories flooded back. She named the boy Muturi Tatton Makomeki with the second name after the boy's English grandfather and a name she had used. She was guessing at the spelling for Lodi's family name as if it were Swahili. She looked at Rebecca and gave the form back. Rebecca smiled as she read the form herself, as if to say, Oh, it all makes sense now. "Is this Mr. Makomeki a teacher at the high school there?" The nurse asked.

"Yes, do you know him?"

"Yes, he and I dated for several months. It did not work out, since I am a strong Catholic and he is…" she paused looking for the right word.

"Crazy? Foolish? Immoral?"

"I hate to say this since he is your husband now," she said and Wanjiru's heart skipped several beats at the nurse's use of the word *husband*, "but I thought he was a womanizer."

"Womanizer? I do not know that word."

"He enjoys sex with many women. I gave him a box of condoms so that he would not spread disease." They both laughed and the baby lost his sucking grip on Wanjiru's tit.

Wanjiru said, "My Muturi would not be here if he had used those condoms! He must have used them all up before he got to me." Again they laughed together.

"Who will be escorting you out this morning? Will it be Mr. Makomeki?" she asked. "I wonder if he will remember me."

"My aunt and several cousins should be coming. Lodi is in Njoro." She said, not wanting her to know that Lodi will never know about the boy… or the boy might end up in America and she will never see the boy again.

"Well, he should be very happy to see you when you get back." Rebecca said apparently trying to be supportive. "I could…" she started but several women and girls came into the ward, shouting and interrupting her.

"Oh, good, you are ready to go!" Wajiko said, then hushing her voice seeing the other women in the ward holding their babies and glaring at the exuberant woman. Wajiko's mother was very quiet but had a huge smile as she took the sleeping baby from its mother. Her other cousin grabbed the bag of baby supplies, and Wajiku took a bag of dirty clothes, helping Wanjiru off the bed. "The manager at the hotel sent his van with Hussein to pick us up and take us back to father's house. You can stay with us for a few days and then go back to work with Hussein."

Wanjiru thought of Hussein's occasional nightly visits and her current soreness, and decided to put off returning to Hussein's as long as possible.

"You need to learn to tie the baby to your back," her aunt suddenly said, "just like the dolls you used to practice with, but you have to be gentler." She handled the baby back and Wanjiru snapped a towel onto her back, bent forward and gingerly rolled the sleeping baby between her shoulder blades, quickly unknotted a large, brightly colored cloth from around her waist and brought it up over the sleeping baby. With some quick knotting the baby was bound to her back. "Oh, that is very good. All that practice with the dolls was worth it." The aunt checked the cloth and the safety of the baby on Wanjiru's back. The baby had reddish brown hair that was lightly curled, and a bronze brown skin. "You are ready to go." They all trooped out of the ward and out of the health center to the street where a van was waiting. Wanjiru could see Hussein sitting in the front passenger seat and a stranger as the driver. Hussein hopped out to shake her hand and congratulate her, and they all found places in the van. Wanjiru sat down and pulled the slumbering baby around to the front of her body for the ride.

They arrived at her uncle's little house, and Hussein got out quickly, opening the large sliding door and helped Wanjiru's aunt and cousins out, but politely pushed Wanjiru back in the seat. "Oh, please, my wives want to see the baby, and you can stay with us." Wanjiru tried to get up, but Hussein pushed her back down again.

Her aunt piped up, "Your uncle can bring you back so we can help with the baby, when Mr. Hussein gives you permission." Wanjiru suddenly felt trapped, knowing quite surely, what Hussein was wanting. Her aunt waved, and Wanjiko shrugged and turned her back to head into the house.

The van pulled up to Hussein's house and two of his wives came out to help Wanjiru and the baby out. They both wanted to carry the baby, but he wanted to suck again, so Wanjiru walked into the house carrying the nursing child. "Did they make a mistake and give you a *mzungu* child?" One of the wives, Nathifa, asked laughing.

Wanjiru laughed back, "You know his father is a *mzungu*, as is one of his grandfathers… So he is mostly *mzungu*… nusu nusu, nusu nusu *Mwafrika*." She laughed again, thinking of half of a half African boy... what will this huge baby grow into? She thought.

The other wife laughed, "He looks as if he is three months old already. Five days in the hospital. What did they feed him?" she asked as they entered the living room. They stood admiring the baby who had his fill and had fallen asleep again. One of the wives insisted on holding the baby. Wanjiru needed to use the toilet, and mentioned the fact, "Oh, Wanjiru, go ahead. Take your time." The wife Nasra said, and Wanjiru pulled the baby cloth over her head and headed towards the toilet.

She relieved herself and washed her hands. As she walked out into the hall, she was intercepted by Hussein. He pushed her into his bedroom and locked the door behind him. "I want to see you now that you are not pregnant." He said, and Wanjiru froze, knowing what he intended, but not knowing how to react. She folded her arms in front of herself and tried to remain neutral, hoping he would lose his lust, but seeing the buldge in his trousers, she knew what was going to happen, and her body was tingling in excitement despite her anxiety about it. He walked over, pulled her arms apart and began unbuttoning her blouse, getting several buttons, then pulling the blouse off over her head, taking her turban with it. Her long, curly brown hair fell down to her shoulders. She thought suddenly that she needed to wash her hair. He unsnapped her bra, and said admiringly, "You are even more filled out with the nursing, and you are slimmer, of course. He unbuttoned her skirt and let it drop to the floor. He waved his hand, and she removed her underwear to stand naked for him to admire. His bulge had grown enormous. Again he waved her to the bed, and obediently she laid on her back and spread her legs, knowing her very sore womanhood would become more sore. Nevertheless, she felt herself dripping from excitement. She watched him drop his trousers and crawl onto the bed, then she closed her eyes as she felt the cold fat of his belly come to rest on top of her, then suddenly she felt a stinging pain.

Chapter 6, Stories Told

The sun had been up for a half hour and Wambui was rushing to her *mzungu's* place. Though it was a Saturday morning, she still needed to be on time. She walked quickly into the school compound, through the back gate into the driveway that led to the house. As she was half way up the drive, Muwera came running up with his head down towards her. She grabbed his sweater stopping him in his tracks. "What are you doing? Why are you running?" she demanded. "You are that boy I caught looking in the teacher's window, are you not?" The boy twisted away, ran down the drive, and disappeared around the tall hedge. She was curious and went around to the front door, and passing the bedroom window noticed the curtains were open, and at the front door, she noticed the door unlocked. She went in the front door and locked it behind her.

It was all different from usual. There were three glasses on the little table by the fireplace and a bottle of gin was nearly empty. The cassette player stereo was humming, but no music coming out. Lodi had brought the player back with him from his visit to America and had people over to listen to music. So, maybe that was it. She went on into the kitchen to start water boiling, began looking through the house, and found Lodi still in bed. He was on his belly on the edge of the bed near the wall with his face in the pillow breathing deeply. His clothes were scattered on the vanity and his under shorts were on the floor. She wondered whom if anyone was with him last night after he escorted her home.

He suddenly rolled over and his eyes popped open then shut again. "*Habari*. Is it late?" he asked. His eyes opened gradually as if he had a hang over. "I drank too much last night."

Wambui had to wonder about her crazy *mzungu*. "Muwera was leaving here when I came. Did he sleep with you?"

"Sleep with me? He might have. He was here when I was drinking last night. He and Kimani dropped by after I had several drinks. Kimani and I had several more drinks. The last I recall Kimani told Muwera to help get me to bed."

"You were too drunk to know what he did. You have no clothes." Wambui said, and Lodi started laughing, throwing back the covers checking around. Then Wambui started looking through the sheets as well, but they both came up with nothing. "*Sijui*. He put you to bed and slept with you?"

"Hmmm. Too bad," he laughed, "I guess I was too drunk to enjoy it, whatever he did." He patted the empty space next to him and she felt excitement. She slipped off her *chupi* and dress and got comfortable next to him.

Half an hour later, Wambui went into the kitchen to find most of her water boiled away, and she started some more, and started the coffee perculator. As she was slicing bread there was a tapping at the back door, and she unlocked the door to let Kimani in. "*Natya*. Is Lodi still in bed?" he asked and Wambui grunted a yes. "He got very drunk last night." Kimani laughed. "We listened to music and Muwera came in. Muwera told me in Kikuyu that he lusted for the teacher." He laughed again.

"He lusted for the teacher... Lodi? Animal."

"Yes, he said he came to the teacher's house whenever he was alone but the teacher would not get the message."

"Message? What do you mean?"

"The story was that the student is lusting for his teacher and comes around always to be with him."

"Yes, Lodi, asked me why does Muwera keep coming around after I leave. What happened last night?"

"I told Muwera that we will get the teacher drunk and you can do what you want, like getting a girl drunk."

"He is an animal. Why do you do that?" Wambui was recalling that Kimani was friendly with her previous *mzungu* employer, O'Conner, who she thought liked boys too much. Kimani was one of them when he was a student, who came around often.

"It is fine, he does not know what he wants or why." Kimani said with authority. "So, Lodi had a half bottle of gin and was acting very strangely. I helped get him into the bedroom, undressed him and left Muwera alone with him."

"What did Muwera do?" Wambui asked, knowing Kimani would not leave Lodi alone with Muwera, and thought he was lying.

"I can only guess. As they say. Muwera was on a mission."

"Who was on a mission?" Lodi said as he walked into the kitchen looking for his coffee. He shook hands with Kimani.

"We were talking about your guest you had last night." Kimani said in English, with Wambui barely understanding.

"Muwera?" Lodi said in Swahili. "Yes, he might have been here. I woke up with a bad head. I hope there are no diseases." He laughed at his own joke as he often did. "Kimani, where did you sleep?" Wambui knew Lodi had no idea what happened last night.

"I slept with Muthoni and Warimu in their hut. You know Esther has her own place now?"

"At least you didn't do me. You slept with Esther's daughters? Wanjiru, too? Is she back?" he asked, but Wambui knew she was still in Mombasa.

"No, just the two. Wanjiru is not Kikuyu enough for me. Besides, she is still away."

"You don't like half breeds? Hmmm. Must be why you don't do me..." he laughed at his own joke. Kimani looked embarrassed, and Wambui knew that her *mzungu* was crazy.

"You a half breed?"

"Well, Scotish, Irish, English, Dutch, German, French, Swiss, and a bit of African thrown in for good measure." he looked a Wambui, who was having a hard time following the previous comment, did understand the question, and grunted her affirmation. Then he asked in Swahili "Do you know who did Esther? Was it really old Tatton?"

"That is the story. Tatton used to live in this house for many years with his first wife. It was a school for *mzungu* children then. His wife had no children. Esther told me the story."

"Yes, I know you like sex stories." He said in Swahili, then in English, "All the grotty details the better!" and Wambui was confused, but went ahead with the story.

"Tatton wife was very nasty just like him, but she like Esther who was once very pretty when she was a young woman. She had Warimu already, and her mother watched the baby. Her mother is dead now. It was when the British ran the country and there was a lot of fighting. Tatton thought the Maumau would come and kill him, and wanted to return to England." She said and handed Lodi a cup of coffee and Kimani a cup of tea. "Tatton's wife took a bath every morning and Tatton would wash her. He would come out and bend Esther over the table ... the same table you eat on now...and do her as a rooster does a hen. Very fast. He did it everyday like that. She got a pregnancy, and started to show.

His wife asked her who made the pregnancy and Esther says her man. Tatton did her everyday until one time his wife saw him do it. She became crazy and returned to England. Tatton went to England. Divorce. Tatton gave Esther money for Wanjiru to go to school until she cannot pass more examination."

"So, Tatton knew Wanjiru is his daughter? I thought Tatton is dead now."

"Yes, I heard he is dead. Before, if Esther told anyone, Tatton will not help anymore. But everyone knew anyway."

"Yes. It seems everyone knows and talks about it."

"Esther is living near my house now. Wanjiru is working in Mombasa and…" Wambui almost said something about Wanjiru's pregnancy and bit her tongue. "She maybe marry an Arab in Mombasa and live in a big house." She saw the look of pain on Lodi's face, and tears welled up in his eyes.

It was not exactly a lie, since she might become wife number four, and it is a house rather than a hut, Wambui guessed.

Chapter 7, Going Home

Wanjiru had the morning off and decided to take baby Muturi to her aunt and uncle's place on Mombasa Island to show how he was doing. The ferry and bus rides were uneventful. Her uncle was working but her aunt was very happy to see her and Muturi, making her comfortable with thick, creamy tea and thick slices of bread with margarine. Her aunt was playing with the light brown Muturi getting him to stand on her lap grasping her fingers. The boy's baby hair had changed over to yellow hair, making him look like an African with a poor diet. His eyes remained blue. He was stocky with bulging leg muscles and a smile that would not stop. Her aunt set the baby on his belly on a blanket on the floor, and he immediately got up on all fours and tried crawling but fell on his belly. He got back up to try again.

"How is Hussein treating you?" her aunt asked, and Wanjiru wondered if she wanted all the details. But then she added, "He is probably too old and fat to fill you is he?" And Wanjiru was surprised at her frankness.

"No, he does me every other night or so... I will probably get a pregnancy again. *Nusu nusu* Arab this time."

"Keep letting the baby suckle you and it will be unlikely." She said. But Wanjiru already knew that missing two periods probably means she is pregnant again. Her aunt continued, "He pays you well I suppose." And Wanjiru did not want her to know how little she got in shillings, and certainly she did not want her to know how much she and Wajiko were making doing the German and English men at the hotel.

"Oh, I am able to save money to put Muturi in school when the time comes." She said being deceptive.

"The government will pay to standard four they say. So, save the money for later. Get a savings account at Standard Bank... Hussein says the British banks are safest." Her aunt was quiet for a while. "Oh, you have a letter here from your sister, I keep telling Wajiko to give it to you, but she keeps forgetting." She got up and out of a box on a shelf she got a letter that had been opened previously. "Wajiko opened it already and said it was not interesting." She smiled. "You can write back while you are here. I have stamps."

Wanjiru began reading and knew that it was her older sister's handwriting. She wrote about her and her sister's boyfriends mostly from the school, and that Esther was doing fine working for her *mzungu*, his new wife and baby. Esther had moved to nicer place across from Bondeni, but that the girls still live in the hut near the school. Wambui says that her *mzungu* went back to America and even though he said he would be six weeks there, everyone thinks he will not return. Wanjiru's stomach turned, and she looked down at the little boy trying so hard to learn to crawl, then back at the letter. The letter was many months old, so Lodi could be back or in America. She could take the baby for her mother to see, and if he has returned, she will return to Mombasa before he learns about his baby.

"This is making me miss my mother. I should go see her for a visit. She will want to see the baby."

~~~~~~~

The overloaded bus strained to get up the hill towards Njoro, while baby Muturi sucked at his mother's breast. Wanjiru looked around at the people in the packed bus, feeling the air getting colder as the bus driver opened the door to get a breeze through the slow moving bus. A fellow on a bicycle was actually going faster than the bus. She was afraid that the bus would break down and she would have to walk the last few miles. As the bus got closer to town, she could see the smoke coming up from the charcoal pits and noticed several of the huge trees missing on the other side of the railroad tracks. Someone had cut them down to make charcoal.

After the bus arrived in the Bondeni section of Njoro, the bus slowly unpacked its load and the fellow on top of the bus was lowering bicycles and boxes off the top. People were screaming at him to be gentle with their things, but the fellow tossed Wanjiru's box of things onto the ground. It was lucky that she saw where he had tossed it, and she was able to grab it before it was run over by a taxi heading out. It was full of clothes and all the things little Muturi needed.

A few hours before, after she had got off the train in Nakuru, she had gone to the Standard Bank and opened a savings account using her government ID card she had obtained in

Mombasa - one with a thumb print and photo - that her uncle had helped her obtain from the government. She had put three thousand shillings into the account for Muturi's schooling some day. She then had them convert the money in the account to certificates in British pounds. Hussein in one of his political lectures said many higher ups in the government are sending money to foreign accounts for safety if Kenyatta dies - mostly Swiss or American accounts. Hussein said that Kenya shilling would become worthless when Kenyatta dies, so put it in pounds or dollars for the future. She chose the pound. Her father is English, so it is only right. Her official name was *Wanjiru Wa Esther Tatton.*

As Wanjiru crossed the railroad tracks she admired the rich black soil of Njoro and the tall maize waving in the breeze. Women were carrying loads of firewood on their backs, while on her back little Muturi was sleeping. The sun was extremely bright and the air fairly cool compared to Mombasa. The high altitude air seemed thin and hard to breathe. She had only a vague notion where her mother was living now, and she did not want to go over to the school looking for her. She stopped at the edge of the pasture that she had crossed thousands of times to her hut near the school. Off to the right was a row of white buildings where they said her mother had a place now. There was a row of very tall trees and there were charcoal pits in the pasture with smoke seeping out. She stopped nervously not knowing which way to turn. She adjusted the scarf on her head when she heard her name being called. Someone on the path on the edge of the pasture... "O, Wambui! *Natya!*"

"Wanjiru, what are you doing here? Not in Mombasa. Baby, I want to see the baby!" Wambui said with a lot of excitement. Wanjiru put down her box and twisted the *kitambaa* around to bring the baby forward. "Yellow hair!" she exclaimed waking the baby, whose eyes popped open to look straight at Wambui. "Blue eyes! Your baby is a *mzungu*!" they both laughed, and the baby smiled at Wambui's huge, toothy smile. Wambui added, "That smile... just like Lodi... holy Jesus... why are you here?"

"Warimu wrote that Lodi had gone back to America." Wanjiru said, "But also I became very homesick."

"Lodi went and came back many months ago. Let me take you to your mother's. She might be there, she works mornings and

evenings like me. Let me carry the baby and you get your box."
The two headed for the row of white buildings, avoiding the
charcoal pits. Several cows were grazing in the pasture, being
guarded by a small boy with a long stick. The boy waved at
Wanjiru as if he knew her, but she could not place him. They took
a footpath through some weeds by a narrow road between
buildings up to a white fence, entering an unfamiliar gate to a
concrete courtyard. Some women were sitting around chatting
when they looked up, and Wanjiru saw her mother stand up and
come rushing up to her. Her mother looked shorter and older than
she remembered, she was darker and more wrinkled, but the turban
she wore was just as clean and bright white as it ever was. Tears
filled their eyes.

She hugged her mother, who demanded, "I need to see my
grandson! Is this him? Wambui, give him over!" Wambui handed
Esther the little *mzungu*. "Oh, poor baby, yellow hair, but
handsome smile. Does he smile all the time?"

"No, mama, he cries too, he eats all the time, and fills his
pants with orange poop."

"That will change when you stop nursing him." She said as
she led them to her room. It was a long white building made of
wood, with places to sit in the courtyard. They went into her room,
which was a large space with a bed and some chairs and stools
around a charcoal burner, which was cooking a brew of tea. The
shelves on the wall were stacked with various foods and utensils.
Wanjiru thought it was a much nicer place than the hut. Wambui
went to the radio and turned it on to some African music. With the
light coming through the windows and the music, Wanjiru felt very
happy to know her mother was so comfortable. She looked very
strong though obviously aged.

"I will go tell your sisters that you are here." Wambui
announced and soon disappeared.

Chapter 8, Secrets

Wambui handed Virginia a tin cup filled with hot creamy tea, "You know Wanjiru, Esther's second daughter, came back from Mombasa for a visit."

"Yes, her sister Muthoni said something, and that she is going back there to work for an Arab man."

"She is like the Arab's wife number four. I think she is pregnant by the Arab. Her baby is a *mzungu* - never say anything to Lodi, but it is his baby. It has yellow hair and blue eyes. It is very big and smiles a lot like Lodi."

"Oh, and Lodi must never know. She is nursing a *mzungu* baby and is pregnant? That is hard on a woman." Virginia said sipping the hot tea. "But I will never tell Lodi about his child. He will want to take the baby to America."

"It must remain a secret. She might lose the Arab baby unless she stops nursing... I heard that happening..." Wambui said trying to ignore tapping at the open back door. "Enter..." she called out in Swahili, and to her surprise, Muwera entered.

"May I please, where is the teacher?" He said as if talking to the headmaster.

"He is taking a bath, afterwards the headmaster's office, then going to the market. Why do you need to talk to him?" she asked suspiciously. "I last saw you coming out of here early one morning, and Lodi later told me you slept with him when he was drunk." Wambui looked at the boy in the white shirt and grey shorts. He had very clean sneakers and white socks neatly folded around his ankles.

"I confess. I am not normal. All I think of is the *mzungu* teacher. I have to be with him."

Virginia exclaimed, "Little dog. What is wrong with you?"

"I said this is not normal. I just want to be with him without you getting me in trouble with the headmaster. I will give you money to help me get him drunk again."

"You are crazy," Wambui said.

"How much money?" Virginia asked, and Wambui looked at her strangely.

"I heard your secret about your *mzungu* and his baby. I will keep that secret if you keep my secret and give you a few shillings." He said and took a crumpled five shilling note out of his pocket and handed it to Wambui." Wambui took it and tucked it into her bra.

"I think you need a woman to get these crazy things out of your head." Virginia said.

"Yes, for five shillings, girls will let you do them all you want." Wambui said. "That is why you come to Lodi's house... *kutomba* and crazy things?" She laughed. "Are there other boys who want Lodi to do them?"

"I don't know... many come around but that is to study... I should ask him." Muwera left the kitchen and headed of to the bath.

The tea began to steam, so she poured some into a porcelain cup, and put it on a saucer. She cut a slice of plum cake and put it on a plate with a fork. She gave the plate to Virginia, who followed her into the bath. The water was still pouring in but Lodi was in the tub already, and Muwera was talking to him and acting very frustrated. She handed him the tea which he set on the edge of the tub, and Virginia handed him the cake.

"What a surprise... so many people want to see me in the bath!" he said, but she saw that he had a washcloth across his privates. "Now, Muwera told me something interesting about Wanjiru." He looked up at Wambui. "Something about a secret?"

"You stupid monkey." Wambui said in Kikuyu and glared at him. In Swahili she said to Lodi, "What lies is this fool saying?"

"He said he heard you tell about Wanjiru's *mzungu* baby. She is back from Mombasa at her mother's house."

"Lie! lie! lie! She has a baby but it is her Arab's baby."

"I want to see her baby. Wanjiru is half-English, so if it has brown eyes... maybe Arab. Blue eyes... maybe my baby." He said, and Wambui was steaming with anger for Muwera. She had to go warn Wanjiru. What does Lodi know about eye color?

"I have to go home now." Wambui said to Lodi, looking at Virginia, who was studying Lodi in the bathtub. She caught her eye as if to say we both should leave.

"Well, I will get dressed and come over to your house, and you can take me to see the baby." Lodi said as he soaped his legs. Wambui turned to leave, and Lodi asked Muwera in Swahili,

"Muwera, what do you want from me?" As if Swahili was not potent enough he said in English, "Every day you come here. What do you want?" Was the last she heard as she turned down the hall following Virginia.

~~~~~~~

"So, this fool of a student overheard me talking to Virginia and then went and told Lodi. I told him it was a lie, but he wants to come here and see your baby." Wambui said, and looked straight at Wanjiru nursing the huge baby, but she did not seem too concerned.

Esther piped up, "We have a plan. When he comes, send your little brother to tell us you are coming before you come. My neighbor has a baby, and we will trade babies. Your *mzungu* will see the African baby, maybe give Wanjiru some money and go away."

"Lodi is not a fool, he will know the baby not *nusu nusu*."

"Say one of the students is the father… he will believe that."

"Lodi is convinced he has a son. Maybe God has told him and not just Muwera. He knows maths and science so he can know it was when Wanjiru worked for him."

"My neighbor's baby is much younger… would that help?"

"We will try." Wambui said, and taking a look at the suckling baby.

Wanjiru finally spoke, "I should not be here. I should return to Mombasa soon. I can earn money there."

~~~~~~~

"You know, it does not make sense." Lodi was saying as Wambui set his supper in front of him. He was using a pen and writing things on paper. "She left in -" he was saying in English, and babbled on about Wanjiru this and baby that.

"The baby should not be that black… such kinky hair…Wambui, is that baby really hers?"

Wambui was stunned, how did he figure it? "Really, it is hers…" she lied. The scheme went off exactly as planned, and Lodi gave Wanjiru twenty shillings and a hug and said something in English about how wonderful it is to have a beautiful baby. Of course it was a neighbor's baby and did not look like Wanjiru … and it was a girl instead of boy, but so what? Lodi even asked her if she was pregnant again, and she asked how did you know, and he pointed out things, but she did not understand how he knew.

Lodi went on like he always did. He would not let it be, "And she is pregnant again already? *Fanya hesabu*, Wambui!" he said demanding she do the math. She had no idea how he knew all this.

"I don't know. Forget it. It is not important." She said, and he looked frustrated and picked at his fish. She went into the kitchen to begin cleaning up.

A few minutes later, he came in with dishes and his food half eaten. "Wanjiru was so beautiful, but her baby. So so." He was muttering in Swahili.

Wambui wanted to get him onto something else. "Is that Muwera the only boy who wants to do you?"

"Do me? Muwera wants me to do him."

"Dirty, dirty. How many want to do you, and how many want you to do them?" she asked laughing at the thought.

"I have been here three years, so many, many students. Just a few *msenge* though. I am afraid of trouble, so… they do not excite me, also. You excite me. Go to my bed and get ready." He said, sending a tingle to her groin. Good he is not thinking about Wanjiru anymore!

Chapter 9, "Miscarriage"

The two women walked off the ferry onto the soil of Likoni, and Wajiko said, "I still do not understand why you left Muturi with your mother and sisters... a baby needs his mother's milk."

Wanjiru felt a shudder going through her thinking about her little son, "I told you several times. Why do you not understand? I am pregnant with Hussein's child."

"Yes, yes, I know, I know." Wajiko said, looking at her cousin, and Wanjiru knew she felt her pain. "Besides, Hussein's wives will be jealous."

"His wives are very good women. This frees me to work better for Hussein and his house." She said as they headed up to the branch in the road, which would take Wajiko to the hotel for work, and Wanjiru to Hussein's house. "I should go to Hussein's house." she said but was wondering what kind of cute men Wajiko was doing these days.

"I have to clean rooms. There is a church group using the hotel and doing services there every day... many holy holy people at the hotel. In a few days, many the tourists come back. Come over this afternoon and maybe we can have some fun." Wanjiko said as she headed towards the hotel. Wanjiru headed down the dirt road among the palm trees and banana plants. The heat was oppressive after Njoro, but the sea smells and breezes were calming.

After knocking a few times, Nathifa, opened the door and gave her a big welcoming hug, "Where is the baby? You leave him with your aunt and uncle or up country?" she said with obviously mixed emotions.

"Yes up country with my mother and sisters. He will do fine there. They started him on the bottle." She said trying to sound fine with the situation as she followed Nathifa into the living room where the children were playing and the two other women were sitting on the floor. Nasra and Wareesha both accepted hugs from Wanjiru, and motioned for her to sit between them. Several toddlers came over, gave her a quick hug, and went back to their toys. Nathifa came back in from the kitchen with a steaming cup of coffee for her. It was rich with cream and sugar for sure, she thought. She sipped as she watched the children play. Wareesha was looking more serious than usual.

She leaned over and rubbed Wanjiru's belly. "You have a pregancy?" she asked. "Is it Hussein's or who?" she asked in an accusatory tone. Wanjiru said nothing but tried to choose her words carefully. She was sure Hussein would brag to his wives that he was doing the cleaning girl just to make them jealous. The young men at the hotel always used condoms, so it was unlikely to be any of theirs.

"You are correct, I have a pregnancy." She said looking at the floor. "I must be honest, since Hussein wants to do me several times a week. I cannot object."

"Do you want to be his wife number four?" Wareesha asked.

"You know I am a simple up-country girl who does sex with any one. I love sex, so I do not object. If God wants to give me a pregnancy, He will make me desirable to the men who He wants to be the father." Wanjiru stated, trying to use the fatalism she learn from these Arab women.

"Wanjiru," Nathifa said, "you know we are not really Moslem, we are as much Catholic. I know you have little choice but to let our Hussein have his way with you."

Nasra reached behind her and brought out a packet of pills all nicely lined into a circle. "We get these at the health center…they are pills to keep you from getting pregnant…also they have a wire they put in the womb to stop pregnancy. You need to do something, else you have a pregnancy all the time." She smiled, "Also we have dawa to end a pregnancy… make it look like a miscarriage, if you do not want the child. You will be sick like stomach for three days, then blood and little fish comes out."

"I will have Hussein's child, and go from there." Wanjiru said, and the three women took sudden, noticeable breaths. "I know it will be such a burden, but Hussein will love it and care for it, I believe." The women groaned.

Nasra said, "Well, do not tell Hussein until it is for sure that it will come. For now, we are behind on the cleaning and need you to help us. Work a few hours and we will make you some lunch… we have some goat and ugali for you." She said, and

Wanjiru thought how she loved their cooking and even after a big breakfast at her aunt's, she would be hungry for lunch.

The house became very dirty in the three weeks that she was away, and Wanjiru doubted that the women did any cleaning outside the kitchen. She cleaned all the floors on her hands and knees with a pail and sponge. After several hours of labor, she received a large plate of goat and ugali. The goat was boney and tough but edible. The ugali was very dry, just like she preferred. It must have been left over from the day before, because it had a strange flavor to it. She was to launder all the bedsheets this afternoon and hang them out to dry, so that they can be back on the beds before bedtime. It was a huge amount of labor, washing the bedsheets by hand with the caustic detergents. She had gotten the sheets off the line and back to Hussein's bedroom after the sun set at 6:30 according to the bedroom clock. She made Hussein's bed as well as the three wive's, her own bed and four older children and three cribs. She was completely exhausted, but made it to the kitchen for her supper.

Nasra told her that there was a plate for her in the oven. The plate was hot, but covered to keep it fresh. She sat down at the kitchen table alone and uncovered it and saw a large pile of mashed potatoes and some chopped beef. There was a warm, wilted pile of chard, which was good for the blood - she grew up being told. There was a yellow spice of some sort sprinkled on the potatoes and chard. She blended it into the potatoes, not knowing what it was, maybe a curry. She ate the food, which did not taste as good as usual, but being so hungry and exhausted she cleaned the entire plate and drank a glass of water from the filter tank. As she was finishing she had heard Hussein come into the adjoining living room. The older kids who were still awake were noticeably louder and having fun with their father. Hussein usually ate at the hotel, so she was not expecting him in the kitchen. She heard Nasra mention to him that Wanjiru was in the kitchen eating. "Wanjiru, come in here and join the family!" he shouted, and she jumped up, but was taken back by the double meaning of what he had demanded. She walked in and saw the rotund man sitting on the floor wrestling with two boys.

"I am glad you are looking so well," she said to him, feeling a bit dizzy and wanting to sit down.

"Yes, I am feeling very well. Now, how are you feeling. Your uncle told me that you told your cousin some interesting news. It makes me very proud and happy." He said, and Wanjiru wondered what Wajiko could have told her uncle.

Her stomach started rolling, and she had to sit down from dizziness. Hoping the news was not about the pregnancy, she glanced at the three women and back to Hussein. The women were silent and expressionless. She deflected by saying, "Muturi is staying with my mother and sisters in Njoro." But this gave him a lead back to his topic.

The two boys continued wrestling with their father as he spoke. "Yes, that is good that you can put your strength to the new baby that is coming." He said, and there was an audible gasp from the three women. Wanjiru knew that everyone knew her secret.

"Perhaps another five months, yes." She wanted to say that it was his, but he obviously assumed that it was, so nothing to add anyway. She suddenly felt a chill coming from the three women, who loved her as a housekeeper and concubine to their husband, but would not welcome her as an equal wife. She was not Arab, but a simple, mulatto, up-country girl. Her stomach gripped and turned and she began sweating, which she assumed was due to the tension of the moment. "I should go to bed. I am exhausted from a long day, and I have a stomach…" she said.

Nasra agreed, "Yes, you had a long day. When you wake up in the morning, everything will be new again." Wanjiru did not pay much attention, but was only feeling the stomach cramping.

She left the room and rushed to the toilet where she thought she was going to vomit, but only had drive heaves that cramped her stomach. She urinated, washed her face and hands and went to her bedroom, and closed the door behind her. As she had learned, she slept naked to make it easier for Hussein's attentions. And soon, despite the stomach cramping, she passed into dreamland.

She dreamed she was back in her Lodi's bed with him positioning himself above her, then suddenly she awoke to Hussein above her in the dark, but with the light from the hallway streaming through the crack in the door. "Thank you," he said simply as he mounted her. Her stomach rumbled and the room began spinning as he pleasured himself, but quickly finished. He left, shutting the door and leaving her in the darkness. She rolled over onto her side curling up with her knees close to her chin, and passed back into sleep.

Again she came back to consciousness with the light from the bulb above her bed burning her eyes, and Nasra muttering something about a miscarriage. Wareesha and Nathifa were holding her legs up, touching her breasts, while sitting on her arms. Something was being ejected from her vagina and Nasra was saying something about taking a deep breath. She bent her head upwards just in time to see Nasra plop a bloody wad of something into a mixing bowl. "It is very sad, but you will not have the burden of another son." Nasra was muttering, and Wanjiru's stomach was cramping in horrible pain. "And we will make sure you do not get another pregnancy while you are in Likoni. We will take you to the health center ourselves and get you a wire."

Through the fog of her pain she heard Hussein's voice, "What is this?"

Voice that was more dreamlike came back. "She had a miscarriage… it is very sad… but it happens."

"Very sad… I need to get to work. Wanjiru we will talk later…take the day off and rest." And Wanjiru assumed she was dreaming, since everything was so unreal. She felt someone washing her clean, removing towels from under her and covering her with a sheet and a blanket. Someone left the room, and she was aware of the cramping in her stomach and the room still spinning. Someone returned with some warm, sugary milk and helped her drink it. It tasted of medicine. She soon relaxed and the stomach cramping ceased. Sleep soon surrounded her and she was back with Lodi and Muturi, sipping tea on his front veranda. Muturi was a two-year old boy sitting on Lodi's lap giggling. She rested her cup of tea on her belly… another of Lodi's children. Again the light came on burning her eyes. She rolled over.

"Wanjiru, you need to get out of bed and move around." Nasra said and pulled the sheets off her naked body, the cold draft gave her a chill. "Please, we have some food for you, it is time to return to the living." Wanjiru actually felt quite fine. There was no cramping or dizziness. She stood up and found some clothes and was soon in the kitchen eating porridge, realizing that she had slept an entire day and night straight through.

~~~~

Kimani looked up and saw the jagged peaks of Mt Kenya break out of the fog, realizing that at fourteen thousand feet, the fog was actually clouds. He looked back and saw his delicate *mzungu* friend, Lodi, gasping for air and in slow motion lifting a foot for one more step over a rock. He looked at his struggling white boy with nothing but affection, and would do anything for him. He wanted to climb Mt Kenya and there he was, totally out of shape but determined to make it or die.

Kimani thought his white boy must be the luckiest around, since they were able to hitch rides from his father's farm thirty miles away and up to the ten thousand foot level of Mt Kenya, then struggle up in thin air to the fourteen thousand foot level. Lodi was gasping for air, taking five hours to climb four thousand feet. Kimani had hoped that he would give up and turn around, since he looked as if he would die.

"My God, that is beautiful!" came a voice from behind him. He turned around and saw his friend collapse onto a thick growth of vegetation, and at the same time Kimani saw spots in his field of vision and everything going black.

He dreamed of being back at Njoro, recalling the time he dropped down from Molo just to see his white boy Lodi. He missed him horribly and could not wait to see him. But the front door was locked and he could not see him. In his dream he saw one of Lodi's girlfriends walk naked across the living room towards the kitchen, so he went around to the kitchen door. In the dream, Virginia opened the door and let him in. He followed the naked woman back to Lodi's bedroom, and Lodi was naked on the bed waiting very much aroused. Virginia said to him, "I teach you to please him." However, instead of Virginia pleasing the white boy, Kimani had taken her place...

He awoke to Lodi shaking him, "You okay? I collapsed from exhaustion, but didn't think you would!"

"I think the air is too thin for us. We need to walk slower. I had the strangest dream."

"Slower? We came less than a mile up in five hours. Look, the clouds are clearing. The peaks are beautiful." He said and Kimani turned to see the sight he had seen before when he worked as a porter carrying supplies up the mountain for tourists. "Hey, I grew up in Illinois and didn't see a real mountain until I was fourteen. See that sign, it says we are now about as high as any mountain in 48 states, and we still have over three thousand feet to go to get to the top.

"Bwana, we are not going to the top are we?"

"It would kill me, I am half dead already. We need to find a warm place between boulders to put the sleeping bag for the night. What was the dream?" Lodi said, and Kimani thought that his white boy was indeed insane to sleep outside on Mt Kenya in a sleeping bag?

"I dreamed that Virginia was teaching me how to pleasure you."

"How?"

"Mouth, but I am suddenly her and you are in my mouth." Kimani said and his friend began laughing so loud it echoed off the hills.

"Did I enjoy it? Did I taste good?" he laughed.

"Uhh, yes." Kimani chuckled. "And I made a mess in my briefs."

"Just now? It'll dry up. I think the shrinks call that homoerotic dreams, when a man has a male friend and is curious about what it would be like to have sex with him. If we have to go a few more days without a girlfriend, I might ask you try what you learned from Virginia." He said laughing again so loud Kimani heard an echo.

They walked for another mile or so on a fairly level ground leading up to a canyon where the huge uplifted megaliths of Mt Kenya hovered overhead, and some cabins lined the hillsides and a colony of green tents were in the distance. The sun was going down very fast, with darkness closing in.

"How about here… I can't walk another step." Lodi said.

"Sleep on the moss?" Kimani wondered.

"Sure, we have heavy coats, a heavy sleeping bag. We can go back down in the morning. We have plenty of food and a bottle of sherry to warm us. It will be cool to see the Milky Way." Lodi said, and Kimani baffled himself as to why he was here. He was too exhausted to complain, even though the temperature was dropping fast. They sat down in a thick layer of moss, watching the shadows fall on the weird plants, which always made Kimani think he was on a different planet. Then his pensive friend stated, "I keep thinking of Wanjiru."

97

"Wambui's daughter?" Kimani tried to deflect, knowing where this was heading.

"No, my sweetie, you know Wanjiri Tatton. I must be in love with her, since she keeps appearing in my thoughts. I still can't believe that baby they showed me was really hers. Her kid should look at least one-quarter white."

"She is half-caste, so that would happen, that is true." Kimani said feeling the cold cutting through his hair, but not yet willing to pull up his hood, and too tired to lie to him anymore.

"Muwera said he overheard Wambui telling Wanjiru's secret."

"Muwera? Him? Oh, the one who wants you to do him."

"Apparently he tried when I was drunk, according to Wambui." He said and Kimani thought that a good gossip could not stop at Wambui. He continued, "She said you helped."

"Bwana, Muwera was so pitiful, and you were so drunk."

"It took me a few days to recall, but I think you convinced me Virginia wanted me. It was you who licked and sucked on me."

"Yes, and you got very aroused. I convinced you that Virginia wanted to do you. It was funny seeing Muwera wearing a scarf like Virginia does, getting on you. But you went limp, so I did Muwera like he…" he was saying as a shout came from one of the cabins.

"Hey, you fellows," came an Englishman's call, "Too cold to sleep outside, there is one stall left in here. Spend the night inside." Again, Lodi was the luckiest man in the world to get to sleep in a cabin and not make a reservation! Lodi stood up and walked towards the Englishman, waving at Kimani to follow, and introduced himself and where he was from, as if his name would get him anything, which it usually did. Kimani thought it was interesting to see the look on white people's faces when his friend Lodi would introduce himself and give his name. What was the magic? He would need to ask him someday.

Inside the cabin were some serious mountain climbers getting ready for bed. The Englishman offered them a lower foam pad just large enough for two people to keep each other warm for the night. They found a place to sit and in the light of a flashlight, Lodi took out some dried beef, a package of crackers and the bottle of sherry, and offered the others some. They all refused, saying they ate already, so Kimani and Lodi had their Christmas Eve feast, while the climbers organized their gear and settled in for the night.

"We are getting up about four to start the final ascent," announced the friendly Englishman. Kimani could barely understand for all the noise the other climbers were making, but thought he added, "It was nice meeting you and your friend. Merry Christmas to you." As the climbers one by one got into their sleeping bags fully dressed, one was wearing only his briefs to Kimani's surprise. The fellow took off his socks and mentioned sleeping with his socks to keep them warm. Kimani thought he would never understand the Brits and looked at his friend rolling out the huge sleeping bag onto the foam padding on the wooden floor of the cabin.

"Pull your hood over your head, I think it will be cold tonight," Lodi warned. "We can keep each other warm, but it has its limits. You get in first and I will zipper up." He whispered and Kimani got into the sleeping bag, followed by his huge friend, who pulled the bag over them and pulled up the zipper locking him in. The Brit turned off the flashlight, and several climbers were already snoring. It was pitch black darkness. While there was at least six layers of clothes between them, his dream, after passing out on the mountain, worried him, since it seemed to tell him of his erotic desire for his white boy.

He was freezing on that side of the sleeping bag so he rolled in closer to his friend hoping for warmth. The giant friend pulled him in close with a gorilla hug and he finally felt warm enough to fall asleep.

His dreams took him to his *mzungu* girlfriend Beth's house. In the darkness of her bedroom, she was working her magic with her lips, tongue and throat, and his manhood felt like it would explode in pleasure. He saw in his dream, her hair was short brown instead of long and black like Beth's in the dark. In his dreams he felt his legs being pushed up and something pleasantly entering him. He saw his white boy above him and Kimani was feeling how it must feel to be his girlfriend being so sweetly sexed - with Lodi saying, "Wanjiru, I love you." Kimani awoke with a start, hearing the cabin door close and the climbers talking outside the cabin, and walking away into the early dawn.

The early dawn light was coming in through cracks in the door and walls, enough to see his white boy barely breathing, laying on his back, while Kimani clung tightly to him for warmth. These *mzungu* were bred for the cold, he thought. It must be minus five C! Happily pressed against his white boy's thigh, his right hand was under his friend's thick thermal jacket. He moved the hand down to see if his friend was aroused also, and he was as well. Kimani was freezing, sliding his head down deeper into the warmth of the sleeping blanket. He explored some more and slid his hand to open his white boy's jeans and found what he was looking for. Overpowered with desire, he had to taste it again. Speaking in his sleep, his white boy said, "Njiru, that feels so nice."

It was later, walking down the mountain on a glorious morning. The thermos bottle full of snow and ice banged against his hip as he walked. His mother will enjoy the ice from Mt. Kenya. It struck Kimani that his white boy now acted as if nothing had happened. As if it were not much different than sharing a shot of gin with a friend, he thought. From fourteen thousand feet up, with perfectly clear skies, Kimani thought he could see the whole world and all of its truths. He looked back at his white boy, who was taking photographs with his SLR clicking away, and asking, "Was that enough breakfast for you?" He was thirty miles from home, and it will be a long, dusty walk if they cannot beg a ride.

Kimani replied, "No, I will want some more later."

Chapter 10, Letter from Home

Wanjiru was waiting in the sultry sea breeze outside the hotel for about an hour, when her cousin Wajiko finally showed up. She was looking her usual beautiful self, and said in a hushed tone, "Wanjiru, sorry for being so late, I was doing a couple of German boys." Wanjiru giggled and shook her cousin's hand. "I have a letter for you from home - thick like a long letter." She looked around inside her bag and pulled out a crumpled envelope. "So, when do you want to help me with the tourists? I get a lot of these boys wanting two girls or two boys wanting one each. Does the wire stop hurting yet?"

"Oh, the last was two days. The nurse checked it. Said my man might feel the string sometimes. Oh it hurt so bad for two days. Like giving birth. She said I could still get a pregnancy, but the wire would stop the baby from growing."

"You can still get disease, so Durexi - unless they want to pay extra." Wajiko laughed. They were walking towards the beach and found a fallen tree, and sat down on the log. The waves were breaking about a hundred yards out, and the roar made talking difficult. Wanjiru tore open the envelope, took out three sheets of paper and recognized her sister Warimu's handwriting. It was a mixture of English, Swahili and Kikuyu. She read it to her cousin.

Wanjiru, Muturi is doing very well. He is standing up by himself but not walking. We are having fun with him. He makes us laugh. Mama took him to the health center and the nurse said he is healthy. The nurse taught her how to boil his bottle and nipple to kill germs so he does not get the zum zum. We got the money you sent at the post office. We bought more diapers and clothes. We buy the BHT milk for him so there are no germs. He is eating some ugali and soft beef. Mwangi down the road asked about you. He said he misses you. He has a car repair shop now in bondeni. He bought Makomeki's motorcycle to fix. He says come back and he will marry you. Pay mama good bride price. Stop laughing. I know you are laughing.

You asked how Lodi is doing. He went with Kimani to climb Mt Kenya to find some snow for

Christmas. Crazy? Kimani is still doing Muthoni but no
pregnancy yet. He say he is doing Miss Beth now, too.
When I thought Lodi left for Embu, I went to Lodi's house
to see Wambui. Virginia and that boy Muwera was there
too. We all laugh at Muwera. He is in love with Lodi and
comes around everyday. He asks Lodi to do him. Wambui
laugh and say she will ask Lodi to do Muwera. I was
surprised because Lodi came in and asked why all the
laughing. Then Wambui say that there are four people
here. All want Lodi to do them, but only one not yet.
Kimani was laughing and walked Muwera into the other
room. He said he would take care of him. Wambui said she
wanted Lodi and left. He went to Embu with Kimani and
will return after Christmas.   I have no more paper.
Send money when you can. With God, Warimu.

"She writes an exciting letter. So this Lodi has some sweet
sperms?" she laughed.

"Sweet enough." Wanjiru said, feeling very excited by the
letter, thinking no one has done her since the miscarriage and the
wire was inserted. The more she thought about it though, she was
sure Nasra secretly fed her the dawa and that caused the baby to
come too early. Nasra had wrapped the birth product in a bloody
rag and threw it into the garbage bin. No *nusu* African baby
allowed. "Why clean house, take care of the children and let
Hussein do me for only twenty shillings a month?" she asked out
loud.

"The German boys asked me to come back later and bring
a friend." Wajiko finally spoke after staring at the crashing waves
for a few minutes. "If you tell them you have the wire - they call it
aiyudii - they pay extra to do without Durexi."

"How much?" she asked.

"A thousand shillings."

"I could send Muturi to school for a year for that." she
said. "Maybe I could do more now. Muturi may not have a father
or uncle to care if he is schooled."

"You could rent a place or get a job with me at the hotel.
They have workers quarters. They charge 50 a month, food is
cheap. You could make a lot of money doing the tourists. I will
teach you to do things they like. You may get a disease but the
health center will give you a jab or a pill and cure it. You never ask

102

someone. It may be police. Always wait for them to ask you. Never do anything before you see money appear on a table. Do not take the money until after." They were quiet watching the ocean roll out and roar back. "Go with me to talk with the German boys." And they both stood up, rubbing their numb rumps, and Wanjiru happily followed Wajiko.

Chapter 11, Coastal Vacation

Kimani looked out the window of the Nairobi-Mombasa train. He and his two teacher friends had a sleeper. Kimani was on a well-deserved school break from teaching primary school girls in Molo, sitting watching the scenery go by while his two, *mzungu* teacher friends were asleep. These two kept him laughing and were always traveling with him. He spent Christmas on Mt Kenya looking for snow and ice. He brought a thermos bottle full of snow back to show his mother. She was impressed how cold it was.

"Lodi," as everyone in Njoro called him, was still asleep on the bench across from him, while his friend Beth was asleep on his bench with her head in his lap. He introduced himself to Lodi a few years back, when someone told him there was an American at the school. He had gone to a Baptist High School in Embu. Beth taught in Nakuru for less than a year, and Kimani met her through Lodi once when he went shopping in Nakuru and they stopped by Beth's place. They were both from the same part of America, but Lodi said he did not find her attractive, at least not as attractive as Wanjiru – always Wanjiru. Beth told Kimani once that she liked Kenyan men better… which he thought meant she wanted Kimani.

He still remembers the day he went to Beth's place alone, a week after she had made her suggestion, and he found her with several of her students, whom she was tutoring. Beth sent the students packing so that she could be alone with Kimani. She was wearing a white blouse and pink shorts that made her paper white skin seem nearly transparent. She was shapely with small breasts and wide hips, and was taller than he was. She offered him a Tusker, which he accepted and sat down on her living room couch. The velvet couch was big enough to sleep a man comfortably, but she sat next to him as they sipped their beers. She drank half a pint, and set her bottle on the little table and began touching him, getting him excited. He recalls asking her if he needed to use a condom, and she said she takes pills, and soon they were naked and copulating on the couch – *tamu sana*!

He never understood why Lodi did not want the give try her. It was something about changing the meaning of a relationship between a male and a female, which he did not understand. It must

104

be an American thing or he has another reason. He looked down at her sleeping on his lap in the train sleeper. The pillow had fallen on the floor and her head was moving back and forth to the rhythm of the train, with her nose against his belt buckle, getting him excited. He was not aware that Lodi was awake, sitting up and watching them. Kimani adjusted things in his jeans because of the motion of Beth's head.

He laughed, "Kimani, should I leave you two alone for a while?" The laughter woke her up and she sleepily opened her eyes realizing where she was. Lodi should be used to Beth touching Kimani so often, since she does it all the time. She looked up, moved her head and seeing the bulge in his pants, and gave it a stroke, but got up and sat on the bench looking at Lodi, who asked, "Do you need to use the *choo*? Might be a line, or you could wait until we get into the station, but then it would be really filthy." She got up and slid open the door and disappeared. "We should try to get rooms first."

"Rooms? We can all share one room." He said thinking how nice it would be to have his two friends in bed with him.

"You two need to be alone. I was thinking at Sea Breezes in Likoni."

Kimani was suspicious, knowing from Muthoni that is where Wanjiru is living. "Why Likoni? You are not looking for Wanjiru are you?"

"Oh, that is where we got Swahili training. It is just a place I know. It is close to the beach. We can spend a couple of nights there and then go on up to Lamu on the bus."

"We could get one room and save money." Kimani offered again.

"Beth is rich, let her pay for you. After all you provide her with stud services… right?"

"Stud services?" Kimani asked wondering if that is an insult. "I never heard of that."

"Oh, if you have a prize bull and other farmers want the bull to inseminate their cows, they pay you for stud services." Lodi said and Kimani thought that men do not get paid to do women, in Kenya anyway, though he heard of dowry that some fathers give a man to take his daughter. Changing the subject he asked, "How much longer before we arrive?" Kimani looked at his watch and thought we should be there already, and looked out the window

105

and by luck saw a sign on the road running parallel to the railroad track.

"I guess about half an hour." He sat awhile, watching Lodi studying a map. "You are looking for what?"

"How to get to the Likoni ferry. Haile Selassie to Digo Road which turns into Nyerere Avenue I guess." He looked up. "We should take a bus, since Beth hates hiking."

~~~~~

The three teachers were filing off the ferry with a large crowd of people heading up the Likoni road. Lodi was digging some paper out of his backpack, mouthing some frustration. Beth was obliviously doing her people watching and admiring the little, brown babies strapped to their mothers' backs. Kimani asked, "What are you looking for?"

Lodi said, "I found it. It is where Wanjiru is working."

Kimani's stomach did a flip, "Why are you looking for Wanjiru? Which Wanjiru?" he asked, and Beth was acting confused, but just followed them up the road. Lodi rolled his eyes as if he did not want to explain. Kimani was aware that Lodi knew Kimani kept secrets from him. It was for his own good. "How did you find out?"

"It is just up here. Mrs. Keogh asked Esther for the address to deliver a gift to the newborn. Esther fell for it! Well actually, I will deliver a nice gift."

"Why do you care about Wanjiru and her baby? You saw her baby at Njoro." Kimani tried to keep up with Lodi's long stride.

"You know, I did not believe it. That baby was all African, and Wanjiru is half-English. They must think I am a complete idiot to try a switch." Lodi laughed, which confused Kimani even more. Why is it so funny? He wondered. Lodi stopped and looked at the address and the map, "This way." They headed up a narrow road. Lodi stopped a man and asked him something in Swahili about a man named Hussein something, and the man pointed at a house. Lodi checked the address again and shook hands with the man and gave him a shilling.

The three walked up to the small, adobe house and Lodi knocked on the door. They waited and he knocked again. An old woman opened the door and said something in Arabic, then again in Swahili, "What is it?"

106

Lodi said in Swahili, "Does Wanjiru Wa Esther live at this house?"

The woman said in formal Swahili, "Sorry, no longer, she works at the hotel and lives there now." The woman looked into Lodi's eyes and nodded in understanding. "Are you from Njoro?"

"Yes, I and Kimani here are friends of Wanjiru. We know her sisters Muthoni and Warimu, and her mother Esther." Lodi said in his best Swahili. "I bring a gift for her baby." He said and the woman frowned, and a tear came to her eye.

"Oh, you did not know she lost the baby. It came early and died." She said, and Lodi looked very perplexed.

"The baby died?" he looked horrified.

"Yes, it came early." She said in proper Swahili, and Kimani thought the old lady was referring to her recent pregnancy not to Lodi's baby, which was the baby that was being kept a secret from him. If he thought the baby were dead all the better.

"Very sorry. Very sad. Thank you. We are staying at the hotel, perhaps I will see her there." He said and shook the old woman's hand. Reached into a side pocket and pulled out some wrapped candies. "Some sweets for the children." The old lady smiled and took the candies. The door closed and they turned to head back down the road.

~~~~~~~

The three teachers checked in at the front desk. Kimani tried to get one room, but both Beth and Lodi said two small rooms would be better. Kimani and Beth got "Shamba Majani" and Lodi got a single "Makanda" and said he was happy. The clerk said that the cleaning girl would show them the way.

"Jambo, I am Wajiko, I will show you your rooms." She said and Kimani thought he heard a Kikuyo accent, and wondered.

"You work here long?" he asked in Embu Kikuyu.

She laughed, and replied in a Kikuyu accent he could not place, "Several years. You from Embu?" she asked as they walked along the path. Kimani thought she probably thought he was chatting her up, but he had his bedmate already.

"Yes, but I teach in Molo, near Nakuru." He said.

"Is that near Njoro?" she asked.

"Yes, my friend teaches there. My girlfriend here," he motioned towards Beth, "teaches at Nakuru." Kimani laughed to himself seeing her reaction to his having a white girlfriend. They arrived at the double and Wajiko unlocked the door and let them in.

"If you need anything call the front desk," she said and handed them the key. "Your Njoro teacher friend is right next door." She added in English. Kimani and Beth entered their room and unloaded their backpacks. Through the bushes that shielded the screened windows, Kimani heard Wajiko talking to Lodi.

He could barely hear, "I have cousins in Njoro... they like it a lot." and that was all he could hear. Beth was undressing and pulling back the covers of the full size bed. He knew what she wanted.

~~~~~~~~

Kimani and Beth were glowing as they left their room to go knock on "Makanda" to find out what he was up to. After Beth knocked once, Kimani pushed the hedge back and peeked through the crack in the curtained, screened window. Lodi was on top of an African girl, who looked like Wajiko, sucking on her nipple. Beth knocked again, and Lodi rolled off the bed and covered the girl with a sheet, and waved at Kimani looking through the window. Kimani could not resist watching, seeing him wrap a towel around his waist.

The door opened and he said, "Beth, would you believe Wajiko here knows Doug." Kimani and Beth walked in and Kimani was looking at Wajiko who was only covered to her waist. She had her hands behind her head showing off her beautiful breasts.

Beth said, "She is beautiful. It did not take long for you to get to know her."

"You have to know how to tip." Lodi laughed, and Kimani thought that it meant that money exchanged hands. He looked around and there were two five-pound notes on the side table.

Kimani asked her in Kikuyu, "I heard you say you have cousins in Njoro. Maybe someone I know?"

"My cousin Wanjiru works here, she is from Njoro." Wajiko said, and Kimani was hoping Lodi did not understand, but the Kikuyu sounded very much like Swahili.

"Wanjiru from Njoro?" Lodi said in Swahili.

Then Kimani said quickly, "No, Lodi, she did not say that."

Wajiko then said, "You are Lodi from Njoro? But that is not what you said your name is."

Lodi laughed, "That is the way folks in Njoro pronounce my name. R's come out as L's, and everything ends with a vowel." And Wajiku laughed and her breasts quaked.

"I should let Wanjiru know you are here. She will want to see you." She said getting out of bed and walked naked over to her clothes on the chair. Kimani's annoyance turned to a feeling of electricity in his groin and he was aroused at the sight of the beautiful woman showing off her body. She first slipped the money into her bag, and then found her bra.

"The woman at Hussein's house said her baby is dead. It is not here?" Kimani said, hoping the old woman was referring to Lodi's kid.

"Which baby? Muturi is in Njoro, and she lost her pregnancy. That baby is dead. It was her employer's son. After it died she came to work here."

"Did you ever see Muturi?" Lodi asked.

"*Rafiki*, you do not want to know." Kimani insisted.

"Big boy, brown like Wanjiru. Blue eyes, yellow hair, big, very strong. But Wanjiru took him to Njoro, did you not see him there?"

"They showed me a black baby with black eyes. Looked like a girl actually."

"Wanjiru afraid you take the baby to America." She said as she finished dressing.

"America? Hmmm, how could I *ever* do that?"

"I do not know. Oh, she said she was at the beach. You want to go with me?" Kimani thought this would not go well.

"Beth, let's go get a beer."

Chapter 12, Reunion

Wanjiru changed the station on the little radio a grateful tourist had given her. The waves were breaking far out, and she adjusted the earphones so she could hear the African music pounding away inside her head. The breeze off the ocean was delightful. She thought about the British tourist boy who had her for the whole night and gave her a thousand and the radio. The money is safe in Standard Bank and converted to certificates worth nearly forty British pounds. The young man did her about five times like an air hammer, and all the while giving her sweet compliments, especially about her breasts. She was very relaxed listening to the music when off in the distance, coming up the sand was Wajiko with a white man in swimming trunks.

At first, she thought she was bringing a customer, then as they got closer it looked like a heavier version of her Lodi. As the two drew nearer she realized it was her son's father, and was wondering if she should run away or stay and see what will happen. She was too stunned to move, and as they stood near, she was dazed like a mouse surrounded by cats. "Wanjiru! Can you hear me?" her cousin was saying and she realized the music was loud in her ears, and she shut it off and stood up. Lodi wrapped his arms around her and give her a hug that took her breath away. "Do you not know the father of your son! Why do you act so strange?" Wajiko said in Kikuyu. Lodi backed off and looked at her.

"You are even more beautiful than I recall." He added and Wanjiru moved in and gave him another hug, dropping her radio in the sand. She had the nervousness that comes when her dreams become reality – not sure which is which. She was dazed.

Wajiko added in Kikuyu, "Wanjiru, I did not realize until this morning that he was your Lodi. I may have all his *manii*." She said as they started walking back to the hotel, but Wanjiru was not listening. Lodi had picked up the radio and put it into Wanjiru's bag. The three walked back to the hotel with Lodi in the middle with a woman in each arm. As they arrived back at Makanda, Kimani and Beth were coming back, with Beth stroking Kimani as she often did. They waved and went on into their room, leaving

110

Lodi with the two women. Soon they were in the room and Lodi found an afternoon tea tray on the small table, and had forgotten that he had ordered it when they checked in. It was a pot of creamed coffee, small cakes, sliced fruit and a bowl of sugar. He offered it to the women, looking around the room for some cups, which he found in the bathroom.

Wanjiru's haze was slowly lifting, and she was able to wonder what was happening. She sat down in one of the stuffed chairs, "Lodi, why did you come here? Were you looking for me?"

Lodi sat on the bed, sipped the coffee and said in English, "You may not know, but I think about you always, and wonder if your boy is my son... Wajiko seems to think it is." Wanjiru looked at the white man sitting on the bed wearing only a swim suit. His skin was so white except for his arms which were brown and his face that was nearly burnt red. His hair had bleached out in the sun, so it had yellow streaks among brown, long hair. His nose was burnt so much, the skin was pealing. He had gained weight from what she remembered.

"If you believe the boy is yours, you will take him away from us to America." She worried aloud.

"I would gladly marry you and take you both to America." He said simply, and her heart fell to the floor... go to America? She thought, who do I know there, and what do I know to live there?

"I could never leave here. Kimani told me that there is a season like being on top of Mt Kenya. I would turn to ice. No, I could never live there." Wanjiru said and both Lodi and Wajiko laughed aloud.

Wajiko said, "Millions of people live there just fine. Who will take care of Muturi... who cares for him besides us women and Lodi... well, Lodi would love him if you let him ever see him." Then she added in Kikuyu, "You must tell him what you told me. It is his boy, and will make sure he does well." Wanjiru looked at the *mzungu* as if he would understand what Wajiko had said.

Then as if from nowhere, it came to Wanjiru, "Mwangi in Njoro, the car repair fellow wants to marry me. It will be good, since I must stay in Kenya and you will not be allowed to live in Kenya." She saw the look of hurt on his face, but he got up and walked over to his backpack. He took out a notepad and pen and began writing.

He said in Swahili as if to be very clear. "You are right, your government does not like white people for citizens. I understand. Also, everyone except Wajiko says that Muturi is not my son, I can do the math, and I am not stupid. Here is my full name and my parents' address in America. If you need anything for Muturi send me a letter and I will send some money to help. I know Mwangi, he bought my old motorcycle. He is a fine man, smart and very reliable." Wanjiru was relieved, he was giving up on the notion of marriage and taking Muturi. She looked at Wajiko, and she looked stunned.

"You give up?" she said to him. "Muturi is your boy, and you go back to American and not take him?" Wanjiru's stomach knotted. Why is she saying that?

"Wajiko, you sweet thing." Lodi laughed, "A man cannot steal a child from its mother. Muturi will have a good life. I am sure. He is living in a wonderful country with many people who love him." Wajiko was nodding and Wanjiru felt that she was convinced. Wanjiru took the paper from Lodi and looked at the handwriting. It was easy to read. The names of his parents she had never heard of, in a place she did not know. Would this be where he would take Muturi?

"That is it? I do not have to worry anymore?"

"Worry? Were you worried? Do not worry. Things will be good." He said, but it did not immediately say how her life would change. Would she need to be doing all the tourists to put money away for Muturi? He said he would send money to take care of Muturi. We will see. All men are liars.

Wajiko was sitting in the other chair, looking at him as he put away the notebook in the backpack, then she looked at Wanjiru and said in Kikuyu, "No worry. Do you want to do him?" Wajiko asked, and Wanjiru shrugged. As he turned towards the bed, Wajiko grabbed his swimsuit by the band and pulled him close.

"Hey," he said, "What's up?" and Wajiko pulled his swimsuit down and moved her head in close. Wanjiru could not see what she was doing, but the swimsuit slid down to his ankles, showing her his very white *matako*. Wajiko's shoulders went up and down and her hands stroked his *matako* gently. Wanjiru was getting excited and suddenly wanted him. She stood up and walked towards the bed removing her clothes as she went. She stood naked on the other side of the bed watching Wajiko's head move back and forth. She lay down on the bed and readied herself.

"*Lodi, mimi ninataka wewe.*" She said, saying she wanted him. It was more erotic for her to say it in Swahili. She was so excited that she felt she could not wait. Wajiko let him go. He stepped out of his swimsuit, walked over and bent down to her and gave her a kiss. Kissing her, he settled down onto her. They were soon connected, sending waves of pleasure throughout her body. He got up on his elbows and looked into her eyes. She looked into his deep blue eyes and felt his slow movement inside herself.

He whispered, "It feels so wonderful - do you have an aiyudii? It feels like one." At least that is what she thought he said, and through the fog of lust, she was able to nod in the affirmative. "Not only beautiful but intelligent." he added and bent his head down and licked her nipples as he thrust deeper and more vigorously.

Through the fog she could see Wajiko climbing onto the other side of the bed, and doing something. Then it hit, sending intense waves of pleasure throughout her body and she felt all her muscles tensing as if she had touched an exposed electrical wire. He stopped and she relaxed, and dozed briefly. She woke to the bed moving and Wajiko's leg rubbing against her hip. Wanjiru opened her eyes to see him connected to Wajiko. He lifted a hand and squeezed the nipple on her large brown breast. She let out a scream, went tense, shuddered and the motion suddenly stopped. Wanjiru stroked Lodi's shoulder and he looked at her then Wajiko. She looked at Wajiko who was pressing her eyes shut and was still shuddering a bit. He pushed himself up and moved over on top of her, to reconnect and gave her a kiss with his tongue playing with hers. As the thrusting continued, the electricity inceased, with muscles tensing all over. Wanjiru could feel his hot sweat pouring down onto her. She felt her womb shuddering, spasming, and felt hot fluid. Lodi suddenly cried in pain, and rolled off her. "God, your aiyudii!" He sat on the bed and she felt down there and pulled the string hanging out of her. Out came the piece of wire all bent, and no longer in a t-shape. "Sorry, I'm afraid I shot the whole thing into you, too." He walked into the bathroom holding his thing. She wondered what he meant, then realized he meant that she had no protection from a pregnancy.

113

"No, I think I got some this morning." Wajiko said. "Maybe we will get a pregnancy together." She laughed.

"Together? I thought you..."

"Only Durex. I was hoping a cute German boy would get me, but they always use Durex, or some German kind." She said as he came back holding his thing. "Did you get hurt? Her wire is bent. The nurse put it in wrong." She took it from Wanjiru and handed it to him. He held his thing as he examined the wire.

"No harm done." he said and pulled back the foreskin to show them a red nick on the pink skin. There was no bleeding. Wajiko took the opportunity to look closer, and leaned forward and gave it a kiss, and he laughed as his thing perked up. Wanjiru laughed and did the same, and he perked up more. Wajiko gave it a lick, as did her cousin. Wanjiru thought there was a fishy smell and salty favor but the fun was licking it to make it get larger and larger. They both petted his fur around his thing and soon he was fully aroused and connecting with Wanjiru, who immediately went into her pleasure-filled shuddering. She imagined that her womb was pulling in all his sperms.

~~~~~

Kimani snapped his jeans and looking at his girlfriend Beth asleep in bed, hoping she was too exhausted for more. Kimani wondered what his friend "Lodi" was up to so he quietly opened the door, stepped out, and quietly latched the door and walked next door. He heard a woman and a bed squeaking, so he pushed back the bushes and looked through the crack in the curtain. He had two women in bed with him, Wajiko and someone else. The three were relaxing on the bed with him in the middle with his arms around the two women. They were petting his hairy belly. He then realized the other woman was Wanjiru from Njoro. They all looked exhausted. Kimani knocked at the door.

"Come in, it's not locked." He heard his friend say, and he walked on in. A sheet was pulled halfway up his pubic hair, and he tried to ignore it. The women covered themselves and had their hands on his chest. "What's up doc?" he smiled his big smile. "Beth exhaust you yet? Is your seminal vesical empty yet?" Kimani shut the door and turned the key, and walked over to the end of the bed.

Kimani laughed, "She turned me inside out. Wanjiru, good to see you. Did you work things out?" He asked, knowing from her sisters that a fellow named Mwangi was wanting to marry her, but here she is in bed with him.

Wanjiru said, "Yes, we worked it out." she said then shifted to Kikuyu, "Lodi will not take Muturi to America with him." She relaxed and stroked the belly some more and Kimani could see her breast clearly, which gave him a tingle.

"Can you afford to raise him? You have money?" Kimani wondered aloud. Wajiko was looking at him critically as if to ask who are you to ask? She also stroked his belly but sent her hand under the sheet to play. Kimani wondered at the woman for being so open.

"Oh, yes," Wanjiru said in Kikuyu, "He said if ever Muturi needs anything he will help." Kimani then remembered other women saying the same thing about their children and how "Lodi would help" them, too. The list gets longer in the telling. As she spoke her cousin was playing with his friend's thing, pushing the sheet down. She must know what she is doing, since he appeared to enjoy it and did not object to Kimani watching.

Kimani also was getting aroused watching the show, and had to adjust things in his jeans. Wajiko moved her head down and pushed the sheet down to show how she was using her mouth to pleasure him. He stroked her back as she did it. Kimani was hypnotized by the show, but Wanjiru continued, "I will probably go back to Njoro. You know Mwangi the motor repair fellow in Bondeni?" she said. He could not help but stare at Wajiko with his thing going back and forth through her thick lips, and the erotic way she used her tongue. Kimani had a weird desire to have a taste, but tried to concentrate on what Wanjiru was saying.

She continued, "Mwangi asked my mother to marry me. He will pay a good bride price and adopt any children I have," she said, but he was watching how Wajiko did him, while he was off in some pleasure place not paying attention to Kimani and Wanjiru. Lodi was fully aroused, so Wajiko moved and mounted him and Wanjiru had to move to continue chatting with Kimani. His friend was moaning in delight as Wajiko moved up and down on him. Wanjiru got off the bed and grabbed a towel, wrapped herself with it and continued. "Lodi has to return to America in four months right? Oh, I see you are very excited." She said and Kimani knew she was right, since he was watching his friend being serviced so nicely. Wajiko moaned and collapsed, rolling off him onto her back on the bed beside him. "My turn." Wanjiru said and climbed onto the bed and mounted the father of her son. Kimani watched as the towel fell off Wanjiru as she repeated what Wajiko had done, sending Lodi back into that pleasure place. Wajiko was spread out on the bed next to them, dozing, her legs spread wide invitingly.

He could not take it anymore, and rushed back to his room and Beth.

~~~~

The mop slid across the floor leaving a wet path as she heard, "Wanjiru! Lodi is heading to Lamu. We should say *kwa heri*." It was Wajiko, and Wanjiru put the mop back into the pail of water. Heading out of the empty hotel room, she locked the door and she followed her cousin to the front of the hotel to see the tall, white man with his backpack standing next to the white woman and the Kikuyu man. They all shook hands, then Lodi gave her a big hug.

"Are you coming back to Njoro before I leave for good?" He asked.

"Yes, I will come and marry Mwangi. He is a good man and my people will approve," she said implying that her people would not approve of her marrying a *mzungu*.

"Yes, my people in America would approve if I married a white girl." he said with a laugh. "We are going up to see Lamu. Lots of Arabs there. Maybe one will want to marry Beth." He said and Beth laughed.

Wajiko pulled him aside and Wanjiru heard her say to Lodi in Swahili, "You should do Beth again. I can tell she wants you."

"*Hapana*, she is like a sister to me, and very annoying. She wants to marry me, you know." They both laughed. "Maybe in America, if I cannot find someone better, maybe I will marry her."

"She looks pregnant. You the father?"

"She is pregnant? Not by me. Probably Kimani."

Wajiko and Wanjiru gave the three each a hug and watched them walk down the road towards the ferry.

Chapter 13, First Steps

Wambui unlocked the back door and entered the kitchen that had been empty of Lodi for the last ten days. Some things had moved around, so he must be back. She dropped her bag and locked the back door. She rushed into his bedroom to find him dead asleep, with his clothes thrown on the floor and his backpack emptied in the corner, making a stinky pile. She sat down on the edge of the bed looking at him lying on his side snoring lightly, which soon stopped. She pulled the curtain open to let in the morning light. His camera was sitting on the dresser, and she picked it up, pointing it at him. An eye popped open. He rolled onto his back. He was not wearing a t-shirt. "*Jambo! Habari gani?*" he said. He pushed the sheet and blanket down exposing his white chest. He put his arms behind his head as she snapped a picture. He laughed, and she doubted the picture would turn out.

"I miss you." Wambui tried to say in English, then back to Swahili, "I missed you very much." She said and studied his face.

"I had a good trip, but it is nice seeing you again."

"Did you make it to Lamu?"

"Yes, it is an old city full of Arabs. Very nice people. Beth and Kimani were fun to travel with."

"Did you do Beth. She wants you very badly. She comes here many times and you do not do her."

"In Lamu we had to share a room, and I woke up with her on top of me. She did me." he said and Wambui laughed. "But after Kimani, maybe I was not as sweet."

"Did she get your sperms?"

"Yes, morning sperm, I dreamed of you, but when I saw it was her doing me I lost interest. She took what she wanted." He said, and Wambui knew he would dream of Wanjiru, not her.

"You are a very bad man. Men must give it to women who want it." Wambui said seriously, she was thinking this *mzungu* humiliates so many. So many come wanting him and he turns them away. This talk was making her want him now, but he may refuse then humiliate her too. She pulled the covers down and he had his morning arousal was sticking out of the top of his briefs. She stood

117

up and pulled her dress over her head, removed her bra and underwear and lay down next to him. He could not resist the invitation.

~~~~

Warimu looked at her half-naked nephew and laughed. Muturi pulled himself off the concrete, stood up, and gave a big laugh. She thought that he would take off walking any day now. He was huge for his age, and his blue eyes, light brown skin and yellow, curly hair made most around here think she was caring for a *mzungu* child. He waved at his aunt and muttered "*Jambo*" over and over.

She was sitting on a blanket in the courtyard watching Muturi and Wambui's two-year-old girl Ruthy. She sipped her hot tea, and wondered if he really was saying "*Jambo*" or just jibberish. They heard a cow mooing on the other side of the courtyard wall in the pasture. Ruthy looked up and in English said "Cow?" and Warimu laughed, knowing that Wambui's *mzungu* was teaching the little girl some English. Wambui's mother was horrified, since Wambui's father had tried his best to exterminate English during the Maumau. Wambui was not allowed to take Ruthy to the *mzungu's* house if he was going to teach her English. Now she is watching Ruthy as Wambui worked, and Wambui's mother was at market.

The two children wore t-shirts but no pants, since it was easier to wipe a puddle on concrete than to change diapers. Muturi laughed again and took off walking towards his girlfriend Ruthy. Ruthy saw him coming and started laughing, too. He reached out trying to grab her, but she ran away and Muturi ran faster and collapsed into Warimu's lap. He fell into place as if he was going to nurse at her breast and began patting the bare flesh on her chest above her blouse. She had a carton of BHT milk for the kids. He was pulling at her clothes demanding food, and she laughed from the tickling. She looked around and she was alone with the two children.

Ruthy began singing in English, "I'm a soldier in the aaammeee." And began marching around. Muturi was pulling at her blouse, so she unbuttoned it. She had no bra, so the boy began searching around for the nipple, as if all women could feed him. She undid several more buttons, and Muturi soon found a nipple and began sucking as if he were starving. She took the carton of milk, bit a small hole, and sprinkled milk onto her nipple next to the boy's mouth. He was sucking the milk in. He looked into her eyes as if she were a wonderful person. As he sucked she felt shooting pleasure down to what she thought was her womb, and she drifted off into delight. She squeezed drops of milk at the corner of his mouth and he continued to suck giving her intense pleasure. Muturi you will be some lover, she thought.

Ruthy came over and wanted to nurse also, but her whining only interrupted the delightful sensations. Wambui still was breast-feeding the girl a few times a day. Muturi looked up and saw his girlfriend looking at him, and was suddenly done and wiggled out. Ruthy quickly took his place expecting the same treatment.

"Monkey!" Warimu said in Kikuyu to the girl and handed her the carton to help herself. She buttoned her blouse and watched Muturi trying to stand up without help, but he kept falling onto his naked *matako*. Ruthy walked around sucking on the carton.

As Muturi was trying again to get up, someone was unlatching the gate to the courtyard. He stood up and watched who came through the gate. He should know who it was, but he just looked trying to place the face. She put down her bag, and Muturi just stared, and Warimu laughed, "Wanjiru! You came back!" Muturi looked at his aunt, then back at the strange woman. She walked closer then squatted several yards from him. He looked at her, then his aunt, then Ruthy.

"Muturi, my boy, I missed you so much." Wanjiru said, and Muturi's face lighted up and he ran to his mother.

To her surprise he said, "*Jambo*." She enveloped him in her arms and stood up with him.

"Oh, you are so heavy." The boy acted as if he knew whom it was and held her tightly. Wanjiru walked over to her sister and sat down next to her on the blanket. "Muturi, can you eat? I am ready to burst." She said undoing buttons to get out a breast.

"I thought you would dry up." Warimu said.

"I have been wet nursing some babies while their mothers work. Two times a day, but the trip from Mombasa takes forever. I even borrowed a baby on the train to Nairobi." Muturi latched onto her nipple and started sucking greedily the syrupy sweet mother's milk. Immediately Wanjiru relaxed and listened to her sister bring her up to date on all the local gossip. Ruthy was sitting in Warimu's lap as she went on with the news.

"Are you living here now?"

"No, I am still at the straw hut near the school. I am still hoping one of the Kikuyu boys will give me a pregnancy."

"You still try? If any baby would do, try Lodi again. He will give you a pregnancy if you ask him."

"No, I want Kikuyu. Wambui say he tried to give Beatrice one."

"I heard her baby is his."

"Her? Oh, you mean Mama's *mzungu's* wife. That might be, but Mama's *mzungu* and Wambui's *mzungu* look the same. No I mean old Beatrice Wachiru."

"Just as well spill his sperm in sand. Every man has tried with her." She looked down at the nursing boy. She switched over to the other side, and he continued. The boy looked up and she realized he had the same color blue eyes as Lodi, and probably her own father's eyes.

"Wambui tells me that he saw you in Mombasa. She say he wants to marry you and take you and Muturi to America."

"We talked. He said he will help, but leave us here. I want to marry Mwangi and live here."

"Mwangi? Yes, that is a good choice. He promised Mama some good money for you even though you are not a virgin."

"Yes, he was always crazy in love with me and too shy to ask to do me. He thinks I am a holy angel or the like." They both laughed at the thought. "I am not a holy angel, but at least I am not *mzungu* who does anything that moves." And Warimu screamed in laughter, making Muturi turn and look at her. Warimu stroked his head and rocked Ruthy back and forth.

~~~~~~

Wanjiru had some news for her sisters, and Muturi was walking next to her on the path across the pasture to her sisters straw house to see them. It was was a crystal clear day, and the air was cool and dry very unlike the steamy days of Mombasa. The sun was hard on Muturi's hair, bleaching it more yellow the more he was outside. So, she tried to use an umbrella for the sun, but she had too much to carry.

As they approached the rear entrance of the school, several cows were eating the grass, and a small boy in ragged clothes with a long stick was keeping them away from some weeds. She thought the weeds would spoil the cows' milk. Muturi pointed as his mother towed him along, "cow" he said in English. God! She thought, Ruthy is teaching him English. Better to learn it now. As she approached the straw house, she saw an older student leave the front door and turn towards the school. She thought he had a very satisfied look on his face. She began to enter through the curtain and saw a young man's *matako* going up and down, obviously doing one of her sisters, so she backed out to wait.

"Wanjiru!" she heard her name and turned to see her sister Muthoni waiting by the hedge. She took Muturi over and Muthoni picked him up for a hug. "Warimu should be done soon." And as if on orders, another older student exited the hut and headed towards the school in a hurry. The bell was ringing at the school telling the students to head for the next class. The two women and the toddler went into the dark hut and found places to sit. Muturi found an old, crushed soccer ball that he usually played with when he visited. He started kicking the flattened ball.

"I just went to the health center for Muturi. He is very healthy says the nurse. The same nurse delivered Muturi in Mombasa. She is here now again. Can you believe she dated Lodi a few years back?"

The two other women giggled, and Muthoni said "Oh, no! She is so black and a Kalanjin. Very holy holy."

"I saw Lodi talking with her the other day. But she is angry with him, now." Warimu said. "These *mzungu's* do..."

"Jambo!" Came a voice and in walked Muwera. "Sorry, I was coming by and heard you talking about the nurse Rebecca."

"Come in and tell us," Warimu said, ready for more gossip.

"Yes, she is still very mad at him for seeing other women. She gave him a box of hundreds of condoms and told him to use them on his whores."

"How do you know this?"

"I was in his kitchen when she came with the box. He said later that it was very funny. Rebecca was not good in bed. He said she needs a bigger man than he is." And the women all laughed.

Wanjiru was a bit disgusted with the gossip, and said, "Should you not be in class?"

"Teacher sick so we wander away." He looked at Muturi. "He has a nice thing."

"You leave Muturi alone!" Wanjiru demanded.

"Your boy is very cute." Muwera said and Wanjiru's stomach knotted remembering Wambui's gossip.

Again, the bell was ringing and Muwera said, "Lunch" and disappeared. The three women looked at each other then at Muturi who was rolling around on the ball.

"Also, I told Rebecca that I had missed my blood, and she asked me to urinate in a glass. She said I am pregnant again. She said that the aiyudii would keep the baby from growing. I told her that it came out the last time I did it. She wanted the details."

"So do I," said both sisters at the same time. Muthoni added, "When was that? Was that when he was in Mombasa doing you and our cousin?"

"Yes. When I decided to come back and marry Mwangi, I became holy holy again until Mwangi. Now I am pregnant."

"Mwangi will not care." Warimu said, and Muturi threw the flattened ball and it went through the curtain to the outside. "Mwangi just wants a family and a good wife. Kikuyu men all know their wives do every man in town, but if they raise a child, the child is theirs. Not like *mzungu* who think their sperm is magic." They watched Muturi run outside after the ball. Wanjiru leaned over and pulled back the curtain to keep watch on him.

"*Jambo*," Muturi said, and Wanjiru wondered who he said it to. She looked outside and her heart sank as she saw Lodi bend down to her son.

"*Jambo, sana.*" He said to Muturi, squatting down to his eye level and in his effort at Kikuyu, "Are you Muturi?" and he held out his hand to the boy. She saw the boy looking intently at the giant man, then shook hands with him as he loved to do with everyone. Wanjiru stayed back in the dark so he could not see her. The sun was so bright outside.

She heard a cow moo, and Muturi pointed and said, "Cow!"

"Smart boy!" He picked up the soccer ball and reshaped it and gave it to Muturi who was again staring at the giant in front of him. He stroked Muturi's yellow hair, then removed his glasses and wiped the tears out of his eyes. "Have a great life, young man." He stood up and disappeared towards Bondeni.

122

Muturi stood for a while then ran back into the hut with the ball. As the boy returned to wrestle with the crushed ball, there was a stony silence in the straw hut.

~~~~

Wanjiru walked up the cinder driveway as she often did when she worked for him or visited Wambui, but now Muturi was in tow. She had heard that this was his last day and he would take a big bird back to America. She had seen the huge birds landing often in Mombasa. She turned to go through the back garden to the kitchen door, having to carry Muturi through the grass. She tapped at the door, and let herself in the unlocked door. No one was in the kitchen, but Ruthy came in from the dining area and saw Muturi and they both giggled. She went into the dining area and Wambui was sitting looking through photographs on the table.

"Where is he?" Wanjiru asked.

"My father took him to Nairobi in the truck. My father the Maumau is taking *mzungu* for a ride to Nairobi." She laughed and wiped tears from her eyes. "Four years, four good years."

"I missed saying goodbye." She said and sank down into a chair. She had finally worked up the courage to bring Muturi to see his father, but now the place was empty. He had sold or given away everything.

"He told me to take the keys to the bursar. See the photos he took before he left? He made copies for me." Wanjiru looked at the photos. The headmaster, the school, the messenger, Wambui and her children. "Take this photo. It is him with the messenger Kamau. It looks just like him." She stared at the photo. He is heavier than when she first knew him, but it looked like him. "He said he looked for you and Muturi.

"Oh, I thought you knew. I am at Mwangi's house now."

"Good house. You will be happy. Just learn to cook. I will teach you. Let us go." Wambui said and gathered up the photos and put it into her bag. Wanjiru and Wambui looked around, and left the place locking the back door. The school was deserted, with the students gone, the workers gone and only a few teachers in the administration building. Wanjiru picked Muturi up because of the gravel and his bare feet. And she followed Wambui and Ruthy into the building and found the bursar. He was a very fussy man who insisted on giving Wambui a receipt for the keys. He also mentioned that the headmaster wanted to thank her. Wanjiru thought, thank her? And she followed the bursar and Wambui into the headmaster's office.

"Wambui!" The headmaster stood up, and shook hands with both of them. He said in the Swahili of Dar Es Salaam, "Yes, I want to thank you for taking such good care of your employer. If it were not for you making his life here so happy, I am sure he may have left after just a year instead of four. And who is this?" He shook hands with Ruthy and motioned to Muturi. "Is this, is this Muturi? He looks just like him. Did you know that my wife is pregnant and if it is a boy, we intend to name it…" and he said the name the *mzungus* used for Lodi – a name she could never pronounce. He took out his wallet. "I know this will be a difficult time until you find another job, so I want to help also." He handed Wambui two hundred shillings. She looked at the currency with Kenyatta's picture on them. She looked up on the wall and there was a similar photo.

"Thank you very much." She said and the two women shook his hand. Muturi wanted to shake also, and the headmaster laughed.

"Young man, you must come to Njoro School when you are bigger." They all laughed, and the women headed back where they came from.

Chapter 14, Year 1987

Kimani turned his motorcycle into Bondeni looking for Mwangi's engine repair. Njoro's bus stop area had not changed, but looked as poor as ever. He found the little sign and several cars up on jacks and motorcycles torn apart off to the side. He recognized Mwangi from the time Kimani was a teacher up in Molo and owned a different motorcycle that Mwangi once repaired for him. He pulled up to where several people had their heads under the open hood of an old Peugeot. He shut off the engine, and removed his helmet. It was very dry and dusty. Sitting on the *piki* he looked around. There were several buses loading up, a minivan taxi, and several pick-up truck *matatu*. There was always room for three more. Women and little girls were lugging large cans of water towards their homes. A fellow with a large bag of charcoal was trying to persuade the bus driver to put the bag up on the roof of the bus, and the driver was saying, "too heavy now."

As usual there were students from the high school out playing around rather than in class. Their excuse always was that they had to buy soap. He stood waiting for Mwangi to come up out of the engine compartment, trying to listen in on what he was doing. Mwangi finally stood straight and saw him. "I remember you, uh, Kimani?"

"Kimani." They shook hands and Kimani got grease on his hands but it would be rude to wipe it off now.

"Kimani! Yes, I recall now. You had that *piki* like a dirt bike, smaller than this one. You are a teacher at Molo, right?"

"Not anymore, I got a job with the telephone company."

"You were a friend of the *mzungu* that my wife was friends with before we got married."

"Yes, you are remembering right. He wrote me a letter and asked me to come to Njoro and make sure all his friends are doing well. He wants to know about Wambui, Wanjiru and Esther and all the children especially. Is Esther and Wambui still living in the same place?" Kimani was not sure how Mwangi related to his old American friend. Was there hard feelings? Was he fine with what happened and the way it happen?

"Yes, the same place for way over ten years I think." Mwangi wiped his hands. "My place now where Wanjiru and the children are is right next to Esther on the same courtyard. You should remember that." He lifted his hands to wave at a little road over the railroad tracks. "Take that road and it winds around but it will get you there." He thought a while. "Tell your *mzungu* friend that buying his broken *piki* was my best business deal ever."

"Really, that *piki* nearly killed him." Kimani laughed, but remembering it was Kimani himself who ruined the engine by not adding oil to the gasoline after he borrowed it from Lodi.

"I repaired it , sold it for a big profit and bought tools and machines for my business here." Mwangi said proudly, and Kimani thought this would be a story that Mwangi bragged about for years, and felt sure he had heard it before.

"My friend hated that machine. He said it only caused him grief from the day he bought it from a Hindi in Nakuru." He thought a moment. "One man's grief is another man's gold." He added and Mwangi at first looked confused, then got the joke and laughed.

"True." He said, and extended his hand for a less greasy handshake. "Be sure Wanjiru does not make you too long." He said making Kimani wonder at his choice of words – maybe he should be speaking Kikuyu instead of English.

"Keep me too long?" he asked, then realized what he meant and laughed. Yes, she was a beautiful woman. This must be one of Mwangi's well-worn jokes about his beautiful wife.

The *piki* got him over the tracks and along the narrow, rutted road. The women carrying their water and bundles of firewood kindly stood to the side while he passed. He waved his appreciation and went on by the fields of harvested maize piled up for drying. He pulled up to a long white fence trying to place where Esther's place was. By luck he saw Wambui with a thin, brown girl following her opening a gate. He pulled up close and she recognized him right away, despite his helmet.

"Kimani, what are you doing in Njoro?" She asked in Kikuyu. He was afraid to speak that language because she had always joked about his accent. He walked up and shook hands with her.

"Is that Ruthy" He wondered. It has been too long. "Why aren't you in school?" He said as he pulled off the helmet and locked his motorcycle. He took a camera out of the side box. He was proud of his Nikon SLR.

"She is in school, but primary school let out early. No school for a month." She said, and opened the gate. "I was to talk with Esther and Wanjiru. Come, they want to talk to you." They went into the courtyard, which had little children running around and playing. Kimani recognized Wanjiru right away sitting in a chair nursing a baby. He walked over and she looked up.

"Kimani!" she exclaimed and they shook hands. He looked down at the black baby sucking at the light brown breast. He thought, no, seeing the breast will not make him too long, like Mwangi said. "What are you doing here?"

He looked the women over and although they looked ten years older than when he last saw them, they were still very shapely, Wanjiru still beautiful, and Wambui still a beautiful, tall Kikuyu woman with huge teeth. Kimani took off the camera lens cap and snapped a picture of the two women sitting together. Then moved in close to take a picture of Wanjiru and the baby sucking; but just before he pressed the shutter, the baby turned and looked at him. Well, a nice picture of a beautiful tit, he thought. The baby went back sucking and he tried again.

"I am on a mission to see if everyone is well and happy. And take a lot of pictures for our American friend."

"Mission," Wanjiru said in English then back to Kikuyu, "Did Lodi ask you to do it? He maybe want picture of everyone."

"Good guess," Kimani answered. Wambui looked perplexed.

"*Ni ke?*" and Kimani explained in Kikuyu that he wanted pictures of everyone.

"Lodi?" she asked in Kikuyu. "He write you a letter?"

"Yes, he says that when Wambui writes that she is always sick and she only ask for money and does not tell enough about how you are doing. And Wanjiru never writes back, even though he writes her many times." He said in his best Kikuyu, but he could see Wambui's judgmental expression appearing, which made him annoyed. "Also, he wants pictures of Wanjiru Tatton and her children." He saw Wambui smile and Wanjiru wince.

Wambui said, "That is true. I write Kiswahili so bad, it takes hours to write a letter. So, I just write about what I need. Why pictures of Wanjiru?"

"He still thinks the boy with the yellow hair is his, of course." Kimani retorted.

Wanjiru said defensively in English, "That is not a secret. I do not write about his boys or anything. I do not need his money. I use my savings from working in Mombasa."

Kimani was shocked, "Boys? I thought there was just one."

"Remember Mombasa? My aiyudi came out. Me and Wajiko both got pregnant."

"You had an IUD?" he said in English, knowing what that was. "It fell out? You both got pregnant? Now that is an act of God!" Kimani exclaimed. "Where are his boys now?" He said looking around. He snapped a cute picture of Ruthy playing with the younger kids.

"They are over at the school playing ball. The one you shoot through the ring."

"Basketball?" he said but she shrugged.

"I do not know the name. They play with the Keogh boy." She said and Kimani remembered that Keogh had a son.

"All these children," he said to the two women in Kikuyu, "how do you pay to send them to school? Or do they not go to school?" Kimani recalled that Wambui was a widow with three kids, and Wanjiru had – apparently – two kids before she married Mwangi.

Wambui spoke up, "Lodi pays for my three kids. I just ask for money and he sends a bank check." Kimani was dumbfounded.

Wanjiru said, "I pay for Muturi and Mumera once he gets to standard five from my savings. Lodi sends money that I do not ask. I put it in the bank." The baby had stopped sucking and she buttoned her blouse back. "Let's walk over to the school. It will be fun. My mama is still working for Keogh."

"Keogh is still there? He used to teach chemistry!"

"Yes, let us see if everyone is around." She looked at Wambui. "Can you watch the children? Make some tea for yourself. There are scones in there also, and plum jam."

Kimani laughed and recalling something, "Remember that plum cake?"

Wambui laughed, "Yes, when Miss Lee lived with him, Lodi would make plum cake and we would eat all at once!"

Kimani saw an angry look on her face, when she added. "I still cannot believe my Lodi married Miss Lee. They hate each other."

Kimani laughed. "Me too! Once he heard that Ann had his daughter, they seemed to fall in love." Wanjiru was frowning. Wanjiru and Kimani stood up, and Wanjiru swaddled the baby onto her back, and headed out towards the school. The layout was a bit different and he noticed from a distance that the grass hut was gone.

"Whatever happened to Muthoni and Warimu?"

"Muthoni works for a Luo teacher, a woman, we could stop by. Warimu died from some disease." Wanjiru said, and a pain shot through Kimani, which always happened when he learned that someone he knew is dead. "The doctor did not know what the disease was, but it made her very sick like cancer. She died of too much puss in lung."

"I feel very bad to hear that." Kimani said, looking out across the game field and seeing the stands. The track was overgrown. He could see a group of kids shooting baskets. As they got closer it looked like three of the eight kids were whites. The other were various shades of dark brown. Two whites and two blacks had their shirts off, while the rest still wore shirts. He watched a while, snapping pictures, and they all dribbled well avoiding the holes in the asphalt court. The kids were all glistening with sweat, yelling and screaming trying to get the ball.

"Muturi, Muturi," Wanjiru shouted as he went running by. "Can you stop for a while?" One of the white boys screamed and everyone stopped, panting for air. "Come here, there is an old friend I want you to meet." All eight of the boys came over. Two of the "boys" were taller than himself, one white boy – maybe ten years old? – was shorter and the brown boys were shorter but looked about ten years old. This is an old friend of Lodi's and mine. He came to meet you to see how you are doing." The boys came in closer. "This is Muturi he is eleven," Kimani shook his hand.

"This is Mumera he is nine." He shook the boy's hand and both had cheerful blue eyes, so much like Lodi's. She turned to the tallest boy, "This young man is Mr. Keogh's oldest boy, David." He shook the hand and again the blue eyes! But Lodi and Keogh were often mistaken for one another. He shook hands with the other boys and listened to their names, but their faces reminded him of several teachers that used to teach there... or still do.

"Please, may I take pictures?" Kimani asked, and all eight boys arranged themselves. He took one wide angle and two zooming in on the three white boys in the middle.

Kimani tried to make a joke, "Be careful on this court, you know Lodi broke his leg in one of those holes and was in the hospital for three days." They all smiled. God! He thought, they all have Lodi's smile. "David, are your parents home? Esther there?"

"Esther is there with my sister, but I think my parents are in Nakuru."

"Well, I just wanted to say hello. Our American friend wrote me a letter and said I should come to Njoro and make a report. Your mother says you are the finest young men in the world." They all smiled and the brown boys all laughed and started teasing them, while the two turned pink with embarrassment. Keogh's boy punched them both on their shoulders. They all turned and started their game where they left off.

"Let us go back to the road through the school to get to Keogh's house."

"I thought he was over by the golf course."

"They moved back to the compound because of the robberies. They did not feel safe over there. Also the balls hit their house all the time." She said and Kimani got an image of raining golf balls. They walked around a row of hedges and back to the road. There were the dormitories, the long houses full of beds and no heat for cold nights. They found the entrance and walked up the driveway, and around to the kitchen door.

"*Hodi*, mama" Wanjiru called through an open window and the sound of a door unlocking. A short, thin brown woman opened the door. She was happy at first to see her daughter, but hesitated seeing Kimani. She obviously was trying to place him.

Then suddenly she said, "Kimani! Yes, yes. Come in."

Wanjiru said, "We saw the boys playing ball and I introduced Kimani to them."

"Good, good." They walked through the kitchen to the dining area where a girl was sitting with a book and writing. "This is the Keogh's daughter, Andrea." Kimani shook hands with her, and she smiled at him... that smile! Green eyes and black hair.

130

Eyes just like Keogh. His wife had black hair and brown eyes if he recalled. Maybe all *mzungu* look alike to this African.

"Come into the kitchen, Andrea has studies." Esther said, and Kimani thought the constant study must be Mr. Keogh's doing. She closed the door to the dining room, took them in the kitchen, and poured them each a cup of warm tea.

"Esther, you are looking very healthy." Kimani said. "How is your daughter Muthoni?"

"Good, good, you should have married her. She cannot find a man who wants to marry her."

"I am already married and have a baby daughter."

"Oh, well take her as your second wife then. She will help the first wife until you give her a pregnancy."

Kimani laughed, "One wife is enough for me. Sweet Jesus knows." He adjusted the camera for the dim light and snapped a picture of Esther, her daughter and grandchild. The baby was breast-feeding again.

"Are you staying the night? There is a little hotel over by the post office. Sleep with Muthoni, give her a baby." The old woman offered. Kimani got a bit aroused being offered Muthoni after all these years. If she has no children by now, she is probably sterile, he thought.

"I came to Njoro to see my old friends and take pictures for Lodi in America."

"Why should he care?" said Esther.

"Mama! He is putting Wambui's three children through school." Wanjiru said.

"He does not help his own children." The old woman scowled.

"Mama, that is my choice. I have plenty of money from working in Mombasa that I saved. Besides, Mwangi says they are his boys." Wanjiru said. It was then that Kimani realized that she was making money as a prostitute when she was in Mombasa, and putting it in savings for her son. The things women do for their children, he wondered. "Kimani, it is getting late. Let us go see Muthoni.

Kimani gave Esther a handshake as he left with Wanjiru and her baby, which was once again swaddled on her back. They returned down the path, past the entrance of Lodi's old place, to the last teacher's house on this side. All the houses were the same,

131

except a different orientation to the driveway. They went around to the kitchen door, tapped, and turned the handle, but Muthoni opened the door seeing her sister and Kimani and started giggling.

"Kimani, my old lover!" She shook hands with him and came outside to stand in the grassy garden. "You have gained some weight… you were so thin before."

"Yes, becoming a *mzee* at thirty-one. You have slimmed down some. Is your Luo working you too hard?"

"No, no, she is wonderful person. Very serious teacher. I am trying to keep myself attractive for an old lady."

"Old? You look very young to me."

"Having no children helps." She sighed. "I heard that you were married." She stated and he merely nodded. "It is getting late, you are not going back to Nairobi tonight, are you?"

"No, I hear there is a hotel by the post office. Can I buy you supper someplace?"

"Sure, if I can get away. Let me ask." She disappeared into the house. Kimani looked at the beautiful Wanjiru who smiled.

"You really should give her a pregnancy." She said. "She has no men she like here anymore. I think you spoiled her for any other man."

"Oh, come on!" he said imitating an American movie. "I am really not that special." He laughed at the thought, but Wanjiru frowned. They waited a few more minutes, and Muthoni came back with her basket.

"My lady says she is eating at the headmaster's house this evening, and I can go." She was all smiles.

"Let me get a picture of you two here, the light is fading fast." They stood with their backs to the hedge and he snapped the picture. They walked down the driveway and heard some voices from up the road. It was Muturi and Mumera.

"Mama, Esther said you were here." Muturi said, looking his mother in the eyes. Kimani thought it will not be long before he is taller than his mother.

"Escort me home, Kimani and Muthoni are going out to supper. I will have the boys put your *pikipiki* inside the fence for the night." The three turned in the other direction and headed off. Kimani turned to go up through the school campus to the upper village where the post office and train station was. It was a road he took many, many times in the past, and it was quite familiar to him. Students were gathering in the dining hall, while others were still in their classrooms studying. Prefects were running around barking orders at the youngers. They left the campus and headed across a narrow path towards a row of buildings, with a middle one saying "Njoro Hotel & Bar" and he thought, get them drunk and take them to bed. The bartender also gave out room keys, and he got the room closest to the common *choo*. "Are you hungry yet or should we check the room? It might be filthy." They went down the hall past two toilets and found a room, and opening the door found a glossy blue room with a wide single bed, and a bedside table with a simple electric lamp. He walked over to set his camera and shoulder bag by the table, and turned around. She was slipping her dress off over her head.

"Muthoni... uh... my, you are beautiful." He studdered but found the old Muthoni chemistry working.

After an hour, they were dressed and ready for some supper, Muthoni having received, what Kimani called, her first dose of baby maker. He had forgotten how sweet she was. His wife was a bit abrasive and demanding since the baby came. But that is expected with the stress, but she was not wanting sex, which invariably made him susceptible to other women. The two will never meet, anyway, he thought. Over one hundred miles apart. They sat down at a table in the bar and asked what there was to eat, and they were directed to the chalkboard menu over the bar. Several tables were occupied with groups of men and women, already having the table full of empty bottles, which was a way of keeping a tab. Kimani set his camera on the table between them, and hoped his bag would be safe in the room.

Calling to the bartender, they both ordered *ugali* and beef stew, and a Tusker for her and a Pilsner for him. He was suddenly concerned about his health and asked in Swahili, "Should I worry about any diseases?" And strangely she just laughed.

She replied in English, in case people were listening. "I have not been with a man for six months maybe. The last gave me something and the health center gave me a jab. I went back a week later for another jab. Then they check. All clean. Told me to use Durex and they gave me a hand full. But I want a baby. So, I wait for a clean man to do me. I am afraid that I had too many diseases and now I cannot have children."

"We will see what God has planned for us." He said just as the food and beer arrived. She was looking so cute, he decided to try a photo in the dim light. "Stay very still." He propped the camera on the beer bottle to keep it steady and it snapped with a timed exposure.

Using the camera caught the attention of a police officer who had come in to talk with the bartender. He turned and came over. "Hello, Muthoni, hello sir. I am very sorry to inform you that there was a camera stolen just this last week and we have to hold such cameras to check the serial number." He took out a writing pad from his side pocket and started writing. Kimani was fuming angry, but he knew he could only make it worse. He pulled out his wallet, and the officer said, "Please do not try to bribe me."

"No, just my ID. I work for the telephone company and want to show you my ID."

"Yes, Sir, that was what I wanted next. I am so sorry to bother your supper, but I have to do this. We should be able to clear this up by early morning."

"May I at least take the film out. I could have it processed here in the morning."

"Yes, sir, feel free." The officer said. Kimani saw that he still had six pictures left, but rolled the film back and popped it out of the camera. He then remembered it was color film so he might have to wait for Nairobi. The officer gave him a receipt and his ID badge back, and left with the camera.

"Well, that was annoying."

"I know him. He is a very serious police officer. You will get it back, but they are very slow, and have difficulty finding records."

"I have been there before to help Lodi get his *pikipiki* back."

"It was stolen?"

"Yes, after I ruined the engine, he set it in his garden and someone ran off with it. It took the police several months to find it and return it. The thief could not get it started and threw it into a ditch."

"Do you still remember using his bedroom whenever he was gone?" Muthoni asked.

"Of course, and the one time he came back early and we escaped out the front to finish in the tall grass?" They both laughed at their lusty youth. "You worked for him for a while did you not?"

"Yes, for a while while Wambui had Ruthy. Just cleaning and laundry."

"Come on, if there was a female in the house he would have to…"

"Yes, I admit it." She broke in. "Just once on the kitchen floor." She said. "He started and changed his mind, so it was the last time."

"He probably thought you were too young for him."

"Short? Oh, maybe, I looked him in the chest."

"So, this talk is giving me the urge. Want another dose of baby maker?" Kimani asked with a smile?

"My Luo is leaving for Nairobi in the morning so I do not have to wake early. So, give me all you have."

~~~~~

Kimani returned to Nairobi after three days stranded in Njoro waiting for the police to check the camera serial number and release it back to him. He had spent most of the time with Muthoni. When not in bed, they rode his *piki* up into the hills, or up to Elburgon and Molo to where he used to teach, then back to the hotel for more servicing.

He was back at work sitting at his workbench cleaning a potentiometer control, thinking what he was going to write to his American friend. He had the photos processed and he realized how much Wanjiru's sons looked like their father. He would know right away and be very upset. As he snapped the component back into place, a secretary brought around his mail and set it next to his case.

"*Jambo, Asante.*" he said, trying to be cheerful. He closed the component, turned the pot, and watched a voltmeter go up as he rotated it. "Smooth, no static." He screwed the lid shut, and looked at the pile of mail. He could see a USA stamp sticking out of the pile, and he grabbed it right away and used a screwdriver as a letter opener. It was a one page letter with two photos. Lodi's wife Ann had a son the month before and the pictures were of him with the baby and his daughter. He looked extremely happy holding the huge baby. His daughter had his same smile, but her mother's eyes. The baby looked quite unhappy, as if it were not

135

used to being outside the comfort of the womb. He read the letter. It was about the birth, his work, and again he asked about Wanjiru and her son. He repeated for the third time, not to fail him and get pictures.

That night back at his apartment, his wife put the baby to bed, and was too sleepy for some fun. He sat down at the table to write back to his friend. After the preliminaries about the new baby, his latest successes and how his wife and daughter were doing he wrote:

> *Now, my friend, I rode the piki all the way back up to Njoro, and visited with Wambui. She and her three children are all doing great. They said to tell you thank you again and again for helping her kids with school fees. After all these years, I was surprised that you are still helping them.*
>
> *My brother, I have failed you so often. I ruined your piki, I lost all the school books I borrowed. I used your house as if it were my own. I slept with Beth, when I knew she lusted for you. That is why I have to call you my brother, since a friend would have dumped me long ago. I succeeded visiting Wambui, but I report failure with Wanjiru Tatton.*
>
> *The pictures are of me, my wife and kid, and Wambui and her kids. I am sorry, but Wanjiru cannot be found. She moved with her mother Esther, and her new husband and no one told me where. I did see her sister Muthoni, but she did not tell me where she moved. They all want me to tell you that Wanjiru's child is not yours. So, do not worry about some child showing up claiming to be your nusu nusu child from Africa.*
>
> *The telecom is sending me for training in London next year, and maybe Montreal the year after. Maybe we can meet there, since it may be years before you make it back to Kenya. Oh, I met the former Njoro headmaster that was at Njoro when you were there. I did not know that his wife had a son after you left, and they named him after you. He says he misses you a lot and to tell you he is expecting a letter.*

He sat and stared at what he had written. It was not *all* lies. She did move from Mwangi's house to a place next to Esther, and no one will tell him, since he already knows. I have pictures of her sons, but he only knows about the one. There is no need for him to worry about those when he has a family in America to take care of. He folded the letter, inserted the pictures into the envelope, and sealed it away. Kimani thought of a chapter out of the bible. This is appropriate for my friend. Let him believe that his seed fell by the wayside.

Chapter 15, Year 1993

Muturi was dressed in his dark school suit and sported a tie as he walked through Mwangi's auto repair shop, and smiled at his stepfather as he headed to the high school. His "*baba*" handed him some money for lunch. "*Niwega muno, baba*," he said thanking Mwangi. His brother Mumera was still eating his breakfast, as Muturi left early for school. Mwangi had moved his auto repair business down to Nakuru when a "Hindi" family, after four generations in Kenya, had "decided" to return "home" to India. Muturi was doing very well at Njoro High School with and was accepted as a day student here to finish his last year of high school, after his stepfather moved his business. His brother Mumera was two years behind him, but their paths at school rarely crossed. He had already had his first classes of the term in his favorite subjects - physics, chemistry and maths. All the other courses were meaningless although simple. One teacher for the physics and maths recently graduated from the University of Nairobi. The chemistry teacher was an American woman who knew her subject but Muturi was confused when she taught the chemistry he had learned already in a different way.

He crossed Kenyatta Avenue and headed down by the sports club then on towards the high school. The air was crisp and the sun rising low in the sky glared off puddles of water in the street. The smell of the public toilets pained his nose, and the strap from his heavy book bag was digging into his shoulders.

The rough looking characters on the street turned their heads whenever he walked by them. He knew it was because he was not easy prey, even at seventeen, being six foot three inches tall and a 100-kilo. His light brown hair and blue eyes also set him apart from others and was intimidating.

As he approached the school, he was excited because there were such a variety of students he did not feel out of place. There were many different tribes of Africans, from short Kukuyu to tall Maasai, Arabs and Hindi, and several Anglo-Kenyans. He was fluent in Kikuyu, Swahili and English, and the husband of his mother's cousin taught him some German when he visited them down in Mombasa.

His first class of the day was chemistry and he arrived at the chemistry lab early. He had seen the boarders leaving the assembly hall and would soon be here to join him. He was supposed to join them for the morning assembly to hear a passage from the bible and get a prayer, but he could never do it. Strangely, no one ever asked him about it either. He sat at the lab table, setting out his book and and notes. He looked up and there was Miss Mills, his chemistry teacher, bringing in a tray of glassware and setting out large bottles of acids and other chemicals. He watched her brush her yellow hair back out of her eyes - blue eyes, a bit lighter than his own. She looked so small up there until she said, "I'm sorry, I forgot your name already." He was suddenly nervous.

"Muturi Makomeki." he said.

"Oh, yes, Muturi, could you help me distribute the glassware." She was looking at all the things on the front desk when he went up to get the tray, and standing next to her he realized that she was fairly tall and strong looking, like the Viking women he had seen in a movie. Standing closer he saw that her hair had a bit of reddish color with the yellow. She wore a long denim dress, buttoned up to her neck and wore what looked like boots - the kind that could break a leg if she used them to kick someone.

"What should I do?" he asked, and she reached over to the tray passing over his left hand brushing it briefly. An electrostatic shock made them both jump and laugh.

"Put one of each at each station. Students can come up here to get the chemicals. We are doing a titration."

"A titration? Mr. Keogh made us do that many times." Muturi said. And she laughed again.

"Mr. Keogh? You went to Njoro High?"

"Yes, until recently. I transferred because my step father moved his business."

"Keogh would make you do everything a million times until everyone gets it perfect. I did my student training with him when I first came to Kenya. Bit sarcastic but a good teacher."

"Yes, that is Mr. Keogh. I remember seeing a woman with yellow hair. That must have been you."

139

"Well you could do a lot worse. Mr. Keogh should be retiring or returning to England one day." She said as Muturi took the tray. "He has a lovely wife, too. You know his son graduated last year? He went to Duke University in America."

"Yes, he is tall like me, we played basketball at Njoro." Muturi began distributing the glassware and said, "My grandmother used to be their housekeeper, so Mr. Keogh made sure I learned everything perfectly." This made her laugh.

"Well that will be a good start for this course then." He finished and took the tray back up front.

As he turned, she patted him on his back, "Thank you." and she began writing some notes on the chalkboard. This touching must be an American thing. He looked at his notes and saw something she mentioned on the first day.

"Oh, I was curious where this Perdue University that you graduated from."

She turned around and said, "Take a map of the United States, just right of the middle."

"My mother has a friend in a place called Illinois," he said pronouncing the "s" at the end, "or something, I saw it on the envelope."

"It is French name pronounced "ill a noy" and is the state west of where Perdue is."

"Maybe I could study at Perdue one day."

"Muturi, you can set your sights higher than Perdue." She said and he was utterly flattered. Students began coming in and sitting down. "Where does your mother's friend live in Illinois?"

"I do not know. I will ask her, but it sounds like a wine." He said and she turned around to finish the notes on the chalkboard. He picked up his pen, and he noticed a girl turned around looking at him as was another boy next to her at the front bench. He waved at both of them and they smiled. They both looked Kikuyu, and seemed to want to be friends.

Miss Mills started, "Today we will be using potassium permanganate to titrate an unknown chemical."

~~~~

Twenty-four year old Martha Mills was watching the last of her chemistry students finishing the lab experiment. The very tall Muturi was explaining the results to his lab partners, two black students one cute girl and a short boy. They were using a combination English, Swahili and Kikuyu, or so she thought. He was using everything to make them understand what he was thinking. She looked through the booklets sitting on the desk, and most listed the numbers and colors, and a short calculation of concentration and various guesses at the mystery solution.

She had been in Kenya for a year and a half, having contracted for two years with extensions up to five years. It was hard living in Nakuru, not like it was for her aunt Beth who did the same thing years before. Lawlessness and ethnic conflicts were much greater. Her place was broken into several times and she had beaten off the intruder with a stoker one time. There were not many Americans around, or if there were, she did not meet them. The Brits were - with a few exceptions - arrogant snobs.

She watched them talk and the girl asked Muturi to sit with her at the cafeteria for lunch, and the other boy invited himself. The two left Muturi writing in his tablet and brought their booklets up to the front. The girl returned to Muturi and shook hands with him saying thank you for his help.

There were cute male students who were a couple years younger than she was who tried to seduce her during the time she was there. There was another teacher, who tried his luck with her only to end up scaring her. There was nothing like the stories that her aunt had written about in her book - those steamy affairs, traveling around Kenya, doing "it" everywhere. That was before AIDS put a big inhibition on such lifestyles. She watched Muturi, and wondered about what brought such a tall, handsome young man into this world - he is so obviously a mixed heritage. Now if he were to put the moves on her, she would not be able to resist... so much for being a professional.

Muturi finished his writing and brought it to the front. "Do you need help cleaning up?" he offered. I have a half hour before lunch.

"I need to bring all the glassware back to the preparation room and the assistant will deal with them." She said and he took a tray and began circulating around the room picking up the glassware. She took all the booklets back to the prep room hoping to talk with the lab assistant. She looked in the physics and biology labs and could not find him. She came back as Muturi was placing the tray of glassware on the prep table near a sink.

"Anything else I can help with?" he offered with a smile. His smile could stop her heart it is so sexy, she thought.

"No, the assistant will do the rest. I will have to grade all these." She said. "Do you mind if I ask a personal question?"

She could see him get suddenly nervous, with his eyes shifting around. He probably thinks I want him to jump my bones, she thought, but said, "You look very different from other Kikuyu. You must have some interesting family." She asked and he became completely relaxed - he chuckled and smiled.

"Definitely interesting. I am a real mongrel. My mother showed me my birth registry document." He said in the Kenyan accented English that Martha loved. "I am one quarter Kikuyu, one quarter English and one half American." He said and she was amazed that he knew the nitty gritty. "It was a time when sexual intercourse was the Kenya's national pastime. America has baseball, but Kenya had sex." He said and she laughed aloud, especially that a young man would be so bold. "My grandmother had an affair with her English employer, and my mother an affair with an American teacher at Njoro." He leaned back on the table, his jacket fell open, and the tie fell askew.

"Is that the fellow in Illinois that your mother gets letters from?" she asked.

"He is paying for my education." He said proudly, and she felt a weird pang in her gut. "My mother says he is a physics professor. He has a family there. He is old now like my mother."

"Old? How old is your mother?"

"She is about 36 or 37 I think." He said and she chuckled.

"I am 24 so 37 does seem old, but she has a lot of years left. You have brothers or sisters?

"I have a brother who is about two years younger, also the American's boy. Then two half brothers and three half sisters who are by my step father Mwangi Guitiri."

"Is Mumera your brother?" she asked about a form two student that was a younger version of Muturi, and he nodded, "Oh, he is big and cute like you." She said inappropriately, wanting to take it back immediately. She could see his embarrassment, turning a red that she had never seen in other Kikuyus.

"I am only human, you are of course very attractive." he said with his red face returning to normal. "I am sure men chat you up all the time." He said, but she laughed.

142

"Not as much as I would like." She laughed again, and her eyes scanned him from his marred black shoes, up his black slacks, to his brown belt. He was solid, with a bit of a tummy, but broad chest and shoulders. "You must have a few girlfriends."

"Me? I am a serious student. But these girls are always offering themselves." He smiled. "And I..." He started but heard the lunchtime bell. "I am meeting friends." They both headed out through the chemistry lab.

"I need to go also. You are very helpful. If you are mechanically inclined, maybe I could hire you to fix some things at my house."

"Hire me? I can fix most things, but I do it free for my teachers." He smiled reaching out to the hand she offered. Before opening the exterior door they shook hands lingering to look into each other's blue eyes. "Let me know and I can come over." He added, and opened the door, leaving first so that she could lock it behind her. He headed towards the cafeteria, leaving her to walk towards the teacher's room.

~~~~

Muturi balanced his bowl of food and looked around the cafeteria for the girl Janie who wanted to lunch with him. She waved and he found a place next to her saved. The fellow Martin was there, and moved so that he sat between them. The cafeteria was a roar of sound, so she was shouting her welcome. Martin was a short, dark fellow, very thin in the face. They had just finished eating their soup, and were sipping tea. "Where are you from?"

"We are both from Embu. We are sister and brother." Janie said, and then it hit him.

"Are you twins?" he asked and they both laughed nodding in agreement.

"I thought you look alike... except your breasts are much nicer than his." Muturi laughed and they both joined in.

Martin said, "Janie said she liked you the first class, so I said let me see if we can make a friend." He tore his bread and ate a piece. The three talked about their prior schools and what it was like. Martin added, "We are day schoolers, we live with an aunt who works as a housekeeper."

"Muturi," Janie asked, "Do you find it difficult being half-caste in Nakuru?"

143

"It was more difficult when I was little in Njoro. Here, there are people from all over who are different. In Njoro, kids would throw rocks at me, but after I learned to catch the rocks and throw them back, it ended. But I was called *nusu nusu* until I was so big they were afraid of me."

"Sorry for that." Janie said and patted his leg, and left her hand there. "When I was little I teased *nusu nusu* children too, but now I feel guilty for doing it."

"I never tease anyone," Martin said, "I like everyone." He patted Muturi on his other thigh, which made Muturi wonder what the twins were up to. Janie leaned forward and Muturi saw as he sipped the last of his soup, that Janie nodded at her brother. Their hands began rubbing his inner thighs, giving him a tingle as he tore the bread, and yet enjoyable enough to see where they were headed, which got a little higher with each gradual stroke. He was getting aroused, but he was curious how far they would go, and Janie reached it first, which at this point had extended down his boxer shorts onto the thigh that Janie was petting.

"Oh," she said and began petting him. "Martin and I would like you to come to tea after classes today. There are no games until next week." He was afraid she would cause him to make a mess in his pants, so he held her hand that was petting him.

"I would love to. I will meet you out front about 4?" he said, and her hand slipped out of his and went back to give him a squeeze.

"I look forward to it." She said and he guided the hand away yet again. The class-warning bell rang and they picked up their trays and book bags and headed in different directions, with Muturi carrying his book bag in front of him until he calmed down.

"Muturi!" He heard a feminine voice behind him, he turned around and it was Miss Mills. "You still want to help me at my house? I have some curtain rods that are falling down."

"I am free either Friday after classes or Saturday afternoon."

"Saturday works for me. Come for lunch. If you want some tutoring, I could help too. Here is my address." She wrote it on a tablet page and tore it out for him. He tucked it inside his jacket pocket. "See you then." She said and hurried away.

~~~~~~

144

Muturi waved at his brother heading home and walked down the path to the front entrance of the school. Janie and Martin were chatting between themselves unaware that he was approaching. Janie was taller than Martin, with longer, thicker hair. She was very shapely, while he was quite lean, or some would say skinny. The school skirt came to just above her knees, and her dark brown legs had a bit of dust from the schoolyard. He could not understand what they were saying, as if they had their own language. He slung his heavy book bag onto his back, and tapped each on their shoulders. They both turned to him with big smiles and handshakes.

"We were hoping you would come." Janie said, "Biology class was hell this afternoon." They started walking, and Muturi kept pace, not knowing where their aunt's place was. "We both are hoping to become medical doctors one day." They headed towards the cricket fields of the sports club and headed towards some row houses made of stone. "How about you?"

"Engineering, I think." He said, "Maybe chemical or mechanical. So, you too do alright in biology?"

Martin said, "It is difficult but we need it, especially the human anatomy."

Trying to be funny, Muturi said, "You both have fine human anatomies, so it should be easy." They laughed, and looked him in the face as if to make sure he was joking.

Janie added, "Your anatomy needs to be thoroughly studied... for comparative purposes of course."

Martin said, "Janie is always playing doctor."

"Martin! You do, too!"

"Playing doctor?" Muturi asked. "That sounds interesting. Like a physical or something?"

"Yes, we had to have physical exams... you did too, right? Now Janie and I want to give each other physicals, but it is too much like incest." He said with a laugh. "Got to practice being a doctor." They crossed the street towards row houses.

"Incest? I doubt it, since doctors do not have intercourse with their patients." Muturi said, trying to be lighthearted, but the word incest set him on edge.

"That's true. But Janie and I grew up together and have no secrets. Twins." Martin said. "So, whatever pops into our heads, good or bad, we tell the other. Here is my aunt's place." Janie took

145

out a key and unlocked the plain wooden door. "Welcome." It opened to a dark living room with a small kitchen off to the right, and beyond three open doors, the middle obviously a *choo*.

"Take off your shoes and jacket, please. Tie too if you want. Hang them on the coat hook. I will start the tea," Janie said and put on a pan of milk, water, sugar and tea leaves to boil. He looked around and noticed the small frig, and a small television in the corner. There was a long couch and chairs everywhere, and a long narrow table near the kitchen. "Come see our bedroom." Muturi followed the two into the little bedroom off the kitchen. There was an unmade fullsize bed, with clothes on hangers on either side. Female on one and male on the other. There was a long desk with two chairs and strangely a microscope and kit on the table. They take their biology seriously, Muturi thought. Janie and Martin threw their book bags on the floor and began taking off their uniforms.

"I should leave you alone," Muturi said.

Janie laughed, "Oh, no, please stay. I don't mind."

Martin added, "Neither do I."

Muturi bent over to study the microscope, and slides. He read the slides, one being "Martin, semen stained." Smiling he looked over to see Janie pull off her blouse and dropped her skirt. She was in her bra and underwear as she hung the clothes up for the next day. Martin was in his bright red Speedos. Muturi put the slide in the microscope and switched on the light. He saw no sperm but did see bacteria of different sorts. He worried it might be gonorrhea. He suddenly felt hands stroking him and he straightened up and turned to see the two were naked. While Janie unbuttoned his shirt, Martin was unbuckling Muturi's belt. Well, he thought, let's see where this leads.

~~~~

Martha Mills sat on the couch in her living room trying to calm down. He is a student, she thought, off limits! Muturi's image popped back into her mind, and again she became aroused. He will be here soon, and if I do not calm down, I will do something I may regret, like take him on the living room floor the moment he enters. She put her hands in her lap and leaned her head back relaxing, following her rules of meditation. Start with your feet, relaxing them. Scan all your muscles and relax them. Close you eyes, and turn off your thoughts, Martha. Nothingness will be. As usual, when she meditated, she felt herself float up above herself. The more she turned down her conscious self the more she floated away. She had once floated back to Indiana. Now she is floating above herself, calming herself down from the excitement of this perfect boy soon to be in her house. The meditation master warned her never to go out of body unless you can see the cord holding your soul to your mortal self. She never saw such a cord, but flew away regardless, thinking it was just her imagination sending her on these out of body trips.

She floated up through the ceiling, seeing the attic, then the roof, then the neighborhood. There down the street, that perfect boy was coming!

Her eyes popped open and she felt refreshed and in control once again.

~~~~

Muturi read the scrap of paper for the fifth time as if the address would change, and realized that he was near Miss Mills' house. It was a formerly an all-*mzungu* neighborhood. Muturi was dressed in old jeans and a t-shirt. He kept pulling the sleeve down over the bruise on his shoulder. He had gone for a penicillin jab hoping to ward off an infection after the romp with Martin and Janie. But he had a little reaction to the jab that looked like a large bruise. Miss Mills would certainly ask about it, and Muturi knew he was a bad liar, and would over state the cause.

He carried a book bag and a bag of tools his stepfather had given him over the years. He was a blend of repairman and student.

He found the address, and it was a large wood frame house, painted army green with a blue green trim. Untrimmed hedges grew all around it, and the grass was overgrown. She had a motorcycle – *pikipiki* - parked at the side of the house. He went up to the door and just as he was about to knock, the door opened. "*Karibu*!" Miss Mills said, opening the door wide for him. He stepped into the living room that was full of very old furniture and strange pictures on the wall. It looked as if the old *wazungu* had died and the government took over and rented it out with everything in it. He looked up and indeed the curtain rods were tilted and ready to fall off.

147

"Yes, thank you." He looked back at her, "I can fix those for sure." She was wearing a sleeveless t-shirt, blue shorts and sandals. The shirt was thin enough to see her bra straps. Her long blonde hair fell down her back and her blue eyes gleamed with cheer. As he looked her over, she did the same and there was a moment of quiet broken by another woman entering the room.

"*Jambo*." Came the voice, and he looked up and it was a tall brown woman.

"This is my housekeeper, Hanna." Miss Mills said and Muturi looked at the woman setting sandwiches on the dining table. She was dressed in a green cotton dress, and had longish hair. She had a big smile as they walked towards the table. He set the bags on the floor, and looked at the food on the table. "You like a beer? You are over sixteen, right?" They sat down and Hanna left and came back with two cold Tuskers.

"I should not drink too much until I get your curtains repaired." He said and bit into the roast beef sandwich. "Very nice." He sipped the beer and looked at her eating.

"I think your Dad fixed my *pikipiki* once. It is broken again."

"Broken? I call my stepfather *baba*."

"The shifter was slipping and then it would not start. Your Baba fixed the shifter once." She took a bite followed by a swig of beer.

"It is an old BSA, it is amazing that it worked at all. Probably just adjusted it before. He will fix it free for my teachers." They quietly ate enjoying their sandwiches, and then he asked, "Where did you grow up?"

"In the state of Indiana, west of the capital Indianapolis, where there are small towns and many farms. My father sold insurance to farmers."

"What kind of name is Mills?" He asked, being curious about where people came from.

"I think it is English, but when they first came to America, they married people from other countries too. The first Mills who came, came as an indentured servant in Pennsylvania."

"Oh, like a slave except for a certain amount of time?"

"Yes, except the owners usually got years added for not working hard enough or some violation. Mine served his time and first headed down to North Carolina. But because of slavery, poor whites could not make a living so they headed to free labor states, like Indiana."

"That is good that you know your family's history."

"I would bet we could find out your father's history, since there are people who can go through all the old records in America and find that information. I have another aunt who does that for people, especially if you know the names."

"I saw his name on envelopes, but I do not know how it relates to my name."

"We could talk with your mother…" she started, but Hanna came in to get the dishes and wipe the table. Muturi looked at her and noticed that she was standing a little too close to him. Miss Mills smiled, apparently knowing what she was up to. "Hanna, what is it?"

"You do him today?" she asked poking a finger into an "O" formed in her other hand. Miss Mills turned bright red, laughed nervously, but Muturi felt a bolt of arousal.

"Hanna!"

"Sorry, but if you do not want him," she said to Miss Mills, then turned to him, "Will you do me?" she laughed and looked at him, and Muturi looked back and forth between the two women, not knowing how to respond. Then Miss Mills said something to Hanna quietly that sounded like, if he seduces me I cannot resist, and Hanna laughed and left carrying the dishes.

After the curtain rods were well anchored and the curtains hanging straight, she asked him to look at her motorcycle. He saw the shifter cable was stretched, and he adjusted it back. Took out he spark plug, brushed it clean, set the gap, and put it back. It started right up and he let her drive it around to see if it worked. She came back after 10 minutes thrilled that her *pikipiki* was working again. "Maybe we could go out to Lake Nakuru and see the birds, or up to Njoro and visit folks."

Miss Mills asked him to fix a broken leg on her bed. He was nervous entering his teacher's bedroom, but she showed the side of the large bed propped up with a pile of books. It was neatly made, and the room itself was sparsely decorated. "I have petrol smell on my hands, I should wash." He went into the blue and white tiled bathroom to wash. He was impressed with the large tub. He came back out and she was returning with Hanna following her. "That is a very nice tub you have in there."

149

"Yes," said Hanna, "Maybe I could give you a nice bath in it later."

"Hanna!"

"Sounds like fun, Hanna." Muturi laughed and said, assuming she was trying to be funny. He looked at the bed leg and saw that a bolt was missing. The two women left the room. He picked up the bed to move it and the bedside table, and he saw a nut wedged under the molding, and the bolt itself came from under the bedside. "This is easier than I thought." Soon the bed was sturdy, and the pile of books were back on a shelf. "All done," he called out and Hanna came back.

"Oh, good, I can make bed safe now." She plopped down on the bed and bounced on it. "You do me now," she said and laid down on the bed and spread her legs. "Martha not mind..." she said just as Miss Mills came in.

"Hanna!" Miss Mills said and Hanna jumped out of bed, and went to the bathroom. Soon the water in the tub was running. "What is she doing now?"

"I give Mister Muturi a bath, I wash him all over. Clean him inside and out." She laughed. Muturi wondered at this lusty woman.

"Hanna, please call him Mister Makomeki, and if he wants a bath he can bathe himself. She turned to Muturi. If you would like a hot bath, you are welcome. I can help you with chemistry afterwards."

"I have never had a hot bath, only showers. I would welcome it."

Hanna said, "You Makomeki boy? I know Makomeki man was a friend of my Beth. He do me good. Gave me my first baby. You have his eyes." Muturi looked at Miss Mills dumbfounded by what the woman was saying. Miss Mills shrugged.

"Okay. You take a hot bath. I need to go to the butcher for some meat. There are some towels on the shelf."

Muturi went into the bathroom and the tub was half-filled with steamy water and soap bubbles. He shut the door and looked for a lock but there was none. He pulled off his clothes and stood in the hot water. It was too hot to sit, so he added some cold water. When the water was right, he settled down into the water and leaned back. The suds covered most of his body up to his chest and

150

he mounded some suds over his privates and relaxed, closing his eyes, soon dozing off.

He awoke with a start. Hanna was leaning over the edge of the tub admiring him. The soap bubbles had dissolved and she was looking at his body in the water. "I wash you now." She said and began soaping up a washcloth. He sat up with a start maintaining his dignity, and she began washing his back. He was about to object but it felt too nice. "I know you fadder." She said.

"You knew my father?" he said stunned.

"He visit Miss Martha's aunt Beth. He gave me baby girl. She die of *zumzum*." She took a plastic pitcher and poured warm water and shampoo over his head and began working in the shampoo into his dense curly brown hair. "Your thing just like his. I still remember." The head massage nearly made him doze off again, but he could not believe what he was hearing. She poured several more pitchers of water over his head to wash out the shampoo. His eyes were closed and he was too relaxed, he leaned back stretching out, but covering his pride with his hands, letting Hanna wash him. She began washing his feet, moving up his legs. Her touching him was arousing, so he gave up and put his hands to his side in the water, letting her see what she had already seen. She was washing his arms and hands, then his chest and belly working down to his pubic hair, which she shampooed gently around his solid shaft. "Yes, just like his." Then she rubbed the soap into it, and pulled back his foreskin. "You fadder not cut, too." She said. Kikuyu boys were cut after age twelve or so, but he never worked up the nerve to have it done… he had an idea that it would decrease the size if he had it done. She rubbed the soap in making him even more aroused. She began to say, "Do you want me…" when he felt the presence of someone else in the room and opened his eyes. Hanna held a firm grip on his shaft, while she was looking at Miss Mills. She was standing there with a huge grin on her face.

"Hanna, can I not trust you with my students?" Miss Mills said, and Muturi realized that she had been watching. He sat up trying to hide himself. Hanna continued to stroke him, and he tried to get her away. Miss Mills slapped her shoulder to make her stop and Muturi covered himself as best he could. She turned on the water, adjusting the temperature, heating up the warm water. Hanna was moving around the room doing something, but Muturi was watching Miss Mills, pulling off her t-shirt and bra, her shorts and knickers, and tested the water with a toe. He was astounded seeing his teacher nude. "Nice." She said about the water temperature, and he leaned back in the deep water still covering himself. She stepped into the tub and stood over him letting him see all there was to see, and he moved his hands up revealing himself through the clear water. "What a perfect body." She said as he stared disbelieving at the white woman with the yellow pubic hair and pink labia standing above him. He was so thoroughly aroused. He thought he would explode from the scene alone. Her breasts were perfectly round with tight, pink nipples, and her yellow hair fell down her shoulders midway to her breasts. Her legs were bending and he could see the glistening of her labia. Her knees reached the water, and she took him into her hand directing it inside her and slowly came down onto him. Ecstasy! He gasped realizing she was a perfect fit, taking him entirely inside herself. The palms of her hands rested on his chest. He reached up with both hands and began carressing her breasts.

"He was mine, just like he fadder." Hanna whined, and left the room carrying something.

"Miss Mills," Muturi muttered, "It never felt so wonderful - never did a teacher…"

"Call me Martha when you are here." She said as her hips slowly went up and down on his shaft while her hands massaged his pectorals, and he pinched her nipples gently and she moaned in delight. Martha turned around and shut off the water, then continued. Her muscles tighten and her fingernails dug into the skin on his chest. Her head went back and she let out a scream and collapsed in the water with their faces touching. He was still deep inside her and he splashed warm water onto her back to keep her warm. Martha began moving again, and Muturi began a slow thrusting until he felt electricity emanating from their point of connection, it moved throughout his body and he went into convulsions and he felt himself erupting inside her, and he nearly blacked out from the pleasure. They were both very still.

Through the fog of pleasure, Muturi then realized that he had actually had sex with his teacher. Even though she was just a few years older than he, there must be some rule against it. Pure lust, and no protection.

Martha pushed herself up and the water dripped off her. His softening shaft was still inside her, but as she got up it made a sucking sound as it withdrew. They laughed. Martha stood up, washing herself briefly and got out to begin drying herself. Muturi began to stand up.

~~~~~~~

Martha was drying off and watched Muturi do the same. She could not believe herself giving in to lust with a student. Never did she have an orgasm so intense. It must be illegal.

She noticed the huge bruise on his shoulder. It reminded her of the penicillin shot that she once got. "Did you get a shot recently?" Martha asked.

"Shot?"

"Oh, a jab." she corrected, forgetting dialects.

"Yes." He said as little as possible. He wrapped the towel around his waist looking for his clothes. Hanna had picked up his clothes and had left the two alone in the bath. Martha was putting her clothes back on and waving her hand hoping to get him to extend the sentence. "Oh, penicillin. " he finished and was looking for his clothes. She fastened her bra, and then was reaching for her t-shirt. "Where are my clothes?" he asked.

"Penicillin? Why? Sex with the wrong person?" She worried about her catching something.

"A girl I was with on Tuesday might have been with someone with gonorrhea. But she was a virgin. So, I got one just in case." Again he looked around for his clothes, and walked into the bedroom

"Was a virgin?" she asked.

"Still is. She has a really tough hymen." She knew he would not find the clothes, since it was Hanna's kind of joke to take clothes and iron them.

"Do I know her?" She asked. Martha assumed it might be the girl, who was cozy with him in chemistry lab. She watched him holding on to the towel and looking in the obvious places for his clothes. She opened the bathroom door and saw Hanna coming into the bedroom.

"Hanna, bring Mister Makomeki's clothes please!" she said to the woman.

"Thanks. Yes it is Janie from chemistry." he said following her into the bedroom. Martha thought that the girl was quite attractive, and he could not refuse her.

"My turn, you do me now." Hanna insisted.

"Hanna!" Martha exclaimed, but the young man stood looking at the older woman as if he had to obey. There was a quiet moment, and then she laughed, "If you can, would you? I know it is humiliating for Kikuyu women to be turned down for sex." She went to the bedside table and opened the drawer and found a Trojan Max, and handed it to him. He was ready for putting it on, considering the bulge. He was using his teeth to tear open the package. She pulled his towel off him and threw it at Hanna who was getting ready on the bed. "At least put this under you. Do her until she says she is tired, please." Martha thought that would be about five minutes.

He was rolling it on as Martha left the room to go into the kitchen to make some tea. After about twenty minutes, as she was pouring boiling water onto the tealeaves in the teapot, Hanna came into the kitchen buttoning her green dress. "Was it okay?" Martha asked

"*Mzuri tu.*" she responded.

"Just okay?" she said as she heard Muturi walk down the hall into the kitchen. He was carrying something wrapped in a tissue.

"No sperms. I love sperms." she said and Martha hoped that he would not understand. "He fadder give me lot of sperms." Hanna said, but Martha did not want to know what she meant.

"Here, I had no sperms left." he laughed, and Hanna opened the tissue to see the used condom was empty.

Hanna acted annoyed and threw the tissue in the trash.

"Miss Mills, uh Martha. I could use some of that tea."

"I have some scones and real butter, too." she added.

"Okay, let's hit the chemistry books."

~~~~~

Wanjiru was helping her husband close up the repair shop and was glancing at him tightening a bolt on a motorcycle. "Mwangi, I am roasting a chicken for tonight is that what you want?"

He set down the wrench and looked at his beautiful wife. "Very good. The kind you make with the potatoes?"

"Yes, but no potatoes… *ugali*." she said as she locked the front door. She started to walk away, when there was a knock at the door, it was Muturi. She unlocked the door."

"*Natya, mama, baba*!" he said and sounded unusually happy.

"Were you able to help your teacher?" she asked as she locked the door.

"Yes, mama, fixed her curtain rods, her *pikipiki* and a leg on her bed." he said proudly.

"It seems like…" she started and another tap at the door. It was Mumera, and again she unlocked the door. She gave the smaller version of Muturi a pat on the shoulder. "Have a good day?"

"I made about a hundred today." Mumera said, and she was not too sure what he did at the market to earn money like that. He had said it was something to do with buying and selling. She looked at the smaller version of Muturi, except longer hair and invariably wore an army jacket.

The family all headed for the kitchen following the smell of roasted chicken. Wanjiru had cut it up into little pieces and served a bowl of ugali with chicken broth, letting Mwangi have first choice of a piece of chicken. He always went for a thigh and a wing, so there was no surprise. The six people ended up sitting in the kitchen with bowls on their knees chatting about things. Wanjiru looked around at her four kids who were there, three others were off at boarding schools, or living with other relatives to help out. Two boys by Mwangi were little, dark brown and skinny, compared to her two oldest.

"Muturi," Mwangi asked, "what kind of *pikipiki* did you repair for your teacher today?"

"A very old BSA. It has a small engine, two stroke thing. It is a wonder that it still works. Next time you might need to replace something."

"My first big repair was a BSA. I bought it from your mother's *mzungu*."

"Really? Why would he sell it, was he leaving?"

"Oh, no, he told me two reasons. He had a bad accident once and was nearly killed." Mwangi said seriously. Muturi knew if the mzungu did die, he himself would not be around to hear the

155

story. "Also his friend Kimani borrowed it, put petrol in it without adding oil mix, and the engine locked up."

"My, his friend must be very humiliated." Muturi said.

Wanjiru spoke up, "Lodi was such a good friend he never said anything, Kimani told me. Other than - maybe Kimani save his life by making him walk instead of kill himself on that thing." They all laughed. "Lodi took me riding on it one day." She added, recalling that day blissfully.

Mwangi said, "He told me about his accident. There was a pack of dogs chasing him, he twisted the throttle to maximum, and it stuck in place just as he came to a turn. Went off the road and hit a fence flew up in the air and landed flat on his back. Had to go to hospital."

"Wambui told me that story also." Wanjiru said, "She thought he would die and she would not have that easy job."

"Did he sell you the *pikipiki* for a good price?" Mumera asked as he chewed on a chicken leg. The two younger boys were punching each other, and Wanjiru tapped them on their heads.

"Yes, eight hundred, the price I asked. But that was when Kenyatta was president and Kenya money was worth something. He let me pay little by little." Wanjiru moaned to herself having heard this story hundreds of times. The boys have heard it, too, but pretended it is all new to them.

"What was he like?" Muturi seemed curious about the man who had fathered him.

"Tall like you, like you, except whiter, and fatter."

"Did you fix it?" Mumera asked.

"Oh, yes, I took the entire engine apart and took parts to Nakuru to be machined and I replaced rings. Put it back together. It ran very fast. I sold it for three thousand five hundred." The two older boys hooted and cheered.

"You must have lived fat for a while," Mumera said.

"No, no, I went and bought more tools to machine parts. I rented a space in Bondeni to repair motors. Later I hired people to help until I married your mother and she became my helper." Mwangi finished his plate and set it in the sink. "I am going back to the shop and finish some work." He walked away, eager to complete a repair job. His two little boys followed him into the shop. It brought back memories of Muturi and Mumera "helping" their *baba* just by being around watching.

"Mama, Miss Mills asked me where your *mzungu* lives in America." Muturi said. Wanjiru felt a pang of nervousness shoot through her. She always felt it whenever Muturi or Mumera asked about their father. She had tried for years to get them to think of Mwangi as their father, but the two never became close to him. They were too different she supposed. She stood up and waved at them to wait. She went to a cabinet in the living room and got a cardboard box full of "his" letters sent to her through her Njoro friend Wambui. She never replied to the letters but he kept sending them. She came back to the kitchen and her boys were finishing off the chicken and ugali. The sun was setting so she flicked on the electric light.

"He moved around over the years. Here is his last letter. He sent a postal draft for two hundred dollars to help with your school fees. I put it in the bank. He sent a picture of himself with his children.

She handed Muturi the envelope, and Mumera moved closer to his brother. Muturi looked at the return address on the envelope. "It is a university address, and on the envelope he ended his name with 'Ph.D.' What does that mean? Is that town the same as that wine with the bubbles? I know 'Illinois.' Miss Mills told me how to say it."

Mumera said, "No, Champagne is spelled with an 'e' at the end."

"How do you know so much about wine?" Wanjiru asked. Mumera acted as if he did not hear her.

He opened the envelope and Wanjiru saw them look at the glossy photo of an older man with a girl and younger boy. "They all looked very happy." Mumera said, "Look at those teeth and smile, just like yours!"

"Mine? Yours." Muturi replied.

"His daughter is very cute. Looks Chinese. How old is she?" Mumera said

"She is a half sister, so do not talk that way. She is thirteen now."

He opened the letter and began reading it, but his mother snatched it away from him. "*Ni ke?*" he wondered.

"It sometimes has personal things in there. Let me read it first." She read it and handed back two of the three pages as properly censored. Wanjiru thought that the two boys would sneak in and read all the personal stuff recalling their afternoons together. The boys read the parts of the letter that would be very boring to young men. It was about his work and his children, and about his wife who spends too much money on clothes.

"Is this Kimani the same one that spoiled his *pikipiki*?" Mumera asked after reading some of the letter.

"Kimani?" She asked and took back the letter, and reread it. "Yes, same one. He visited there because he had training."

"What is this snow that he is complaining about? Is it that bad?" Muturi asked, and his mother laughed aloud. "Is it like the stuff in the freezer?"

"Yes. Many letters complain about snow. When he was here, he missed snow and climbed Mount Kenya to find some. A few months each year in his country, it becomes so cold outside people die if they go outside without heavy clothes. Sometimes the snow is so thick that no cars can move around." She sorted through some envelopes in the box and found a letter with a photo. It was of him in snow up to his knees holding his daughter when she was smaller. "Here, his snow picture."

"*Gai!*" Mumera exclaimed. "How does anyone get around in that stuff? Look at the heavy coats they are wearing. It must be very cold. Is that his house? It is very big. Is he professor?"

"He started as a professor but he says he does something about electricity and machines that do maths."

"Computers?" Muturi asked.

"That sounds right." She was happy they were taking the conversation that way, instead of asking the question she always dreaded.

Mumera read something in the letter, then wondered aloud, "We could be in that picture, brother." She hoped this was not it, and Mumera looked up at his brother. "Why did he not want us with him?" he asked, and her heart dropped to the floor. The two boys looked her in the eyes. She averted her eyes, feeling horrible. "Mama?"

"He asked me to marry him and return to America with him. I do not know anyone in America. Everyone said I would be very unhappy there."

"But we could go to school in America!" Muturi said.

"That is true, he said you could. I would be crazy with worry. I would miss my wonderful sons. I would die I think." She said with tears welling up in her eyes. She looked at the two, who were staring in disbelief. She had not been so emotional in the past, never telling them how attached she was to them.

"Mama," Mumera started, "you have seven children, why are we so special?"

Wanjiru had thought about that many times. Any woman would be very proud of any of her children. Her *nusu nusu* boys were special. "I think it is because I so dearly loved the boy who was your father." She then realized how that sounded for Mwangi. "I like and respect your baba, and he married me because he loved me, and we have a fine life. But there is not a day goes by that I do not recall the deep love I had and I think still have. You are my love children."

Chapter 16, The Affair

Muturi was walking up Kenyatta Avenue with his family returning from church, when he looked down the street and saw in front of the repair shop that Miss Mills sitting on her *pikipiki* in the shade of a tree studying what appeared to be a map. Mumera then noticed and said, "Isn't that your chemistry teacher?"

"Yes, I fixed that *piki* yesterday. I wonder if it is broken already."

Wanjiru said, "Your chemistry teacher? She is so young. She does not look much older than you do, Muturi."

"When we get closer, she will look older." He said, or at least he hoped. Wisdom comes with age, so he was sure his parents would think she is just an empty-headed child. They approached the shop, and his baba unlocked the door and pulled up the overhead door, thinking the *piki* needed repair. "Miss Mills, this is my family. Mwangi, Wanjiru, you know Mumera, and my two little…" Muturi looked around and his little brothers were gone already.

"It is a pleasure to meet you." Miss Mills shook hands with his parents.

Mwangi asked, "Is the motorcycle still working?"

"Oh, yes, just fine. I was wanting to take it out to Lake Nakuru and see the birds and animals."

Wanjiru said, "A woman should not go alone out there, especially on a *piki*. It could break down. The giraffes will step on you." She laughed, as did everyone else.

Miss Mills smiled, "Well, perhaps my student here can escort me. It would be for just a couple of hours."

Mwangi took a closer look at the *piki*, and suggested, "It will be slow Muturi on it, but then it would be safer." He chuckled at his own joke. "Muturi, if you go, take your tool bag with you."

"You mean I can go?" Muturi asked, knowing he would miss the traditional after church lunch.

"Of course. Keep your teacher safe." Mwangi said.

Wanjiru added. "Do you have enough food?"

160

Miss Mills was glowing, "Yes, I have food and drink in the side box, and enough room for tools on the other side. You will need to change your clothes." Muturi was quite excited.

Wanjiru said, "Come in while he changes clothes." Miss Mills followed Wanjiru in, with Muturi following. She was wearing jeans and a leather jacket, and her hair was pressed down from wearing a helmet.

He headed for his room, but he heard his mother chatting with Miss Mills. Of course he worried about what was said. Thinking for the best he changed from boxers to blue briefs, changed into jeans, a sweat shirt and some heavy shoes. He had a hooded jacket that he carried, to put on later.

In a few minutes the piki was packed with food and tools, and he was wearing a helmet his father insisted he wear. She gave the *piki* a kick and it started right away. He got on the saddle behind her, "Hang on tight... don't be shy... we've done it already." She said over the roar of the motor she was revving. He wrapped his hands around her waist, and she set it in gear and gave it petrol. His helmet tapped against hers as they hit bumps. They headed east, hung a right going south looking for Flamingo road. Literally, huge swarms of birds were flying off in the distance in front of them. It was fairly fast on the *piki* to get to the front gate of the park where the guard looked over a pass she presented and waved them on. This time of day the tourists would be at lunch.

Martha seemed to know where she was going. She pointed to several giraffe running gracefully in the distance, then upwards to see what seemed to be millions of birds circling in the air. She took the road near the beach and saw yet again what seemed to be millions of flamingo, painting the lake pink. Their reflection in the still, blue water doubled their numbers. She drove the *piki* quietly on the road around the lake, with it disappearing for a while until they came to a very narrow path by a stream through the trees towards the lake. She took the path winding through prickly trees avoiding thorns that could puncture the tires. She drove up to the point where the trees and bush ended and the beach began, opening up on a spectacular view of the lake. All around was a ridge of blue hills. Everywhere was a lush moss, and in the distance some gazelle, or so he thought. He had heard there were rhino around, so it worried him a bit. The flamingo and pelican were overwhelming

161

in numbers, color and noise. The edge of the lake was not the place to go, so she shut down the *piki* and leaned it against a tree.

"I could watch the birds all day." She was saying as she was pulling the things out of the side box. She took a large blanket she had rolled up under the front headlight, and laid it out on a thick layer of moss. They sat next to each other looking at the spectacular show. She handed him a bottle of wine and a corkscrew, which he had never used before. Then thought how to get the cork out, and then decided screwing it into the cork and pulling it out, and handing her the bottle. "That was quick," she laughed. "It is red wine." She took a sip from the bottle and handing it back.

"This will be my first red wine." He said tasting it. "Hmmm sweet but bitter, more alcohol than beer." She was unwrapping sandwiches handing him one. It was the same roast beef that he had the day before, that he enjoyed so much. They ate and drank while watching the birds circling and diving, pelicans diving for fish, flamingoes skimming the water with their beaks. The wine was half gone, and he was feeling quite relaxed. He had worried at night about becoming a father and curious about what she used to avoid that. "May I ask? We gave into our desires yesterday, and did not use anything…"

"Oh, I should have said. I used birth control pills and hope we have no diseases. Other than AIDS and herpes, a shot will take care of that. But I was hoping you have been responsible."

"I get Durex from the health center and get a jab when I think something is wrong." He looked over at her, and their eyes caught. "You must come out here often." He observed.

"Yes, this is an incredible place. There are preserves in America where birds come and spend the winter. Flocks of geese fly in from northern Canada. Millions of noisy birds, fields of corn just for them, but things about this place are special. I feel so close to life and nature." She looked back and forth between the scenery and him, but he was mostly watching her. "Oh, after you left yesterday, I looked through my aunt's book about her time in Kenya."

Muturi wondered what she was talking about. "You had an aunt that was here before?" He took a bite of the sandwich.

"I didn't tell you? She was a teacher here in Nakuru and left about 15 years ago. She went back to America and wrote a book telling about her life here." She said and Muturi repressed an urge to get too excited about a story that might be related to him. "The problem is that she changed the names of the characters, but an American teacher at Njoro sure sounds like your father."

"Maybe I could read the book?"

"It is very steamy."

"Steamy? What does that mean?

"Oh, she gives details about everything especially sex."

"You know young men only like to read those kinds of stories. Such a book would sell very well in Kenya."

"It was banned in Kenya because it could corrupt young people." She laughed, but he thought she was joking. "I will give you my copy. I will ask my aunt to give me another when I get back."

"Get back? You are leaving?" he felt the pain that comes with separation anxieties. Making such a wonderful friend and the thought of losing them pained him.

"My contract is for two years, but could go up to five. Let's see what happens. My aunt stayed only two years, and went back to Indiana. She got a job in a nuclear plant and wrote the book. Anyway, I read last evening about a trip she took to Mambasa and Lamu with the Njoro teacher, 'Ron' and her Kenyan boyfriend 'Vince,' who was a primary school teacher. In Mombasa, Ron was looking for a Kenyan girlfriend of his who was from Njoro and he found her working in the hotel."

"I was born in Mombasa." he said, getting excited about the story.

"She said in the book that they spent a few days there and Ron spent the entire time in his room with his Njoro girlfriend, while she and Vince saw Mombasa during the day and made love all night."

"Made love?"

"Make love is a nice way of saying they had sexual intercourse. I would say what we did yesterday in the bath tub was making love even though it definitely was coitus." She said and they both laughed. "She said that Ron was never interested in her, and all he would talk about was this Njoro girl, and how he wanted to marry her and take her back to America. But on their way to Lamu on the bus, he told her that he was going back to America alone, that the girl did not want to marry an American and leave

Kenya. My aunt Beth had always been interested in Ron and tried to seduce him in Lamu. She said she took advantage of him one morning in the hotel room the three were sharing."

"Took advantage? How does a woman take advantage?" He thought it was impossible.

"What do you wake up with every morning? If you are sleeping on your back it is very easy for a woman to mount you. Men will think it is a dream until they come." She giggled at the thought and he caught the imagery right away, thinking she must have done it before.

"I think you have done this mounting a man in the morning." He wondered.

"Yes, a boyfriend I had in college."

"You must tell me about him someday."

"He was fun for a while but I would rather forget him."

"So what did your aunt do in Lamu?" he asked, thinking it would be an arousing story.

"Well, Ron had always turned her down. She visited him many times in Njoro. He came to her place in Nakuru, but he never wanted to make love with her."

"Why would he not want to enjoy it?"

"He told her that he did not find her attractive, but liked her as a friend."

"If that is my father, I need to talk to him about manners. If a woman wants it and man just does it." He laughed.

"In America it is very complicated, so I see his point. There a man must pay the cost of raising his children, and here it is optional. So, breeding there can be very, very expensive." He thought it over, and realized that is why his mama's friend is sending money to help with his school fees. "I tried to figure the years and all the people she mentioned, and I bet they made your brother in Mombasa in 1977." She laughed, then realized that saying that may have hurt his feelings.

"Mumera? Mama never gives the details other than saying she could not resist the *mzungu* boy.

"*Mzungu*? Oh, right."

"I wonder how many other half brothers and sisters I may have. He seems to have been very busy."

"Yes, for sure. That reminds me." Martha took a sip of wine and staring at a flock of birds landing along the edge of the lake. "She wrote about showing up at his house in Njoro on a Saturday afternoon after she got to know him and no one answered the door. Aunt Beth thought she could seduce him. She waited a long time on the front veranda until she saw him and some white woman entering the living room from the bedroom area. He let her in, but the woman said something with an Irish accent, and left."

"Irish? Mr Keogh's wife is Irish. I saw her around the school a lot, helping students with studies. So, perhaps Keogh's oldest is my half brother? "

"You said you knew him, so I looked that story up in my aunt's book."

"Did he ever make love with your aunt?"

"He introduced a friend to her, and they got together. When Aunt Beth got back to Indiana, she wrote him letters inviting him to pay her a visit. But she was too busy working on a p. h. d. and raising Franny." She said and that reminded him of the envelope.

"P. h. d. What is that?"

"She wrote in the sand 'Ph.D.' is for doctor of philosophy. In physics, one earns a B.Sc., which is what I have in chemistry, then a M.Sc., which is what I want to get when I go home. Then the highest is Ph.D."

"Did your Aunt Beth ever have children?"

"Yes, a daughter, my cousin, who is younger than I am. My aunt did not marry. She says she went to a sperm bank, although I doubt it."

"Sperm bank! Sperm bank?" he was horrified.

"Some women want children but cannot find the right husband, go to a sperm bank." She said but he was thoroughly confused. "Men go there fill out a form with all their information and ejaculate in a cup and get a few dollars. Usually it is college men." "And they get paid for this?"

"Yes, then the sperm is frozen until a woman picks it. It is thawed and injected in them on the time of the month they are the most fertile."

"You *wazungu* do very strange things. I heard of farmers doing this to cows. *Gai!*" They laughed together. "So, do you really believe it was what you call a sperm bank, or maybe a boyfriend that she did not want in her life?"

"Good point… you are a wise young man." She was quiet watching the birds and he watched her thinking, her lip trembled, "I would have to have the father of my child involved in my child's life, I think." A tear rolled down her cheek. "I love my dad so much, I cannot imagine growing up without him." He saw the look on her face mentioning her father, and wondered.

"Is your father well? Are you worried about him?"

"He is well for an old man. Mom and dad call me at the school every Monday at noontime. They are very proud of me."

"That is very nice."

"Would it be bad for you to write your American father a letter?" she asked.

"Write him?" he said nervously. "What would I say?"

"Just tell about your life and what you are thinking of for your future."

"I will give it a try, if you and mama help me."

"I would be honored to help." She said, and he was feeling excited and hopeful for the future. The huge display of birds was an example of the boundless energy of life. He passed her the wine and pondered the scene.

"Do people other than yourself come here?"

"Sometime people walk along the shore. Why?"

"In case my desires become too strong." He said, and she smiled. She sipped the wine and handed him the bottle. He looked at it and there was just a little left, he drank about half of it and gave the bottle back. It was getting warm and he took off his jacket as she finished off the bottle. She took off her leather jacket. She was wearing a thin sleeveless blouse, and he thought she was not wearing a bra. The wine made him less inhibited, thinking of her as his girlfriend rather than his teacher. He reached over and unbuttoned the top button on the blouse, then the next and next until it was opened, then pulled it out of the jeans, and he saw her thin bra. The snap was on the front and he twisted the snap and released her beautiful breasts. She turned and helped him pull off his sweat shirt, and she turned laying on her back on the blanket. Her hair radiated from her head. She unbuttoned the top of her jeans and zipped them down pulling them down to her boots.

"Help me take these off," she said. He slipped off her boots, leaving her socks on, and pulling off the jeans. He could not resist stroking pubic hair. "Take off your clothes, too." He was soon out of his clothes except his socks, and lying next to her stroking her body. She pulled his mouth to hers and let their tongues lick each other. Her hand stroked down his side to his hip to his shaft resting on her thigh. She rotated her hips, and pressed her hand on his hip trying to get him to mount her. He rolled onto her, and on his own found his way deep into her. The sensation was better than he could ever imagine.

~~~~

Martha felt him slide deep within her, creating a sensation of euphoria she had never experienced before. She almost passed out, but opened her eyes to see the curly brown hair on his chest, then looked up and saw curly brown hair on his chin, then his beautiful blue eyes looking into hers. The roar of a million birds faded to nothingness, as he began a slow thrusting, sending her off into another state of consciousness.

She felt all her muscles tingling and suddenly she was hit with a long intense orgasm that continued as he moved in and out of her. She felt as is she were leaving her body far behind rising up into space to fly among flamingos and pelicans above the lake looking down at the couple making love in the moss near the trees. She felt as if she were soaring with the birds and the sun was burning her skin making it tingle. As quickly as she flew away she returned to see him up on his arms above her, his whole body quivering and convulsing, then collapsing on top of her. The roar of the birds returned and she looked into his blue eyes and enjoyed his pearly white smile. They were still connected, but slowly separating.

He rolled onto his back on the blanket next to her, and she rolled onto her side and rested on an elbow so that she could study the naked fellow next to her. Her bra and blouse fell forward. She stroked the hair on his chest, which felt very soft despite its curly appearance. He rested his head on his folded arms, relaxing and letting her touch him as much as she pleased, and she took advantage exploring every square inch. He fell asleep. Worshipping his body was not enough. She got up, pulled her camera out of the bag, and snapped a picture of her sleeping Adonis.

The petting went of for a while, until she woke him up. "I promised your parents a few hours, and we are past due. Let's not worry them." She said, knowing that there will be other times. She sat up on her knees and snapped her bra and buttoned her blouse as he began getting his clothes on. They were soon dressed and picking up and rolling up the blanket. All packed and ready she turned the *piki* around and gave it a kick-start and nothing happened. She hated that feeling. Three more kicks and still nothing. "It is a long walk back!" she laughed.

"How much oil did you add to the petrol?" he asked and she indicated more than necessary. "Gummed up spark plug. I'll clean it." As he did the day before he took a wrench from the tool bag, removed the spark plug, "Yes, see all the oil deposits?" He brushed it off, put it back and she tried again with success. She revved the motor and blue smoke belched out the back, scaring some birds, which took to the air.

"Whoops, too loud. Sorry birds." She laughed, relieved that she would not have to walk home. He got on the back and felt she had not tucked her blouse in as before and he snuck his warm hands under her jacket onto her belly. She thought it felt good. She gave it gas and their helmets tapped together as she followed the stream path back to the main road, and back to the main gate to Flamingo Road. They quickly were back at Mwangi's repair shop and his home. Mwangi still had the overhead door open so she drove the *piki* right into the shop. Mwangi was with the two little boys and Mumera organizing tools, and they all looked to see them pull in and waved.

After shutting down and parking the *piki* and removed their helmets, Mwangi asked, "Any trouble with the *pikipiki*?" She thought he was wondering if that was the reason they were late getting back.

Muturi said, "Yes, the spark plug was fouled. Need to add some petrol to the tank… too much oil, is all."

"The two stroke is such a bad motor if you get the mix wrong. Too little and motor locks up, too much and the spark plug. Go see your mama, she was worried. Miss Mills, please go have some tea."

~~~~

Wanjiru had spent the afternoon with her sister Muthoni and her five year old boy Kimani. She doted over the boy like he would be the only one she would ever have, which might be the case. She had just returned from putting her sister and nephew on the bus, when Wanjiru heard the motorcycle pull into the repair shop and hoped it was Muturi. She did not worry if he did his teacher, since he would do any woman who wanted it, it was the motorcycle she feared the most. It is so dangerous, but then they were going to the park. She put water and milk on to boil for tea, and sliced some scones that she got from the market. She heard the door to the shop open. "Mama, we are back." Muturi said cheerfully, and in front of him was the tall teacher with the yellow hair. She was wearing a leather jacket and jeans. Muturi was pulling off his jacket as he entered.

"I am making some tea for you. I hope you had a good time at the lake."

"Wonderful time, Mrs. Guitiri. Your son is such a gentleman." Miss Mills said.

"Please call me Wanjiru."

"I will if you call me Martha." They sat down in the kitchen waiting for the tea to boil. "We saw millions of birds and had a picnic. The *piki* did not start, so Muturi knew what the problem was and fixed it. Its okay now."

"I am so happy to hear." Wanjiru said. She studied the two, fairly sure they were engaging in things that a young man and woman would do on a picnic. She stood up, "let me get these toys out of your way." She bent down to pick up the toys in front of Martha and taking a sniff, she knew she was carrying her son with her. Well, she thought, at least my son is attracted to very hardy women. She took the toys and put them in a box, thinking that woman is strong enough to pick up Mwangi and throw him in the air. She laughed to herself as she checked the tea which was boiling and the brown color she liked. She poured the brew through a strainer into three cups which were on the tray with the scones.

As she brought the tray over, Muturi said, "I would like to write a letter to your friend in America and thank him for all his help." She was surprised, but yet she was expecting it. Lodi had written that when Muturi suggested it, he would love to get a letter from him. "Maybe Mumera would like to join."

"Lodi said if you want to someday, he would love to read from you."

"Lodi?" Martha asked

She saw Muturi smile, "That is how Kikuyus in Njoro pronounced his name and it stuck, and everyone knew him as

169

Lodi." Muturi said with the authority of hearing the stories many times. Wanjiru sat the tea down and went to the door and called to Mumera to come in. She went to the box of letters and brought them into the kitchen just as Mumera came in. "Mumera, I want to write our American father a letter. He wrote mama so many letters. We can write to tell him we are doing well."

"If you mean mama's friend Lodi, yes, I am curious. What do you think, Miss Mills?"

"Well, I guess from all those letters he is very interested in keeping a friendship with your mama."

Muturi said to Mumera, "Let's go to our room and write it." He then looked at Martha, "Miss Mills could you wait until we write something so that we do not say the wrong thing?"

Wanjiru looked at the yellow haired woman who merely nodded, and the two young men disappeared. The two stared at each other. She looked at the young teacher, who said "Wanjiru, you must be very proud of your children."

"There are a couple of problem children, but not these boys. I could not ask for finer sons."

"Yes, remarkable."

"I think you also are seeing Muturi as someone very special." Wanjiru said not knowing the right English words for what she was thinking.

"I can see him growing into someone very special, if you know what I mean. I am supposed to be his teacher, but I am here for only a short while. I think he could get into college in America possibly on scholarship."

"I will miss him very much. But it is good that he try his best. Lodi has told me he makes a lot of money and has plenty for all his children to go through college."

"My, he must be a very good friend. I mean you have two children together."

"Yes, whenever I saw him I could not resist, I only wanted him. It was like a magic he had over me." She looked into her blue eyes, "I am afraid my son may have that magic over you."

"Magic? I think you are right. I have had a few boyfriends and none had the magic that Muturi has over me. "

"Be careful. That magic makes babies." They both laughed. "I had an aiyudi after Muturi was born."

"An I.U.D. but you had Mumera…"

"Magic. The aiyudi fell out just right time to make Mumera."

"That is magic or an act of God."

"Maybe God. I worked for Arab man and his family, and he gave me a pregnancy."

"An Arab? Where?"

"In Mombasa. His wives were jealous of me and gave me *dawa* that made the baby come too early. It died, or they killed it."

"That's horrible. They gave you an abortion."

"Abortion? Is that the word?" Wanjiru recalled the word, and continued, "His wives took me to clinic to get the aiyudi."

"And you still worked for him?"

"No, I then worked at hotel in Likoni." She smiled, not really telling the whole story. "That is where Lodi find me."

"He came looking for you?"

"Yes, he got my address from Keogh's wife, who got it from my mother. He said that he would send Muturi baby present."

Martha laughed, "Looks like the present was giving Muturi a brother." Now Wanjiru was laughing. "When he found you in Mombasa, were you happy to see him?"

"Likoni was where he found me. I was very surprised. Then I know he love me, too. He told me he wanted to marry me and take me to America, but I did not want to go. He said he take Muturi and raise him there, but I say I die if Muturi so far away. He said he take care of his child, and I should write whenever I need help."

"Good. It worked out. From all those letters, he must think about you often."

"Fifteen years of letters. I never reply, I never asked for money, but he sent money anyway. My friend Wambui said she wrote." She said and saw that Martha had a very perplexed look on her face.

"Muturi said that his American friend paid his school fees."

"Lodi send some money, even though I never ask. It is what I told him. I made good money in Mombasa. I bought British certificates and I never needed anything from my Lodi. Please do not tell him. Muturi would not understand. I want him to think all the money was from America."

~~~~

171

"I am not sure I understand, unless you are not proud of how you made money." Martha said with a serious face.

"Yes, my boys would not appreciate what I did for them." Wanjiru said feeling a heaviness in her chest. She looked at her box of letters. "I would like..." she started to say as the boys returned with their writing.

"Here is what we have..." Muturi started.

~~~~

Wanjiru promised her boys that she would take the letter to the post office while they were in school. She looked at the letter, with the return address "Muturi and Mumura Makomeki" and the address to some unknown place in the "USA" by airmail. She sat the letter in a cooking pot while she got a match. She set the letter on fire. She watched the flames jump out of the pot until there was nothing but ashes. She put the pot under the faucett and added water, stirred until it was a black flakey soup, and poured it down the drain.

~~~~

Martha was watching her chemistry lab class writing up their results and again Muturi was explaining to Janie and Martin in three languages why the results were as they were. Both touched Muturi a lot, which on one level was arousing and the other made her jealous that she could not do the same right now. "Muturi, before you leave, I have some papers for you." She said and he looked up, and only Janie looked up to see. Muturi stood up and came to the front desk to see what it was.

"I am now curious, I must know." He whispered and chuckled.

"Sorry, I just wanted to make sure you got these forms." She whispered and handed him some papers, and he looked through them a bit perplexed. "I sent off to universities for application forms for graduate schools, and they sent forms for graduate and undergraduate. I thought you could apply for some of these universities. Also they sent information about taking their entrance tests in Nairobi."

"That is very nice of you. Maybe we can go to the same university." He said, and she felt a tingle of excitement.

"Yes, let's see what happens." She said and he was quickly reading through the forms. Other students were handing in their booklets.

"I have to send 50 dollars for the application."

"I have US banking accounts, and can do that for you."

"I will work for you and pay you back."

"If you must." She giggled. He smiled and went back to his work. Martha thought she heard Janie say something about inviting him for tea again, which sent a pang of jealousy through her. But he shook his head no, but Janie whispered something into his ear and then he shrugged a maybe. She heard Martin say something about her seeing a nurse. Muturi shrugged again and went back to his writing. The rest of the class was turning in their booklets and leaving. Martha was feeling very lusty seeing him there writing. She got up and locked the door to the preparation room, as Janie and Martin handed in their writing and left. As she sat down again she reached under her dress and pulled off her panties and put them in her purse. He was done and putting things away into his book bag. She stood up and locked the door to the lab, leaving them alone together. He looked around to see what was going on.

"Are you locking people out?" He asked and looked back towards the windows, and she turned off the lights so no one could see in on a bright sunny day through the dirty windows. She lifted her dress to show the yellow hair he loved to see. He walked around to the door where she was standing. She undid his belt and opened his trousers, which fell to the floor. She could see that he was very aroused. Martha turned and sat on the edge of a lab table, lifting her dress and pulling him towards her. He pulled off his boxer shorts and she saw how aroused he was. She pulled him close and he found his way deep inside her. She felt a million volts of pleasure hit her, convulsing her immediately into orgasm. He began thrusting and she felt herself fly out of her body to hover above the couple making love in a chemistry lab. In the distance the lunch bell was ringing. Waves of pleasure washed over her as he was convulsing and sewing his seed into her. They both collapsed face to face on the table with her legs wrapped around his torso, and their blue eyes locked hypnotically. He suddenly looked guilty and said, "Miss Mills, I cannot believe I just did this to a teacher in a classroom." He withdrew making the sucking sound that made them laugh despite the guilt. They both stood up and Martha took lab towels, handed him one and dried herself off.

"I cannot control myself." She said, not resisting watching him dry himself off and pulling his clothes back in proper order.

"Should I come over after school?"

"I would love that but I am tutoring a group of students. I have to drop down to Nairobi on Saturday to pick up some more birth control pills. You want to go with me?"

"On your *pikipiki*?"

"No, take a taxi *matatu*. I will pay."

"I will ask my parents."

"It would be just for the day. Need to get there by 11, and we will be back by 5."

"When can we do this again?" he asked and she felt a tingle of excitement go through her.

"Let me figure that out. I am expecting my period."

"Period?"

"My month, my moon, period of bleeding." She giggled. "Most men stay away from their women."

"Oh, of course. How do you know when?"

"The birth control pills. I stop taking them and a few days later it comes and then I start a new month for the pill cycle."

"You should show me these pills sometime."

"On Saturday I will show you when I get more." She gave him a hug and a kiss. "We gotta run."

~~~~

Muturi was feeling thick in the head from thinking so hard all day. Being seduced by his teacher in the Chemistry class took some energy out of him, which for a young man he was recouping fast, as he saw Janie and Martin waiting on the street. Just as he wondered if they were waiting for him, they were waving at him. He was curious because Janie had whispered to him that she had seen a nurse to clip her hymen.

"So, you want to come to our place?" Janie asked. Muturi was not too sure, and she added, "I am bigger now. I practice with cucumber."

"What?" he at first thought it was strange, but then he laughed and said, "Oh, how did it feel?" They crossed the street heading towards Janie and Martin's place.

"Okay, a bit cold. But the nurse suggested it so that I don't heal back." She said, but he never heard of such a thing and just shook his head.

174

Martin chimed in, "We both got jabs too for gonorrhea. So, we should be clean."

Muturi knew better. "Not for AIDS or herpes of course, but most things."

Janie whined, "Does that mean you won't share your seed with me?"

"I don't want AIDS." They reached the house, and Janie unlocked the door.

Martin said, "She never did anyone to get AIDS, I am sure. Is that true, Janie?"

"Just some virgin boys with little, skinny things." She opened the door. "Just come in and decide over tea." They went in, but unlike a week before he sat down in the living room on a couch while they went to start the tea and change clothes. He turned on the TV and tried to find something clear and interesting. He found a fuzzy Nairbobi station that was showing some game park safaris. He could barely see the picture for the static. Martin came out of the bedroom wearing only his red Speedos and went to the kitchen. Janie came out wearing a bra and knickers and helped him with the tea. After a few more minutes watching the TV, they brought over tin cups of tea and a saucer of scones. Muturi sipped the tea watching Martin sit next to him and Janie sit in the chair across from him, with her legs open, sipping her tea.

Martin started, "Now Janie wants your seed, but you are afraid of AIDS. I have an idea. Just do her with a condom, and afterward she can poke a hole in the end and have your seed."

"Why do you want that? You want a pregnancy?" He asked, astounded that they were so insistent.

Janie smiled, "Yes." She said simply and continued sipping the tea. Muturi had to admit that he was very aroused at this discussion. If a woman wants his seed, it is rude to refuse.

"Okay," he said, learning from Martha a new way of saying yes. Her eyes lit up and she set the tea down and stood up and disappeared into the bedroom, and returned with a condom, scissors and her cucumber. She handed him the condom. Martin got up and sat down on the chair, and she took off her bra and knickers, standing naked in front of him. He stood up and dropped his pants and shorts. Being very aroused, he put on the condom, but she turned around and bent over. Muturi looked at the target in front of him and desired to try it. He bent his knees somewhat, held

175

onto her hips and slid in a ways and was stopped halfway. She squealed in delight, and he began thrusting and he saw Martin smiling at the show. He kept thrusting as Martin turned to get a better view. Muturi was feeling his muscles throughout his body tightening and she was squeeling each time he went in, and finally he erupted into the condom, and nearly collapsed on top of her. She was shaking. He withdrew and the condom nearly fell off. He handed her the used condom and she sat down on the couch. He did not want to see what she did with it.

As he was getting dressed, Janie asked. "Can you do me a few times a week until I get a pregnancy?" She inserted the cucumber in the condom, snipped the end and inserted in herself. Muturi thought of a farmer inseminating a cow, and felt ashamed for thinking it. The poor girl wants my baby, he thought, but I am afraid of diseases because her brother goes with men.

"We will see." He said, not knowing what the future brings. He admired the beautiful girl on the couch, and it suddenly occurred to him why she wanted his baby. "It just came to me, you want a pregnancy by me, because the baby will not look like your brother, so people will think there is no incest."

"Oh, you very smart." She said, putting her legs across his lap. Martin had fallen asleep. Muturi began petting her pubic hair, thinking how scratchy it was compared to Martha's soft hair. He stroked her belly and played with her breasts, which were sensitive and she pushed his hand away. She smelled of his semen. He moved his hand down the pubic mound until his thumb slipped between her labia and he found her bud, and gently rubbed it until she began squirming obviously enjoying it. The nipples on her breasts hardened to points and all her muscles were tightening as he continued. Her eyes shut tight and she let out a little scream and shuddered.

He stopped and she relaxed. Women have told him that they thought that what she just experienced would suck the seed into the womb and give them a pregnancy. He was not sure that was true, but she obviously enjoyed it.

~~~~

Martha was a bit early, not expecting Muturi would be at the market on time. But there he was standing by the entrance to the market with a couple of girls chatting him up. He saw her coming, waved, and began walking towards her. Not wanting to draw attention, they headed towards where the Nairobi taxis usually sought passengers. There were three drivers next to their white minivans shouting "Nairobi, Nairobi!" and Martha looked at the one nearly full of people. She knew the usual price, and gave the man the price for her and "her student." They got into the back seat of the minivan next to two little women with a baby, packed in very tightly. They needed one more for the front passenger, and it was another five minutes before a heavy set man in a business suit got in. There was a lot of chattering and the taxi roared out. Muturi was next to the window, and Martha was next to the woman with the baby. Martha picked their jackets off the floor and put them across their laps so she could play with him if she wanted.

They headed out of town and headed southeast on the Nairobi road. Off in the distance three giraffe were eating at tops of trees. She could see thousands of birds in the distance flying in circles. The baby began to cry. The woman moved around, pulled out a tit and the baby began sucking happily. They sped on down the road seeing the volcanic cones off in the distance along with more lakes and an incredible landscape of contrasting terrains. Greens followed by barren desert, followed by lakes and volcanoes. Soon they were racing through Gilgil. Sometimes the volcanoes would be smoking as if ready to explode. The minivan roared on past Lake Naivasha, which also had multitudes of birds and pink patches here and there. Then on to Longonot an active volcano, that for some reason made her want to stroke him under the jackets. They started climbing up the escarpment towards Nairobi, giving them the sensation of flying. At higher elevation, they looked out across the Rift Valley for what seemed to be hundreds of miles.

Things turned lush and green heading into the city, the traffic got more vicious, but soon they were heading close to the office where she would be checking in. The taxi was heading for a place about ten blocks further on, but Martha begged the driver to let them out early. He pulled over to let them out by a park, and she gave him an extra twenty. She tried to get oriented trying to recognize the building, and she looked at her watch- plenty of time. She looked at Muturi who said, "Looks like Nakuru here, except for the tall buildings over there."

"True. I have to go over there to check in and get my pills. You want to wait in the park? They make you go through security, and if you don't have an American ID, you will have to wait outside anyway."

"Why?"

"It started after that bombing of that big building in New York city. There are people who want to bomb Americans, I guess."

"I heard about that – they will never bomb Nairobi." Muturi said hopefully. "I will wait over here."

Martha squeezed his hand and headed for the office. It was an ordinary business office with dirty walls and a little plaque saying what it was. Inside a security guard took her ID and let her in. She took the stairs up to the medical office and saw a new receptionist that she had not met before. She handed over the ID,

"You're early but the doctor is free." She smiled and pointed to a chair in the empty waiting room. "I'll let him know you're here." Martha waited for a couple of minutes, and she saw her doctor coming out of his office.

She stood up as he said, "Martha, you're looking good. Come on in." The doctor had black hair laced with grey, and was fairly chubby. She went into the exam room and he pointed her to the exam table, and set her file down to read. "What's up? You okay?"

"I need more birth control pills, I am all out."

"I suppose that means you're sexually active. I suppose I have warned you about AIDS and other STDs." He took off his reading glasses and looked very concerned.

"Yes, I try to be careful about who I interact with. I ask a lot of questions."

"Good, good, don't be shy - it is your life, not just discomfort nowadays. Do you mind if I take swabbings for STDs?"

"I hope you would." She said, but not liking the process.

"Stand up, drop your jeans and panties, and bend over the table, and I will take swabbings and look under the microscope for the bad things." She did as told and felt cold plastic swabs reaching into her vagina and his moving it around. It actually felt very pleasant, but she would not say so, but rather let out a wincing sound as if it hurt. "All done, I will make a slide and take a look, hang on." He disappeared, and she pulled up her clothes and sat there for ten minutes staring at the pictures on the wall. He came back, "Almost good. No Chlamydia, or gonorrhea, but you do have e coli, which usually means you are wiping back to front. Wipe front to back, or you might get pelvic inflammatory disease or cysts."

"Guilty as charged. I try to wipe two birds at once. Any other diseases I might catch?"

"Thousands of them. I could take some blood and send it off to the lab." And she nodded. Soon he had a vile of blood and was writing her name and ID number on it. "It takes a while to get you the news. You want a call either way?"

"Yes, call the school at noon hour, I am usually in the teacher's room."

"Now, we have to change your prescription. They found that the daily dose was much more than what you need. But I have to tell you it may not be enough yet. So, we need to watch this. If you do miss a period come in for a D and C."

"Is that like an abortion?"

"We don't do abortions. We would give you a month off to go back to …" he looked at her record. "Indiana and get one done."

Martha intellectually said yes, but if it came to that she doubt if she could go through it. "Okay." Was all she could say. He disappeared again and came back with four months of pills, and she tucked them on the zipper pouch on the front of her jacket.

"See in four months, or earlier if you have a concern." They shook hands and Martha was soon out on the street looking across the street to the park. There were about a hundred people but he saw him, of course, with a couple of girls standing next to him chatting. She walked over to him.

"Hey, handsome, want a beer?" she said, and laughed. He stood up with a big smile towering over the two girls who walked off. "Got my pills, and the doc said no diseases. The shot you got must have cleared up anything you might have had." They started walking towards downtown, looking for restaurants for lunch.

"Good. I never want to give you anything bad." She looked up at him and really wanted to hold his hand and walk like lovers, but maybe in America. "Oh, I wanted to tell you I filled in all those forms you gave me. You really have enough money to cover all those fees?"

She looked into some of the shops, and saw displays of personal computers. "Don't worry about it. You will love this. These are a lot better than the school's." She pulled him into a store with some British made computers. One had a spreadsheet program running, and she began entering a formula into a cell. Then typed some numbers down a column, then copied down the formula, grabbed a graph icon dragged it down, click it, then selected her data, and as if by magic a graph of the data appeared.

"Wow, that's great."

"Very, very overpriced here though. When you are in college in America we can get you one much cheaper than this."

"We?"

"Assuming we go to the same university of course." She laughed. They left the shop and began looking for a restaurant. They came upon an Indian restaurant, a place Martha recalled having eaten at when she first arrived in Nairobi. "You like spicy foods?"

"*Pilipili*," he said, "is good going in and coming out, Mwangi says."

"Or there is another place, straight bland everyday food."

"We are in Nairobi, let's go exotic." He suggested, guiding her into the Indian restaurant. They were quickly shown a table and handed dirty menus. The table was a bit sticky, but Martha convinced herself that it was because the table was just wiped clean and it was still wet. He looked around, "You think we get the *zumzum*?"

"Maybe, help clean us out and we can start fresh." She looked at the menu and everything was a curry of some sort, not like her favorite Indian restaurant in Lafayette, Indiana. There was one masala.

Muturi was looking around at what other people were eating. "The chapatti looks very good. I should get a stack of those." The waiter suddenly appeared and they both chose a chicken curry, and he added, "Some extra chapatti, too, please." The waiter just smiled and disappeared. They both were studying the people in the restaurant. Half were Asian, a few whites, the rest looked Luo. He added quietly, "I think Luo like the *pilipili*."

"I may be wrong but I heard that, too. Was that because so many of the Hindi railroad workers ended up out in Kisumu with the Luo?"

"I do not know, I would be guessing." He said, but he obviously enjoyed speculating, she thought. Suddenly the food showed up, with two people laying down plates, napkins and tableware. Muturi lifted a plate cover and there was a stack of chapatti just as he ordered. Martha looked at their plates, piled high with a variety of chopped vegetables and chicken in a greenish-yellow sauce. Then a pot of black tea and several cups showed up. She jabbed at a piece of vegetable and took a bite, and the flames of hell engulfed her oral cavity. She could feel her face burning and sweat breaking out on her forehead. She watched him take a scoop of vegetables and chicken and put it on the chapatti, and took a bite. "Hmmmpf," and a grunt. "Delicious!" She laughed for inflicting such pain on herself, like a masochist, but he seemed happy with it.

"If this does not give me *zumzum*, I don't know what will." She laughed.

"Tomorrow maybe, not now." He stated, on a mission to devour everything in sight. Martha poured some tea to calm her mouth, and she sucked on a lemon, then tried again. By the time she was able to get a third of her plate done, he had consumed all the chapatti but one and cleaned his plate.

"How about some tea?" she asked and pushed her plate away from herself.

"Do you not want that?" He asked. She shook her head and he traded plates with her, and soon had finished it off. The waiter brought the tab and gave it to Muturi. Martha looked at it and was stunned how cheap it was, and put down a few notes to cover it plus gratuity. The waiter came back, and Martha said, "The change is yours." The waiter gave a polite bow and disappeared.

Back on the street, the city had clouded over and turned chilly. Martha knew where the taxis back to Nakuru was, but asked, "What time did you tell your parents you would be home?"

"In time for supper, about *saa moja usiku*, I mean about seven PM."

"What are your plans for tomorrow?" she asked, thinking another Sunday picnic somewhere might be fun.

"Family day tomorrow. Mwangi wants to take us all in his truck up to the top of Menengai Crater for a family picnic. We will all be packed in like canned fish."

"Sardines?" She offered, but thought she might tag along on her *piki*, but suggested for now, "We could tour Nairobi for a while, or go back to my place and get naked." She said. "I leave the choice to you."

"That is no choice," he laughed, "Let's find a taxi or *matatu* or bus back."

They started walking faster. "Taxi is fastest. Now my period is due, so you may want to wear protection, I have some at home."

"Not as sweet, but if your period is due, I hate getting bloody..." he said.

~~~~~

Hanna had come in to prepare supper for her *mzungu*, and was trying to read Martha's note, which was written first in Swahili, then English. The Swahili was nearly incomprehensible, and she did not know how to read English that well. It was something about a soup, she thought, and maybe bread. As she finished reading, she heard some noises coming from the bedroom. Martha must be back from Nairobi early. She went to the bedroom door, which was opened a crack. Standing in the darkness of the hallway she saw the two naked people connected with Muturi on top and Martha's legs entwined around his. Their faces were turned away from her, so she watched as she heard Martha letting out little screams of pleasure, and his butt going up and down rapidly then suddenly stopping. Both relaxed, and he rolled off to her side. He took off a condom and dropped it on the floor. He rolled over with his back to the door as if smothering her with hugs.

Hanna had wanted his semen, because, she thought, she wanted his pregnancy. Maybe, she thought, "get same girl his fadder gave me." The time Martha made him do her, it was not what she wanted. These days all the men are afraid of that sex disease that kills slowly, so they only want to do virgins, not older, single women like herself. She was old, too, at thirty four, but still young enough to have the baby she wanted. She had two babies, but they died of *zumzum* and dehydration.

She watched for a while and it looked as if they had fallen asleep. She opened the door and quietly snuck in and picked the bloody condom off the wood floor and snuck out just as quietly. Looking at the condom she knew that Martha is having her moon. She closed the door and went into the kitchen to look through the vegetable bin and found a plump carrot, chopped off the green and inserted it into the condom, washing the blood off in the sink, then holding it up so his seed would run down. She snipped the tip of the condom with a paring knife. She sat down on a chair, lifted her cotton dress, and pushed her underwear aside to insert the condom-covered carrot. She felt his seed still warm inside her. She stuck it in as far as she thought the womb was. She moved it back and forth as if it were a man doing his thing, until she felt the tingle and her muscles all contracting. As the old women say, the womb is sucking up the seed. She let out a little scream, then felt a fine bliss settle over her. She could feel the seeds planted in her womb, or so she thought.

She sat for a few minute, then thought, he will look for the Durexi. She took the carrot out of the condom and washed it off, placing back in the vegetable bin. She went into the bedroom and stood over the naked couple entwined like snakes. The two looked up. "I want him to do me now." Hanna said.

Martha laughed, "He is all mine now. No share." Hanna looked at him and he was too busy playing with her breasts to care about Hanna.

"I clean up for you," She held up the condom so that Martha could see. Martha was stroking down there. "He will need another." Hanna opened the little drawer and took out another and handed it to Martha, who just giggled. She one-handedly tore open the packet with her teeth, squeezed it out, tossed the empty packet to Hanna, looked at the plastic thing, then expertly rolled it right onto him.

"Go fix my supper, Hanna, I want soup and bread, just me, he has to do me then go home." They both giggled together. Hanna was dying of jealousy.

She left the room thinking the boy might produce more seed for her, and feeling that this might be her most fertile time of the month... since all she could think about was men... she might get a pregnancy by this giant, *nusu nusu* Kikuyu boy.

She went back into the kitchen to start the soup, and after a long while she heard sound in the other room and a door opening and closing, then Martha, wrapped in a white robe, coming in looking for food. She was all aglow, which gave Hanna more pangs of jealousy. However, she made a large bowl of soup – more like a stew – on a plate with bread and butter. Martha sat down humming and sipping her soup. Hanna snuck her trusty carrot and headed into the bedroom, and found the condom in the bathroom waste bin wrapped in a tissue. His valuable seed was still warm, and she closed the toilet lid, sitting down, and planted more seed.

Chapter 17, Harrassed

Muturi was frantically writing the notes from Mr. Watusu's maths lecture. He was flying along proving a formula on the chalk board, and finished it with a "QED! Well, not really, but you see how I got there? The room was silent as everyone looked at the board then their notes. Muturi saw it plain enough after he stopped writing. No one else wanted to admit that they did not, so the room was silent. "There is not enough time to do another, so you can leave early." There were the rushing sounds of students putting away books and notes, but Mr. Watusu added, "Mr. Makomeki, please stay a moment I would like to ask a question or two."

Muturi was suddenly very nervous. Mr. Watusu - or Joe as he tried to get students to call him - was an average mixed tribal Kenyan, very, very black with an oval shaped face, and he was apparently proud of what he carried in his pants, which was intimidating to some male students and exciting for others. That is, Mr. Watusu was well endowed and wore trousers that emphasized the fact. He was very bright, but had told the story that it took him very long to get through college because he would have to quit school for a while to earn money to pay for his younger brothers to get through school. The fact that he was not married made him the subject of rumors about liking boys rather than girls. So, is he going to chat me up? Muturi wondered. Then he laughed at himself and was curious what would happen.

"Mr. Makomeki, I hope you do not mind," he started but someone came to the door. It was Janie's brother Martin, who waved at Muturi. Mr. Watusu turned his back on Muturi to speak quietly to Martin. Martin was asking something, and he could barely hear the teacher say, "Please, do not bring your sister, though." He turned around and Martin had a mixed expression of excitement but anxiety about something. The teacher walked up to where Muturi was sitting. He looked a lot shorter now that he was off the lecture stage.

"Mr. Makomeki, I hope you do not mind, but I was curious about your name, and I looked up your record. Your second and last names are very interesting, especially since you were a day student at Njoro." His voice was very pleasant, and now that he knew the topic less threatening. Muturi was distracted having those packed trousers staring at him, so he got up and sat on the table so that he and the shorter teacher were more on the same level.

"When I was in form two at Njoro, there was a teacher with your name, spelled differently but just about the same."

"Yes, that is true."

"I know this is very personal, but that teacher, I was very fond of. He was very funny and treated me and my friends like his young brothers."

"Yes, I have heard of stories." Muturi gave a big smile.

"And your smile, Mr. Makomeki, is identical. I would swear I am looking at him now."

"That is because he is my biological father."

"Oh, and I joked that he had spoiled all our women and left nothing for us. It looks like my joke had truth in it." He thought a moment. "Anyway, it was an honor to know your father. My friend Muwera and I often went to his house to hear music and drink orange juice."

"Muwera? My mother and her friends told several stories of a Muwera."

"Muwera is, what they call these days, gay. Well, was, he is dead now. He died of a cancer caused by that sex disease... uh."

"AIDS."

"Yes, that is it. Anyway, Muwera was in love with him probably as much as your mother." Mr. Watusu said, and Muturi nodded acknowledging the truth of the statement. "Muwera was always hanging around him, hoping he would do him. If you know what I mean." Muturi thought of his experience with Martin, and simply nodded. "It was pitiful. Unrequited love."

"Unrequited?" Muturi said not knowing the word.

"Like with a girl you love, she never lets you do it with her." He laughed and Muturi smiled. "Anyway, he told me to introduce Muwera to a certain gay prefect there, and Muwera was happy after that.

"My mother and her friends always wondered what happened to Muwera. He was such an odd person for them. I will let her know this evening. They never talked about you, so you must have been very ordinary." They both laughed together.

"I think I left an impression on certain boys who liked to watch me take a shower."

Muturi was perplexed then it hit him, "Oh, you still have some boys who are curious about your manhood." he laughed.

"Yes, I know. I do at least know what your father went through with Muwera. There are gay boys here who keep asking me." He laughed. "Several have made some interesting offers."

Muturi was interested, although feeling that he was chatting him up, perhaps wanting Muturi to do something for him. He did not mention girls wanting him, which is more likely. "For example?"

"Umm... you know. I'm sure you get offers all the time." Muturi was wondering why he was saying this to him, other than he is chatting me up, he thought, and to see if I get aroused talking about these things.

"I get that too. But a lot more with girls." Muturi said and wondered out of curiosity where this would go. "Can I ask you for some help?" he asked.

"Of course."

"I am applying for many universities, some in America, and I need to do well in my studies and have good references from my teachers." Muturi thought this might be a interesting to see where he takes it.

"I give tutoring for my students, and once I know them I give references." Mr. Watusu said. Muturi thought, is that know them in the biblical sense? If he is chatting me up, at least I will know if that in his trousers is real or just padding. Mr. Watusu started writing something and handed him a scrap of paper. "Here is my address, students can come over for a while around 4 everyday. I usually shoot basketball around the side of my apartment, so if I do not answer the door, come around the side."

"Thank you. That will help me very much."

"Good, I can get to know you." He said, and Muturi thought, there he said it again. Will we know each other in the biblical sense? Curiosity.

~~~~

Muturi could not resist the call of his curiosity. Was Mr. Watusu chatting him up or just being a concerned teacher. He was skipping Janie just to find out. He found the house easy enough since it was in Miss Mills' neighborhood in an apartment building,

187

a corner unit on the ground floor. He heard a basketball being dribbled on the side and went around and there Mr. Watusu was only wearing white shorts and athletic shoes, and of course, the shorts emphasized his manhood. He made a nice lay up, and came up to Muturi. "Need some help?"

"Mr. Watusu, I was on my way home, just stopped to say hello."

"Come on in, Mak. Please call me Joe. Your father's mzungu friends called him Mak." He said and Muturi followed him in the back door of the apartment through the kitchen. He pointed to the dining table and Muturi set his book bag down and turned around. "Come in here and talk while I shower." He said and Muturi felt a shot of nervousness. He went into the bedroom and his teacher was already naked walking away from him towards the bathroom.

It was so dark the black man nearly disappeared into the shadows. He switched on a light and put the toilet lid down and said, "Mak, have a seat and talk." Muturi saw the demarcation of very black back to the merely black buttocks as he got in and pulled the clear curtain shut and turned on the water. He was saying something he could not hear, so he went in and sat on the toilet lid like a chair, worried that his curiosity may spell his doom. In the shower, Joe was saying something about liking to work up a sweat after teaching. The shower shut off and he stepped out reaching for a towel at the same time, and indeed, he had the longest and biggest set of manhood he had ever seen coming out of a shower, and he had seen a lot from years of showering after basketball at the dormitories. What have I got into now? Muturi thought to himself.

~~~~

He had escaped from Watusu with his dignity intact. He knocked at the door and Hanna opened it and let him in. "You want me or you want Martha?" She asked. He looked around as if she would be there. "She at school. Her time on paper in kitchen." He followed her into the kitchen and remembered that she taught labs until seven. "You do me now?" she asked. He thought she would do. She said in Kikuyu, "You do me and use Durexi. I have no disease. You only one who do me." She bent down pulling off her knickers, and pulled her dress up and over her head, standing naked in front of him except for plastic sandals. He was

completely aroused, but he still thought she would give him a
disease, and looked through his book bag for health clinic Durex,
and found several in the inside pocket. She got up on the edge of
the dining table getting ready for him.

~~~~~

Martha closed her front door and locked it, sliding her bag
on the floor and kicking off her shoes. She was thinking she had
seen Muturi a block ahead of her jogging as if hurrying home. She
recognized his book bag for sure. He must have stopped by. She
thought, I need to give him my schedule so if he wants to drop by,
he will not be raped by Hanna. She chuckled at the idea. She heard
some noises in the kitchen, so she headed that way and stopped at
the sight of a naked Hanna masturbating on the dining table. She
was using a large carrot and what ... a condom? Hanna was giving
off lust grunts and her hips were gyrating, then she went limp as if
she were done. She pulled out the carrot, but the condom was
stuck, and she was groping for it when Martha asked, "Hanna,
what are you doing?" Hanna jumped off the table to grab her green
dress, which was draped across a chair. The condom was hanging
out of her vagina as she tried to put on her dress.

"You home early." Hanna said, and Martha laughed, and
as Hanna was pulling the dress over her shoulders, Martha
snatched the condom, and sniffed the end. Hanna pulled her dress
on and began looking for her knickers.

"Muturi was here." Martha said. Then she saw the tip of
the condom had been cut off.

"Maybe."

"Hanna, are you trying to make Muturi a father?"

"He no fadder. I just use his sperms." She found her
knickers and pulled them on. Martha thought there was something
pathetic about her friend Hanna being unable to find what she
wants out of life that she has to seduce students who come around.

"How many times have you done this?" She asked, simply
curious. She felt Hanna was too pathetic to feel angry at her.
Hanna counted with her fingers and held up three. "Okay, I know
you miss your children, and Muturi would have some healthy
sperms. That is true. It is good you use a condom. Thank you."

"You not angry at me?" she wondered.

"Angry? I love you too much to be angry. I understand."
Martha said. "Now make me some supper, I want a quick shower."

189

A few minutes later in her living room, Martha found the number in the phone book, picked up the telephone and began rotating the telephone number in. She had the telephone installed after her father said he would pay the cost, because he did not like getting up at 4 or 5 AM to chat with her at her lunchtime. It rang five times before the voice came on "Mwangi's Engine Repair" in Mwangi's voice.

"Hello, this is Miss Mills. How are you? Can Muturi talk on the telephone?"

"Oh, Miss Mills, I am doing very well. Yes, Muturi can talk with you. Supper will be ready in a half hour, so do not make him too long." He said and chuckled. She at first thought he had bad English, then realized what he was getting at, and she chuckled too.

"He is a young man," she stated.

"Please hold," he added, and she waited a couple of minutes.

"Martha? Your first call. This is nice." He said cheerfully.

"I just had to hear your voice, I know you have to stay in and study, so I won't make you too long."

"Keep me too long?"

"It is your baba's joke." She said and heard him laugh. "Say, Hanna tells me she has been using your sperms."

"What?" came the voice over the phone.

"Yes, she has been taking your used condoms and inseminating herself. I thinks she wants your baby." Martha laughed.

"Did she tell you I was there after school today?"

"No, but I caught her using your condom"

"Interesting. Well, she would make a good mother."

"I don't know about that. She had two babies but they died of diarrhea."

"*Zumzum*." He stated obviously for understanding. "Mama say it nearly kill me a dozen times. Also, Hanna claims her firstborn's father was my father."

"Really? I'll ask her what the story is."

"Oh, should I tell you about Mr. Watusu?"

"Joe? What did he do now? He showing off his dick again?"

"Dick?" there was a silence. "Oh, his long, black snake?"

"Oh, did he show you? It is amazing. When I saw it, I just had to jack him off."

"Is that American?"

"Oh, I guess. What did you do?"

"I went over hoping to get a recommendation for college. He told me to talk while he took a shower, then came out and got an erection in front of me."

"Same here. It looks like a deadly weapon... or like you said a long, black snake."

"Yes, I could not resist. It was like I was hypnotized into thinking it was *my* snake. I wanted to see it spit poison like a snake!" They both laughed so hard that Martha had tears in her eyes.

"I did it in his bathroom sink. Then he grabbed me and tried to get me aroused."

"Did he?"

"Men make me shrivel up." Came the distant voice, and she laughed.

"Well, make him happy sometime, close your eyes and pretend it is me and let him jack you off. He will give you a good recommendation. Even better if you let him -"

"Martha! Shame on you!"

"Muturi, you are right, teachers should not be having sex with their students."

"I never said that. I am surprised that you are not jealous."

"Jealous?" She was perplexed. "Because all these people want to do to you what I want to do?" There was silence again. "I mean, after we get married you have to be all mine."

"Yes, when we get married." Came the voice across the line. "I have only known you for a few weeks, so I guess we should wait a while before the wedding." He said and Martha laughed, but did not know what to say. There was a long pause. "Sorry, did I say the wrong thing?"

"No, it was very sweet. Not only a great lover but a gentleman, too. What a guy." She said. Over the line she heard a child saying something either in Swahili or Kikuyu.

"I am being called for supper. Good evening to you." He said.

"You, too. Good night." She said and hung up. She stared at Hanna wondering what she wanted. "Hanna, are you done?"

"You know my nephew, right? He your student." She said, and it never occurred to her, since the young man usually showed up when she was somewhere else out of the house.

Martha looked at the boy, "Oh, Martin, yes. How are you doing? I hope you are studying your chemistry."

"Yes, Miss Mills. I study hard." He said, and she wondered if that had a double meaning. "Janie and I study together." He said. Martha thought of Martin's twin sister. They seemed a little too close at times. Both were hitting on Muturi! Then she worried that Hanna would tell Martin that she is seeing Muturi, but then she would let the cat out of the bag about her using him... or at least his sperm. Oh, is it getting complicated? She asked herself. Martha then realized she had too much sex on her mind.

"Well, if you or any other students need tutoring, let me know." She offered.

"Maybe Janie, I and Muturi come over and learn some things." He smiled, and she thought, what does he mean by that. These horny teenagers only have sex on their minds.

"Maybe just you and Janie. Janie obviously has too much Muturi on her mind to learn chemistry when he is around." And they all laughed at the idea.

~~~~

Mumera was sitting on his bed looking through "the" box of letters and photographs, and heard his brother flush the toilet down the hall, and appear at the door a minute later. The taller version of himself came in pulling off his shirt, and dropping his trousers, folding them to use again tomorrow. His brother walked past him in his boxer shorts, and looked him in the eyes, "What are you doing. Isn't that mama's private things?" Muturi asked.

"It is very sexy stuff. Mama was very beautiful when younger." Mumera stated holding up a photograph. Mumera took it and, turned it over.

"Egerton Castle, it says. They did it in Egerton Castle? You're right, she was beautiful. Well, she is beautiful now, but my..."

"Muturi, you are getting happy." Mumera laughed. "That is your mother!"

"She is naked with a white man and he has his hands on her belly in Egerton Castle no less!"

"That white man is our father, *manii*!" Muturi exclaimed.

192

"I think he knew you were in that belly."

"Mama will kill us if she knew we were getting happy looking at her naked pictures. Here, I will put them back." Muturi said, and Mumera shrugged, since both were "happy."

Muturi returned and turned off the light and settled into his bed on top of the sheets. There was a glow from the streetlights keeping the room from being totally dark. Mumura saw that his brother was stroking the hair on his chest.

"You mind if I ask?" Mumera was curious about his brother's life outside the home, and his brother shrugged as if to say, ask away. "Who are you doing these days. I heard mama and baba say you are doing Miss Mills, and at school there is a girl saying you are doing her."

"It would sound like I am bragging." Muturi said.

"I am your brother - you are supposed to make me jealous." Mumera laughed.

"Okay," he said, "The last few weeks, Tuesdays and Thursdays after classes, I do Janie. On Mondays and Wednesdays after classes, I do Miss Mills' housekeeper. Then Friday evening through Sunday evening, I do whatever Miss Mills wants." Mumera was getting aroused, hearing the story.

"I heard stories you do her in the chemistry lab also."

"*Gai*! How did you hear that?" he asked.

"Lots of stories about you, but most of them I know are false, like I heard one boy claim he did you. This one sounds right." Mumera offered.

"Yes, once or twice a week, I stay after class and she locks the doors and turns off the lights."

"Then you do Janie or the housekeeper the same day?"

"Sure, I am young. I make sperm like Tusker makes beer." He laughed, and Mumera was very aroused stroking himself. "She usually tells me to help her clean up, then lifts her dress and shows me her yellow hair, and I cannot resist. I have to do her there."

"Where?"

"On the chemistry lab table. The one away from the windows."

"Now that is what I call learning chemistry! Then after classes you are ready for more?" Mumera wondered, and was stroking himself in excitement.

"Yes."

"Are you going to give these women pregnancies?"

"I use condoms with Janie and Miss Mills' housekeeper. And Miss Mills takes pills."

"Lots of Durex." He said stroking himself more quickly.

"They both cut holes in them later and inseminated themselves like cows." He laughed. "So, they will probably have two kids by me next year."

"And Miss Mills? You think that she really taking pills?" he said feeling the tingle of the coming eruption.

"I see her take the pills several times a week. But maybe she want a pregnancy. Who knows. If a woman wants it, a man must give. She wants so much - I think I might cancel out the pills." Muturi laughed and Mumera groaned and made a mess in his briefs.

"*Gai*!" He cursed and went into the bathroom to clean up.

~~~~~

Muturi was sitting next to Mumera on the tailgate of his baba's pick-up truck looking into Menengai Crater. His baba loved bringing his family up here after church with a picnic lunch on beautiful days. There was a tall sign there pointing to various places on earth and how far away they are. The volcano is long extinct with the hot spot moving on as the Rift Valley widens. Looking out over the valley he tried to imagine it millions of years hence at the bottom of a sea. He took a bite of his sandwich and watched his little brothers running around, then up to the sky to see billowy clouds floating by. Mwangi and his mother were sitting in the cab chatting, and Mumera was watching other people who had come up the steep hill to see the crater. He recognized a few German phrases, and assumed that they were either tourists or teachers from Egerton College. As one of the older Germans passed by he said, "*Wie gehts*?" The fellow's face lit up.

"*Sehr gut, danke*." He said and switched to English. "You know a little German?"

"Yes, my mother's cousin married a German. They live in Mombasa."

"Very nice. Yes I teach at the college in Njoro."

"Egerton?" Muturi said, and the man nodded. "I thought you were a tourist or a teacher." As he said this, he heard the familiar revving of a motorcycle coming up the hill. Mumera jumped down and ran over to one of the little ones getting too close to a drop off.

"It is beautiful up here." He said. "My car barely made it up the hill."

"We sometimes have to get out and walk." Muturi said and turned to see Martha driving her *piki* up to the back of the truck. She got off the *piki* and walked up to Muturi and gave him a hug, and shook hands with Mumera.

"I thought I would find you up here." She said and the old man walked back to his family. Mwangi and Wanjiru got out of the truck's cab, and Martha gave Wanjiru a hug and shook Mwangi's hand.

"Martha, it is good to see you. How is everything? You look a bit worried?" Wanjiru said, and Muturi wondered at how his mother had determined that she looked worried. Is it a secret greeting that women have?

"You have a good eye. My mother called and said that my father had a mild heart attack and spent the night in the hospital. He is back home and feeling better." Martha said. Muturi was a bit shaken, feeling how it is when a loved one is hurt.

Muturi said, "You must feel very bad."

"At first, but my mother said that he is doing much better. If it gets worse I will want to fly back."

Wanjiru said, "We should pray for him. My father died a few years before Muturi was born, but I did not know him. I know I would feel horrible if I lost my mother." Mwangi nodded in agreement. "Martha, I have an extra sandwich if you like to join our picnic. We feel closer to heaven up here."

"No thank you. I slept late and had a big breakfast. I was going for a ride and hoped to see some friends, and I did – joined some friends close to heaven." Martha took out a camera out of the side box and snapped a few pictures of Muturi and his family standing there talking to her.

"If you are driving around," Mwangi suggested, "Muturi should go with you. It is not safe for a white woman driving around alone." Muturi thought it great that his baba was getting him together with a woman.

Muturi chimed in, "Mama, is it okay?" Mwangi was getting a few tools out of the back of his truck and putting them in

Muturi's backpack, as Wanjiru nodded approval. Muturi thought his mother had that I-know-what-you-are-after look on her face.

Martha asked Mwangi, "On the way up I saw several grass huts off the way all empty and overgrown, do you know what that is?"

"Oh, those were the workers for a big farm owned by *mzungu*. He sold the place to his workers and moved to Australia. The workers all moved into the *mzungu* house."

"Do you think they would mind if I look inside? I have never been in a grass hut." Martha said, causing Wanjiru and Muturi to burst into laughter. She looked at them, "What?"

Wanjiru tried to be polite, "I lived in one for years before my mother moved to a wood house."

"Mama, I still remember playing around that hut with my aunties."

"Oh, right, Muthoni and Warimu lived there for a time before Warimu died." Muturi saw his mama flinch at the mention of her sister's death.

"Well, Muturi, you will be my guide on living in a grass and stick house." She said as she put the camera away, got back on her piki, and bumped it off its stand. She put on her helmet.

Mwangi said, "We left your helmet at home. Young lady, please go very slow with our boy on your back." Muturi put on the backpack his father handed him and got on the back of the *piki*, knowing his baba was trying to make another double meaning joke.

"No worry, Mwangi, he is very safe with me. We take it nice and slow. He likes to hang on tight and take a slow ride." She said as she kicked the engine and revved it up. Soon they were rolling down the hill in second gear with the engine whining and complaining. Muturi gripped his hands together under her leather jacket and bumped his head against her helmet with every rut in the road. Large white clouds floated above the horizon, threatening to turn into an afternoon shower, as was often the case around the lake and crater. They drove the windy road down the crater, through some scrub trees that opened into farmland. Muturi saw her point towards the row of grass huts on the other side of a field of maize. She looked for a gap in a barbed wire fence and took the *piki* up a narrow footpath towards the huts. She pulled up to a large hut surrounded by some smaller ones, stopped, and shut off the engine. They both got off and looked around. She took out her camera again and snapped a picture

"The smaller huts were for women with fewer children. The men usually had their own huts - young single men would have tiny huts. A woman with young children had her own, where all the children slept, but the men would come to eat and chat." Muturi said.

"Where did they have sex?" Martha asked as if that was the most important thing. Not where did they get water, or food, or clothes. Rather, where did they do sex? He laughed to himself, knowing that is something she had on her mind.

"Usually the man's hut, then when they are done, the woman goes back to the children. Or if a man must have it, in the woman's place after the children fall asleep - or in front of the children for their sex education."

"Really? The thought of seeing my parents having sex is kind of..." she stopped looking for words.

"Natural? Beautiful? Inspiring?" he laughed. She went to the largest grass house and bent over, pushing aside a leather curtain, looking inside. "It will be dark." He said and she went inside with him following into the dark hut. There was light coming from the smoke hole at the top about four meters above. As their eyes got used to the dark, they could see the row of beds along the wall, and a large bed behind two posts. She was fingering the rubber straps on the bed.

"What is this?" she asked. She stood back and snapped a picture of Muturi next to the bed.

"They took the rubber from tire inner tubes, and cut them into straps and weave them into a rubber mat. Then they nail the straps to the wooden frame." He pointed to the row of nails.

"Looks bouncy." She said and flopped down on the bed. He looked down at her. Her leather jacket fell open to show her t-shirt and her beautiful breasts. She wore loose fitting jeans without a belt. She handed him the camera, and he looked through the lens, adjusted the aperture until a little needle was centered, then clicked.

"You see the walls?"

"Looks like adobe." She said, sitting up and taking off her jacket.

"Cow dung and mud." He said, and watched her take off her boots.

"Cool." She said. He took off the backpack and put the camera inside for later.

"Not really, the fleas hatch out when it is fresh and they eat people." He laughed, remembering flea bites as a kid. "But this is dried out and falling off. No fleas."

"So, if a Kikuyu woman wants it, does she just get naked and wait for it or what?"

"They just say they want it, and their man must give it to them. Or it will humiliate them so much that…"

"*Ninataka kitu hiki*," she said pointing at his groin.

"You want this thing?" he repeated in English, thinking she must have been looking through her language course materials to piece that together. "Just this thing or something more?" he teased.

"*Mimi ninataka chote na manii yote*", she said getting him quite excited.

"I *must* give you what you want." He smiled and began removing clothes.

~~~~~~~

Martha awoke slowly out of a dream that she was nursing a beautiful baby at her breast. The image of the infant dissolved into the ceiling of the grass hut that she and Muturi were making love in. The sky through the smoke hole was grey and blue as if the rain was moving on, though she was warm and dry where she was lying. She followed the line of the curving sticks and woven reeds that made up the roof. A few places needed repair were letting in light. Straight above the bed the grass was water tight and she felt warm and comfortable with the heat of the young man's body pressed against hers.

Muturi should be exhausted by now, but he was toying with the nipple of her left breast and giving it a lick once in a while. Their bodies were entwined among their clothes being used as covers. Her leather jacket was a pillow. She was thinking of the dream and that several weeks ago she did not get her period during the break from the birth control pills. She had been nauseated several mornings, in fact vomiting several times. She was sure, despite the birth control pills that she was pregnant. No use alarming anyone. Just wait to see if it takes. She thought to herself, if I miss the next period, I might fly back to Indiana to nip it in the bud, or whatever...

"Hey, you think your father and mother made love in a place as strange as this?" Martha wondered.

"My biological father? And Mama?" he laughed, "You know my Mama has her box of private things, and Mumera showed me a picture of mama and my father in Egerton Castle naked!"

"No! You got to be kidding!" she felt the excitement sweep through her.

"In color! Not cheap black and white. Mama was very sexy when she was young."

"I'd love to see that picture. Hey, do you know how to get to Egerton Castle? I got my camera." Martha laughed.

"I do but I think, some church group runs it now. We would just go over to the Kisumu Road, go up a ways and take a left. It's a mile or two."

"Let's go, since it's not that far."

~~~~~

Martha's motorcycle came to a halt on the north side of the castle, and Muturi was thinking this could be big trouble, but very exciting. Mama and my father did it here! Why can't we? He thought. They got off the *piki* and parked it in some bushes in case someone would see. Muturi said, "The church group uses the old ballroom for services all day, so we might be able to walk in the front door and head upstairs without being seen." They ran up the front of the building as if they were commandos on a mission, and tried the large front door. It was not locked. They peeked in and the once fabulous rooms was filled with all sorts of odd furniture, but they headed up the grand staircase and headed down the large hallway. Muturi was looking through rooms for the windows that he remembered in the photograph. He found the room filled with three desks and office equipment, with large posters of Jesus, and the phrase "Njia Moja!" or one way. He pulled her into the room and pulled a desk in front of the door.

"Is this the room? Where were they?" she asked.

"If I remember right, where the couch is."

"Where would I put the camera?" she asked and he looked around, trying to figure angles. As he looked around he heard hymns being sung in Swahili, and an organ playing. "This might

199

be a religious experience." Martha laughed. He pointed to the old battered shelf with bibles on it. Martha moved a few and set up the camera, as Muturi started taking off his clothes and moving the couch out of the way. "I have plenty of film." Muturi was standing naked by the window as Martha was taking off her clothes, which aroused him no end. "Okay, ten seconds!" she said and clicked the timer on the camera. She ran over, and Muturi positioned her and himself as he remembered his mama, with a second to spare. They made two more at different exposures, making Muturi so aroused, that he led her to the couch and found that she was even more excited to be making love in Egerton Castle.

~~~~~

Muturi was sitting in Miss Mills' chemistry class waiting with the rest of the students for her to show up. He was very worried that something bad happened to her. He could feel the growing pain and anxiety in his gut. Janie and Martin turned to him as if he would know.

"She is never late, she is always here waiting for us." Janie said.

Martin began, " And I usually…" But the headmaster opened the side door and came in with a very sad look on his face. Muturi's heart fell through the floor. This cannot be good, he worried.

"May I have your attention." The headmaster said, pausing for attention. "Miss Mills called me this morning to let me know that she received some sad news from home last night. Her brother called to tell her that her father died of a heart attack yesterday. She told me that she is too upset to come and tell you herself. She is very sorry, but she must fly back to Indiana to be with her mother at this time." Muturi's eyes blurred with tears at his double loss. He would never get to know Martha's father, and now more painfully Martha is gone. He does not know if she will come back, and whether he will ever see her again. "Students, this is difficult of course, but we will get a substitute. I used to teach chemistry and will do my best until the TSC sends someone. For today, I will let you take the day off if you need. I called Father Kennifick, and he will talk with anyone who is upset about this news." He frowned and left as he came in.

Janie turned around, "I feel very bad for her. My auntie works for her, so she might be out of a job."

Martin said, "This affects so many of us. We know you were her special fellow. It must hurt." Muturi appreciated his friends' concern, but it did not help.

"Yes, it does very much." He said with his voice cracking. The headmaster left and the class soon cleared out and soon it was just the three of them chatting.

"Come to our place and we will try and cheer each other up." Janie said.

"Will your auntie be there?" Muturi worried that she would tell everyone about the insemination services he provided her.

"I think she would be at Miss Martha's place. She said she also needs to go to the health center for her pregnancy."

"What? She is pregnant?"

Martin sighed, "Come on, you think we do not know?"

"This is too much news in one day." Muturi said, and Janie stood up. Oh, he looked at her stomach and he thought, she wants one too, like some sort of competition with her aunt Hanna.

"Are you coming to our place after classes? I need my medicine." She said. "You know, to cheer us up." Janie said, and looking down at Martin who was standing up.

"No, I need to go home and tell my parents. They liked Martha very much. They will want to know." Muturi said, standing up. Martin went to the door and Janie followed but was pulling off her knickers. Martin shut, locked the door, and shut off the lights. Janie sat on the table edge of the table near the door. Muturi was at first confused, then realized what she wanted. She leaned back, lifting her legs apart and pulled up her dress showing herself, making Muturi instantly aroused.

"Don't worry about disease, you're the only one who does her." Martin said, standing waiting for a show.

Muturi thought a man must give a woman what she wants…

~~~~

Wanjiru was hanging laundry in the courtyard behind the shop when he heard Mwangi greeting Muturi. He was home early from school, and she knew why. She heard the two talking and they both came out to the courtyard.

201

"Muturi, Martha came by this morning hoping to see you." Wanjiru said and seeing the sad look on his face. "Did they tell you at school what happened?"

"Yes, mama. It is very sad. We all will miss her very much."

"You more than any other, I am sure."

"Yes, mama. I hope it is only for a short time." He said and Wanjiru patted him on the back. She got a little too close and detected the smell of a woman on him. Do these girls ever leave him alone? She thought to herself. She deliberately dropped a wet shirt in front of him and bending over she sniffed and confirmed that he was busy this morning. They think we will never know. Life goes on.

"Without a teacher, it may be more difficult," she said in English, "so study with your friends and relieve yourself." She paused and thought about what she had just said to a young man who was turning 18 in a few days. At his age he will "relieve" himself at least three times a day if he could. She looked into her son's blue eyes, and saw only concern and no reaction to her poor choice of words. He always acted as if he enjoyed it when she used English and massacred the language.

"You are right. I will need to study harder."

"She left you a letter. It is on the kitchen counter. Would you read it to me?"

"Of course," Muturi said, but she knew he would leave out the interesting parts. Mwangi went back into the shop with Muturi following. She continued with the laundry and Muturi returned with the letter having opened the envelope already. As she continued hanging laundry, he began reading:

My Sweet Man;

I got a call that my father has died of a heart attack. After his minor heart attack, I was afraid this would happen. I called the office in Nairobi and they said the embassy always has seats available for us to fly back. I should be back in Indiana tomorrow night. My family will need me at this time. I will miss you like crazy. I will try to call after I get there, maybe before you go to school. Do NOT skip school. Also, tell Hanna to keep working I will pay her. Check the mail for me for our applications should be coming back with a decision.

I have something to tell you. They said that since I have only a couple of months left on my contract, they might not pay to fly me back unless I extend. I will have to make a decision on that since I want to go to grad school. Complications!

I will tell you that I will miss feeling you...

He stopped reading, looking at his mother, and she knew that it was getting too personal to read aloud. He continued to read to himself. She picked up the empty laundry basket and led him inside. She turned and saw tears streaming down his face.

"What is it?" she asked in Kikuyu. "You love this woman? What is it?"

"You will be so angry with me."

"Angry? What did you do?"

"She says she might have a pregnancy, but is thinking to end it."

"End it? How do you end it?" Wanjiru began a scolding sound, then remembered Hussein's wives and how they ended a pregnancy for her. "That is not for you to think about. Many pregnancies end on their own, without a doctor's help." This reminded her of the dawa that they had tricked her into taking. And the pain. She could see by the look on his face that he was depressed by so much news. "But if she keeps it? Do you want to be the father or simply the fellow who gave the *manii*? You have to think about that."

"Yes, mama. The future looks so complicated. If she keeps it and we go to the same college it would be easy for me to be father. If I cannot go to America, I would be the one who gave *manii* only."

"Just as my Lodi, and my mother's Englishman." She mumbled, not intending for Muturi to hear it.

"What?" he looked at her wanting her to repeat it.

"Do you have a class this afternoon?" she diverted, switching to English.

"Yes, I do, may I eat lunch here?" he asked in English

"Then after classes find some friends and relieve yourself." She said, then paused. She thought, there she stupidly said it again. "I mean relax with your friends." She corrected.

He looked at her, "Yes, I should stay confident that things will be good." He said and gave his mother a huge smile with his beautiful teeth.

Chapter 18, My Indiana Home

Martha was dead exhausted. With bleary eyes, she was trying to distinguish her luggage from all the other bags on the baggage carousel at Indianapolis airport. Having missed her flight in London, she spent the night in the airport hoping for a seat on the next flight to JFK. Once in JFK, she had to transfer to LaGuardia for an early morning flight to Indianapolis, which was delayed. She could not sleep on the plane, thinking of her father and mother, missing Muturi, and wondering if she was pregnant or not. She was afraid of missing her own father's funeral, but if her older brother Dan was there, he could make it work. Most of the crowd had taken their luggage and the remaining black case must have been hers by default. Grabbing the heavy case, full of her life in Kenya, she set it on the floor, pulled out the handle and headed for the taxi stand, hoping her brother would at least be waiting there.

"Martha!" A familiar, yet unwelcome voice echoed. She turned and it was her exboyfriend Bobby. A pit rose in her stomach, reserved for those who you once thought you loved but now loathed. He rushed up and gave her a bear hug and a peck on the cheek. "It is great to see you again. Dan is outside waiting."

"Bobby, thanks for helping Dan find me." She said trying to be civil. She had hoped that he had moved on. He grabbed the handle of the luggage as if rolling it was too difficult for a woman he used jokingly to call "his Amazon." At other times, his "Viking mama." That was nothing quite endearing, to say the least. When she first heard it, she knew he had some complex about being shorter than his girlfriend.

"No, problem. Your mother actually asked me to help out, since she and Dan were involved with the funeral arrangements." He said, and she then knew it was her mother's idea since she liked Bobby so much, and thought they should get married. Yuk, she thought. They exited the arrival area and she saw her brother at his huge Lincoln waving at her and then waving at a cop who was apparently telling him to get out of the taxi lane. Bobby threw the luggage in the trunk, while she got in the front passenger seat next to her brother, giving him a hug. Strapping on a seatbelt, she got comfortable in the soft seats.

"Thanks for picking me up, Dan." She said feeling exhausted and seeing just as much exhaustion in his face. "This is too much of a shock for us all, isn't it?"

"Martha, that's not half of it. Dad left exact funeral arrangements as if he knew he was going to die young. Mom is extremely upset, as is the rest of the family."

"He was fifty-eight..." she started to say.

"Grandma said he had rheumatic fever as a kid," he said pulling the car into traffic. "which probably damaged his heart for life." The Lincoln felt like it was floating as it pointed towards I74 West. Everyone became very quiet.

"I haven't slept for two days..."

"By all means take a nap. It'll be an hour before we get to Mom's." She did not worry about Bobby in the back seat. He could take care of himself. She pressed a button on the side of the seat and heard a motor tilt the seat back. In seconds, she was sound asleep on her way home to her mother.

In an instant, she awoke to her mother kissing and hugging her inside the car. "Come on in," she said. "We still have two hours for the funeral. The visitation was yesterday evening." She was saying as they walked into the well-kept Victorian style home. Walking up to the large wrap-around porch, she noticed the spring leaves on the oak trees were still small, and the grass was still trying to turn green from winter's rest. "Several hundred people showed up. Your father must have sold most of them insurance. Farmers from all over came. People I never knew."

Though still groggy, Martha was able to say, "Dad loved the farmers... really admired them."

As Bobby opened the front door for them, her mother said, "You will love to hear, your aunt Beth is here helping out. She drove all the way here in just a few hours after Dan gave her a call." Martha knew that her mother's youngest sister Beth was always very close. Her mother bound all Beth's letters from Kenya and gave them to her to write her best-selling book.

"Martha! My errant niece!" Came Beth's voice from the dining room, and she came running as Martha was removing her coat. Her aunt gave her a bear hug. "This is not the way I wanted to see you again." It was then Martha saw that everyone's eyes were red and on the verge of tears.

"I know, it is such a shock to me. I feel like I am in a nightmare. The only sleep I got in the last two days was the drive from the airport."

Dan interrupted them, "Martha, I have to get to the church to arrange the music and readings with the pastor. Dad was very specific about what he wanted, and by God, I will make sure it is exactly what he wanted." He gave her a peck on the cheek and headed out the door.

At the large Methodist Church in Crawfordsville, after finding a black dress to wear among her old clothes, she was escorted with her mother and siblings to the front row near the open casket where her father's remains were on view. Her legs went weak and she could not contain the tears. He looked so young, peaceful and strangely healthy for one lying in a casket. He wore the same suit he would wear for church. She gave the cold forehead a fond farewell kiss. She prayed there was a heaven where she could meet her father once again.

The pastor was a good friend of her father's, and was the one officiating and leading the service. Her father loved the old time spirituals and she had a hard time with "Lord I Am Coming Home," trying to sing it with an old-fashioned attitude that death was all around, waiting to take you away at any moment. "I wandered far away from home... now I am coming home." She sang, thinking her father must have meant it for her being so far away in Kenya. "I've wasted many precious years..." she sang, "Now I'm coming home..." There was not a dry eye in the church when done with the song. The pastor began a reading from Mark chapter four, reading in the old English that Dad loved. "Harken; Behold, there went out a sower to sow:" She recalled that chapter, since Muturi recited it often, even though his interpretation was not about receiving the word of God, but about his own father's spreading seeds around Kenya. "And it came to pass, as he sowed, some fell by the way side, and the fowls of the air came and devoured it up." She had to think of her father's sense of humor on these things to have something that could have such a double meaning to young folks. "And some fell among thorns, and the thorns grew up, and choked it, and it yielded no fruit. And other fell on good ground, and did yield fruit that sprang up and increased; and brought forth, some thirty, and some sixty, and some an hundred." With that, she found herself rubbing her own belly thinking of the seed that "sprang up" despite the birth control pill that was too low of a dose to keep an egg in her ovaries. The final song before the procession to the cemetery was "Amazing Grace," a song that had meaning for others, but none for Martha.

Martha, her mother and siblings were at the lead behind the hearse of the long procession to a cemetery on a bluff above Sugar Creek north of town. It was a huge cemetery, and Martha tried to memorize how to get to the gravesite from the entrance. By the time they got out of the limo, the staff with the hearse had already moved her father's casket above the open grave. Martha followed her brother Dan who led them to an open tent where the closest family was to sit. Her brother, a huge man as tall as Muturi, she thought, making her feel short, put his arm around her shoulders and gave her a quick hug and went back to talking quietly to his wife. Her mother handed her a piece of paper with the graveside service listed.

The pastor was there between them and the grave. It seemed hundreds of people were gathering, many well to do and not so well to do farmers were there to pay their last respects to a man who helped them stay solvent through failed crops, wind storms, late frosts, tornadoes and barn fires. "We are here today to lay to rest," the pastor began in the microphone, "John Ladson Mills, the son, grandson and great-grandson of Indiana…" he went on, and Martha was too upset to read the paper everyone had received. Over the loudspeakers, they played a slow version of Ashokan Farewell "Will we climb the hills once more? Will we walk the woods together?" the words came. The image of her father was replaced with Muturi, and she wondered the same thing. Being only a few days separated, she was embarrassed to say she missed him more than her own father. Her reverie about Muturi helped to clear her tearful eyes to read the paper with the song her father wanted people to sing as they lowered him into the ground.

Dad you sentimental old fool, she thought looking at the paper which had the lyrics to "O, Danny Boy." She knew her brother would not make it through the whole song. She had seen him sing it with her father and they both would break down into blubbering fools. The pastor led the crowd in singing the old, sentimental ballad, but as they sang the fourth verse, "And all my grave will warmer, sweeter be. For you will bend and tell me that you love me" her big gorilla of a brother collapsed into his chair weeping like a child. Her mother switched places with her as the crowd finished the song, while the casket lowered by electric motors into the grave. His wife and mother tried to comfort Dan who would miss his father very deeply.

The pastor led the crowd in the Lord's Prayer, after which everyone milled around hugging and shaking hands with the family. Martha was benumbed accepting hugs and best wishes from dozens of people she never knew.

Chapter 19, Blackmail

Muturi looked at his physics lab notes, and looked around the class. He was always last to turn in lab results. He was thinking of Martha also, which slowed him down. She must be in a lot of pain going through the funeral of her father by now. He looked again at the results of the parallax method for determining the focal length of a lens. Simple concept, but annoying method he thought. He looked up and Mr. Watusu – Joe - was staring at him. He was now alone with the black snake, and was getting nervous. Joe had closed the door, and Muturi was worried. He decided that perfection should not get in the way of a quick escape. Standing up to turn in his lab booklet, Muturi looked his teacher in the face. He was standing between Muturi and the door.

"Mr. Makomeki, I need to talk with you. The headmaster gave me some forms. Four universities want references from your school." Joe said, and Muturi felt a trap closing in on him, and he simply nodded. "I would like to give you a good reference but I would like to get to know you better, if you know what I mean."

Muturi felt that he was cornered, and he looked around for escape, but he really wanted to go to one of those universities. Acting naïve might help. He had heard the rumors about Joe and some willing boys, but he would not put himself in that group. "Sure, that makes sense. You need to be able to write good things about me." He walked towards the door, as if Joe would step aside, but instead he backed up against the door blocking the way.

"Yes, I want to get to know you much better, inside and out." He smiled, reaching out and grabbing Muturi's belt. Muturi thought of what Martha told him, if it was harmless and got him somewhere, what is the harm?

"You want to return the favor, now?" Muturi asked. But without responding, Joe pulled him, turned and exchanged places with him, pushing him against the door. He knew he was going to be molested, but wanted good references for those universities. He closed his eyes and imagined Martha seducing him, unzipping his pants, finding his manhood and arousing it to be long and stiff. He substituted her voice for Joe saying how handsome and white it is,

210

feeling "her" taste it. He imagined that she was stroking it for a quick one. In his mind's eye, he ejaculates and she giggles at the eruption shooting out a few feet. With eyes closed he senses Joe letting loose and turning away. He puts himself back in order and notices his semen on the floor under the front desk.

Joe was wiping his hands with a towel. "Come to my house after school and I can get to know you better." Joe said, and Muturi knew that he was wanting a lot more than what Martha had suggested. Getting "jacked off" was not enough to satisfy Joe. Another male before never did Muturi, though his baba warned him about men who enjoyed that sort of thing, giving Muturi and Mumera all the mechanical details. His baba warned about the new disease going around. Be careful with everyone, he warned. Recalling a rough prostate examination for the school physical, Muturi was sure he was not one of those who would enjoy that kind of sex.

Through classes the rest of the day, Muturi's thoughts rambled like a bad nightmare. He had mixed feelings about what to do. He worried about Martha, and how they would they get back together if he did not get any of the university scholarships. They would be thousands of miles apart.

At the end of the day, he was walking as if he were a convict headed for the gallows, looking at the ground. "Muturi!" Janie's voice came through his fog. He looked by the gate and she was waiting.

"Where's Martin? You are always with Martin." He said as if it was a wonder of the world to be separate from her twin.

"Rumor is that Joe trapped you in his classroom. Did he make you squirt?" She giggled.

"Janie! How do people know this?"

"So, it is true. Do you have any left for me?"

"I have to go to Joe's house." He said and started walking in that direction.

"*Gai*! You're the one?"

"What do you mean by that?"

"Martin said that he and Joe were going to do some boy after school."

"What? Joe said he wanted to talk to me about university references."

"Martin says Joe has some medicine he puts in boy's tea that makes them too weak to resist, and Joe does what he wants with them."

"That's rape, why isn't he in jail?"

"What boy will testify against him? It's too embarrassing to say anything! And boys like you who need something from Joe, will pretty much do what he wants." She said, and he knew she was right. He would do anything he wants to get those references.

"We need to think of something to get me out of this." Muturi said as they were getting closer to Joe's place.

"Anything you can blackmail Joe with?" she laughed, and he could not think of anything. An idea hit he remember that he still had Martha's camera in his backpack. He stopped. He took off the backpack and pulled out some books until he found the small camera. He pointed the camera at her, rotated the lens, adjusted something and clicked a photo of her. Then he put the books back and camera on top, closing the backpack. They started walking again.

"This is very complicated idea…"

~~~~~

Janie was extremely nervous - since Muturi's plan was so complicated, she wondered if it could possibly work. She was outside waiting for Muturi to walk past the front window scratching his head, when she saw him walking by without his sweater, scratching his head, just as he said. She walked up to the door and knocked. Joe came to the door. "Hello, Janie, can I help? We are very busy right now." He was only wearing his gym shorts and a tank top.

"Martin said he would be here, his auntie told me to tell him not to forget something before coming home."

"Martin, come to the door and talk with your sister." Joe demanded sounding annoyed. He stood there waiting, and Martin showed up wearing only his Speedos. This rather shocked her, but then that was Martin.

"Hanna wants to make sure you stop at the butcher for the beef. She said she gave you money to buy a few pounds."

"Auntie is a *mjinga*, she gave me nothing."

"She said she did. Do not forget!"

"She gave me no money."

Joe was getting annoyed, "I will give you the money, and he will pick up the beef. Now, go!" The door shut in her face, and she thought that was enough time to switch teas if it were to happen. She sat down on the steps waiting. Cars would pass, people would walk by, and she thought it must be twenty or so minutes, when Muturi came to the door in his boxer shorts.

"Fun time!" he said and she got up to follow him in.

"Why are you in your underwear?" she asked noticing there was no one in the living room where she had seen him. "Where are they?"

"I pretended to be under his *dawa*, until they got my shirt and pants off they lost their strength. I carried them to his bedroom." Janie noticed he picked the camera out of his backpack, and followed. "I will take pictures like someone was watching from the window." He said as they walked down the hall. In the bedroom on the double bed, her brother was in his Speedos next to Joe who was still in his gym shorts. They were groaning with their mouths open and eyes rolling. This is going to be fun, she thought. "You get to pose them anyway you want." He said, and she felt a tingle of excitement. He turned on the overhead light and opened the wide window to let in the light from the cloudy sky. She went first to Joe and pulled off his shorts and athletic strap.

"*Gai*! I heard stories, but this is amazing. It is like a black snake. "I will pose them like the stories Martin told me, so it will be true." She rolled her smaller brother's head onto Joe's belly, moving arms and legs around to look natural and inserted the black snake into her brother's drooling mouth, and placed his hand on Joe's thigh. She stood aside and heard Muturi snap the camera. She then moved Joe's hands to look like they were blessing Martins head. Click. "Help me move them around." She said, pulling Martin's Speedos off and tossing them on the floor. She thought, he shrivels up so much when he is afraid. Muturi came around and picked him up like a rag doll and rolled him over, then went around picked Joe up and positioned him on top of Martin. Janie had fun moving legs around and turning heads so that their faces would be in the picture.

"Looks like Joe is getting to know Martin from the inside out." He said and moved back to the window to snap two pictures, with two settings.

"One more. Martin says they suck each other at the same time." She said and saw the weird look on Muturi's face. "They should be on their sides." She started moving them, and he came to help. Soon they were on their sides pointed 180 degrees, posed as Janie suggested. Click. She moved hands and legs. Click. Joe suddenly moved his arms, and Janie realized that the *dama* was wearing off. "Time to go." She said and they left the two where they were and headed out. Muturi found his clothes. He was putting them on, when she noticed papers with Muturi's name on them. "Are these the papers you were talking about?"

He buckled his belt and walked over. "Yes, those are the ones. He filled them out and signed them already. That dog was lying." Janie started reading what Joe had written.

"These are very nice words. He thinks you are a great student and will do very well in university." He picked up the rest of the forms and read them.

"Well, I will mail them for him at my expense, before he changes his mind." He laughed and took the forms and envelopes. He heard someone talking in the other room, and they both ran out the front door, slamming it behind them. "Janie, I owe you a lot." He was telling her as they started walking up the street, going in the wrong direction for Janie. "You saved my virginity!" he laughed, and she knew what virginity he was referring to."

"Well, I expect a lot of return services." Janie laughed, realizing she was going in the wrong direction. "Now that Miss Mills is gone, and my auntie is already pregnant, and Joe won't bother you now, you will have to do me until you go to America." She said very confident that her *manii* boy would make it there. "I am going in the wrong direction. See you tomorrow. Let me know if Miss Mills calls. Love you!" she said. Gai! She thought. I see too many movies.

~~~~

Muturi was reading and re-reading a page in his physics text, when Mumera came in, and plopped a photo envelope on the book in front of him. "My friend said some of those pictures could land him in jail, but I told him we needed it for the police anyway, so he said he would forget what he saw when he developed the photos."

"How much do I owe you?"

214

"Nothing. He does not want to get in trouble. Leave no records. He said." Muturi opened the envelope and there was a thick stack of black and white pictures. They started off with duplicates of pictures that Martha took around her house – Hanna is showing already – and around the school. Then the pictures from Menengai crater. Mama and baba will like these, and he separated out one copy each showing all of their kids and themselves on top of the crater. Then there were the pictures in the abandoned grass house. The pictures in Egerton Castle – Martha is so beautiful with my hands on her belly! Such sweet memories he thought – will life get any better than that? There was a photo of cute Janie. I will have to live in Kenya, he thought, so that I can have four wives. Yes, Martha, Janie and two more will do. He laughed at himself. Mumera looked over Muturi's shoulder at the picture of him and Martha, "Gai! She is very sexy! She is better naked than what I imagined in her chemistry class." Mumera said, and Muturi elbowed him in the stomach.

Then the pornography… well maybe modern art, he thought, and he heard Mumera snicker. "Is that Joe, and who is that boy… looks like that Martin who is always chatting me up."

"You stay away from Martin. One pit of disease that one. Stay away from Joe, too. *Gai*! Now I have to worry about my brother!" Muturi felt rage steaming through himself.

"Muturi! Calm down."

"If I see those two near you, I will kill them, I swear! Never drink anything at Joe's place, no food, nothing! Understand?"

"*Gai*! I hear you already."

"I will do anything, just stay away from them and their likes. They are *msenge* rapists."

"Okay, okay!" Mumera said. He looked at the photos. He was interested in what Martin was doing. "How did you get those pictures? From a window?"

"No, they tried to give me *dawa* and I switched it on them. Janie posed them the way Martin told her they do it."

"It looks like fun if it were legal." Mumera said.

"That is not legal?" Muturi asked.

"No, well, maybe not in Mombasa. It is the Moslem laws that Kenya has. Sex between men is a death penalty."

"I don't think so, or all the sex tourists would be hung."

"That's what I heard, is all. I didn't know a man could use a boy like a woman that way." Mumera said and took another photo and said, "I would like someone to use their mouth on mine like that, that looks like it feels good."

"Yes, it does, but they have to know how to do it right." Muturi thought of how well Martha did it and how badly Janie did it. "Yes, you have to know how."

"Maybe you would do it to me sometimes." Mumera said.

"What?" Muturi exclaimed, not believing what his brother said, wondering if this were blackmail again.

"You said you would do anything to keep me away from Joe and Martin." Mumera said, and Muturi thought, so this is how he boxes me in again. Mumera was looking him straight into his eyes. He was not joking around, he was curious about how it felt. "I tell you what. I give you a week to help me find a clean girl who wants to do that for me. If not, we are like one person - anyway, it would be like you doing it to yourself." He laughed.

"Or else?" Muturi said, knowing full well what was coming.

"Or else, I tell Mama about these pictures and you're blackmailing Mr. Watusu."

"You would do that just to get this?" He said and showed the photo. He heard his parents coming in from the shop, and he took the pornographic photos and hid them in a pocket in his backpack.

"Yes, it looks like it is the best feeling. I want it. You know how to do it right." Mumera said.

"This is not normal. I cannot agree." Muturi said just as his parents entered the kitchen.

"What does the bible say about it?" Mumera asked.

"What is not normal? Bible say what?" his Mama asked, giving her two boys pats on the shoulders.

"I got some pictures, Mama." He said in Kikuyu, knowing that pictures diverted any question. His mother loved pictures.

"Is this from Martha's camera? You forgot to give it back to her?"

"Yes, Mama, but she says I should bring it when I come to America. She is very sure I will go there." She began looking through the pictures, and stopped at the one of Martha sitting on the bed in the grass house. She stared at it a long time and tears started flowing down her cheek. Muturi looked over her shoulder of the available light photograph of a blonde woman leaning back on the bed with her jacket open, looking so attractive and full of love for the fellow behind the camera.

"She is so beautiful. I see she loves you very much. Is this the woman who will steal my son from me?"

"Mama, you will always be my mother. And you still have Mumera and the others." She looked at Mumera and gave him a hug.

"You two are almost twins, but each has your own wonderful soul. I want you all around forever, but..."

Mwangi interrupted, "Wanjiru, where is supper?" he laughed, as if he knew she was getting overly sentimental and would end up spending the evening in tears. "You two go to your room and study until your mama gets food ready."

Muturi picked up the books and photos and headed for his room, Mumera headed for the bathroom. He set his backpack on the bed and tried reading the physics text again. Mumera came in, locking the door behind him, and immediately Muturi knew what was up. "You said I had a week." Muturi said.

"I changed my mind. I want it now. I washed it just for you."

"No. Go study!"

"No, you love me too much to refuse me. You don't want me going to Joe or Martin or people like them." He said, and Muturi knew he was right.

"Okay, if I can't find you a girl. But you must never tell anyone." Muturi said surrendering to his younger brother. The pastor at the church never said it was a sin, but then how would a pastor ever bring up such a topic in a church service?

~~~~~~

Muturi tried to sneak out of Mr. Watusu's class early, not wanting to confront him yet. "Mr. Makomeki, could you wait after class, I need to talk with you about your references. Muturi was anxious and ready to leave, but Joe added, "We could discuss it here in front of the class, or wait until everyone is done with their lab." He hissed sternly, so he sat down and read until everyone had left, only then standing up to confront Joe, who had closed the door and was standing in front of it.

"I am not sure what happened the other day, but I did not get what I wanted. You seemed to have drugged me with something. You will come to my place, and you will do what I want, then I will send those references."

"No. I thank you for the very nice references, but I posted them already to America." Muturi said as he was reaching into the inside pocket of his backpack. "You will do your job as a teacher and stop thinking about doing me." He said and handed him the pornographic pictures of Joe with Martin. "In a few years, when I know you cannot bother me or my family again, I will send you the duplicate photos and negatives." He smiled and said, "Great pictures aren't they? Very clearly see the who, what and where." Joe was looking through the pictures getting both angry and aroused. "Thank you for being a very good teacher, just stop raping your students." Muturi stuck his hands under Joe's arms and picked him up as if he were a child and set him down on the lecture platform. "See you later." He said and left.

Chapter 20, Acceptance

Muturi's eyes had just popped open from a great night's sleep, when he heard his baba calling him to the phone in the shop. At this time in the morning, it must be Martha. He ran into the shop in his boxer shorts and grabbed up the receiver. "Hello?"

"Hey lover, I got some news, some good and some bad about our applications. I called the registrars' offices yesterday to get news. I am sponsoring you so they gave me the scoop."

"I hope it's good."

"Well, Duke and U of I rejected both of us. Northwestern accepted only you but no scholarship. Purdue accepted both of us, but for me it is West Lafayette campus, and you the Indianapolis campus in mechanical engineering with full tuition scholarship – from the McCormick Foundation for African Students. I get an assistantship. But my father left me a lot of money, so we can decide. We would be about an hour fast driving apart."

"We still can get married right?" he worried, recalling other conversations about keeping the baby. They had set their minds on marriage.

"Yes, of course, with the baby coming we will work it out." She laughed, "The little Makomeki will be kicking inside soon. Another good soccer player I'm sure." They both laughed.

"Or basketball. I wish I could be there."

"Well, you already got your passport, and once you get the letter from Purdue accepting you, you can get a visa. You can spend some of the summer with me at my mother's place in Crawfordsville. When we get married, it will get a bit easier with immigration."

"It will be very exciting. Oh, Mwangi sold your *piki* and sent you a bank check."

"Yes, he told me. Well, I am very sleepy. Time for bed. Love you!" Came the voice from eight thousand miles away.

"Love you too. I am always thinking of you." He said and hung up the phone. He went back to his room, thinking he will tell his Mama later, otherwise she will start weeping.

Mumera was still in bed, wide-awake and obviously waiting for him. He pulled back the sheet and pulled down his briefs expecting servicing.

"Mumera! What are you doing?" Muturi complained, looking at his naked brother on the bed.

"Time is up." Mumera demanded, and Muturi thought how this kid had him 'by the balls,' as they say in the movies.

"You should be able to get someone clean."

"I am too young, too big, too white, too Kikuyu, too something. No one is interested. No one likes *nusu nusu*."

"I need more time. Janie will need a boyfriend now."

"Janie? She is damn cute! You think she would like me?"

"I would bet more than me. She's crazy over blue eyes."

~~~~~

It was late Friday night as Mumera stood on the dark Nakuru train platform waiting for the train to appear. His mother and older brother were standing near him listening for the the train whistle. The three of them were waiting for his mama's cousin Wajiko and her three children, who were paying a visit from Nairobi. The passengers who were going to board the train continuing onto Kisumu were milling around with their boxes of possessions, grumbling about the train being late. He looked again at his older brother, who was a few inches taller than himself - a taller twin of himself. Mumera had learned that Wajiko's oldest son is actually his half brother, and that they were born a week apart. He was born in Njoro and his half brother – and second cousin - in Likoni. He met him once before when the family went to Mombasa for a visit.

"Is that a whistle?" his Mama wondered, obviously very excited about seeing her cousin.

"Is Wajiko's husband coming, too?" Muturi asked in Kikuyu, and Mumera looked him in the eyes wondering where that question came from.

"No, he went to Germany for business." His Mama said quickly in Swahili, looking down the tracks just as the light from the train engine glared down the platform, having made the bend in the tracks. The little narrow gauge engine rumbled slowly by and quietly the passenger cars came to a slow halt. The train looked packed but people were trying to get off pushing people who were trying to pile on at the same time. Mumera always thought it was funny how no one could get on or off because of the pushing. "Wajiko! Wajiko!" His Mama was screaming at a woman following a large *nusu nusu* boy, who was pushing back several very black Luo's who were blocking their exit. Mumera and Muturi ran up and took their luggage from them and his Mama and Wajiko were hugging each other tightly. He always thought the two were closer than most sisters. Actually, he thought again, as close as he and his older brother.

As they were hugging, they were all exchanging handshakes with the three kids, the tall Hans, and two girls, Maria and Christa, who were twelve and fourteen. They went by their family name Weiss, which his mother pronounced as Waisi. Mumera was thinking that Hans looked more African than Muturi – or himself, and was several inches shorter than himself. His skin was darker, probably from years of living in Mombasa before moving to Nairobi last year.

Wajiko looked Mumera and Muturi saying, "You two just get taller and taller. Look just like your father!" she said, and Mumera knew she did not mean his baba. Wajiko was always very open about who bred with whom to get which child, and was the one that informed Mumera that Hans was his half brother. The six people began moving through the train station trying to get out on the street. "Where is Mwangi? Is he home asleep?" Wajiko was asking.

"He went up to Njoro for a few days to see his sick mother. He took the little ones with him."

"Should we check into a hotel?" Wajiko asked politely, obviously hoping there would be room at home.

"No, no! Never! You can sleep with me, the girls can sleep in the little one's room, and Hans can sleep with Mumera." His Mama said, and Mumera looked at Hans who just smiled and slapped Mumera on his butt. They headed out onto the poorly lighted street for the walk to their place. Along the way Wajiko was asking about the supermarket, and his Mama was saying it was not as good as hers in Nairobi. They made it home very late, with everyone very exhausted, but his Mama and Wajiko wanted to stay up and chat. As they were putting the two girls to bed, Muturi was using the bathroom.

"You don't mind sharing a bed again, do you Hans? I could sleep with Muturi." Mumera asked, recalling a few years back in

Mombasa he shared a small bed with Hans without problem. Hans was taking off his clothes, as was Mumera. He was thinner and not as muscular. He was wearing white briefs, which did not seem to have much in them. Mumera stripped down to his red Speedos, and sat on the bed waiting his turn for the toilet.

"If it doesn't bother you, I don't." He said as Muturi came in and began taking off his clothes. Hans went into the toilet.

Muturi said, "You alright sharing your bed?" he chuckled, obviously knowing he had no choice. "I hope you will not be blackmailing me while they are here." Mumera shrugged, as if to say, no promises.

"I will sleep in the truck or with you if Hans gets too close." He said and his brother rolled his eyes. After a few minutes, Hans returned, and Mumera went for his turn. He peed and brushed his teeth, and returned to his bedroom, which was dark already. He tried to slip in next to Hans into the single bed without too much contact, but there was not much room so he soon had his back pressing against Hans' back, even though he was on the edge of the bed. Oh, great, he thought, I might have to go out to the truck to get a decent night's sleep. Just then, Hans flipped around slipping one of his arms under Mumera's pillow, and the other wrapped around his front as if hugging him from behind. That feels much better, he thought, and was so tired he started dozing off, and soon fell asleep. He awoke with a start as Hans began molesting Mumera's manhood. Mumera grabbed Hans' hand and rolled out of bed, moving over to sleep with Muturi, but he had to use the toilet

He got up and rushed to the toilet and by the time he got back, both Muturi and Hans were snoring. He heard his mother and cousin Wajiko talking, and was curious about what they were talking. He walked a little closer, feeling a shiver from wearing only his Speedos. They had a fire in the fireplace and were talking in Kikuyu about their days in Mombasa.

"I put most of my money in the Standard Bank in British pound certificates. I have enough to get my kids through school."

"That was very smart. I spent my money on clothes and good times. I have enough to get Hans through school."

"You remember that day Lodi came to the hotel?" his Mama asked.

"Day? Days. Didn't we spend three days in bed with him?"

"It may have been three days, but it seemed like only a day."

"I recall how he jumped out of bed when you lost your aiyudi." The both laughed aloud. "Shhh we will wake the children. He acted like you sliced off his thing.

"Was that when he was doing us both?"

"It might have been, but remember how he shared his *manii* between us."

She laughed, "And now we have Hans and Mumera. Two wonderful boys."

"Hans. Wonderful?" Wajiko said.

"What does that mean?"

"He seems to like boys better than girls."

"Really? Boys have so much *manii* they squirt it everywhere." Wanjiru giggled, "Even on other boys." They both laughed. "I would not worry, once they try a female, they will think only of that…"

"The first girl has to be great or they think of boys again."

"Does he do boys?"

"Not that I know of. No, I am sure no *kundu* but just rubbing. I find their messes. It is as bad as having chickens in the house." They laughed.

"My boys are good about hiding their messes. Muturi has a girlfriend I think. Then of course there is Martha in America he wants to marry." Marry? Mumera thought – well that makes sense. "He is going to university in August in America. He said they will get married. "

"Why marriage, does she have a pregnancy?" Wajiko asked.

"Yes, I am sure that is why. These Makomeki spread their seeds everywhere." Mumera was getting very sleepy and headed back to his room. In the dim light Hans was pressed against the wall, so Mumera rolled in gently next to his brother, and fell asleep.

~~~

Muturi woke with the sun streaming through the curtains, sure that he slept in late after picking up Wajiko and her kids at the train station. He sat up on one arm with his younger brother next to him hugging the edge of the single bed. The sheet had fallen on the floor. Hans was face against the wall, obviously having slept without clothes. He was skinny and brown with round buttocks. Muturi needed to use the toilet, so he took a book, went in, and sat down. After the first dump, he gave it a quick flush and continued reading.

The door opened and Mumera walked in. "Hey, he tried to screw me last night."

"What your *kundu*?" Muturi was appalled - his brother might get a disease.

"No, he tried to jack me off." Mumera said, getting aroused again talking about it.

"So, are you saving yourself for me?" Muturi laughed. "That explains why you were in bed with me." Muturi said.

"I guess it is just brotherly love." He said standing in front of Muturi, and someone knocked at the door. "Minute." Mumera took off his Speedos and got into the shower. Muturi finished, washed his hands and opened the door. It was his Mama.

"Mumera is taking a shower." He said, which she never minded and went in to use the toilet.

~~~~

Muturi glanced at the setting sun ready to slip below the horizon, "We should hurry, Mumera, or Mama will be annoyed with us for being so late." He looked behind at his second cousin Hans – and half brother - who was trailing behind.

"You gave Janie some good lessons, she is good. But not as sweet as I thought it would be." Mumera chuckled and looked back at Hans as if hoping he did not hear.

"She has big teeth, but she has more going for her than her mouth you know."

Mumera laughed, "When you come back from America do you expect to get her back?"

"She was never mine. If she wants you, she will definitely tell you."

"Okay. I am still going to miss you." Mumera said, but Muturi hoped that Mumera would do well. He had a few days left before he flew off. He got his leaving certificate from the high school, and his student visa for the U.S. Martha had arranged the air transportation. He would fly from Nairobi to Liberia, then to New York where Martha would meet him and fly on to Indiana. The complications!

Hans caught up with them and complained, "That Martin boy is really queer." Muturi chuckled to himself thinking that is like the warthog telling the baboon his is ugly.

"Why?" Muturi asked.

"He kept feeling my privates. I had to punch him."

"Is that why he left?" Mumera asked. "I thought you were watching the telly."

"We were, and then he moved in on me." Hans whined. "He wanted to make a mess in me." Muturi looked at Mumera and they rolled their eyes at each other. They hustled on home and arrived just as Mwangi was closing the overhead door.

Chapter 21, America

Martha watched Muturi as he peered out the small window as the jet gained altitude over New York City, having just taken off from LaGuardia. "That must be at least ten times the size of Nairobi! *Gai*!" he said. It was blue skies and all the skyscrapers were clear. The plane began a turn and the window filled with blue sky. Martha suddenly became aware of his crushing her right hand in his. She patted his hand and he relaxed as the plane seemed to point west but continued to climb. "I flew all across Africa and never saw anything like this. Some interesting volcanoes, but no huge cities." He said in his Kenyan accent. She hoped he would never lose it.

As the city got smaller, Muturi leaned back, caught Martha staring at him, and smiled broadly. He was even more beautiful than she remembered, and photos did not do him justice. His smile could melt your heart. "You will see several more cities, but none like this, no mountains and a lot of farm land."

He looked down at her belly and gave it a rub, "You are showing. You look beautiful."

"You're sweet. My mother is kind of embarrassed to have a pregnant daughter living with her."

"Once we get married, will she be better with it?"

"We will see. She is still missing her husband, Dad, and going through big changes. She is talking about moving away to live with a sister." She said and he nodded. "Now, tell me. Did you have a big going away party?"

"Oh, yes, friends and relatives from all over came. Mwangi got the use of a restaurant for the celebration. Lots of *pambe*."

"How many girls wanted you?"

"What? What do you mean?"

"I've heard at these things there, all the girls want one last bit of you." She smiled seeing his embarrassment. "It is okay to say, we are not married yet."

"I had a pocket full of condoms that I pretty much used up."

"I think they wanted more than good feelings."

"Yes, true, but I did not want to bring a disease to America. Besides, after the first two it was all dry stuff anyway." He chuckled. She felt the plane leveling off and the seatbelt light blinked off. A flight attendant came up to the man sitting next to her, telling him that she could upgrade him to first class. The well-dressed man quickly put his things together and left. Martha suddenly felt more relaxed, but wanting to make love with him so badly, she was nearly in pain.

"I hope you saved some for me."

"Yes, it has been a few days." He smiled then frowned. "I worry about my brother. I think he might let the likes of Watusu or Martin seduce him. Then I worry about that disease."

"AIDS?"

"Yes, and if Mumera gets that I would go crazy with pain."

"Even if he is seduced, they are not so stupid as to take chances are they?"

"Martin goes down to Nairobi a lot to hang out with tourists."

"I see. I hope your brother is as smart as you about these things."

"Smart is one thing, lust is another. I lust after more women than men, but I think it is the other way with Mumera... more boys than girls."

"Are there men that attracted you?" she was curious about this side of him.

"Some. More young men than older. But then I get aroused seeing myself naked in a mirror."

"Haha, me too. People will think we are weird or crazy."

"But we already know that, do we not?" he laughed.

"How do you resist your own brother? He is so damned cute!"

"You think I can resist?" he admitted. "I would do whatever he wants." He said, and she felt a tingle go through her body. "If it keeps him out of trouble, that is."

"I see now why you are worried about him."

"You remember Janie? I got them together. I hope they will be very happy."

"I thought she slept around."

"Sleep around? You mean do many men?" he asked and she nodded. "No, I think she is crazy for a baby now, and wants to know who the father is. And the father can not look like her brother Martin. She says everyone believes she does incest."

"Really? Mumera is ready to be a father?"

"Not a father, but as you say, sperm doner." He laughed and looked out the window. "What city is that?"

"I would guess Cleveland." I think that is Lake Erie. "The planes don't fly in straight lines, they have to follow what they call air corridors. So, you think Mumera will father a kid?"

"I do not know." He said. They were quiet as the attendant brought some snacks and drinks.

"Before we head out to Crawfordsville, I thought I would drive you around your university. Also, I have a surprise for you."

"Really? Sounds like fun."

"Maybe. My mother is a genealogist, and looked up your biological father and found some interesting things."

"What is a geny...uh"

"Oh, they are people that find records to say who your ancestors were and where they lived."

"How many ancestors did she find?"

"She was able to follow the fathers line back about 300 years to a place in Northern Ireland."

"Ireland?"

"Well, they were Scots who settled in Ireland and were driven out because they were not Catholic. They came to America rather than return to Scotland. They married French, English and Irish Protestants."

"So, you must know about your ancestors, also." He said

"They were English, Irish and French Protestants."

"Sounds like history repeating." He chuckled and added, "My mother is half English, half Kikuyu. So, my genes have done a lot of traveling."

~~~~~

Muturi was sweating from the heat and humidity, standing on the bank of the White River staring east to the skyline of Indianapolis. He felt as if he had come home. There was a large bridge across the river, no longer used for cars, but was a walkway across to a park. Martha was pointing to a large rock. "Read the plaque." She offered. "He is one of your great great great grand

228

uncles. Where we are standing is the site of the first house built of this city."

"Oh, it was a log cabin, here on this river?" He read some more. "Oh, that was about 200 years ago."

"Your university is right over there. That is where you will be studying." She pointed at some buildings. "We could get you a dormitory or rent an apartment. I put a reserve for a single dorm room for you, but if you want an apartment…"

"What will you be doing?"

"I am going to live at my parents' place and commute." She said. "For the first semester if the baby does not come early."

"We should get married soon to make the baby legal." He said seriously, as he stared at the rock.

"My father would have liked you very much. Too bad he won't be there."

"Oh, yes, he will be there. Some of his blood is in you and your baby… so, he will be there." He said with such certainty that it brought tears to her eyes.

~~~~

Mumera was thinking that his brother should be in America by now, and maybe getting married as he was determined to be. He was walking over to Janie's place, hoping for some "affection" as he called it. Mumera had to think of getting back to school, so that perhaps in two years, he too could join his brother in a place called Indiana… if his lust did not divert his plans that is. He was not sure this Janie was going to suit his lust needs. She is not forgiving about things. He tapped at Janie's door, and the door opened "Jambo," Hanna greeted him, then switched to Kikuyu. "You want Janie? She here waiting. You do her good today, she want a pregnancy."

He laughed, "You look like you might give birth now."

"You be good boy. I have two more months, maybe. This your brother's. Going to be a big baby. Strong like him." She smiled as she escorted him to Janie's room. Martin was watching TV, but he turned to ogle Mumera. Mumera took off his army jacket and hung it by the door. Janie was asleep on her bed, and he wondered if he should go. "She has a stomach, lose her breakfast. Dizzy too. Probably need your sperms." Hanna said, as if sperms were the cure for all diseases. She waddled away leaving him standing by her bed. One of her eyes popped open and she smiled.

"Muturi?" she mistakenly asked, then turned and opened both eyes. "Mumera!" she turned over and the covers fell down exposing her breasts. "Close the door, please." He closed the door and slid the lock so they would not be disturbed.

"You have a fever? Malaria?" he said and began taking off his clothes.

"No, just lost my breakfast and felt very tired." She kicked back the covers, laying on her back. As he pulled off his jeans, he eyed her beige knickers. She pulled them off as he pulled off his Speedos. He stood waiting and she arranged herself. Without foreplay, he climbed onto the bed and connected with her, feeling delightful, staring down at her smiling face, thinking this was so much better than oral sex... no teeth.

"You are" he thrusted a few times, "probably pregnant by my brother..."

"Uuuuhh." She mumbled as she was concentrating on the pleasure. "Hope so." She added and held him very tightly wrapping her legs around him. He was transforming to a different state of mind, wondering if his sperm would somehow poison his brother's baby. Then he thought he felt a lump and then theorized how the womb would close up and protect itself from such things to incubate the baby... if she were pregnant. His mind drifted away from that concern back to enjoying the here and now. He exploded and passed on into oblivion.

He awoke to Janie crying out in pain and someone pounding on the door. Janie was shrieking and the door was pounding. He got up and unlocked the door and Hanna burst in, "What did you do to my niece?"

"Nothing, I fell asleep and woke up to her screaming." He looked down at the naked girl on the bed, she was curled up and screaming in pain. Something was being expelled from her vagina.

"She is having a miscarriage. Leave us! Get water and towels." Hanna demanded. He grabbed his clothes on the floor and went to the kitchen to get a pan and water, dropping his clothes on the kitchen floor. He looked for clean towels and returned to the bedroom just in time to see Hanna pull something bloody from Janie's bottom. He put the pan of water on a chair and gave her the towels. Hanna dropped the bloody something into the pan. As the blood dissipated, and tissues floated away, it was like a little brown, rubber doll about an inch or two long, but curled up. "You will be fine. This happens." Hanna was saying trying to reassure Janie. "At least you know you can have babies." Hanna turned to him, "You get your clothes on!"

Mumera became aware that his clothes were still in the kitchen, and he turned and Martin was blocking his way out. Martin grabbed Mumera's privates oblivious to his sister's suffering, "Oh, nice." He muttered, stroking him, but Mumera pushed him out of the way to head towards the clothes on the floor. Martin was saying "Let me do you. I do you nice." As Mumera bent over to get his clothes, Martin reached from behind grabbing Mumera's testicles, pushing him towards the kitchen table. Mumera grabbed at Martin's hands trying to get loose and rid of the pain.

"No I promised my brother. Only clean girls." Mumera said as if in delirium, trying to get loose, but Martin held on tightly.

Martin was saying, "I will do you fine. You will like it. Bend over table, hands on head." He said, squeezing harder until Mumera obeyed, feeling the cold table on his belly and the shooting pain in his groin. Mumera could not believe this skinny, little boy had overpowered him, just as Muturi said he might. Mumera tried to get up but Martin squeezed harder. "Don't move!" Mumera tried to relax and Martin reduced the grip somewhat, but he felt something greasy being rubbed into him. "Nice. This will feel good. You will like it." Martin was muttering. Mumera knew that Martin was intending to rape him. He struggled again, and the crushing pain was so bad he passed out, and time skipped to the next conscious scene.

"Mumera, why are you sleeping on the table?" Hanna said waking him up. The pain in his testicles and rectum was sharp and unforgettable. "I told you to get dressed and you come in here for a nap?" She slapped his bare bottom. "Get dressed!" He stood up and found his clothes, and felt something trickling down his leg. Either I am bleeding, he thought, or... "Go talk to Janie, she asked for you." The pain was fanning the flames of his rage towards Martin. He looked at the pregnant woman putting a kettle on the electric stove. "Oh, Martin said he wants to see you again tomorrow."

Mumura thought, I will see him in hell first, if not dead. He probably gave me a dozen diseases. He turned and went in to see Janie. She was under her blanket holding what looked like a

231

folded towel, but as he got nearer he saw that it was the little two-inch fetus, curled up in the cloth. Mumera's rage turned suddenly to sad sympathy for Janie.

"Can we give her a burial?"

"Her? Well, I suppose. My mother told me about a miscarriage a friend had. It was cremated and they buried the ashes in a church cemetery with other miscarried babies. I will talk to the health center people." He promised, thinking he will be going to the health center anyway.

"Could you do that now?" she begged.

~~~~

Mumera was fuming angry, leaving the health center in the dark. Having to wait so long for that humiliation, he thought. At least he found out the Catholics have a ceremony for miscarried babies, and that they offer cremation and a service twice a year.

Then he had to tell the nurse that he was raped by a man, and he had to show the nurse, who took samples. She wanted to report it to the police! He thought. *Gai*, why not increase the humiliation? He only became angrier as he had to bend over and have more things stuck into him for various tests. Then he needed the penicillin jab in the butt to add to the pain below the waist.

Then there willl be more humiliation in a few months, when he will have to go back for a blood test for AIDS! *Gai*!

It was after dark before he finally was on his way home with anger clouding both his vision and his judgment. His path home brought him past the infamous apartment of Joe Watusu. Mumera recalled Muturi's photos that were used for blackmail. Martin surely was there now he thought. He made a turn down the walkway to the backdoor of the ground level apartment. He heard some sounds, and walked around to an open window. From the dark, through a crack in the curtains, he looked in to see two black figures obviously engaged in vigorous intercourse. In the dim light, as the top figure moved, he could see the bottom figure was Martin on his back with his leg pulled up to his chest. He was making sounds like lust filled pain, while Joe was dancing up and down, then went rigid and slid down next to Martin, who lowered his legs. Soon, they were relaxed, if not asleep.

Mumera's rage got the better of him, thinking he would go beat Martin, and went to the back door. Even though it was locked, the window next to the door was open. He stuck his arm in and felt around for the deadbolt, and unlocked the door. He walked in through the kitchen, seeing cooking knives on hooks, his rage changed his mind about a beating. He took one with a long blade and a splintery wooden handle, and walked quietly into the bedroom. The two were snoring, obviously regaining energy for the next round. In his slumber, his teacher was affectionately embracing Martin, with his hand resting on Martin's belly. Mumera felt an incredible, violent rage and hatred for these two, for these who intended to rape his brother and the one who did. His hands were shaking and he heard nothing but the snoring and his heart pounding in his ears. He gripped the knife with both hands, still feeling the pain of Martin crushing his testicles earlier in the day. He raised the knife over his head, imagining Martin's thing inside his own body, he plunged the knife down to where he thought Martin's heart should be. He felt the resistance of bone, the knife sliding through the bone maybe three inches, then breaking off. Martin stopped snoring instantly, while his teacher slept soundly, snoring loudly. A dark puddle of blood oozed out and ran down touching the teacher's arm. Mumera laid the broken knife in the puddle of blood and left, shaking like a storm blown tree. His rage was subsiding; replaced with disbelief at what he had just done.

~~~~~

Mumera's eyes popped open to see his brother's empty bed across from him. Pangs shot through him, missing his brother and fear for what he had done to Martin. He was not able to sleep the night of the murder and was finally able to get a couple of hours before the sun came up just now. Yesterday, he spent in the market helping to carry things for tips, hoping as well to hear some news. Late in the afternoon, he had heard the rumor that someone had stabbed a high school student to death, and police had arrested his teacher. He worked vigorously in the market just to keep himself from shaking and hearing the roar in his ears. Why do I miss my brother so much? He leaves and I am in so much trouble in just a few days.

He pulled himself out of bed, and sat in his boxer shorts on the edge of his bed for a while wondering what time it was, since the sun through the thin curtains seemed high. There was a tap at the door, "Mumera, you there?" The door creaked open, and there stood Janie. She was wearing a school skirt with a tank top that emphasized her breasts and a kitambaa around her shoulders. Her legs were shiny and she was barefoot, she put the kitambaa on Muturi's bed. "Your mama said I should wake you up. I have been waiting about an hour. Your mother thinks you are missing your brother and not sleeping."

"I heard about your brother. Very sorry." He lied. She came in, closed the door behind her and sat next to him. She rested a hand on his bare thigh.

"I lost my baby and brother the same day. The police arrested Joe. It does not make sense. The police came to talk to me. They found pictures of Martin doing sex things with him, so they think Martin was blackmailing him, so Joe killed him."

"Hmmm." He mumbled. "What happened?"

"The police told me that a neighbor, who was coming home late, saw Joe's back door open and went in and found Joe with Martin naked on the bed sleeping and Joe had a knife in his hand and blood all over the place." She said and Mumera knew that was an exaggeration. At least the neighbor did not see Mumera leaving… and leaving the back door open was probably a mistake on one hand, but worked otherwise. "The police still have Martin's body for evidence."

"How are you? Are you feeling better?" he asked.

"I am back to normal. The baby was smaller than a finger, so it did not do any harm. I took the dead baby to the health center, and they will put it with other dead babies and turn them to ashes. They will all be buried in a couple of months by a priest."

"And your brother?"

"Mama is coming to take his ashes home after the police are done."

"When is that?"

"After they collect evidence. If Joe confesses, they will release him earlier." She said and absent-mindedly stroked his inner thigh.

"I guess we both lost a brother." He said, looking down her tank top and admired her beautifully brown cleavage. His eyes turned to her hand stroking his leg, getting him aroused.

"I lost Martin months ago when he fell in with Joe. He spent most of his time at Joe's place. Only came to Hanna's when Joe was doing someone else." She said and as if by second nature, pulled his boxers up to stroke his manhood. As if being connected was normal conversational mode, he laid back on the bed. She stood up, removed her knickers and his boxers, and mounted him. Mumera felt perfection being coupled together with her. All his concerns vanished. "So, I al..." she moved her hips, "got used to him..." she rested the palms of her hands on his chest, "not being around already, but Muturi helped."

"I really," he sighed, "miss my brother. He was so good to me. But you are helping me." Her eyes were closed as her hips were moving gently back and forth as they talked. He heard the door creak and saw his little half brother peering through the crack. He reached up and pulled up on her tank top, pulling it over her head to show off her beautiful breasts. He turned her skirt around to open the buttons and pulled that over her head. She was beautifully naked so his little half brother could feast his eyes.

She continued, "My mama wants to meet you," she gasped as if reaching a peak and scratching his chest, "and your family." He reached around and put his hands on her butt lifting her up a bit to show off his shaft. The boy was gradually getting both eyes on the show and his lips made an O shape. Mumera pulled her forward and began thrusting in and out and watched the boy's concentration on the dance, until she squealed and he exploded into her. She collapsed onto him into a deep hug. "We can start on another baby," she sighed. He looked over at the boy who was getting bored. The boy disappeared, leaving the door open. He pulled the blanket from the side of the bed over Janie to let her rest and mumble on top of him.

"You do know I am not sixteen yet?" he said.

"I know. But I am done with high school and likely not get into university. I should get married." She said and his manhood shriveled out of her.

"Will your father arrange a marriage for you? Some old man?"

"Yes, unless I find a good man on my own. Someone like you."

"I still have two years of high school, then college."

"Maybe Mwangi let me live here."

"You want Mwangi to marry you?"

"No, you, you marry me, and I live here."

"You think fast. I would have to work to pay for support. And does your father want a bride price?"

"Him, no. He would give me money to start off though. He acts like he is *mzungu*."

"Really. So, he would not mind your marrying someone who is mostly *mzungu*? I am only one-fourth Kikuyu."

"No, and tell Mwangi and your mama that I can tutor you in your subjects. I can also find work."

~~~~~~~

Wanjiru heard the telephone ringing in the shop, and Mwangi laughing and joking with the person in Kikuyu. At first, she thought it was a friend or customer until he shouted, "Njiru! Muturi is on the telephone from America!"

She thought her heart would burst running to the telephone. "Muturi, you made it! How is everything?" she said in Kikuyu.

"Very nice, Mama. Such a clean country. Everything is so big. The farms have so much food! The cities are very, very large."

"How is Martha and her mother?"

"Doing well, still sad about Mr. Mills. I will start university in a few weeks. Martha is helping very much."

"When do you get married?"

"We get the papers tomorrow, and we see a judge, then there will be a party at her mother's house on Saturday.

"I wish I could be there."

"I will send a lot of pictures. When we come back to Kenya we will have a second wedding party, with *pambe* and lots of dancing."

"Yes, for sure. I am so happy for you. Mumera seems to like Janie a lot. I am so glad you helped them get together. She is here now."

"How is she doing?"

"Bad, bad news. Her brother was murdered and his teacher Mr. Watusu was arrested for murder."

"Murder?"

"Yes, the newspaper says Martin was blackmailing Watusu, so that is why he murdered him.

"Unbelievable. I will tell Martha, but she may not believe it."

"Yes, Martin was stabbed in the heart with a kitchen knife. A neighbor found Mr. Watusu in bed with the dead body."

"That is so sick!" came the voice from eight thousand miles away." "Martha wants to say hello."

"Martha? Martha? Hello my soon to be wonderful daughter!"

She heard laughing, "Yes, your wonderful son is going to make me and the baby legal!" Wanjiru had forgotten about the baby in the talk of the murder.

"Is everything going good?" she asked.

"Yes, mama," Martha said, "everything is fine." And hearing all the joy, Wanjiru could not be happier. Her son going to university in American, getting married and giving her a grandchild.

"I could not be happier. Send my regards to your mother. Tell her I was so sad for her loss, but so full of joy that she will be like me a grandmother."

"She is going through a lot of changes, and sad times. So, wish us luck. I love you dearly, Wanjiru. A woman could not have a better mother-in-law!"

"You are good to say so. Bye for now." And Muturi came back on the line.

"Mama, so many changes. I hope I do well and not let you down."

"May God be with you, Muturi."

"And with you, Mama. Bye for now." He said and she heard the phone go dead.

She looked over at Mwangi working on a motorcycle. "He sounds like he is doing fine." She said and he waved back. She wanted to tell Mumera, and walked off towards his room, then thought about Janie being there, so she walked quietly noticing his door was open. She looked in and they both were under a blanket talking. She tapped on the door and walked in, thinking it was still her home. "I just talked with Muturi."

Mumera rolled Janie backwards, and Wanjiru smiled to herself to see briefly the older girl's beautiful breast before it was covered by the blanket. "Is he in America?"

"Yes," she answered looking down at the girl's clothes on the floor, which in turn were on top of Mumera's boxer shorts. "He is doing fine. He said he is getting the marriage papers tomorrow. Martha is going to make me a grandmother." She said, but thought, knowing my boys, I may be a grandmother already.

237

"That is great..." Mumera started.

"May I ask something?" Janie interrupted.

"Of course."

"I want to be Mumera's wife. At least one of his wives." Janie stated honestly.

"It would not cost him anything. In fact my father would pay him a dowery like the English do."

"What?" Wanjiru felt a sinking feeling. "What about his schooling and going to university?"

"I would work and take care of myself and any children. He can support us later."

"He is still fifteen you know. He may look fully grown, but he still has two years of high school. And you are what eighteen?

"Yes, I just turn eighteen." She said, speaking with her hand caused the blanket to slip down. She got up on one elbow to express herself. "I cannot live without Mumera. I will do anything to be with him." She said, and Wanjiru thought she was being very immature, but young people are like that. If they fall in love, the world will end if they cannot be together.

"Mumera, what do you say? You want a wife and children? What if you get bored with her?"

"Bored? I do not think I will. But she said I could have other wives, too. "

Wanjiru looked at the half-naked girl. Then back at her son who had scooted up in bed. Her dark, young skin against his light brown skin was interesting. He was quite large in the small bed. Janie was stroking his stomach "Well, where are you two to live? With your aunt? Or here?"

"Well, we..." Mumera started.

"I would live here. I could pay for my food and expenses. I can work some in the shops, keep books. I could be a help with your kids." Janie said, and Wanjiru thought that she would love some help.

"I know you just lost your brother. I hope you are thinking clearly, and not regret it." She worried aloud.

"No, my brother went his own way for several months. Joe seduced him into that kind of life. It disappointed my father very much."

"We will talk with Mwangi, but I am sure it will be fine. If you want a legal marriage we can arrange it, or if you just want to live together as you suggest, that is fine with me." Wanjiru thought back over her own life and thought, who am I to tell even my own children how to live their lives?

Chapter 22, Montreal

Kimani waved good bye to the bright red taxi and turned back up Boulevard René Lévesque. He thought, his old friend "Lodi" was already looking like an old man. Kimani was in Montreal for several months of training in cellular technology for his company, and Lodi brought his wife and two children for a visit to Montreal. They flew in from Chicago, saw the city with Kimani and his workmates and were flying back today, two days later.

Kimani was still recovering from the shock that he had a daughter in America. Lodi told him that his old friend Beth had written a book, which said that Kimani was a father... well father yet again. Kimani had lost touch with Beth, after he met his current wife. Beth had never told him.

"He is a very funny man. Does he ever take anything seriously?" Kimani's workmate Bernard was asking. Kimani smiled at the old Kalenjin with the white beard.

"You do not want to know him when he is serious." Kimani laughed. "He has a temper like a hungry lion."

"His wife is very pretty." Kimani's other workmate Paul said.

"Paul," Kimani looked at the chubby young man, "every woman looks beautiful to you. She has too much hair and is shaped like a boy. She is well educated but acts like she is stupid."

"Yes, I noticed. But she must be good in bed, since he has two children with her." Paul responded.

"Lodi said they had several more that died after birth."

"Died?" Bernard said, "That is bad luck. But that happens often. Does she work, too?"

"Yes, I think she is a teacher." Kimani said.

"I wanted to take her to bed." Paul said, and Kimani laughed at him. Paul was wearing a West African outfit even though he was East African. He said the girls would always stop to talk with him when he wore those clothes.

"Lodi tells me he thinks she is sleeping around."

"Sleeping?" Bernard asked.

"*Kutombwa na mabwana mingi.*" Kimani said

"Many men?"

"He has no proof." Kimani said.

"His daughter is cute. I would do her, too." Paul said.

"Paul, she is still a child."

"No," Bernard said, "She told me she was fifteen. She is developed!" As they walked, Paul stopped to chat with a brown skinned girl. Kimani turned and saw another girl coming out of a bar behind the first. Kimani stood waiting with Bernard, while Paul chatted up the girls.

"Kimani! Remember these girls from Haiti? You bought them drinks last week."

Kimani replied, "Sure, I remember, but I do not know French."

"They were mad we did not invite them up. I told them we have some beer in our apartment." Paul said.

Kimani was getting excited at some prospects. "If they want to come. Let them know." Kimani walked over to listen in.

Paul said something like, "*Venez a ma maison et buvez de la bière avec nous.*" The girls laughed, and Kimani knew that Paul's French was off the mark, but at least they laughed, and began following Paul. The light brown-skinned girls both had short-cropped hair, and were wearing flashy jewelry, short skirts and light, translucent blouses. They carried little purses. Kimani let Paul lead the way, following a bit behind to check out the catch of the day as Paul would call them. Kimani listened and heard something like "*Vu etay les filles tray douces.*" And again the girls giggled, and Kimani wondered what he was trying to say. They turned into the long term stay hotel, and took the stairs to the second floor. Inside the suite were three bedrooms, a kitchenette and a sitting space, where the two girls sat on the couch near a window.

Bernard said, "I am an old man who needs a nap," and disappeared into his bedroom. Kimani sat in a chair across from the two girls noting the catch. The girls smiled at him.

"I am sorry, I do not know French, *mon nom est* Kimani. *No parlez.* Sorry."

"I know English." Said one. "I am Margaret and she is Mary. She only speaks Haiti French." Paul brought over the beers for everyone in opened beer bottles. He sat on the couch next to

241

Mary, having already targeted Mary. He began talking in his pidgeon French, making Mary giggle.

"Margaret, how long you live in Montreal?" Kimani asked.

"Two years. We work at the Haiti embassy. I am a receptionist, and she cleans. We will go back in a year, and maybe go to some other country."

"Is this your first job. You both look young."

"Yes, outside Haiti. Mary is my cousin."

"Yes you look alike. We are from Kenya and are here for training."

Paul and Mary stood up. "Excuse us, Mary wants to see my artwork." They went off to Paul's bedroom carrying the beers.

"His artwork?" Margaret said. Kimani knew what Paul meant by that, and pointed to his own privates, and Margaret laughed. "Oh, he is proud of his artwork. *pénis d'art*." She said, and Kimani at least knew that much French.

Kimani looked towards Paul's bedroom, and the door had drifted open. He could see Paul exposing himself and Mary pulling her top off. "You and your cousin have beautiful bodies. Are your breasts as beautiful as Mary's?" Kimani boldly said, and pointing his nose to what he was seeing. Margaret leaned forward, saw, and giggled.

"Mine are better." They both watched as the couple in the other room undressed. "*Merci*! They work fast!" She said is Mary fell down on the bed. "I think she is like a cat in heat."

"In heat? Oh…" Kimani said, as he watched Paul connect with Mary. Margaret moved over and sat on Kimani's lap to watch the show. Kimani was quite aroused and was pressing against her. Her blouse buttoned in the back, and he felt compelled to start undoing them to see if she objected. Once opened he stroked her back and felt no bra. She giggled as the blouse slipped forward and down. "My you are right. Much prettier." She turned to give him full view and began unbuttoning his short sleeve shirt.

"You are a skinny thing aren't you?" she said.

"Makes it easier to slide between your legs." They laughed, and his cell phone began ringing. It was a rather large thing that was used mostly by his boss in Nairobi contacting him, but sometimes his wife. Caller ID only said out of area. As he picked up the phone, Margaret scooted down to the floor and turned around to work on removing his pants. "Hello?" his said into the phone. "Hello? Oh you are calling late. Is everything okay?" He said, then pressed the mute button. "It is the boss," he lied since it was his wife, "so, please be quiet." He unmuted it, and said in Kikuyu, "How are the girls?"

"We are fine," she said, while Margaret began removing his shoes, socks and pants. "My account is running low, and I need to check if you transferred some money yet." She said, while he moved up so that Margaret to pull off his clothes, with his little stiffy pointing upwards

"Yes, I did. I put the usual amount in." he said and Margaret sucked the whole thing into her mouth and he nearly screamed in delight. Her large breasts were resting on his knees as her head went up and down. He thought, she must be trying to make it bigger. What she has is all there is.

"I have to pay the girls' school fees, you know. And my mother needs some medicine." She said, but he was having trouble concentrating. Margaret stood up and trying to pull him into the bedroom, he stood up and continued.

"I will go and add some more then." He followed Margaret into his bedroom, watching her walk out of her skirt and panties. "Are the girls still awake?" Margaret pulled his open shirt off him and pushed him onto the bed.

"No, they are asleep." She said, and Kimani was naked on the bed with Margaret climbing on, with his stiffy as big as it could get. Margaret was looking disappointed. "I could not sleep because I worry about money and my mother." Margaret straddled Kimani's skinny, little body and connected. Oh, very nice, he thought, nearly gasping.

"I miss you very much." He offered as Margaret began gyrating on top of him, creaking the bed. Kimani put his free hand down to rub Margaret's clitoris

"Oh, sure. You are probably doing all the women in Montreal. Tell me the truth." She accused him.

"No, that would be my workmate Paul. Now, listen, I know Kikuyu women have needs too and there are plenty of men to do you. Now you tell the truth." Margaret suddenly doubled over in orgasm and was breathing so heavy, Kimani covered the mike.

"You jealous man. You know I do not do that."

"Yes, you are very holy. That is why I love you." Kimani felt like he would explode any second, but Margaret had stopped moving, apparently regaining her strength.

"Yes, I know. I love you and miss you, too." She finally admitted. "This is an expensive call, now. You be good." She said.

"Yes, and give the girls my love." He said. "Bye." And he heard the phone go dead. He set it by his pillow and rolled Margaret over so that he could get on top.

Chapter 23, Champaign

Martha could see through the front window of the car the sign referring to the Neil Street exit. Beth turned around and looked at her, "This is where we get off." Beth then turned to her sister in the front passenger seat, "How are you doing?"

"You drive fast. What did it take two hours?"

"About an hour and a half."

Martha turned to Muturi, "This is where your bio father lives and works. You nervous?"

"Happy."

"Well, I was not able to contact him. I was hoping if we just show up at his place, it would be a nice surprise. Beth knows him, so it will not be all strangers."

Her mother turned, "I thought Beth and I came over to see our sister?"

"That's true, Mom, I was just saying if it works out, Muturi can meet his biological father."

"I still think that would be too much of a shock." Her mother protested. Beth was reaching the end of the off ramp stopping at the intersection.

Beth said, "I know him well, he will welcome every one of us in with open arms. I never met a person who did not love him and vice versa."

"I wrote him letters but he never replied. He wrote my mother though a lot." Muturi said.

"Sounds like him," Beth added. "Are you sure the letters were mailed?" She headed the car south amid congested traffic.

"Martha, my sister lives on Church Street across from a park." Martha's mother was worrying. Martha had never visited this aunt but in turn worried about her mother, who seemed to have aged ten years since her father died. For a woman in her fifties, she acts like an invalid at times.

"Well, Muturi," Beth said, "if I were your mother, married to someone else who adopted you; I would keep the biological father out of the picture until my child was old enough to appreciate what his adopted father did for him." She made a right turn onto Church Street, and began driving very slowly looking for the house.

"See how pretty it is here?" Martha's mother was mumbling, "I just might move in with my sister."

Muturi said, "Mwangi? He is my *baba*. He is. But I am curious about the man who loved my mother so." Martha thought about the symmetries. History repeats itself.

After several hours at her aunt's house - so that the three sisters could visit - Martha asked Beth to drive them over to see if Muturi could meet his biological father. They drove south through town to a mini mansion area with ponds in the back yards. Beth had been there before and knew the place, or so she thought. After a few wrong turns, she found the house and pulled into the drive.

"*Gai*! This is bigger than Egerton Castle!" Muturi exclaimed. As they got out of the car, packs of kids on bicycles rode by. Of all the houses, this looked the least occupied.

"It's not that big." Beth stated.

"You think anyone is home?" he said and Martha worried he was right. The house was a modern house with a large front porch, and a three-car garage attached near the back.

The three walked up to the front porch, and Martha noticed the morning paper still there. Beth rang the doorbell, but no one answered. Martha turned and saw an older man going through the mailbox by the road, and then walking up to them carrying a few magazines. "They are gone to Montreal for a few days. I am keeping the mail and feeding their cat."

"Oh, that is too bad. We are heading back to Indiana this evening. You know when they will be back?"

"Well, they left yesterday, so, I think they get back tomorrow night. But I will keep watching until they get back. I don't want their cat to croak. "The man smiled at Muturi, who flashed a smile back at the man." Are you related?" he said staring at Muturi.

"Yes, I am." Muturi stated, and Martha felt a shot of pride at his forthrightness.

"Well, if you are half as nice as Mac and his family, it is an honor to meet you. I am Samuel Beck."

"Muturi Makomeki. This is my wife, Martha Mills, and her aunt Beth Kropp. Beth knew Mac when she taught in Kenya." Martha felt strange being introduced as a wife. She had decided to keep her surname name so that she would not have to deal with all the record changes.

"Beth? I think I met you once before at a BBQ here. Mac told about you two there." He laughed.

"Wow, good memory, Sam." Beth said. "I remember you now. You were always carrying the cat around.

"That's me." He smiled again. "Well, Beth, Martha and Matary, I will let them know you stopped by."

"It's Mu tu ree. My mother might be moving to town, so we might see you again." Martha suggested, as Sam shook hands all around. Martha watched as Sam walked back to his house, and looked around. She saw the pond out in back through several trees. The house looked recently built.

They hopped back into the car and headed back to her aunt's house. Martha often thought her mother and older sister could be twins. They had always been close.

"I am going to stay a week or so with my sister," Martha's mother said.

"But you didn't bring any clothes," Martha stated.

"I'll wear my sister's."

"Well, you have everything you need I guess." Martha was happy that she would have the house alone, but knew she would miss her mother.

"We should get going. My daughter said she would be coming up to Crawfordsville this evening."

"You have a daughter?" Muturi asked surprised. "I thought you never married." Martha would swear that she had told him about Beth's daughter.

"Martha, you never told him?" Beth acted stunned.

Martha's mother piped up, "Just like Martha, Beth came back from Africa knocked up!"

"Mother!"

"I'm not being judgmental, just stating the facts." Her mother said. "You should get going, it is getting late." After a few minutes of hugs, they were back in the car driving east on the interstate.

The car was quiet for a long while, until Beth broke the silence. "Frances is sixteen and went to boarding school and starts Purdue the same time as you do." Beth stated. "Martha never told you? She was born premature, and I thought she wouldn't make it."

"I gave him your book to read." Martha said defensively.

Muturi said, "The sexy parts were all I read. Sorry." Then Martha saw the lights go on in Muturi's eyes. "Mombasa?" he asked.

Beth laughed, "Mombasa? Well, actually Lamu. Didn't you get a brother from our trip to Mombasa?"

"Yes, and a second cousin."

"What?" Beth wondered.

"My mother's cousin Wajiko had a boy she later named Hans."

"Wajiko? I know her. When we were in Mombasa, she and your mother were partying with Mac."

"Wow," Martha exclaimed, "talk about a population explosion."

~~~~

Mumera's stomach was turning as he looked into the police officer's face. The officer had said he was a detective investigating Martin's death. He was sitting at his mother's kitchen table with the officer. His mama and baba having left them alone.

"Don't be nervous, Mumera, we just have to talk with everyone who saw Martin the day he died. I understand you saw him earlier in the day."

"Yes, I was visiting with his sister, Janie, and saw him there at Hanna's apartment. He was watching TV. Janie had a miscarriage and I was helping Hanna."

"Miscarriage? Did you get her pregnant?"

"No, I have seen her for a short while. It was a surprise to all of us that she was pregnant. Even Janie. I saw the baby it was less than two inches long."

"Janie and Martin were twins, right?"

"They were? I thought Janie was older. She is over two years older than me, but she likes me for some reason." He said seriously. The officer looked mixed tribe and had proper English, slipping into very proper Swahili at times. He looked small next to Mumera.

"So, it was very surprising to everyone about the miscarriage?"

"Martin did not seem surprised. Me and Hanna were panicking and Martin acted like it was nothing."

"What did you do?"

"I got towels and a big bowl of water."

"Yes," the officer said, glancing through his notebook, "Hanna said you helped. She said she came out and Martin was doing something to you on the table."

"Really. What did she see?"

"She thought you were asleep and Martin was having sexual intercourse with you."

"When I came out of Janie's room, I was naked, because Janie and I had just done it." He looked up beyond the officer and he could see Janie was listening from the bedroom.

"Yes. Hanna said as much."

Skipping a few details, Mumera added in a quieter voice, "In the kitchen, Martin grabbed my testicles and squeezed so hard I passed out. Hanna woke me up later. I was naked on my belly on the kitchen table."

"I learned that you went to the health center." The officer stated.

In a quiet voice intended only for the officer, "Yes, I suppose you did. I had blood and *manii* running from my *kundu*."

"You told the nurse that a man raped you."

"I was embarrassed that such a small man raped me." He said quietly, hoping Janie could not hear.

"Yes. I understand. Where do you think Martin learned to do that?"

"There are rumors at the school about Mr. Watusu, using *dawa* to rape boys. But I have no facts." He lied.

"Yes, several boys came forward to say that Watusu raped them by grabbing their testicles or using a narcotic." The officer was very serious. "Others say they consented to have relations with him." Mumera could see Janie straining to hear the conversation.

"Are you saying there are some boys who would like to see Joe or Martin dead for one reason or another?" he said almost in a whisper.

"Yes, boys like you." The officer stated in very quiet tones as if he feared Mumera's mother was listening.

"I must say I was angry enough to kill Martin, and if he were at Hanna's when I woke up, I probably would have strangled him there. It would be very easy for me to snap his neck." Mumera said, and finally the officer cracked the smallest of smiles.

"From what I learned," the officer leaned very close and whispered, "Martin probably got what he deserved. The blood is on Watusu's hands."

"Oh, no," Mumera lied, "that should be up to God to decide."

The officer looked very solemn, and nodded. "Indeed. Well, I should get back. I may need to talk with you some more." The officer stood up, and Mumera showed him out.

Janie was right behind him as the officer disappeared. "Why is he talking to you? Does he think you killed Martin?" Mumera turned and looked into Janie's eyes.

"He did not say so. He knows I saw him the day Martin died. I had to tell him about the miscarriage."

"Yes, Hanna and I told him about it, too."

"He asked me if I was the father of the baby."

"Yes, the officer thought Martin was. Like it was incest. I told him it was one of my boyfriends."

"Oh."

"I had to convince him that I did not kill my brother."

"Why would he think that?"

"I think it his job to accuse everyone until someone confesses. He could say Martin raped me or something."

"Oh." Mumera sighed.

"Hanna told the officer Martin was doing you on the kitchen table."

"What? You knew that? You did not tell me."

"She said you were not awake. So, I thought you did not know what he did to you."

"I came out of your room to get dressed in the kitchen. As I bent over to pick up my clothes, Martin grabbed my testicles so hard I passed out. I woke up with blood and *manii* running out of me. I went to the health center."

"That animal. Had I known I could have killed my own brother."

"Did the police say what was Joe's motive for killing Martin?"

"Joe was mad at Martin for giving him diseases. Martin kept dropping down to Nairobi to prostitute."

"You think he gave me something?"

"I don't know. Just go be tested." She shrugged.

"I got some tests and penicillin. I have to go back later for an AIDS test."

"What is that?" she looked perplexed.

"Slim." He said.

"Horrible. Now, I would kill him for sure."

"Don't let the police hear you say that." Mumera said and saw his mother coming in from the courtyard.

Wanjiru walked up and asked, "So, what did the *askari* want?"

Mumera smiled at the choice of words. "He needed to talk with anyone who saw Martin that day."

"Oh, fine. I hope they do not accuse you instead of that dirty teacher."

"The officer said that Watusu had blood on his hands. I think they will charge him for raping boys and sexing boys underage." He stated flatly. Wanting to change the subject, "Did you talk with baba about Janie living with us?"

"Yes, Mwangi says fine, fine. But Janie have to help with food, cleaning and laundry. Not to worry about rent for bed. He says you two will sleep together anyway."

"Do we need to marry?" Janie asked.

"If a baby comes, then marry." Wanjiru said. Mumera was feeling aroused that he would have a girl sleeping with him all the time with his parent's permission no less!

~~~~

Kimani pulled the letters out of the postal box, closed and locked it back up again. He looked through bills and saw a letter from his old *mzungu* friend that he had seen in Montreal a couple of months back. Feels like photos. He looked on and found a letter from Beth Kropp, and his stomach turned acidic. He left the crowded post office, headed down the street to the park, and found an empty bench to sit on. Do I want to open this, he thought. Staring at it for a few minutes, wondering what she had to say after, what? Fifteen, sixteen years? Kimani recalled the letters he sent with no reply. His last letter told about getting married after his first daughter was born. Beth left, wrote a few times, saying she was in love with someone else and stopped writing.

He took out a penknife and gently opened the letter. "Kimani, I know it has been forever since I wrote you. Mac came back from Montreal and called me. He scolded me for not writing

251

you and keeping secrets from you. He insisted I write and send some pictures, and be honest with you. He said he knows the pain of being deceived, and would not wish it on his worst enemy. So, here I write."

Yes, you did a good job of keeping secrets! Kimani thought, but then realized he tried the same. He stopped reading and looked through the photographs. Beth was first holding a baby, and in several with a skinny girl with dark hair, at various ages. Kimani thought of the long affair he had with Beth, but would swear he had always used condoms. In the more recent photos oddly enough looked very much like a young, pale, female version of him. The girl had his skinny, bony structure rather than Beth's meaty one. He started reading the letter again. "You recall I left Kenya at the end of my contract, but did not say good bye since you were working in Molo. Had you seen me, you would have known I thought I was with your child at the time. I named her Frances, but her friends call her Franny. She is smart and friendly. She started college already, going to a school here in Indianapolis. Her cousin Muturi by marriage is also going there. You may remember him as Wanjiru Tatton's first son. Muturi married my niece Martha who was a teacher at Nakuru for a while. He also went to Njoro." Muturi, cousin by marriage? She said that he married her niece? He asked himself. I need a piece of paper to write down all these relationships. He looked closely at a photo of a family gathering with a lake in the background, and looked at the names on the back. The tall *nusu nusu* man in a t-shirt and shorts was Muturi, standing next to Franny, who was in a bikini and on his other side his wife Martha, who wore a tank top and shorts. Next to his daughter was Beth who added, like himself, a few pounds over the years. There was also several older women listed as her sisters and a nephew. Muturi had his arm around his wife, who looked like she might be pregnant. His daughter Franny looked like she had a hand on Muturi's back… well actually a bit lower. He thought about it, and realized Franny and Muturi were about the same age. Like the protective father, Kimani assumed that Muturi would be hitting on his daughter, but this Martha looked huge in comparison to his skinny, little daughter. Not someone you would want to make a mistake with, he laughed to himself.

"Finally, for years I told Mac that Franny is your, but I think that morning in Lamu when I finally connected with Mac was all it took to make Franny. Mac's mother had dark complexion and was skinny - so I do not know. Franny looks more like her than you. Only a blood test for sure. Sorry, if this is a short letter, but write if you want Franny to write back. She would be interested in your family and all the details of your life." Kimani was dumbfounded, still not knowing if Franny was his or not.

Chapter 24, Perdue

Muturi looked out his "dormitory" window to see the Indianapolis skyline, but recalling the dormitory at Njoro High School, he laughed. Actually this was a one room apartment, and because he was married he got extra perquisites from the university. Being an "international" student got him some leeway, too. He glanced back at his calculus textbook and re-read a homework problem that was due on Monday. He was one of those weird students that studied on a Saturday morning rather than nurse a hangover.

He was still in a t-shirt and boxers studying, but still felt the glow of having talked with Martha, who described the baby as kicking and very strong. She was sure it was a boy from what others had told her. She was very happy, and the commute to West Lafayette four times a week was easy enough. She did worry about winter, but since he never experienced an Indiana blizzard, he had the ignorance of a child going to a dentist the first time. He was looking forward to taking the train up to Crawfordsville in a few weeks at what they call Thanksgiving. Her mother finally had come back from Champaign to help with the baby if it came early.

He had gone out to a movie last evening with Franny, the skinny, little daughter of Beth Kropp. Actually, since he is married to her cousin, was she legally a cousin? Did he figure that right? Compared to Martha, though, Frances was a frail little girl, with dark wavy hair. Frances was living at her mother's Indianapolis home. She took the bus to classes. After the movie, they went for a pizza, but she had to leave before the last bus. "I would love to spend the night with you, but mom would kill me sleeping with a married man." She said, and he did not take her seriously. There were plenty of guys around, she did not need to bed a married one.

He was on his last calculus problem, when there was a knock at the door. At the door was Frances carrying a purse and a cardboard box. "I have a real treat for you!" she said, barging in. "No, I'm not going to have sex with you. I have pictures!" She was wearing a red sweatshirt and blue jeans, like a real college student.

"Pictures?"

"And letters. From the guy mom says is my biological father." She said. "Apparently, you met him." She suddenly realized he was only in his underwear. "Nice outfit."

"You did not give much notice. I met him?" he asked. She kicked off her shoes, sat down on the couch and set the small box on the coffee table. Muturi sat down next to her, and suddenly thought of Janie and felt a tingle go through him. She leaned forward and their legs rubbed together.

"Yes." She opened the box, took an envelope from the top, and opened it up, setting out the photographs. He recognized himself at about ten years of age and his brother, Mumera. Oh, that is David, too.

"We were playing basketball and my mama came by with a friend of hers. He took some pictures. He was a little, skinny guy. You're built like him."

"Thanks a lot."

"Well you are rather flat-chested." He said, knowing he did not have to flatter a cousin-in-law.

"Well, I'll have to show you later that I'm not." She laughed, "But, here is a picture of my father."

"That was the guy who took pictures of us, and said he was Lodi's friend."

"Lodi? Your father? Mom calls him Mac. Here is the letter from my father."

"Read it to me."

"Dear Beth. I really have been thinking about you. I went up to Njoro on a mission for Mac, who wanted me to get pictures of his son. You know he still believes he has a son here. I told him a hundred times Wanjiru's boy is not his, but somehow he knew. You said you visited him. That is good. Tell me more details. You can give him these pictures if you think it is all right. Wanjiru told me she never wrote back to him." She unfolded the letter and another picture fell out.

"He is wearing red Speedos!" He said. "Anything on the back."

"Yes, it says, 'Please don't forget me.'"

"Your mom wanted..."

"I am not sure. Here, I read this, but what do you think it means. 'Yes, to answer your question, I loved him very much and would do anything he wanted. But he did not want much, anyway.

He showed me ways of love I never thought of.'" She stopped and looked at her cousin, "What do you think that means?"

"I know what he means. Sometimes two people have to express their love and concern physically." He thought of Mumera. "I was that way with my brother. I would do anything to make him happy and protect him… absolutely anything." He said and looked into her eyes, and suddenly realized she had a hand on his bare thigh moving up on the cloth of his shorts. He removed the hand, and slid down to rest his head on the back of the couch.

Suddenly changing the subject, she said, as if insulted by the rebuff. "And I am not flat-chested!" She put the letter back in the box and stood up, pulling off her sweatshirt. She was not wearing a bra, and she was flat chested, or nearly so. She had small handfuls with pink nipples. She was so skinny her ribs showed through. Muturi was almost embarrassed for her, but nevertheless was getting aroused. If a woman demands it, Muturi thought, a man must give it.

~~~~

Gai! He thought. Martha will be so disappointed in me. He looked down at the skinny woman under him, feeling her hip bones cut into his.

"Whoops. I promised my mother I wouldn't do that." Franny whispered as if her mother would hear. "My mother will kill me. She said do anyone, but not Muturi!"

He sat back on the couch, tucking himself back into his shorts, and looked at the naked girl at the other end of the couch. "I'm not sure what Martha would do. She is so pregnant though." He said as if that justified it. She was not embarrassed, sitting there as she did.

"Hmmmm. Well, as long as you give her all the sex she wants, you are okay, and I will never say anything. I have wanted you since Martha sent a picture of you." Franny said, and Muturi thought that was leading in for her to get more from him, so long as Martha got all she wanted. He reached for a fresh towel in the kitchenette. "I have to admit something."

"What is that?"

"You are my first guy I'd seen, you know…"

"Really? Not even in books?"

"What books?" she laughed.

"Not even in high school did you have a boyfriend?"

"Nope! Never got asked out. I asked guys, and they said I was too skinny."

"Wow." He wondered. "You were a virgin for sure."

"I read books, but never imagined what a penis was like."

Muturi felt bad for her to be so ignorant. "You want to study mine? It is quite average." He pulled off his clothes to let her examine his body. She moved in closer as if to do a medical exam.

"Hmmmm. It is not like it is beautiful or anything." She said looking at his limp thing. "These are testicles?" she asked and he opened his legs. Your hair is just wavey, like mine.

"Your hair is not kinky like African girls."

"You saw African girls naked. How many?"

"I don't know. A lot. First my aunts when I was little."

"Oh. Then your mother?"

"She was *nusu nusu*, though."

"What's that?"

"Mixed. Like me. Her father was English and mother Kikuyu."

"Oh. My father was Kikuyu and mother European, right?"

"I guess. Would you like to meet your father."

"Sure. Someday. I am curious. May I touch?" she asked and he nodded. She lifted it and pulled back the foreskin. "Hmmmm it is getting harder. So, if I touch it will it always get harder like that?"

"Usually. You should not make it harder unless you want it inside you." She suddenly let loose, letting it flop down, and he laughed. As if having a second thought, she began touching it again until he felt rock hard. He slid down on the couch as she climbed on top of him.

"That feels soooo good." She sighed, and he sailed away on a sea of pleasure.

Chapter 25, Murder Trial

Mumera was sweating - staring at the defense attorney, wondering whether could stop shaking. He was sworn in, and he could not believe that he was expected to say something nice about Joe.

"Mr. Makomeki, how do you know the defendant?"

"He is a teacher at my high school and I have seen him around."

"You were never his student?"

"No."

"Do you know anyone who was his student?"

"Yes, my brother, my girlfriend Janie and her brother Martin."

"The deceased?"

"Yes."

"When and where was the last time you saw Martin?"

"I saw Martin at his aunt's apartment, on the day he was murdered." Mumera said concentrating on answering exactly the question and nothing more.

"What was he doing when you saw him that day?"

"He was watching TV."

"Yes, and later?"

"He came into his sister's room to see why she was screaming."

"And why was she screaming."

"She was having a miscarriage. His aunt Hanna was helping Janie and he came in as I was going to the kitchen to get towels and a bowl of water."

"What were you wearing at that point?"

"Nothing." Mumera said, and the audience murmured.

"Nothing? You were naked?"

"Janie and I were having sex when the miscarriage began. I did not have time to dress before Hanna and Martin came in."

"Naked? Did Martin see you naked?"

"Yes." Mumera said and there was more murmuring.

"The court has seen evidence that Martin was an active homosexual. What was Martin's response to seeing you naked?"

"He pushed me in the kitchen and said he wanted to do me." He said and again the audience began mumbling.

"You expect the court to believe that boy half your size pushed you in the corner?"

"I had bent over to get my clothes, but then he grabbed my testicles and squeezed very hard. I tried to get loose but he squeezed harder and he ordered me to obey or he would squeeze harder." There were moans of anguish from several men in the court room.

"How did you get away?"

"Your honour!" The prosecution stood up demanding. "How is this relevant?"

The judge simply stated, "It is obvious! Continue."

Mumera answered, "He rubbed something in my anus, and I tried to get away. I passed out from the pain, and woke up later on the kitchen table when Hanna woke me up."

"What do you believe happened to you when you were unconscious?"

"I do not know, but I had blood and what looked like semen coming from my anus." Again another gasp, and some male voice stated out loud that Martin deserved to die, and the judge pointed his gavel at the man and ordered him to leave the courtroom. The large, well-dressed man stood up and left.

"Did you assume that you were raped by Martin?"

"I had good evidence to that effect." Mumera stated factually.

"Did you go to the Health Center?"

"Yes, and I got tested and some penicillin."

"Did you report it to the police?"

"I did not, but the Health Center did."

"Why did you not report it to the police?"

"I was too humiliated."

"Is it true that you intended to get revenge on Martin and did not need the police?"

"Objection!"

The judge turned to the defense lawyer and stated, "Stick to the facts."

"After the Health Center, did you go to Joe Watusu's apartment?"

"No." he lied.

"You have been there before, is that true?"

"I had never been in there before." He said truthfully, thinking before that night, he had never gone inside... walked by yes, but inside no.

"Did your brother tell you he had gone there before?"

"Objection. Hearsay!"

"Did your brother tell you Mr. Watusu seduced him?"

"Objection. Hearsay!"

"Mr. Makomeki, did you hate Martin?"

"Objection. Relevance?"

"Mr. Makomeki, did you test positive for AIDS."

"No!" he answered quickly.

"Mr. Makomeki, did you test positive for any sexually transmitted disease?"

"Yes."

"What and where was it?"

"Herpes in my anus." Mumera answered miserably feeling the itching in his anus as he spoke.

"Your honour, the victim is not on trial here. The defense is justifying the death of the victim."

The judge looked down, then to the defense attorney. "I agree. You are making the victim look worthy of capital punishment. I order this testimony be stricken and the jury to disregard this testimony."

"Your honour, it was my intent to show that Mr. Makomeki had motive to kill the victim."

"Motive, just as a dozen others. But you have provided no groundwork evidence. You must lay the evidentiary groundwork before showing motive. The fact that the victim was generally hated does not nullify the physical evidence against the defendant." He glanced at Mumera. "You are excused."

Unbelievable, Mumera thought, they are letting the murderer off! The details of the rape even made the judge sympathetic to him as a witness. The judge probably believed that Joe deserved to go to prison, regardless whether he killed Martin or not. As he walked out of the courtroom, he saw Janie in a corner seat. She waved at him and smiled.

Later that day, Mumera was sitting at the kitchen table with his younger brothers doing homework. Occasionally, one of the boys would ask about an arithmetic problem, and Mumera would help. His mother was boiling ugali and frying some beef with onions and carrots, making him very hungry.

Janie came in through the shop looking very glum. She walked up to Mumera and gave him a hug and kiss. "The jury took maybe five minutes to find Joe guilty of raping boys, but innocent of murder." Janie said, and Mumera's stomach turned.

"Innocent of murder?" Mumera was stunned.

"I heard from some people they think the jury believed Martin deserved to die."

"That is a piece of – " Mumera started.

"Was he punished yet?" Wanjiru asked in Kikuyu.

"I heard the prosecutor chatting with someone and he thought Joe would get life in prison."

"He will like that," Mumera said. "All those men!"

Wanjiru sighed, "They even put boys in prison with men, so Joe will be very happy there."

Mwangi came in expecting food to be ready, having heard some of the conversation said, "No, Joe will be miserable there. They hate *msenge* there from what I heard." Janie sat down next to the two little boys doing homework.

"Very good, boys." She said to them.

Mwangi laughed. "I have some good news for you Janie. I was bragging about my future daughter-in-law helping my boys with their homework. The headmistress of the Catholic grade school said she needs women like you to help with the teaching. They may be able to get teacher training for you if you do well with the children.

"I would love that!"

"Well, we can give her a call tomorrow and you can go talk with her for a job."

"Hey, we might have two teachers in the family." Mumera stated.

Wanjiru furrowed her brow, "What? What do you mean?"

"I think I want to be a science and maths teacher. I really enjoy helping the boys learn." Mumera looked at his mother, and she had an expression as if he said a foul word. Then he remembered about his biological father.

Mwangi laughed, "Mumera, it is in your blood! Lodi was a science teacher. Fine man! He sold me his *piki* and helped me get my business going. If not for him, no business and no two fine sons!" Mumera was stunned. His baba was the most understanding man he knew, but this was more than he could believe.

Wanjiru spoke with a testy voice, "So, you do not want to join Muturi in America?"

"I could, but Kenya has a very good science teachers college. A lot of Swedish, but still good. That is years away."

Wanjiru acted like steam was coming out of her ears. "I bred with a very smart man to have smart children." She said to Mumera's astonishment. "I saved and saved so you could get a good education to become a wealthy man, but you want to be a poor teacher in some bush school?" Mumera was feeling the wrath of Wanjiru and began to shake. Wanjiru was scooping out food onto plates for everyone.

"No, mama, I will go to school until I cannot learn anymore! I will become a college professor."

"You will become a scientist or engineer. And then if you are not good at that, you can teach!" she demanded.

"Yes, mama." He cowered. "But Lodi was a teacher!"

"Yes, he came here because he not want to be a soldier. He is now a scientist in America. Muturi says he has a big house on a lake. He teaches at a university. He is not some bush *mwalimu!*" She handed Mwangi a plate of food and a fork. Mwangi laughed and sat down next to Janie. Wanjiru passed out more plates.

Mwangi said, "Boys! Promise your mama that you are going to learn all you possibly can and be the best you can!"

In unison, they all said "I promise." Including Janie, and Wanjiru began laughing as she sat down next to Mwangi, who reached over and gave her a quick hug. Mumera felt very happy to be with his family, but felt a pang of guilt looking at Janie, knowing he had murdered her brother.

They ate in silence, enjoying the food, until Mwangi asked, "You said you got a letter from Muturi? What is the news."

"He is studying a lot. Misses all of us and Martha, since he only sees her every two weeks or so. Oh, do you remember Kimani? Muthoni's boyfriend?"

"The one with the *pikipiki*?"

"Yes. That one. Apparently, when Martha's aunt was a teacher in Nakuru when Lodi was teaching in Njoro, Kimani did Martha's aunt and she had his daughter."

"You must be joking?" Mumera asked. "I remember him. I remember his taking pictures of us. Skinny little guy."

"So, Kimani and Beth's daughter is named Frances and she is going to the same university with Muturi."

Mwangi tried to figure it out, "So, this Frances is Muturi's wife's cousin. So, Muturi is her cousin by marriage?" Mwangi took a big forkful of ugali in his mouth.

"Yes, I think that is right."

"Should we worry about Muturi getting her pregnant?" Mumera laughed.

"Mumera! What a thing to say." Wanjiru said and Mumera felt a bit embarrassed at his remark. "Why would you say such a thing?"

"Women are crazy for his body. I never knew why."

Janie laughed, "You? You do not know why?" Wanjiru and Mwangi laughed also. Mumera looked at his little brothers enjoying their food and looking perplexed at the laughter.

"Muturi said that she is short and very thin, but has my coloring, since she is *nusu nusu* like me.

Then Janie blurted out, "Frances cannot resist seducing Muturi."

Mumera was surprised, but even more surprised when his mama said, "Like Lodi, I would do anything for him." Then he remembered his brother's love for him, doing anything to keep him out of trouble.

~~~~

"I have a test this morning. I can catch the train in the morning to Crawfordsville." Muturi was saying to Martha on the phone. He was stretched out on the couch talking with her.

"I have to leave for a test about the time you will get here. You okay with being alone with my mother for a while?" Martha worried.

"Your mother? Why not? I will bring a lot of books to study."

"She is making a big deal out of Thanksgiving. My brother and his family will be there too. Beth and Franny are coming. We

263

may not be alone much, but I am so big, we might have to be creative to connect."

"We will figure it out. You said Franny, too?"

"Of course. They always come." Martha said, but Muturi thought how Franny was always attacking him. "What? Are you afraid of that little girl? I hope you are taking care of her."

"Little? Yes, I let her do whatever she wants. So, what are you wearing?" he asked.

"Nothing. I am in the bathtub."

"Nice. Rub your button for me, imagine it is my tongue." He said, and he saw the knob on the front door twisting, and the door slowly swinging open. He covered the mouthpiece. Franny's head peeped in around the door, and he pointed at the phone.

"I'm imagining."

"Hey, boy!" Franny said, dropping her jacket and book bag on the floor.

"Speaking of the devil!" Muturi laughed.

Martha said, "Franny there? You be good to her."

"I am. She wants me to help her with algebra."

Franny asked, "Is that Martha? Hey, Martha!" She lifted leg over Muturi's reclining body and straddled him, taking the phone. "Hey, Martha, your husband is a good teacher. I got an A on my last algebra test." Muturi could not hear the answer, but Franny pulled up his shirt and began petting his chest hair, and rubbing her jean bottom against his groin. He was getting aroused. "Here." She handed back the phone, and scooted down to unsnap and unzip his jeans.

"I'm back," Muturi said. "You still rubbing your button?" He asked as Franny pulled his jeans and shorts down until she found what she was looking for.

"But of course I am imagining taking off your clothes and tasting you all over. Is Franny in your pants yet?" Martha asked just as Franny began tasting him.

"Oh, uh, yes." he whispered into the phone, "talk like that and I will get aroused in front of Franny."

"That's okay, she knows we talk dirty. I want to make you hard as a rock and feel you inside me." She said just as Franny slid him to the back of her throat.

"Hmmmm." He said. "Keep talking like that and I might make a mess."

Martha laughed, "Make it in me, please." Franny, got up and pulled off her jeans and panties and mounted Muturi, digging her fingers into his chest. "I am rubbing myself thinking about you."

"Hmmm, wish I could be there and be inside you." He said, and continued the phone sex talk with Martha as Franny rose up and down, sending flashes of pleasure through him. He could hear Martha's lust grunts on the line. "Oh, Martha, nice." He said, and heard her little squeal she usually got when she had an orgasm. He saw Franny about to do the same. She let out a little squeal also, collapsed on his chest, and he popped out of her. "How was it my beautiful wife?" he asked.

"Not as good as the real thing. But I swear I can feel your hot semen in me now." She laughed. "Sounds like Franny is happy. I need to get going. I can't wait to see you. Love you like crazy. Bye for now."

"Love you like the world!" he said. "Bye." He reached out and hung up the phone. Franny was getting her energy back. "Franny, time to study."

"I didn't satisfy you."

"Reward me later."

~~~~

Mumera wondered if he were dreaming, but it is so real. Muturi is in America, wasn't he? Where is Janie? Mumera was in bed stretched out on his back, and Muturi was down there doing his magic, or was it Janie? He looked down and he thought he saw Muturi's head go up and down, and the pleasure was nearly perfect. Then Muturi got up and gave him a smile, "Hey, brother, you're awake!" Muturi climbed up and straddled Mumera as if to mount him. Muturi would never do that! Ohhh! That feels so fine! Then strangely, Muturi said "You murdering *msenge*!" and dug his fingernails into his chest, waking him up. Janie was going up and down on him, her beautiful breasts swinging back and forth, taking advantage of his morning arousal. She went rigid and collapsed on his chest.

After a while she said, "You must have been dreaming about Muturi."

"Why? Did I say something when I was asleep?"

"Yes, you said 'Muturi that feels great' when I was sucking on you." Janie said casually.

265

"Oh." He said non-committally, not remembering if he had told her anything.

"You probably miss your brother. Don't I do it as good as he did?"

"I wanted him to, but could not persuade him. Only you."

"Yes, I love doing it. You need to get to school and I need to get to work." She announced.

~~~~

Muturi winced as his brother-in-law, Daniel, shouted at the TV, "Damn, another touchdown!" Muturi was still perplexed about this game where rows of men pummel each other and throw an odd shaped ball around a soccer field. He smiled at Martha as she and Franny walked through the living room heading upstairs.

"We are done cleaning up. Are you understanding the game yet?" Martha and Franny dressed alike, both wore white blouses and skirts to their knees, except Martha's were maternity clothes.

Muturi was determined to learn the game and felt frustrated. "No. I am getting there, though. Daniel is a good teacher." Muturi looked at the older fellow sitting next to him on the couch, who kept slapping Muturi's leg every time something exciting happened. Muturi was thinking Daniel might be a bit *msenge* himself.

"Beth and mom are heading out to visit their sister this evening. My brother is taking them after the game."

Muturi knew at least there was not much time left to the game. "It says two minutes on the clock."

Martha laughed, "That means half an hour with commercials."

Her brother looked up from the TV. "Franny is not going with us is she?"

Franny said, "I want to stay here and let the three sisters chat."

Martha said, "Dan, what are you going to do there? Can't Beth drive herself?"

"My wife wants to do some shopping there tomorrow morning. Should be some great sales."

"We had too much turkey and need to take a nap. We said good bye already." Martha said and headed up the stairs with Franny following.

Martha's brother stroked Muturi's leg. "Those two have always taken naps together after a big meal. Hope you are not jealous." Daniel said, and his big, blue eyes twinkled. Commercials came on the TV and he changed his focus to Muturi.

"Jealous?" Muturi wondered. "No, not really." He added and his brother-in-law belted out a very loud laugh and slapped him on the leg. They watched the game for a while.

"You know, Martha and Fanny should be naked by now, you want to go watch them?"

"Watch them do what?"

"They have been making each other for years. We can watch through a vent if you like. It used to be fun when they were younger. Now that Martha is pregnant, maybe not."

"What did they do?"

"Lots of kissing, touching and licking. I learned what women like from watching. Helped make my wife happy, I guess." He said as three women came strolling through the dining room and stood next to the TV.

Beth looked at the score, "Indiana does not have a hope of winning. Shall we get going?" Muturi stood up to give each of the women a hug. His in-laws, he thought, all good folks, just like Martha. Daniel was pulling on his coat as the women had disappeared into the mudroom.

The four in-laws were soon out of the house and driving away. The house was dead quiet, so he slowly climbed the stairs looking for his wife. He walked by the room Franny was using and she was snoring away. He went on and found Martha on the king size, guest bed awake. The woman was huge as if she could deliver now rather than in three weeks. Muturi lay down next to her and rubbed her belly.

She said, "It's a boy you know."

"How do you know that?" he wondered.

"I had a sonogram done, and there was a hangy down thingy."

"What is a sonogram?"

"It is a machine that uses sound to make pictures inside the body... like sonar." Martha leaned over to the bedside table and took a piece of paper.

"That is nice." He said.

"See, it is clear as day." She said, and pointed to the black and white printout. "I think he has a boner." They both laughed. "So, I guess we name him the only name we both like."

"Thomas? Thomas Mills Makomeki?"

"Yes, unless we change our minds in the next few weeks."

"We have changed our minds about fifty times." Muturi said staring at the sonogram. "This is amazing."

"What's amazing?" Franny asked from the doorway. Muturi looked up at the skinny girl and felt a tingle go through him. She was wearing a white blouse and a black skirt, which was looking a bit wrinkled from her nap. She came around to Muturi's side of the bed to see what he was looking at.

"Join us, Franny," Martha said, moving over and pulling on Muturi to make space for the girl on the huge bed. Muturi felt somewhat suspicious, wondering if this were all right with Martha. With both of his lovers on either side of him, he was feeling a bit erotic. Frances and Martha were staring at the picture. He put an arm around each woman who had laid their heads on his shoulders.

"Yes, I would say a boy. And definitely Muturi's!" Frances pronounced. *Gai*! Muturi thought, Martha will know.

But Martha agreed, "Yes, definitely Muturi's." Then Muturi looked at Martha who laughed at him and began pulling at his belt undoing it. Frances placed the picture on his belly and helped Martha undo his pants and pull his manhood out for comparisons, as if there was one to be made. Martha held it up and Frances giggled as she held the picture above it.

"Definitely Muturi's." Frances said again. She tossed the paper on the floor and joined Martha stroking his elongating manhood. The pleasure was intense. "Martha, may I?" she asked as if the two cousins knew beforehand what the plan was. Frances got up and straddled Muturi, raising her skirt to show she came prepared. As an accomplished equistrian, she had him inside her within seconds, then pulling off the rest of her clothes. Muturi felt waves of pleasure roll through his body, and quickly forgot his concern for being unfaithful to Martha. Martha reached over and began stroking Franny's and Muturi's pubic hair. Muturi watched as Franny moved up and down while Martha rubbed Franny's "button." As usual, before he could explode, Franny screamed and collapsed onto Muturi's chest, and Martha giggled.

"Franny, you sure come quickly. Now move over, it's my turn." Franny rolled off Muturi, leaving his wet shaft pointing upwards getting a bit of a chill. Martha got up and straddling him and showing her lack of panties, as if this were preplanned with Franny. She slid down smoothly onto him, letting her baby belly rest on top of his belly. She pulled off her clothes while he enjoyed the wonderful feeling of being inside her. He and Franny both stroked the large belly while Martha gently went up and down pleasuring herself, but pressing her hands into his chest. This went on for many minutes with Martha coming several times and Muturi going insane with pleasure. Franny began kissing him and putting her tongue into his mouth, while stroking his ribs under his shirt. The electricity was building up, Martha was moaning, and suddenly he exploded just as Martha tossed her head backwards. She was rigid for nearly a minute then collapsed onto the bed next to him. Franny held onto is flaccid shaft as if it were a puppy she were afraid would escape. Her stroking it gave him secondary quakes and more electricity shooting through his body. She soon stopped and relaxed beside him.

"That was very nice." He said to Martha. "Did you and Franny plan on sharing me?"

"Good guess. We have been kissing cousins for a long time. She had the hots for you since I sent a picture of you from Kenya." She played with his pubic hair, and added, "One from our first trip to Lake Nakuru."

"Which one was that?"

"You were asleep. Sorry."

"What? I must have been…"

"Yes, very."

"How did you get the picture processed?"

"There is a automatic place in Nairobi." She said and they both laughed. "I'll show you the pictures sometime. I'm surprised Franny did not show you."

"She had a box of photos, but we never got through them all." He said as Franny moved snuggling close. He looked down at her little tit compared to Martha's huge pink tit resting on his white dress shirt. Martha began playing with the buttons on the shirt, undoing them one by one.

"Why is that? She always was jumping your bones?" Martha laughed. "You know she tells me everything."

"She does? And I was afraid you would be angry."

"Not if Franny does you."

"And if I do Franny?"

"Then I would get jealous. She said it was great that you would just lay there and let her do whatever she wanted. You are such a gentleman." She said and opened his shirt so that her tit would rest on his chest hair. She stroked his chest and Franny's breast, causing the nipple to tighten up.

"If a woman wants it, a man must give." He said and stroked each woman's bare shoulder with his hands. Franny began stroking his belly and Martha's breast.

Martha looked at him and said, "You need to get Franny pregnant so little Thomas will have a brother or sister."

Muturi was shocked, "Why not get you pregnant again?"

"You can. The more kids the better." She said, and Muturi wondered if she really believed that.

"Yes, good idea," Franny piped up, "I'll be your second wife. Can't you have four in Kenya?"

Chapter 26, Photographs

Wanjiru laughed when she looked at the picture and handed it to Mwangi. Mwangi, Janie, Mumera and the little ones were enjoying the photos that Muturi had sent. Wanjiru felt a warm glow going through her, knowing her son is not only in university but also married and soon to be father. Who is that skinny girl in so many of the pictures?

"Mumera read this and tell me what he is saying. His English is too big for me." She laughed. Mumera took the letter and began translating into Kikuyu.

"He says. University is easy and his teachers like him a lot. They are giving him good grades. It is all very interesting. Martha is doing very well. She is as strong as a water buffalo, but still goes to university also. She says her mother will take care of the baby so she can continue her studies. She will be done with classes in June and finish her masters by August. The skinny girl in some of the pictures is Martha's cousin. She is her Aunt Beth's daughter."

Wanjiru felt a shot go through her. Beth has a skinny girl? Kimani? She thought excited. "Wait, wait, Beth has a daughter. Very thin? Let me see those pictures again." She looked more closely at the skinny girl in the photos. "That could be Kimani's daughter!"

"Kimani?" Mwangi laughed. "That skinny little man with the *pikipiki*?"

"Yes, he came down to Mombasa with Beth and Lodi. That is why Mumera is here." She laughed very loudly, and Mwangi joined in. Mumera was looking quite perplexed.

"Do you want me to read?" Mumera said, and the two adults calmed down and motioned for him to continue. "Her name is Frances or Franny. Martha and I care for her very much. She wants to be my second wife and Martha likes the idea. Beth does not, and gets very angry. She says there are plenty of men, but said that she cannot stop Franny from doing stupid things, after all she did stupid things to make Franny!" Mumera stopped and looked at Mwangi, "Baba, did you ever want a second wife?"

"Second wife? Your mother is worth six wives. I am thankful that she finds me adequate. What else does he say?"

"Just one more. He says, the next time I write I will be a father and will send you pictures of your grandson and nephew."

"What? How does he know it is a boy?" Wanjiru asked.

"I think that is the funny picture." Mumera said. "Read the back."

Wanjiru turned over the black and white picture and read in English "So no gram, doctors have machine to look inside the womb at the baby. You can see it is a boy." She turned the picture over and stared at it. "It is a boy! That is wonderful. America is amazing place. They have machines to watch a baby grow inside the mother." She said and handed the picture to Mwangi. "There is your grandson!" Mwangi had a huge smile on his face and a tear in his eye. She looked at Mumera who appeared very upset. "Mumera, what is it?"

"I miss him so bad, I think I will die." He said.

"Study good and you can join him soon. Janie," Wanjiru said, "take Mumera to your room and make him feel better."

"Yes, Mama." Janie said, and the two disappeared.

Wanjiru looked at Mwangi who was smiling. "What?"

"You are still young enough to have many more children and now you will be a grandmother."

"I do not feel old." She said and noticed the youngest kids had disappeared. Little monkeys are probably watching Janie and Mumera. She picked up the photos and began going through them yet again. *Gai*! Beth and Kimani!

~~~~

Beth looked at Dan, who had just given instructions to his wife where to meet them in the mall later. "You should be with your wife shopping, not your cranky aunt."

"My cranky aunt likes to shop in the same places as I do, and my wife doesn't." he said looking ahead at the music store. "You always have great suggestions for CD's."

"Well, I..." she started to say when she heard someone call her name, turning to see her old friend from her Kenya days.

Dan was saying, "Hey, Mac, it's good to see you old man... who is this?"

Beth said, "That's Job, you remember him." She said and gave the tall man a hug. She looked at Mac's son – a handsome

272

mixture of Mac and Ann, she thought. She joked about his name, "Hey, *Lodi, Habari gani*?"

The blue-eyed fellow had put on a few pounds since she last saw him, but he said, "*Mzuri tu*. Where's Franny?" he asked giving his son a hug to catch his attention. "Job, go check out the video games." And the boy disappeared.

"She is still in Crawfordsville with Martha and Muturi."

"Oh, damn, how many times have I missed seeing them again?"

"How old is Job now, he looks ten." Dan asked.

"He's seven now – pretty big isn't he? Hey, Beth, did you send Kimani a letter."

"Yes, Mac, I wrote Kimani a letter. I told him the truth."

Dan was wondering, "Kimani is the guy you say is Franny's father?"

"I insisted she do it after meeting Kimani in Montreal. He is married and has two girls of his own, and another kid on the way. He ever write back?"

"He wrote before he would've received my letter and said he was heading off to Sudan to install telephone towers. But I am sure he got the letter."

"He called me from Sudan, testing the tower, but never mentioned anything like that. All he would talk about is his temporary marriage to a Sudanese girl."

"What?" Dan exclaimed.

"Yes, he marries a girl for the six months that he is there and divorces her just before he leaves. It is a Moslem thing he says. He thought it was a great idea to have a wife in the desert like that."

Beth rolled her eyes at the two men, "You think that is great don't you both?"

Mac got very serious. "My son Job doesn't know, but Ann said she hates me and wants a divorce."

"No!" Beth could not believe what her old friend was saying. "You have an affair or something?"

"No, I am just not the guy she married. Too fat and lazy."

"Well, you two fought like cats and dogs in Kenya, so I never understood why you married her."

"Yeah, yeah. Our daughter needed a father, then along came Job. So, how is Muturi doing?" Mac retorted with a question.

"He is doing great, at Purdue in Indianapolis. He married Martha, and she is due pretty soon with a boy... going to make you a bio-grandfather."

"Wow, just like my older brother. A father at eighteen!"

"Where is your daughter?" Beth asked.

"Alicia? She is with her mother shopping for clothes. She is developing fast and needs something she can fill in."

"I remember you said she is developing early." Beth recalled.

"Yes, I think she gets that from my side of the family, but her personality is so much like her mother's. I do worry since my grandmother and a female cousin both died young of aneurysms. She is very social, very bright." Beth thought, bitchy like her mother I bet! He looked sad, and his big blue eyes were moist when he added, "You think I should drive over and try and meet Muturi sometimes, or should I wait for him to come to me?"

"I would wait for him to try again. Oh, you know he tells people that it was you that paid his school fees and got him through high school."

"Good story," he said. "Wanjiru never asked for money from me. I sent her some, though. Wambui sure did, but I don't think she wanted to tell Muturi where most of her money came from."

Dan blurted out, "She was a hooker, right?"

Beth looked annoyed. "She just got good tips for what she would do naturally anyway."

"Yes, I recall Wambui told me that once. A guy she wanted to do her gave her five shillings and she was quite pleased. She got the man and the money!" He laughed. "They did not think it was prostitution if they were 'tipped' after sex."

Beth laughed, "Yes a hooker gets paid first." This caused Dan to belt out a laugh. She looked behind Dan and saw a her old friend and a younger girl approaching. Dan turned to see what she was looking at. "Dan, you met Mac's wife and daughter before?"

"No. Wow, Mac, your daughter is a looker." Dan said and Beth gave him a kidney punch.

"Dan, this is my wife Ann and my daughter Alicia." They both shook hands with Dan, and gave Beth her old friend a hug.

Ann looked Beth over, "Beth, you are staying in great shape. How is Franny doing?"

Alicia asked, "Is Franny around?"

"No, she is back in Crawfordsville. She's still skinny as a rail."

Ann asked, "I am really hungry, where's Job? You want to join us for lunch?" Beth realized that what she liked about Ann in Kenya was her bitchy-ness. Perhaps I changed, she thought.

Dan spoke, "I need to find my wife. We promised lunch with her."

Beth got the impression that Dan took an instand disliking for Ann, who was still a beautiful Chinese-American with a harsh temper. Beth could only guess that she must have been good in bed, otherwise she would not have two kids and several more miscarried pregnancies with Mac. A pain shot through her thinking how in love she was with him in Kenya. She literally threw herself at him – yet the memory of that morning in Lamu sent a tingle through her. Will he punish her forever for rejecting him twice? Beth thought about all the men she had dated since returning, but they did not compare, and Beth was determined not to settle for second best. Well I'm 42, Beth thought, maybe Ann will dump him, and I will finally look good to him. Dan, Ann and Alicia drifted away looking for her son, with Dan pointing the way.

"Beth, it was great to see you again. If it were not for my two wonderful kids, I'd confess to you that hooking up with Ann was probably one of my biggest mistakes."

"Never say that. We should not regret the past if it has brought us something we could not live without."

"I always thought of you as a sister, but I know you had a thing for me… everyone knew it. I am sorry I did not try harder with you."

"Give me a hug, Mac. Love me like a sister if you must, but please love me." Beth said, and a tear ran down his face, and gave her a hug. Dan was returning with a look of frustration.

"Let's see what the future brings." He said.

"Your old lady is waiting for you." Dan said, and he waved as he hurried away. "Aunt Beth, you still have a thing for him?"

"Damn right I do." She laughed. "He still has that smile."

Chapter 27, Baby

Muturi cringed as Martha belted out a scream. The doctor, whose name Muturi had already forgotten, checked Martha's birth canal and told the nurse. "Ten centimeters. Make sure the fetal monitor is ready."

"What is that?" Muturi asked.

The doctor smiled and said, "It attaches to your son's scalp so we can keep track of his heart. If he gets too distressed we can rush Martha in for a c-section." Muturi's stomach did a flip thinking of slicing his wife open to pull the baby out. Martha was relaxing and taking rapid breaths. Somehow, she looked beautiful. Franny came over with some ice and put it on Martha's lips. Martha sucked the ice in and smiled. Muturi felt a bit faint and looked around the "birthing room." The doctor had disappeared, but the chubby, little nurse was still hovering around with a very confident and professional mannerism. Franny was very happy, and Martha seemed to be on some other planet.

Martha's mother was sitting on the rocking chair reading a book as if nothing special was happening. She stood up with her book and came over to Martha. Everyone had to change into hospital scrubs in a pale green color. This included Martha's nonchalant mother.

"I'm going to get some lunch. If I am right, it will be a couple more hours. Hang in there love, if anyone can do it, it would be you." She gave her daughter a kiss on the cheek and disappeared.

"Muturi, Franny, come close." Martha said and scowled at the nurse who turned her back to look at the fetal monitor trace. Muturi and Franny leaned in to Martha as if to hear a secret. "Franny is ovulating today. Muturi, you need to give her some..." she began to say as a contraction started.

Franny laughed, "Martha, are you nuts? You're thinking of that now?"

"What is she talking about?" Muturi wondered.

Franny explained, "She wants you to knock me up today."

"Why today?"

Martha groaned, "Humor me. Use the toilet in the hallway." She whispered so loudly that Muturi thought the nurse heard. "Plant your seed in her." Muturi wondered if he could even do it with all this pressure, but Franny headed for the door staring at him. Martha slapped the back of his hand, "Go!" Muturi gave her a kiss on the lips and the nurse smiled at him. Martha added aloud for the nurse's benefit, "Get some lunch and come..." she groaned and grabbed her belly. He patted her belly and left the room.

Half an hour later, Muturi was happy that he could do the deed and keep his women happy. He opened the door to the birthing room slowly just as Martha let out a scream and began puffing air. Her knees were up as he and Franny came back in. He thought he could see the baby's head crowning as she gave a push, but then the head withdraw back in. He could see where the wire attached to the baby's head. "Okay, relax for a while and get your energy back. The baby's heart is doing great."

Martha's mother came back in, "They closed the cafeteria. I got there too late," she complained. She stopped by the bed, "You are looking good, Martha. Won't be long now. Nurse, call the doc."

"Thank you Mrs. Mills, I already did that, he should..." the nurse was saying as the doctor came back into the room, and began putting gloves on.

"Martha, we could speed it up with an episiotomy. It looks like a huge baby."

"Do it when you think, doc." She said just as another contraction was beginning. She took a deep breath and began pushing with all her might. She was squeezing Muturi's wrist, and he thought she would crush it. He looked down and saw the top of the baby's head with the wire clip attached, popping out. The skin of her vagina stretched tight as steel, and Muturi wondered if any baby could stretch or rip that skin. The doctor took what looked to Muturi like little scissors, and gingerly inserting a finger between the baby's head and Martha's skin. Snip! The baby's head popped out. Seeing Martha's skin cut like that made Muturi's stomach turn. Glad there is no food in there to lose!

"His shoulders are stuck." The doctor calmly stated, while inserting index fingers from both his hands past the baby's head and hooking the baby's armpits. The doctor gave a tug and the huge, blue baby went flying out onto the bed between Martha's ankles. "Oxygen!"

Muturi was stunned expecting the baby to cry right away. He is all blue! The nurse put a clear mask over the baby's face and pressed the baby's belly. Muturi watched the miracle of life as pink spread out from the baby's chest as if oxygen rich blood were spreading throughout his son's body.

Muturi could not contain himself, "Breathe, Thomas!" As if on command, the baby jerked, took a deep breath and began crying hysterically. The nurse clamped the umbilical cord and handed Muturi scissors. He proudly snipped the cord, after which the nurse took the screaming baby over to the scales. "Eleven pounds, one ounce. Nearly two babies!" Muturi heard Martha say something and he turned to see the afterbirth on the plastic sheets and the doctor was beginning to stitch her up. The nurse was now rubbing the brown, greasy stuff off Thomas's skin, and the baby was putting up a noisy fuss. Muturi wanted to help, so the nurse handed him the rag. Martha's mother was snapping pictures of him cleaning the greasy baby boy. The nurse was cleaning up the mess on the bed, wrapping up the afterbirth and cleaning up an unconscious Martha. Franny was holding Martha's hand with tears streaming down her face.

He noticed that the nurse was faster cleaning up the bed and Martha than he was with the baby. She came over to show him how to put on a disposable diaper. Thomas was bright red at this point and looking very angry. "Hey, *manii*, you angry because your mama kicked you out of the womb?" he asked in his best Kenyan accent, and the nurse began laughing, causing Thomas to begin crying again. The nurse put a little t-shirt on the baby and wrapped him in a flannel baby blanket and handed the boy to his father. Martha's mother snapped two more pictures.

"My, is he red or what? He is going to make such a wonderful Christmas present for the whole family." Muturi wondered at his mother-in-law: was she finally coming around and accepting him. "Son, give me my grandson, and take a couple of pictures with me by his mama." Muturi's heart nearly stopped being called "son." Up until now it strangely has been "Mr. Makomek," or "Mr. Muturi."

"We'll come back in a while to check on you all." The doctor said, as if one of them besides Martha would need medical attention.

"Get Franny in the picture, too." She said, but Martha was still asleep, and Franny holding her hand. He snapped two different pictures. "Franny, switch places." By the time Muturi got into place for the picture, Martha woke up and wanted to hold the baby. Franny snapped a few pictures.

"Let's see if he is hungry." Martha said and pulled down her gown and presented a nipple to Thomas's mouth.

"Martha, it takes a while, don't be too anxious."

"Muturi, you're looking very pale," Martha said, "please sit down before you fall down." Muturi wondered how a woman who had just given birth could be so aware. He sat down on the rocker and watched the three women around the baby. He was utterly exhausted, and thought it amazing that Martha was thinking of feeding the baby rather than taking a nap… well, I guess she did, he thought, but not very long. He set his head back on the pillow and was out.

When he woke up, his wife was on a wheel chair holding the baby, and Franny was shaking him. The nurse chuckled, "We are taking your wife to her room and the baby to the nursery. You can come back tomorrow morning after eight. They will need lots of rest." The nurse started to roll her away.

"Wait, wait." Martha said, "I need to tell my husband something." The nurse backed off a bit, and Martha motioned for him to come in close. She gave him a warm, wet kiss and whispered. "Fill Franny up. I want her holding her own baby in nine months. Understand? I love you more than I can ever say." She gave him another kiss with a bit of tongue included. The nurse wheeled her out.

Franny asked, "What did she say?"

"If you are not holding your own baby in nine months, I am in serious trouble."

Chapter 28, Kimani Visits

Wambui looked up from a letter to see her twenty year old daughter Ruthy. And I thought I was ugly, she laughed to herself. Not only ugly, but she has a certificate from a business college and cannot find a job. Her daughter was all bones, with a flat face and most of her hair shaved off. She has to stay here, she thought, because Ruthy has no place to go. Men do not want her. She is too ugly and looks very weak. She cannot even carry a bag of charcoal. It amazes her that Ruthy still has her monthly since she is so thin.

"*Ni ke?*" Ruthy asked, suddenly aware that her mother was staring at her. A toddler came up to Ruthy wanting to sit on her lap. Wambui looked at the other children playing in the courtyard. If it were not for her father living into old age, she herself would not have a place to live. Her only job is to watch the children of other women while they work. Wambui's two older children are off in Nairobi. Her other daughter has kids and her stepson has a good job. He sends her money. Lodi has not sent money since Ruthy got her certificate. He says it is time to throw the bird out of the nest and see if it can fly.

Wambui could never do that. The best she could do is to leave the door unlocked for Ruthy to join her stepbrother in Nairobi and look for a job there. She went back to the letter. It was from Lodi, written in Swahili, which over the years has gotten more and more difficult to read. He would write to Ruthy in English giving her advice, but it was useless. The sun getting low in the sky made reading even more difficult. Time to get in.

"*Natya!*" Came a male voice from the gate, and looking up she saw her old friend Kimani. He had gained quite a bit of weight, compared to the skinny young man she remembered.

"Kimani, what are you doing here?"

"My crew is in Nakuru for a few days. We are driving up to Juba in the Sudan to install telephone towers." He shook her hand. "This is Ruthy?" Kimani shook her hand. "What a beautiful young woman." Wambui thought he was trying to be nice to her ugly daughter, or he has not had a woman for a while and is in need.

"Yes, yes. She got a business certificate and is looking for work. She does not want to leave Njoro."

"Stay in Njoro?" Kimani acted stunned. "Maybe Nakuru or Nairobi, but not in Njoro. Our old friend Wanjiru and her family even moved their business to Nakuru. Did you talk with them?"

Ruthy spoke up, "That is a good idea. I will drop down and talk with them. I can keep books, and come back to take care of mama on Sundays."

Wambui was annoyed that Ruthy would claim she needed to be taken care of. "Monkey! You get a job and worry about me later. Or you will spend your life working in the *shamba*." Kimani sat on a bench next to Ruthy as if he were truly interested in her. On the other hand, Wambui thought, it is too dark to see how ugly she is. Maybe I could get him to sleep with her, and get her interested in men instead of boys. "Kimani, you know Muthoni got married. After she had yours, she met someone."

"She did? Very good. It was been years."

"Lodi writes that you told him that your wife has another on the way."

"Yes, I am hoping it will be a boy this time. My wife is not happy with me. I think this will be the last she does for me."

"Why? You are making good money now."

"Yes, but she is lonely." Kimani frowned. "I am gone all the time. She wants more than me coming long enough to give her a pregnancy and leaving."

"Can you stay here for a while?" Wambui wondered, thinking it would be nice to have a man around.

"Yes, I was going to ask if I could stay. If you have an extra bed now."

"Yes, I have a cot. I will sleep on it and you sleep with Ruthy."

"Mama!" Ruthy was obviously abashed, but Wambui did not care for her holy holy attitude. "I should decide that." Ruthy added. See, Wambui thought, not holy holy.

"If you don't want him, you sleep on the cot and he can do me." She laughed, "Kimani, how old are you now?"

"Thirty-eight."

281

"You can do a twenty-year-old or a forty-eight-year-old. Or do both, if you have the energy." She and Kimani laughed, but Ruthy was quiet, looking Kimani over. Wambui looked at Kimani and saw that he was getting aroused at the conversation. "You should take Ruthy to Sudan with you so that you have someone to do everyday if you want."

"We have to get special permits and visas. As much as I would like that." Kimani said and Wambui was very surprised.

"Ruthy, if you want Kimani, go get ready in bed."

"Mama! Let Kimani ask me."

"If you want him, you ask him. Look, he wants you." Wambui pointed to the bulge in Kimani's jeans.

"I remember you from when I was little. I want you," Ruthy simply said, "I will go get ready." Kimani merely nodded a yes, and Ruthy went into the apartment.

"She is not a virgin. She lets the boys practice on her. They are too young to have sperms. How many days do you have here?"

"Two nights, then we drive out in five trucks. It will be six months before we come back."

"Do her, and when you come back do her again, if you like. Make her a woman. Maybe she will finally grow up." Wambui stood up and escorted him in.

Wambui awoke to sunlight coming through the window and the sounds from the other side of the curtain were of Kimani doing Ruthy. She still sparkled from Kimani's attentions, and was glad that Kimani had some left after Ruthy. She put on some clothes to go outside to use the *choo* and wash up. When she came back, there was silence on the other side of the curtain. Wambui started making tea and Ruthy came out from behind the curtain. "Put on some clothes, monkey!" But Ruthy came and sat on the stool to watch her make the tea. "You should go wash up." She stared into her daughter's eyes. "Monkey, what is wrong?"

"Nothing. He taught me how to use my mouth to pleasure him. That was very strange for me. He said I was good at it. Am I bad to say I enjoy doing that?"

"No. But I could never do it. My *wazungu* asked me many times but no."

"Kimani is such a vigorous old man.

"He is not old. He is at his best."

"Fat."

"It feels good on the belly."

"How do you know?"

"He did me after you complained."

"Oh, yes, I recall. You were very quiet."

"He did me until I passed out. I forgot how nice it feels. I thought I died and went to heaven." Wambui laughed.

"Yes, he is so much better than those little boys." Ruthy laughed also.

~~~~

Mumera looked up from his studying at the kitchen table to see his mama in the shop chatting with a very skinny girl, as if they knew each other. She wore a dress with frills on the shoulder. When she turned she had wide hips and nice breasts, he thought. No hair to speak of and a skeleton-like face. Mumera laughed to himself, I'd have to turn out the lights. His mama brought the girl into the kitchen. "Mumera, you remember Ruthy Muigai? Wambui's daughter?" And he suddenly remembered her back in Njoro, but she was plumper and had some hair. He recalled doing her in the grass out behind the basketball court – or was that someone else? She has a huge mouth. I wonder if she…

"Hi, Mumera," Ruthy said. "I remember you very well. I always thought you and your brother were so cute. Remind me of Lodi." Right! It was her! I did her a few times, he recalled. His mama took the business books and papers off a shelf and sat them on the table.

"Could you look these over and tell me and Mwangi if you can help us with the business taxes?" Wanjiru said, and Ruthy began looking through the papers.

"Yes, I see you have the forms. I will see if I can help." She sat down across from Mumera who was entranced by her mouth and the way her tongue popped out when she pronounced an "s"

"Mumera, finish your work and let her check the books." His mama said, which meant not to start chatting her up. To add to the point, she said, "Remember Janie." Ruthy looked down, and began sorting through the papers. "Mumera, I have to go to the market. Mwangi is working, and the little ones are in the courtyard." She disappeared, and he looked at the ugly girl across from him, who began sucking on the end of a pencil.

He looked at his book and tried to concentrate, but blurted out, "You have very nice lips." Immediatedly felt embarrassed, but under the table came the sounds of her kicking off her shoes. He felt her bare foot on his... instant arousal. "I guess you are pretty and smart." He lied, well half lied, to see what else she intended.

She was sorting out the papers while stroking his foot with hers, then her foot began exploring his bare leg. He was glad now that he decided to wear khaki shorts instead of jeans after classes. He looked up at her and noticed that she had unbuttoned the top of her dress to show off the tops of her brown breasts. She scooted down in her chair, and he felt her bare foot exploring his inner thigh, then she slid a toe up inside the leg of the shorts into his boxers. Contact! He was staring her in the eyes as her toe caressed the tip of his manhood, her mouth opened and her tongue came out licking her lips. He closed his eyes to enjoy the sensation, when it suddenly stopped and he heard some motion. He opened his eyes to see she had disappeared only to feel her under the table pulling his stiff shaft out of the leg of his shorts. It fired off an early round, and he wondered where it went. Then he felt her grasping at him and taking him into her mouth, sucking gently. "Oh, that is wonderful!" he said aloud. He felt the tingle of electricity surging from the focal point and quickly he fired. She continued sucking and licking until he became hypersensitive and pushed her away. She suddenly appeared back at her chair.

"You taste very good." She said in Kikuyu. He saw Mwangi coming out of the shop area, so he pulled his clothes back together and pretended to study.

"Ruthy," Mwangi asked, "can you help us?"

"Yes, it will take about a month but I can do it for you. They trained me to do this. I will need to use your adding machine."

"Yes. How much do you want to do the taxes for us?" Mwangi asked, and Mumera saw him staring down at her, and assumed he was looking at her breasts, but then he saw it on her shoulder.

"The standard is one percent of your gross, but that is if I have my own office. If I could do the work here, half that would work for me."

Mwangi smiled as if he was getting a deal. "I think I could manage that." Mwangi held up his greasy hands. "I would shake on it but my hands." Mwangi paused, and Mumera was wondering if he saw it. Mwangi got a paper napkin off the counter and handed it to her and pointed to something on the shoulder of her dress. Mwangi walked away back to his shop. Ruthy stood up and wiped her dress.

Ruthy laughed at Mumera, "I thought I got all your *manii*." She stacked the papers and books together. "You didn't have any when you did me in Njoro, remember?"

"Yes, but I can make much more for you."

"Oh, good. See you tomorrow?" she asked and he nodded a yes before she disappeared out onto the street.

Chapter 29, Sudan

Kimani liked to work in the equipment building instead of out on the tower, since it was air-conditioned and the desert air was oppressive. He was still shaking from an accident that day. One of the crew fell off the tower, but was saved by a safety line a few yards from the ground. Such is the grace of God, he thought. He looked at his watch and backed out nine hours. It is a Saturday morning in Illinois - maybe I can reach him. He took out his wallet and got a card of telephone numbers, and punched it into the computer. He will call this testing the equipment. He could hear it ringing and a familiar voice came on the line, "Hello?" came the voice through the computer speaker.

"Hey! I'm calling from the Sudan!" he said, speaking into the computer mic.

"Kimani, *rafiki yangu*! How are you doin', old man?"

"I am fine. We are putting up a microwave tower in the desert. One of the crew fell off today. I thought he was dead, but the safety line saved him."

"Wow, you must be really shaken up. Do you climb those things?"

"I get dizzy, but I stay down and monitor the electronics. How is everything there?"

"*Hivi hivi*. I recently saw Beth." He said and Kimani felt a stabbing in his guts. "She said that Frances is in college, and hanging out with Muturi."

"She likes Muturi, I bet. It would be like you and me - friends for life."

"Muturi married Martha and had a kid already. I think he was doing her after chemistry class or something." He said and Kimani laughed aloud.

"If he is anything like you probably did her several times a day." Kimani chuckled.

"Me. You make me sound like a jack rabbit."

"You said that remember. If it moves, do it!"

"Well, I think my phrase was a bit cruder than do it. I'm trying to be more upstanding since I have kids to raise."

"Upstanding?"

"Holy holy as Wambui used to say."

"Oh, I saw her and her daughter Ruthy before we headed up to the Sudaan."

"Ruthy? She sent me a picture when she got her business college certificate. Ugly as sin. She used to be such a cute little girl. She was 20 a couple of weeks ago."

"As you used to say, turn out the lights and they all look alike."

"Saying that, you must have done her." He cackled.

"I was there a couple of nights, and Wambui insisted."

"That must mean you did Wambui, too."

"*Gai*! What are you a mind reader?"

"No, I know you and Wambui. Wambui dried out yet?"

"No, I chatted her up first. Her daughter is great."

"Ruthy?"

"Yes, I taught her to use her big mouth for more than eating and talking."

"Hmmm." Came the voice from nearly nine thousand miles away. "If anyone could teach that, it would be you."

"I was a teacher," he laughed, "and you never know when such skills will become valuable. She might need it for job interviews." They both laughed.

"Kimani you forget, I read your book on the girls' school you taught at."

"That was so corrupt! Just as well I couldn't get it published. All those primary girls were over the age of consent, and most of the teachers had no license." Kimani thought back on the place where some teachers acted as if their classroom was their personal harem. It gave him the shivers and then thought about his own daughters now heading soon to primary school.

And as if reading his mind as usual, "Think of your own daughters now. What would you do if they had teachers like that?"

"Such teachers would be eating their own testicles for sure." Then he thought about the daughter so long unknown to him. "How come you never told me about Frances before?"

"I did. I said that Beth told me she adopted a girl. I recalled your affair with Beth, I asked questions and did the math."

"With that math, Frances could be yours, too. Beth did you in Lamu, remember."

"God! And I think she got at least four hundred million of those little swimmers. Frances is skinny like you though."

"What kind of kid is she?"

"Beth says she is people smart, but not good with math and science. She has to work hard for her grades. She is short and slim, except nice hips and smallish breasts."

"You would notice that wouldn't you?" he laughed. "Have you met Muturi yet?"

"No. He came over when I was visiting you in Montreal. He is pretty busy now with college, a new wife and a kid."

"Who is paying his college."

"Beth said he was accepted several places but went for the one with scholarships. I think a foundation for African students."

Kimani looked at the time on the computer screen and worried about it costs. "I stopped to see Wanjiru when I went through Nakuru." Kimani added and heard a bit of a gasp at the other end. "She is still quite beautiful for a *nusu nusu*, and her husband is really great. They have a good business repairing engines. I saw your other love child, Mumera." Kimani heard a moan come out of the computer.

"It's breaking my heart. You denied it for so many years."

"Sorry about that, but I thought I was saving you some pain. Mumera is looking good, though. Looks like a light brown version of you when I first met you." Kimani said. "Has a cute girlfriend who is a couple years older than him. She has a job in some clothing shop while he is still in high school. I get the impression she was Muturi's girlfriend before he left."

"She cute?"

"Beautiful. I'd leave the lights on." He laughed. "I think it is a matter of time before she makes you a grandfather again."

He heard laughter coming from the computer speaker. "Yes, a bio grandfather, since I was excluded from their lives."

"Wanjiru told me long ago you offered money but she refused."

"Beth says that Muturi brags that I sent school fees from America. But Wanjiru told him that to hide from her boys how she got most of her money."

"Oh, right, tips from boyfriends in Mombasa?"

"Yes, I think I told you that before. The last time I saw her I only gave her a few shillings."

288

"That was back when a shilling was good money though." Kimani laughed. "I never helped Beth though."

"She made a bundle from her book. She did fine."

"Hey, man, in Montreal I detected some tension between you and your wife. Is it going okay."

"No, I have changed too much for her, or so Ann says. We got married for my daughter and the sex. I'd give the marriage a couple more years. I imagine she is out looking for someone else at this point."

"Well, that opens new doors." Kimani suggested.

"Yeah, she might be out opening her doors to other guys is all. Have to wonder what diseases she will be bringing home. Can't be too safe these days."

"You mean with AIDS?" Kimani asked, knowing he had not been too safe lately. Then he started worrying about his stay in Njoro and whether they were clean or not. Then the Sudanese girl that he "married" here did not seem to be a virgin. He thought, I better use protection and get tested.

"Yes. That was a cold shower for the sexual revolution."

"So, you don't trust your wife, what are you doing for sex?" Kimani asked as if doing without sex was doing without food and water.

"My hand is my lover until my wife finally dumps me. Then I will start looking."

"You ever think about Beth?"

"Yes, I think about her as a sister." Came the voice over the computer, just as a co-worker entered the building.

"I have to go now. It was great talking with you."

"Yes, love you, brother!"

Kimani said, "Bye." He disconnected. He looked at his co-worker, the one who survived the fall. "Did the doctor say you are okay?"

"Just a stretched tendon on my knee. Your wife came back from town with a lot of food."

"You need to get yourself a wife." Kimani said, knowing his friend would want to share his food, and maybe his wife. He shut down the computer - left the equipment shed and went over to his small trailer. It was big enough inside for a bed and small camper kitchen. It had air conditioning, which was good during the day. He went inside and Bishira was making sandwiches for supper. He was thinking, more canned fish, but saw that she had sliced beef. She was all in black, looking more like a Catholic nun than a Moslem wife. She was good for six months, but he could not see longer with this girl. He paid her "father" the going bride price with no guarantees. When he has to go back to Nairobi, he will return her to her family having "divorced" her. All the better for the family that she will have no babies.

Kimani and Bishira ate the sandwiches in silence. "Do you like living with me?" He asked in Swahili.

Bishira smiled, "It is an easy life. Nice house, good food. Very comfortable bed. You do not beat me. My father enjoys beating me. Yes, I like it with you."

"You are very obedient." He said sipping milk from a carton.

"Yes, thank you. I like living with you. I know you will go away, but perhaps when you come back I can live here again."

"That is possible. You need to learn how to use your mouth better. Too much teeth. Your *mkundu* is very tight. I like to start with mouth, then *kuma*, then finish with *mkundu*." He patted her on the shoulder. "Only your *kuma* is good. This morning when I was using your *mkundu*, you complained about the pain, and I could not finish. Next time you will tell me feels good or be quiet."

"Yes, Kimani." She said nervously. She finished her food and sat waiting.

Kimani said in Swahili, "Stand up and remove all your clothes. Obediently she did as she was told, while he slowly ate his food and watched. She was an Arab, with much lighter skin than his wife's was. She stood naked before him. She had long black hair, small breasts, wide hips and jet black pubic hair. "Turn around and bend over." He ordered and she did as she was told. For some reason he liked this view. He could see her anus, vagina and mouth all on a line. Three opportunities for pleasure. He finished his sandwich and carton of milk. "Lay on the bed and prepare yourself for sex." He began removing his boots and clothes as she lay down on the bed, raised, and spread her legs and began masturbating. Kimani wanted her to arouse herself to prepare for his pleasure. The air conditioner turned itself off, and the only sound was Bishira's lust grunts. He stood naked watching her and was very aroused as he rolled a condom on. He crawled onto the bed and mounted her to begin his evening of entertainment.

~~~~~

Wanjiru walked into her kitchen carrying a bag of food and set it on the table. Mumera's books were on one side and the business books and tax forms were on another. *Gai*! Can these girls leave Mumera alone to study? She went towards his bedroom and heard the rhythm of his bed squeaking. She looked through the crack in the door and he was on top doing Ruthy. His pants were down to his thighs and Ruthy had her dress up and knickers down to her ankles. She thought, he did Janie in the morning, and Ruthy after school. She went back to the kitchen to begin supper, and after a few minutes, the two came back to their books and papers as if nothing had happened. Mumera patted his mother on the back but said nothing.

"How is school work?"

"I am getting one hundred percent on on my tests. Just fine."

"Is school too easy for you? Do you need a tougher school?"

"This school got Muturi in college. It will me, too."

"Ruthy, how are the taxes going? You worked all day. Did Mwangi do the receipts and expenses properly?"

"He did fine. The tax forms are very complicated. My head fills up and I need to relax a bit." Ruthy said as if to apologize for seducing her son... still underage son at that. She had to wonder if her son was even making sperm yet, or even enough to make these girls pregnant.

"Potatoes or ugali, Mumera. I will let you decide."

"Ugali."

"Ruthy, can you stay for supper?" Wanjiru asked as Ruthy was putting away the papers, knowing that Ruthy would not want to confront Janie.

"No, I need to catch the bus back." She said, and Wanjiru worked on supper as Ruthy got her things together and left.

"How is Ruthy? Better than Janie?" Wanjiru boldly asked her son.

"About the same. Ruthy skinny, but is good with the mouth. Janie has little talent there." He said, and she was shocked that he would trump her boldness with more boldness. He was writing out math problems as he spoke, so she decided that he was being honest because he was not aware to whom he was talking.

"You can still do Janie *and* Ruthy?"

"I could do more." He said, "Wasn't Hans and me made on the same day?" For Wanjiru, this brought back the memory of the day Mumera was conceived.

"How do you know that?"

"Hans told me. My *mzungu* father also had plenty to share." Mumera said as a matter of fact. He continued writing out his math problems. This made Wanjiru think of her "Lodi" and it was getting her very aroused. She turned off the stove and went looking for Mwangi. "Where are you going?" he asked, as she walked off towards the shop. "Oh. Mwangi is working on an old Peugeot. It has big back seats." He said and she laughed. She thought to herself, the kids have caught her and Mwangi many times doing it in the backseat of the cars he was supposed to be repairing.

She checked on the little ones playing in the courtyard, went and locked the front door, turned the sign around to "closed" and found Mwangi playing with the wiring of the radio.

"*Ni ke*?" he asked.

"Come here." She said and opened the back door of the car and lay on her back on the cold leather seats. He pretty much knew what she wanted, and never failed to give it. "She closed her eyes and imagined her Lodi inside her.

~~~~

"I did fine on my math test." Muturi said into the phone.

"Just fine?" Martha asked, her voice over the phone was just a bit accusatory.

"Ninety-five."

"Okay. I was worried that Franny was taking up all your time." She said. He heard the baby crying in the background.

"Thomas okay?"

"Yes, I just fed him and mom is changing his diapers."

"Classes going okay?"

"Pretty simple stuff."

"Yeah, sure." He looked across the room to the door to see Franny coming in. "Franny's here. She looks like she is going to attack me.

"She needs her rest." She said and he thought back a few months ago when Thomas was ready to pop out, Martha was insisting that it was time to do Franny. The things he does for his women. "Oh, Beth told me something interesting."

"What's that?"

"Your bio-dad is teaching for a couple of months at the Kenya Science Teachers College."

"Really. I thought the only white guys there were the Swedes."

"Beth said they asked him for some reason. Anyway, you might want to tell your Mama that he might show up unannounced."

"Would he do that? Mumera would drop out. Mama would take him to bed." He laughed.

"Muturi, she would never do that."

"You don't know? We talk about her *mzungu* and she has to go sex Mwangi."

"Hmmm is that what happens when I talk dirty with you on the phone?"

He thought a bit, "Well, Franny seems to be around when you start that. You get me hot and she takes advantage. I think you two plan it that way."

"Oh, Thomas gave me an orgasm again when he was nursing. Some sort of resonance, I think."

"Is that incest?"

"Of course not. It is a baby's way of rewarding his mama. You probably did the same thing." He watched Franny take off her coat. She was wearing sweatpants and a t-shirt. She pulled down the sweatpants, turning sideways to show what she off the bulge. He thought she will be waddling soon. Martha continued, "Is she okay?"

Franny came close to him and bent over into the phone, "Hey Martha!" He pulled down her sweatpants and lifted up the t-shirt.

"She is getting chubby, and there is quite a bulge. He lifted up the t-shirt trying to get her to take it off, which she did. Then he pulled down the sweatpants, taking her panties with them. She stepped out of them. He reached for the snap on the front of her bra and opened it. She was there in her glory. "The extra weight looks good on her."

293

"You got her clothes off yet? Taking you a long time."
Martha laughed.

"She's working on me now." He said as she tugged his
jeans and briefs off him. It was very arousing. "She's getting on me
now."

"You on the bed?"

"No the desk chair."

"Hi, Martha, he's inside me now. Feels really good."

"I get the picture. Muturi you still there?"

"Mmmmm."

~~~~

Wambui sat in the courtyard drinking her thick tea when
she heard children shouting, "*Mzungu, Mzungu*!" They came
running in the gate. She had been expecting a visitor since her Lodi
wrote that he was teaching for two months in Nairobi. He wrote
that he wanted to take a *matatu*, bus and walk to Njoro. Since he
wrote, she was extremely excited, and could barely sleep for
thoughts of the past.

"Wambui!" She heard the familiar voice, and the huge man
gave three little kids some pieces of candy. He had a backpack and
several shopping bags.

"Lodi!" She stood up and the chubby man gave her a hug.
She stepped back and her Lodi now had a reddish brown beard that
reminded her of his pubic hair, which made her giggle.

He said is Swahili, "You look the same. Are you still
sick?" he asked. She laughed since every letter she wrote she
would complain about being sick. The only time she would write
was when she was sick.

She replied in simple Swahili, "I am not sick now. You are
fatter than before. You have no grey hair yet."

"I pull the grey hair out. Soon I will have no beard."

"Why did you grow a beard?"

"To tickle my wife's thing." He said, and Wambui laughed
loudly. He always wanted to lick her down there but she always
refused.

"I am still your wife." Wambui stated flatly, in Swahili,
"Miss Ann is wife number two in America. But I am still wife
number one." She laughed. "That thing," she pointed at his groin,
"that thing is still mine."

He laughed. "You have more tea?" he spoke in his Americanized Swahili that she had so missed, but could only read the last number of years. She waved for him to follow her into her place. "Where is Ruthy?" he set the backpack, bags on the floor, and took off his coat. The sun was coming in the window, making the room quite bright and warm.

"She is working for Wanjiru's husband."

"Your sister Wanjiru?"

"No, Wanjiru Tatton… she married Mwangi remember?"

"Yes, our friend Kimani has told me by telephone. I think he is still in the Sudan. I hope he gets back before I leave."

"You talk with Kimani?"

"Yes, he told me he had a good visit before he went to the Sudan." Wambui felt a bit of guilt, since she knew men liked to brag about having sex. "He especially liked Ruthy."

"She is ugly but has a good *kuma*."

"How did Kimani treat you?"

"I forget." She lied laughing.

"Gave it all to Ruthy?"

"No, *Durexi*." She lied again and poured some of the thick strong tea into a cup and handed it to him, and watched him sip it. "Ruthy should be back in an hour or so. What is in the bags?"

"I brought some food, tea, milk and coffee. And here in this bag are bottles of Tusker." He said. She thought he knows how to put a smile on her face. She took a bottle of beer opened it and took a long drink.

"I want that thing. Would Ann care?"

"I do not do her anymore. She hates me. We live together to raise the children. We do not sleep together."

"You have a girlfriend? Or are you a holy holy priest?"

"Priests get more sex than I do."

"If you want…" Wambui started to say but Ruthy came in. "Ruthy, you are early." She said, and he stood up and shook hands with her. Wambui was annoyed that she talked instead of getting his clothes off.

"Lodi!" Ruthy said. "That smile. You do look just like Mumera." She spoke in English with Wambui barely understanding.

"Mumera?"

295

"Wanjiru's second son." She added. "I get to thank you in person."

"For what?"

"I went all the way through school and business college because you sent mama money."

"You're welcome. I still remember you as a kid. You used to sing for me, soldier in the army. You were so cute." Wambui opened a bottle of beer, and handed it to Ruthy, who sat down on the cot next to him. "Didn't you just turn 20 last December?" He asked as if she were not old enough to drink. She drank half a bottle like a professional.

Wambui said, "She has been drinking since she was eighteen. A police officer bought her her first one at the Njoro Bar."

Ruthy laughed, "That is how my sister came to be..."

He laughed and said in Swahili, "Your mama told me that story many times."

"*Ni ke*?" Wambui asked wondering which story, but Ruthy ignored her.

"Our friend Kimani visited here."

"Yes, he told me you were good to him." He said in Swahili.

Wambui thought she was getting too familiar with the older man, but she was talking in English and Wambui was not following Ruthy very well. "Do you want to stay the night?" Wambui asked, hoping he would. She worried that Ruthy would seduce him first.

"Yes, that would be good. Ruthy, are you working at Mwangi's tomorrow?" he asked and she realized that he might want her daughter.

"Yes, until the afternoon."

"I want to see the school in the morning, but I will travel to Nakuru in the afternoon to see Wanjiru and Mumera."

Wambui offered, "You can stay another night here."

"Thank you that would be nice." He said, and Wambui noticed that Ruthy kept stroking his leg.

~~~~

Mumera shifted his book bag to one side as he was nearing the shop, and saw a sign in the window. "Out on a call, Will be back" and in Swahili it said tomorrow morning. He was surprised that Mwangi was ever gone that long for a breakdown. He went in and saw Ruthy at the kitchen table. The shop was empty and the little ones were not around.

"Ruthy, where is everyone, mama and baba? The little ones?"

"I am here. Mwangi took his children up to Njoro for the afternoon. I think he wanted to leave your mama alone."

"Why?"

"Lodi is visiting."

"My father? Where did they go?"

"In the bedroom."

"What?" Mumera exclaimed. He stood next to her and set his book bag on the table.

"Shush!" she said. He looked down at her and she was looking at the zipper on his slacks. "The bed stopped squeaking twenty minutes ago. They are probably sleeping. She reached over and pulled the zipper down, and he simply moved in closer. She reached in past the boxer shorts and fished it out, as it was stiffening up. "Yes, it looks just like Lodi's."

"What? You saw his already?" he felt strange that "his" girl had seen his father's. She took it into her mouth, licking and sucking. It felt so good he almost missed her next comparison.

"Tastes the same." She said and sucked it back into her mouth. She did her trick with her tongue and he ejaculated with his legs nearly buckling. She opened her mouth to show the *manii* on her tongue, and then said, "Yes, same taste, different from Kikuyu." She said as if knowing the difference in brands of beer.

"You did my father, too?" he said putting himself back into his pants and zipping up.

"I had too. He put me through school. How else can I say thank you? He is not my blood. Anyway it felt very good." Ruthy explained. Mumera was in a quandary, since his biological father was in his baba's bedroom with his mama.

"Does Mwangi know what is happening?"

"Yes, it was his idea." She said. "Something about two wonderful sons and Lodi helping him start his business."

"Oh, that." Mumera said, "Mwangi always talks about that as if no one ever heard the story."

"Mwangi also said something about giving your mama another son like you would be good."

"What is he..." he started to ask, but heard the bed squeaking in his baba's room. He started to walk in that direction.

"Don't go in there. Leave them alone." He continued on. He decided he would use the keyhole as his brother taught him when he was little. As he got closer he heard his mama moaning as he had often heard her with Mwangi. There was a man's moaning as well. The door was closed but the large keyhole was like a little window. The sun was lighting the room, and he saw the large white man doing his mama from behind. Instead of getting alarmed or hurt, he was getting very aroused seeing the man's thing going in and out rapidly, and his mama's head turning back and letting out lust yelps. His mama lost her strength and went down on the bed with him next to her. He rolled over and his stiff thing was silhouetted against the lighted curtain. Ruthy shoved him on his back trying to get him to stop snooping.

She hissed, "Get away from there."

"Okay." He whispered, but he wanted to try what he had just seen. He pushed her into his bedroom, and whispered in her ear. "Get on your hands and knees." She gave him a weird look, and looked as if she decided this might be fun, and they both got down on the rug between the beds. He lifted her dress and pulled down her knickers to her knees. Her pundenda made a perfect, glistening target. He pushed the dress over her head and admired her beautiful brown skin. He opened his trousers and pulled out his stiffness, and slid it easily inside her. They both gasped in delight. Being deliciously inside her, he stroked her back, and stomach, under her bra to her ample breasts, then down to her "button." She let out a joyous moan. He heard something behind him, looked up, and saw the white man smiling at him, and then his mama pulling the door closed.

~~~~

Wanjiru was both embarrassed and proud at the same time that her Lodi saw her son copulating with Ruthy. Didn't they know that they should close the door? She stood next to her Lodi in the hallway. He pressed her close in a big hug. "We should get dressed, so we can talk when they are done. Is that Ruthy with him?" Wanjiru knew what he was talking about since he said that he slept at Wambui's the night before. Knowing Wambui and Ruthy, they both would need a man if they shared the same room. There were little lusty screams coming out of Mumera's room, and

Lodi chuckled. "Wanjiru, you are still the best!" he said as they went back into Mwangi's room to get their clothes. "I wish things could have been different, and I could have stayed in Kenya and been your husband."

"If so, Wambui would want to be wife number one, and I only wife two." She laughed at the idea.

"Wife number one is the one with my children surpassing others. You have two of mine. Ann has two."

"She had four." She said remembering well his letter about their twins dying the day they were born.

He mumbled in English, "I think she aborted them without telling me. She did not want twins. Too much work." He buttoned up his shirt and complained, "Things could have been so different."

"Life is life." She said pulling up her knickers last and following him into the kitchen.

"I brought some gin to make us a drink if you like." He said and opened his backpack and pulled out a small bottle of gin and a bottle of tonic water. "I even found a lime. Is there some ice in that fridge of yours?" he said looking at the half size refrigerator in the corner. She bent down and pulled out a tray of ice her family never used, and found a couple of glasses and a knife. She could easily drink the gin straight, since some of the tourist in her Mombasa days gave her shots to loosen her up, but her Lodi liked his special mixing way of making a drink. Soon he handed her a chilly glass sparkling with dew, smelling of lime and gin, tasting of the bitter tang of quinine. He sat down at Mumera's book bag and pulled out a math book and some loose papers. She sat down and just watched her Lodi. "You should be very proud of your boy, this is tough math and his test here is very good."

"Thank you!" Spoke a voice from behind. Wanjiru looked up and Mumera was standing there. "You Lodi Makomeki? I have always wanted to meet you."

"Well, actually Rrrod Mak Korrr mek," he pronounced each syllable in American, pronouncing the harsh r-sounds like an Irish priest, standing up and shaking hands. "It is great to see you face to face rather than just photographs." The two were standing nearly eye to eye, since her sixteen year old son was just a bit taller than his father. "It is like looking into a mirror and seeing myself at sixteen with curly hair!" he said and Mumera could not be stopped.

He gave the older man a big hug, and it was returned. Wanjiru felt tears come to her eyes.

Wanjiru heard her son say, "I'm a bit browner, I'm sure."

"After a summer in the sun back in Illinois, I used to be your color." He laughed, and the two separated to look at one another. "Of course my ass is always white as paper, and from what I saw, yours too." They both laughed. Wanjiru sipped her drink and noticed that Ruthy had come in from the toilet.

Ruthy said, "Mumera needs to learn to close the door." She sat next to the business books. Wanjiru enjoyed seeing the two sit down next to each other as if they had always been friends.

Mumera asked, "How long do you have in Kenya?"

"Six more weeks, but I teach only four days a week."

"We can see more of you then."

"I think Mwangi's generosity has its limits. He may not like this big, white guy hanging around on weekends with his wife and kids. Maybe you all could drop down to Jamhuri and pay me a visit. They gave me a nice guesthouse there.

"Could I bring a friend with me?"

"Sure, that would be fine. I gave the address to your mama." He added, and Wanjiru knew he was hoping that she would come down, too, but she did not want to leave Mwangi alone.

"What are you teaching there?" Mumera asked and Wanjiru wondered why he would be interested in that.

"Oh, it is about how to introduce high school students to quantum mechanics. We will have to start younger if kids are to understand computer electronics of the future."

"I would love to learn that stuff. There was a teacher at my school who said he knew you when he was young and you were a good physics teacher when you were at Njoro."

"Oh, really, who is that?"

"Joe Watusu."

"Watusu? Yes I remember. He liked me a little too much… came to my place often." He said and laughed. "I should meet him while I am here."

"He is in prison." Wanjiru spoke up. "He did too much sex with his students. Killed one of his students who was, how you say, *alilazimisha*…"

"He was being blackmailed and did not like it."

300

"Blackmailed? What would be so bad to kill?"

Ruthy said, "The rumor was that the student had pictures of them naked together."

"Oh, they were gay."

"Gay? Homosexual?" Mumera asked.

"Yes, at school I thought his friend was gay. Would a teacher lose his job if he is gay?"

"No, if he keeps it private. It is forcing a student that is against the law. But he could not help himself." Mumera said.

Ruthy laughed, "Mumera was a big news item. He was a witness at the teacher's trial."

"What on earth would you have to say? Did you see the killing?"

"No, the defense claimed I had a motive to kill the victim."

"What the hell did he do to you that you would kill him for?"

"That animal," Wanjiru spat, "raped Mumera."

"Raped? Holy mother of God! I'm afraid I would kill the buggery boy for that! I'm very sad you went through that. It happened to me a couple of times, but I was drunk or drugged. Were you?" He asked, and Wanjiru was stunned that her Lodi would admit that, but knew he was trying to relate to her son's misery.

"I was unconscious." Mumera said. "I guess we are even more alike than I thought." Wanjiru was trying to understand what this would mean to men. Mumera asked, "Do you mind if I ask how it happened?"

"I'll swap stories with you." He said and Mumera nodded.

"I was in teacher training when I first came to Kenya. I came down with dysentery, but got well, but still very weak. Three boys asked me to bring my camera and food for a hike around the country. They gave me some of their *pambe*, which had something in it that made me so weak I could not lift my arms, though I knew what was going on. They stripped me and spent the afternoon buggering me. They left me out there, and the drug didn't wear off until after dark. But I found my way back to the school. I was too embarrassed to do anything about it. I never saw them again anyway."

"*Gai*! Unbelievable!"

"Your turn."

"I was doing my girlfriend, when she went into a miscarriage. Her aunt came rushing in and sent me off naked into the kitchen. Her brother was there and grabbed my *makodo* and squeezed so hard I passed out. He used me when I was out." Wanjiru knew from what he said in court there was a lot more.

"Jesus, forgive us all!" Lodi said. "Was Watusu convicted?"

Mumera answered, "He was convicted of raping boys with Martin, and having sex with his students."

Wanjiru interrupted, "The jury said Watusu was innocent of the murder though." She felt that there was no justice for the murder. "It is sad that people think Martin deserved to die."

"Yes, that is for God to decide." Obviously changing the subject, Lodi said. "Well, Mumera, with these school grades, it does not look like you are giving up on the world."

"No, I want to do well to get to university with Muturi." Mumera said, and Wanjiru felt a shot of pain through her. Her Lodi looked at her and gave her a wink, as if to say it will be okay.

"I missed meeting Muturi. I have only heard good things about him."

"I miss him so much I feel like I will die sometimes."

"Well, don't hold me to this, but I will look into flying you, and your mama if she wants, to Indiana to visit him. What do you say?"

"That would be wonderful to see him and his new son." Wanjiru said as she heard Mwangi's truck. The little ones were making a lot of noise as usual after an afternoon with Mwangi's mother. "Speaking of children…" The younger children were running up to their mother when they stopped and stared at the *mzungu* stranger. Mwangi came in with a big smile on his face.

"Everyone in Njoro is well. My mother is still complaining about her stiff joints. Pali Chege dropped by while we were there." Mwangi always mentioned her to make Wanjiru jealous, but she was not feeling insecure today, so it would not work.

Wanjiru said to Mwangi in Kikuyu, "Is she still without child, this Pali Chege?"

"Oh, yes. Looking old and miserable, too." He replied in English. Lodi, what is that you are drinking?"

"Gin and tonic. I could make you one, but I know you like Tusker." He got the attention of the little boy and told him in

Swahili to fetch his father a Tusker from his bag. He pointed at the bag and the little boy shot over and brought Mwangi a warm Tusker. "When Janie arrives," he continued in Swahili, "I want to take pictures of the whole family with me."

"You still have that camera that takes pictures by itself?" Wanjiru said in English, remembering the photos Virginia showed her and the time in Egerton house.

"No, a much better one, but it also has a timer, you must remember something about that camera."

"Virginia showed me pictures." Ruthy laughed.

"Yes, Virginia showed pictures to everyone."

Mwangi looking at Wanjiru confused. Wanjiru explained in Kikuyu, and he retorted in English, "That should remain private. But remind me the next time I am in Njoro to see those pictures." Everyone laughed, except Mumera who felt left out of the conversation.

"Mumera, you must not understand. I was with Virginia and set up the camera to take a picture by itself then went over…"

"Oh, as if there is someone else taking pictures of you doing her?" Mumera laughed. "Hmmm. Where do I get such a camera?" And everyone laughed.

"I will loan you mine."

"What is so funny?" Came Janie's voice, and Mumera jumped up to give her a kiss.

Mumera put his arm around her and introduced her, "This is who everyone calls Lodi. He was kind enough to provide the sperm that made me." They shook hands.

"*Gai*, now I know what you will look like when you are an old man." She said.

"Me, old? I just turned forty seven." He laughed pretending to be offended. "You are beautiful, but I am sure Mumera tells you that every day."

"Yes, he has his way of telling me." She giggled.

"Well, you are extremely attractive, no man could resist you."

"You make very handsome sons. You have more like him?"

"Yes, just one, my son Job. He is very much like Mumera, except straight hair and brown eyes."

"You should have more sons with blue eyes." Janie suggested.

"I had a vasectomy so no more." He sighed.

"Oh, I read about that in my medical book. You should get it reversed and have more sons like Mumera… many more." They both laughed.

Mumera acted confused and said, "Lodi invited us down to Nairobi, well Jamhuri, to visit with him before he flies back to America."

"Yes, that would be great. I can't wait."

"While everyone is here, let's get my camera take pictures of all of us together."

Mwangi laughed in English, "Do we need to undress up for this?" And Lodi was the only one that chuckled at his attempted joke.

Chapter 30, Jamhuri

Janie thought she should be sleepy. However, she was too excited being in "Lodi's" Jamhuri apartment. Mumera had just headed to the bathroom to take his turn after Janie and his Dad used the *choo*. She had pulled off her shoes and jeans while she admired the furniture in the guest room. His Dad gave them money to come down to Nairobi for the weekend, and they all had fun in restaurants and the museum. The old man spent much of the time together removing Janie's hands from secretly touching him inappropriately. Janie could not get the old man out of her thoughts. She wanted him very badly. She had discussed her passion several times before with Mumera, and like most Kikuyu men did not care so long as he got his desires met. Janie obsessed on how to make it happen, and as well wondered why she was so obsessed. Was it because of Muturi and Mumera, and the old man would make it a third huge man with blue eyes that would do her? She pulled her tank top over her head as she heard a tapping at the open bedroom door, and she saw the old man poke his hairy face around the door. "Are you two doing okay? Anything you need?" He suddenly was aware of the fact that she was standing there in her bra and knickers. "Oh, excuse me. Sorry." But he just stared. "I must say, you are even more beautiful than I imagined."

She unsnapped her bra, tossed it on the bed, and stepped out of her knickers to let him look. "I think we are good. Mumera is about done in the bathroom." She said.

"Very nice." He chuckled and disappeared as he heard the bathroom door open in the hallway. Mumera came in and smiled at her standing there, and began removing his clothes. She walked up to him and stroked his back.

"I want to try Lodi tonight." She stated quietly.

"What? The old man?

"It is all I think about. Besides, he is alone."

"He is used to it." Mumera said as he tried to lead her to the bed. Janie saw that he was excited, but twisted away, grabbed his wrist and led him into his Lodi's bedroom, the door to which was open. The old man was on the far side of a king size bed

305

dozing with a book on his chest. Janie slowly walked in and saw that he had been reading, but was nodding off asleep.

~~~~

Mumera woke up to the sun lighting the curtains, and he realized he was holding Janie's back against his stomach and she had an arm around Lodi, who was asleep with his back to them. The beautiful brown girl turned to look at him. "*Habari*?" he asked.

"*Mzuri*." She said in Swahili but switched to Kikuyu. "Your Dad still sleeping?" she asked and knew the answer, but saw Mumera's face, "What is the matter?"

"If you get a pregnancy, how will I know if the child is mine or Lodi's."

She laughed, "He said he had a vasectomy."

"What's that?" he asked.

"A doctor snips the tube that carries sperm to be ejaculated. He has the seminal fluid without the sperm. Good for fun, but no babies."

"When did he tell you that?"

"Back in Nakuru."

"Was that what you were talking about? I thought he was chatting you up."

"He was, but I thought he was saying he could sex me but I would not get a pregnancy." She said. "I told him I thought it was sad that he would not make anymore sons as nice as you." She chuckled. The old man began stirring and turned around under the blanket, and turned around.

"Good morning, Janie, Mumera. What are you talking about? Anything that would interest me."

Mumera said, "She was telling me about the thing a doctor did to you so you cannot give pregnancies to girls."

"Oh, yes, didn't I tell you about that, Janie?" He said and Mumera noticed how small Janie looked under the blanket with her head peeping out. He looked up at Lodi on the other side of the huge bed, with his reddish-brown beard and blue eyes. "When I get home, I have a precedure scheduled to reverse it, since it causes me a lot of infections - epididymitis."

"I'm hot." She announced and kicked off the blanket. "Can you show me where they cut you?" she asked the old man. "Is there a scar?" Mumera was appalled at her boldness, but he thought lying naked next to two big men had to make her bold. She sat up as if he was going to show her. Lodi bent his knees up and pulled down his boxers and Janie pulled them off and tossed them to the floor.

The old man laughed, "You want to play doctor?" and lay back to let her do her examination. She turned around and got up on her knees.

"Oh, the scars are small. The doctor must use a microscope." She held his manhood up and looked closely at his scrotum. Mumera leaned in out of curiosity.

"More like binoculars,"

Mumera wondered, "If you knew then what you know now, would you have had it done?"

"My, what a great question. I would not since it caused me so many problems and my wife was just using it as an excuse for a lack of libido."

"Libido?" Mumera asked.

Janie answered, "Desire for sex." She was stroking the old man as she said it and he was stiffening up.

"Something you have plenty of." Mumera smiled, and she noticed that Mumera was getting aroused watching. She leaned forward and began sucking on Mumera, who said, "Ouch."

"Wait, wait" Lodi said, "make sure your teeth don't cut." It was good for a few seconds, Mumera thought, but he pushed her away. "Watch my tongue," Lodi said licking and sucking his thumb. Janie tried it, and Mumera thought he would pass out from pleasure. Lodi talked like a teacher. "Better, now but no teeth. Let is slide to the back of your throat. Good, good." He said and leaned back to let her continue, and Mumera started moaning and his hips starting jerking and his legs shaking. Janie giggled, and got up. Mumera was wanting more. Lodi looked at him and said, "Get on top of her and I will photograph you."

Lodi got up and came back with a camera. "Let me take a picture of you two lovers together. Mumera get on top of her." Obediently, he got on top of Janie and connected with Janie wrapping her legs around him. The naked man adjusted the camera, and took a picture from a low angle. Adjusted the camera again and took one more. "Well, I will leave you two lovers alone and I will make some breakfast."

Chapter 31, Franny

Muturi had just hung up the phone having talked with Martha and her mother about Thomas. Thomas had another ear infection and was on medicine. He sat worrying, but knew that Thomas was getting better care than he could provide. He stared down at his homework. One differential equations problem was stumping him. He heard the key in the apartment door and saw the deadbolt knob turn. "I am here with offerings!" Franny announced, waving a large envelope. "Mom got a letter from your bio-dad about his visit to Nakuru."

"Great. Any pictures?" he said standing up and giving her a quick hug. "How are you doing?"

"I have a wicked headache aspirin won't touch, but you will love the pictures!" she exclaimed, sitting down on the couch. She pulled out several five by seven color photos of so many familiar faces. "My legs hurt like crazy. Too much running around I guess.

"If it does not improve, get your mama to take you to a doctor."

"I'll be okay. Don't worry about me."

In the first picture, they were all in a group around his mother. His bio-dad was on one side and his baba on the other. Mumera with Janie, who had a hand as if rubbing Lodi's belly. The little ones were there and who was that? Ruthy? "Why is she there?"

"You know Ruthy? The letter says she is working for Mwangi now as a bookkeeper. Well, it says a lot more." She said and he recalled the time he and his brother shared her in the tall grass out behind the basketball court.

"Yes, Lodi had a housekeeper, Wambui, and Ruthy is her daughter. The story I heard was when she was pregnant with Ruthy, everyone assumed Lodi gave her the pregnancy."

"Knocked her up?" Franny asked, translating his Kenyan dialect into American.

"It turned out to be some guy Mwangi, and of course everyone then assumed it was my baba, but she was not telling."

"So, Ruthy might be your step-sister?" Franny giggled. "I'm sorry, but she is so skinny and ugly."

"You mean skinny like someone else I know?" he laughed and rubbed her bulging belly, then tickled her skinny ribs. "Well, look at the picture, Mwangi has an arm on mama's shoulder and one on Ruthy's at the same time."

"Well, it could be just a family thing. But they don't even look alike. What is Janie doing to your Dad?"

"Knowing Janie, she wants to taste every man with blue eyes, and Lodi would be no exception. Ruthy looks like a bad version of her mother."

"Here is an interesting one. It is your bio-dad with your mama. Very nice portrait. She is very beautiful. He looks like a white version of you, except the beard, of course, looks like your pubic hair." She laughed and he joined in. She looked at another. "It says Mumera and Janie. Very cute couple. I would swear it is you with some other woman though."

"Mumera and Janie want to get married if she gets pregnant, but I have not heard. We used to be a couple. She lost our baby."

"Oh, right, you told me that whole story, the murder and the trial. Horrible - I could see why she hooked up with your brother, though."

"He is smarter with school and people than I am."

"You're being nice." She smiled, "He had you to help him study and explain people, I bet."

"Now you're being nice." He responded and they both laughed.

"Your bio-dad wrote my mom a letter. She said it was personal, but I found it in her bedside table and had to read it."

"That is private, we should not read it."

"You need to tell me who these people are. Makes me hot reading it. It says he visited Wambui and Ruthy. Who's Wambui?

"Ruthy's mother, his housekeeper when he was a teacher there. She called my dad her husband around the village. Like my husband sent me money for school fees. That."

"Oh, it says his friend Kimani visited them and 'did them both.' Does that mean what I think it means?"

"Perhaps. I think it means that he had sex with both Ruthy and Wambui."

309

"He says, he visited and did the same. And apparently 'Kimani taught Ruthy some new tricks.'" She said, and he was getting aroused from all the sex stories. "It says he visited your mama, as you know, but Mwangi insisted your mama spend some time with her first husband. He said it was just like old times, very sweet. Here is something interesting. He and Wanjiru saw Mumera doing Ruthy in his room. He said he thought it interesting that father and son did the same girl within a day."

"Wow, and I thought I was corrupt."

"You're not corrupt, you just do what your women want. Pussy whipped, but not corrupt."

"Pussy what?" he asked.

"Never mind. She said. "Here is something cool about having the same girl. Mumera and Janie visited him every weekend for a while. They went out to eat, movies, museum. They all slept together."

"Mumera?" he said, at first thinking his brother would want sex from the old man.

"No, silly, Janie." She said. He then realized for Janie, she would have to taste the old man – you could not stop her. "The first time, she did him, I guess, and when he woke up in the morning, Janie and Mumera were in bed with him."

"No!" Muturi was afraid that Mumera was after the old man.

"It doesn't say he did anything with Mumera, but that they were sharing Janie." She said and looked inside the envelope. "Here is a great picture." She said. He saw a picture of Janie and Mumera obviously in bed together, with Janie on her back and Mumera on top, with her legs wrapped around Mumera. The skin tones were beautiful, with his light brown against her darker brown. Her nipple was hidden in his chest muscle and they were looking directly into the camera, with her big brown eyes and his dark blue eyes. A curl of his brown hair fell onto his forehead. "Makes me jealous seeing you with another woman."

"It's not me! This picture is making me... uh..."

"Horny?" Franny laughed. "Okay. I need your help on this paragraph. Your bio-dad says 'I guess she was conceived that morning in Lamu. If Kimani always used condoms, and what you say is right, she is our kid.' Can you guess what that means?"

"You ever read your mother's book?" Muturi asked, recalling how important the island town of Lamu was to Beth.

"Vaguely -it has been awhile."

"Beth did an American guy one morning while he was asleep. She called it the best sex she ever had."

"Who was that American?" Franny asked, and it suddenly dawned on Muturi.

"That would make you my..."

"Sister?" Franny shouted and stood up quickly and immediately her legs buckled and she collapsed unconscious. Muturi was stunned speechless.

~~~~

Muturi looked over at Beth holding her daughter's hand. Franny was in the emergency room bed with tubes and wires all around her. A machine was helping her breathe. The mound under the cover was his baby, who might die if they could not bring Franny back. Beth sat with tears in continuous flow down her cheeks. Muturi looked back at the doctor, through his own tears.

"No, she said she had a very bad headache and took some aspirin. She complained of being weak, so I thought she was just tired. But we were looking at photos and she stood up," he continued, "and she just suddenly dropped out. He said shaking, recalling the moment she was getting ready to seduce him then suddenly dropping as if dead.

"We were wondering if that was not the case. I told Frances' mother all this and she asked me to explain to you. We think she had a grade five ruptured brain aneurysm. It filled the area around the brain with blood and cutting off oxygen to parts of the brain. Taking the aspirin made the bleeding worse, unfortunately."

"Will she recover?" he asked his eyes so clouded with tears he could barely make out what the doctor looked like. Would he be judgmental about his being with his wife's cousin, or did he even know that?

"No, she may go on for another week or so in this condition, but no I do not see how she will recover." The doctor said, and Muturi could see Martha and her mother standing in the hallway. The doctor continued, "It would be a miracle. I am also sorry for the baby, since it is still too young to survive even with all we do for premature babies now. If Frances survives just one more month, the baby might have a chance. A week? No." The doctor took Muturi's hand. "I am very sorry." The doctor left and Martha came in holding a sleeping baby Thomas wrapped in a blanket. Her mother quickly went over to console her sister. Everyone was in tears. He gave his wife a hug and took his son, allowing Martha to go stand next to her cousin.

Beth was thinking about signing a do-not-resuscitate order, which she had to explain meant that she thought Franny was brain dead and would never be the same, so if she died, the hospital would not try to bring her back. Beth looked at her daughter then at Mumera. "We could put her on a machine to keep her alive until her baby is big enough to survive."

"I wish we could do that, but I do not have money for that."

"Of course, I know, but I have plenty. I just need you to promise to be the baby's father."

"I swear on my son to be the best father I can possibly be." He said looking at his son.

"I never had any doubt. You will be the father and maybe the uncle to the child." Beth said. "I am sorry I never knew for sure who her father was."

Each time he looked at the dying girl, he heard her mimicking his quoting his mother's "life is life" saying. Not having lived a long life, she said she thought that saying was pretty empty.

He looked down at his sleeping son, with his reddish blonde, curly hair and reddish complexion. My son, I hope we gave you the best of us and not the worst.

～～～～

Muturi's eyes were sore from crying as he looked down at his son in his arms. Thomas was staring and smiling at his "uncle" Job sitting next to him. "How old are you now, Job?"

"I'm eight. You're a cutie!" the boy tickled Thomas's cheek and the baby giggled. Muturi was not sure if his half brother Job had known Franny very well if at all, but his Dad brought Job to Franny's funeral. "Can I hold him?" Job asked, and Muturi looked at the boy, who looked twelve instead of eight, and reminded him so much of his brother Mumera at that age.

"Sure. Be careful, he will wiggle." He said and Job took the baby and was patting his belly and kissing his head. The baby loved it. He looked over and his Dad was hugging Beth yet again, and was very upset for her. Martha was in the same circle chatting and crying and hugging, holding Frannie's baby as if it were her own. Neighbors had brought food to the house and set up a table in Martha's mother's living room. People had been coming and going since everyone had come back from the burial. She was buried in the same cemetery near where her uncle was buried last year. Muturi recalled how upset Martha was at the loss of her father, and now her cousin and best friend. "Did you know Franny?" he asked his half-brother.

"Yes. She was very nice to me. She brought me M&Ms whenever she and Auntie Beth came."

"Auntie Beth?"

"Yeah, Dad says she is not a real auntie, but is like his sister. She looks like my real aunties, too." He said and kissed the baby. "Babies have such nice smells. I have a kitten. They scratch."

Muturi was wondering why his half-sister did not come as well. "Where is your sister today?"

The boy pointed at Martha, "Martha is holding her."

"No, not Thomas' sister, I mean your big sister."

"She was in a play at school."

"What do you do for fun?" Muturi asked, trying to get to know his brother better.

"I play baseball now. Dad put up a basketball goal."

"I used to play basketball all the time in Kenya. Maybe we could play sometimes."

"Yes, but I like playing games on Dad's computer better."

"Games. You can play games on a computer?" he was surprised an eight year old was using a computer. He was learning computer programming, but that was a mainframe. He used personal computers in the library, but an eight year old using a computer?

"Sure." He tickled Thomas who giggled and stroked Job's face. "He's sooo cute! I play Quest and Space Invaders."

Muturi was thinking he should talk with eight year olds more often to see where the world is headed. "Quest?"

"Yeah, you're a knight who has to rescue someone and you have to pick up things along the way that gets you inside a castle or something and…"

"Is he talking your leg off?" his Dad appeared and he looked up. "How's my grandson doing?" Muturi looked at the baby in the boy's arms, each smiling at the other. "Are you two getting to know each other? Job loves computers and anything with wires."

"Wires? Like electricity and things?"

"Yes." He answered, paused, and then stated, "Muturi, little Frances is beautiful. If you need any help, feel free to ask. It is very painful to lose a child, but..." his voice cracked. "I had two, twin daughters born early, and died the same day. Very sad. But life goes on, and you have a wonderful son and daughter, and a lot of family here in America and in Kenya who love you deeply." Tears were glissening in his Dad's eyes, and Muturi felt his heart pounding in his ears. "Muturi, I last saw you when you were about a year old when I was leaving Kenya, and I thought I would never see you again. I want you to know how happy it makes me to see that you turned out to be such a fine man. Your mother and Mwangi did a wonderful job of raising you." Muturi was overwhelmed. He looked at him and thought. Did my mama refuse this man?

"Thanks, Dad, my mama and baba are wonderful people." Muturi said and he could see how happy it made him to call him 'Dad.'

"Beth asked me to get a PCR paternity test. Franny was my daughter." His Dad said, making Muturi cringe at the thought of having had an affair with his half sister.

"Mac, can I talk with you privately?" Beth suddenly appeared and took his Dad away.

"Muturi, I think he wet his pants." Job said, and Muturi saw some leakage around the top of the diaper, reminding him how long it has been since the last changing.

"You want to help?" he asked the boy.

It was hours after the house was empty, save Beth in the guest room with baby Frances. The baby Thomas was asleep and Martha was telling Muturi about what others told her during the day. Most of the people did not know Franny that well, but did know Beth and tried to console her. Martha added, "Your brother Job let a cat out of the bag."

"Cat out of the bag?"

"He blurted out something that was supposed to be a secret about your Dad. As Job said, he went to the hospital so he could have more babies." She laughed, thinking how a kid says the most inappropriate things at times.

"Was Dad there? Who else heard this?"

"Yes, he covered Job's mouth and said that was private. Job said, 'Mom is mad as hell.' And your Dad turned bright red."

"Where was I?" Muturi wondered.

"With Thomas. Anyway, he said that he had a vasectomy to make his wife happy, but it only gave him chronic infections and recently had it reversed. He said, Job is a blabbermouth, it is no big deal. Job was excited that he could have another baby brother like Thomas or sister like Frances."

"What is this vass thing?" Muturi said, not knowing what she was talking about. "Have I heard of this before?"

"A doctor cuts a hole in a man's scrotum," she said and Muturi felt a sharp pain shooting through his genitals," and pulls out the tubes that carry the sperm, then burns them shut."

"*Gai*! Where do the sperm go?"

"They get backed up and die, then get absorbed in the body, except his caused infections all the time."

"He had such wonderful children why not have more?"

"I agree, you are wonderful. Mumera is wonderful. Job is wonderful. Your half-sister is a brat. Three out of four ain't bad."

"Dad told me that Franny was his daughter, too." Muturi saw the look of disbelief in Martha's face. She was so stunned, that she could not speak. "Hans is a brat, too, and very – what should I say? Unusual. So, four out of six."

"Hans?"

"If you don't know, you won't want to know." Muturi responded using his best American deflection, he knew.

"Anyway, your Dad's wife kept having miscarriages and didn't want anymore problems, but surgery for women is too complicated."

"He told you all this today?"

"No, Beth gossiped a lot before. Anyway, your Dad and Beth disappeared for an hour."

"Yeah, she came and got him when we were talking."

"She told me he finally stopped thinking of her as a sister."

"Holy, what does that mean? He did her?"

315

"I think so."

"He must think since they had a kid together anyway. Isn't she too old to have babies? She won't get a replacement for Franny."

"She has a couple of fertile years left. Having more children is never a replacement, any more than Mumera is your replacement."

"True enough. How do you know that Dad did her?"

"She followed after he came back down after an hour, and she was wearing a different outfit and looking less depressed than before."

"Different clothes? That doesn't mean he did her. Unless you checked out the guest room." He said and looked at her and she nodded. "You're serious. You smelled her sheets?"

"The bed was not made, and it looked like some romping around. And there were the smells."

"Martha, you must really want your aunt to find happiness."

"She has been waiting a long time for him, like there is no other man like him in the universe." She said and paused as if thinking about what she had said, "Well, you're the only man like no other in the universe."

~~~~

Mumera awoke to the sun streaming in the window lighting Janie's beautiful, sleeping face. He heard the telephone ringing in the shop and heard his mother running through the house to answer it. He was worried for Janie now that she was pregnant, and for Muturi who in turn was worried about his and his wife's cousin, brain dead in the hospital growing a baby for him. He thought only in America could someone die, but they keep the body alive to grow a baby. He rolled out of bed to let Janie sleep some more, and he could learn the news from America if it were Muturi on the phone. He stumbled into the bathroom, did his business, cleaned up and returned to his room to dress. He went out to the kitchen to see if his mother had started *chai* yet, and she had not. He started making it as she came back through the door to the shop with tears streaming down her face.

"*Ni ke*, mama?" He asked.

"That was Muturi. They cut the baby girl out of Franny and let her die. Muturi said the funeral for Franny was yesterday.

They named the baby Frances Beth Makomeki for her mother and grandmother. So, Muturi has two children now."

"Three. Don't forget Hanna's boy."

"Yes. Sweet baby he is." Wanjiru smiled through her tears. "And now Janie has a pregnancy again. I hope she does not lose this one. "

"Janie said she thinks Martin gave her *dawa* to lose it."

"Oh, no, what kind of animal would do that?" she said, and Mumera thought back on what kind of animal he was killing Martin. Such is the way people justify such things. "So, Muturi say Martha wants to adopt the baby as her own. More babies. Like you, my wonderful son." She said, and a pang of guilt shot through him, wondering yet again, what would his mother think of his murdering someone? "Muturi said that Lodi will buy us plane tickets to come visit."

"Gai! You think Janie, too?"

"Muturi say Lodi expect at least me, you and Janie." She said, and Mumera thought would his Dad want to do his girlfriend if she were pregnant? Maybe he will teach her more pleasure skills, he thought.

"Mwangi said you could never get him in those metal birds, so he will not go." Mumera stated, then thought if Lodi and his mama are alone again, will he give her a pregnancy? "You know, if you go, Lodi will do you. Maybe give me a little brother like Muturi."

"I can not refuse him. Another child like Muturi or you would be wonderful." She smiled, and he could feel his mother's excitement.

Chapter 32, Happy Beginning

While nursing baby Frances, Martha watched Muturi playing with Thomas, and smiled. He asked, "Your birthday is coming, how old are you going to be?" and Thomas looked at him, and held up one finger. "No, that is how old you are. You will be two, see, two."

"One, two, three!" Thomas said. "Two!" and he held up two fingers in a victory sign. The toddler stood up and ran towards Martha, "Nurse, nurse." Little Francis sucked one breast dry and fell asleep. She handed her off to Muturi.

"I guess you're hungry!" she said as Thomas climbed up on her and tried opening her blouse. She looked at her mother on the couch then back at Muturi sitting on the floor. She opened up the other side for Thomas who started sucking ravenously. Her mother rolled her eyes and went back to knitting. Muturi just smiled and watched, looking down at the sleeping baby Frances, the tiny pink girl with the curly brown hair. She had recently started walking, later than Thomas, but then she was premature.

Her mother said, "Beth called me today. Mac signed the divorce papers last month and they drove up to Las Vegas and got married."

"Wow, that took a long time."

"He wanted to make sure Ann was still part of Job's life even though they were living in Santa Fe."

"Job didn't want to live with his mother?"

"Job couldn't stand her boyfriend, and he wanted to be near his new, little brother and sister. His daughter had her friends and could care less about her parents. So, she is staying in Champaign."

Muturi said, "Job will make a great big brother. You see him with Thomas… he is a natural for a father."

"Like you," Martha said, and he just smiled back.

"That's true!" Her mother agreed and continued knitting. "How did Mac end up in Santa Fe?"

Muturi replied, "He is teaching in New Mexico. They found a place near Santa Fe. He told me he would come back when he can. Beth wants to get a teaching job there. Beth say how the babies were doing?"

"Both Nora and Donny had ear infections. Good now."

Martha laughed, "Trouble with twins. You would think a boy and a girl would not get sick at the same time."

"Same bug for both kids. She's too old for kids." She added, and Martha wondered where that came from. Her Mom continued, "Oh, Dan called and invited us all over. Purdue is playing Northwestern and he is all excited about it."

Martha laughed. "Muturi, I think Dan just likes having you around." She looked at Muturi, and he looked down. She was recalling what Muturi had told her about Dan's affectionate attention.

Her mother looked up from her knitting, "I always thought Dan liked boys a little too much. I caught him a few times feeling up his friends."

"Mom!"

"You also caught him a few times. You told me."

Muturi chuckled, "Martha, you embarrassed your brother?"

"No, he was not embarrassed and his friend was enjoying it. Mom, you told me to leave them alone."

"Better that than out knocking up some poor girl." Mom said and they all laughed.

Muturi said, "So, Dan is qualified?" and Martha rolled her eyes. "Had I known -" And Martha kicked his shoulder with her bare foot.